Look for these titles
by Mary Hughes

Now Available:

Romantic Adventure
Edie and the CEO—Crimson Romance
Falling ~~on~~ for the Billionaire
Cin Wikkid: April Fools For Love
Hot Chips and Sand
Bad Boy Billionaire's Lady: Lovless Brothers
Playing With Fire: The Battle of the Bands

Biting Love/The Ancients
Bite My Fire—Entangled
Biting Nixie—Entangled
The Bite of Silence—Entangled
Biting Me Softly—Entangled
Biting Oz—Entangled
Beauty Bites—Entangled
Downbeat—Entangled
Assassins Bite—Entangled
Passion Bites—Entangled
Biting Love Nibbles
Night's Caress —Entangled

From *Hot Chips and Sand*

She tiptoed back to the third floor landing. Panting, she cracked the door.

A hallway stretched before her with a ratty red runner and chewed plaster walls picketed by narrow wooden doors. Her mind clicked through and discarded possibilities as fast as a multicore processor. Open closed doors, possibly meet more goons.

Run back downstairs, definitely meet the kidnappers.

If only this were a computer game. A save game would be nice about now. Or a pause button. Why didn't life have a pause? Then she could try each of those doors, restoring each time one opened to a monster.

But no. If she screwed up, it'd be Game Over. Her stomach knotted.

Shouting. Footsteps on the stairs pounded down. She glanced back at the stairwell door, her throat tightening.

Hide. Didn't matter what might be behind the room doors, she definitely knew what was flying toward her in the stairwell. With a deep breath for courage, she scurried to the first door on the left and cranked the yellowed glass knob.

Locked.

She ran across the narrow hallway to grab a second door knob. She turned and pushed.

It gave.

She half-ran, half-fell into the room, slamming the door closed behind her, her chest heaving with relief.

Hiding place. Skyler scanned the room—and froze.

Standing mid-room was a giant.

Half-naked. Sun-bronzed chest. Very, very male.

And staring at her with eyes so blue they were pure cobalt fire.

Hot Chips and Sand

A kidnapped geek, a daring rescue…

When brilliant, hot-tempered IT tech Skyler Jones is kidnapped, she manages to almost escape, only to be cornered in the hotel room of a half-naked, enigmatic truck of a man. As the kidnappers burst into the room, the man hides Skyler by covering her body with his—and kissing her. The man, known only as Cliff, races Skyler through hot narrow streets and hides her on a boat going home.

Skyler thinks her troubles are over, but Cliff is really Sir Humphrey Hawkesclyffe, genius inventor of the next gen supercomputer. He's zeroed in on Skyler—he says for heading his software development team, business only. But as they work together, Skyler starts to fall for the lonely boy genius who's become a rugged man of action.

He seems to fall for her, too—at least their sizzling kisses suggest more than simple chemistry. But is Cliff just mixing pleasure with his business? Then the kidnappers come back for round two...but it's not Skyler they've come for this time.

Hot Chips
and Sand

A Romantic Adventure

Mary Hughes

DEDICATION

Thank you to Stacy D. Holmes for superlative editing helping this baby walk. Some stories need more love than others, and your wisdom and patience with this one are proof of your big heart.

Thanks as always to my husband Gregg, for believing in my stories from the beginning. Thanks, too, to my kids, who amused themselves, mostly without breakage, while Mommy played novel.

Chapter One

Skyler Jones was deep into coding a project her boss had shoved onto her last minute yesterday, due in two hours. She'd gotten her teeth into it and was thinking she might actually pull off a miracle and get it done, when said boss appeared in the opening of her cubicle like *Office Space*'s version of a grim reaper.

"Drop everything, Skyler. We have a new client." Phil Westerby smacked a letter on Skyler's desk. He cheerfully acknowledged his beer belly and three-hair comb-over was less a graceful slide toward middle age and more stealing the base. But his management style was all *Art of War*. "Rush-rush."

"They're all rush-rush." Skyler turned from her computer screen to give her boss her full attention. "You know I have at least three projects due this week, right? Including the one you gave me yesterday."

"Colonel Fahrrad takes priority." Phil thumped the letter in underscore. "Potential international client. Could be big money."

Irritation ruffled Skyler's nerves, the curse of a redhead's temper. Not that she bought into the stereotype, but she was a redhead, and she did have a temper. "Naturally, you'll forgive any of my missed deadlines."

"Would a little overtime hurt you? Besides, this is for a security system, the kind of project you love."

She stifled a sigh. Normally she did love her job at Fitzwater Software and Consulting. It was the perfect combination of meeting new people and problem solving. And she *wanted* to be helpful. "All right, let me take a look."

She lifted the paper. Good quality, with dented print like an impact printer or a real typewriter instead of a laptop and inkjet. Possibly the client had a secretary who simply loved the feel of an old-fashioned typebar, but more likely a client helplessly mired in the last century.

Reading the letter, she started getting a whole lot of bad vibes. "This Colonel Fahrrad already contracted with another vendor. Do you think the other vendor knows he's sniffing out the competition?"

"Sure. I think. Probably. Does it matter?"

"That he might be going behind the vendor's back?" A wave of annoyance made her clench her teeth. Like the high school guy who brought a girl to a dance, then left her alone so he could chat up other girls. Or fiancés who'd test-drive other models before he even got a woman off the showroom lot. Not that she had experience of that. Much. "Yes. I have to ask how serious this guy really is."

"Serious enough that I scheduled you to meet him today at two."

"The conference room is booked—"

"Boardroom."

That stopped her. Usually only upper management used the board room. "You must really want this client."

"The company president does. International, Skyler."

"That's nice." She pushed the letter back across the desk at him. "But I don't think I'm right for this."

"You know what I think? I think you have an appointment at two." He gave the letter one final thump and stalked away.

She closed her eyes for a moment to get her frustration under control. She prided herself on being professional, but sometimes, like now, it was hard.

Deep inhale. Breathe frustration out. Five of those and she felt calm enough to open her eyes. Time to do a little research on the colonel. She pulled up a browser and abruptly lost all the calm she'd fought for.

Boris Fahrrad had been secret police back when the KGB was cool. He'd been run out of several countries for archaic interrogation techniques.

In February of this year, he'd been hired by a progressive Middle East prince to help stabilize the small country of Middle Yemen.

Then, on the first day of June, Fahrrad staged a coup.

She sucked in a breath. That sure as heck explained the desire for a palace security system. He'd want to make sure no one would pull the same trick on him.

Checking dates, she saw that was only a week ago. This guy was a real winner, kicking out the old regime then off on a shopping spree within days.

Despite her churning gut, she put the two p.m. appointment in her calendar. Fitzwater had given her a job at her lowest point. Her loyalty couldn't be bought, but it could be won. If Jerry Fitzwater wanted this contract, she'd do everything she could to secure it, including meeting a scary dictator dude.

Besides, this was her job. While at one point, she'd dreamed of having it all, having a balanced life—a nice job, a nice family, even a nice house with a white picket fence— her fiancé had screwed that over when he screwed *her* over. Her career was all she had left.

She was very serious about her career.

Breathe in, push pain out. Turning from the deep pang of memory, she set her mind to finishing rush-rush project number two and clear the deck for the new number one.

A few moments later, her calendar chimed. She looked up, disoriented. She'd been deep in her work.

"Two p.m. boardroom" blinked on her screen.

"Two, already?" Panic goosed her to grab her phone and a client welcome folder then dash to the boardroom. She threw open the door to meet Colonel Fahrrad.

Seated at the long, glossy table was a slight man with a toothbrush mustache wearing an over-designed uniform and too-big hat. His beady eyes were glued to a sales brochure before him.

Her first impression was Classic Dictator ala *Mission Impossible.*

"Two-oh-one. You're late." He spoke without looking up. "Mr. Jones, the president told me you were the very best your company has to offer, but this tardiness does not speak well." His gaze rose. And stopped, shocked. "*Ms.* Jones."

As she introduced herself, he sat transfixed, gaze avid on her.

Because he was expecting a man, or did she have lunch salad in her teeth? She sat cautiously beside him.

"What an unusual color for hair." He reached out and grabbed a curl.

Alarm spiked her. She automatically swatted the strand from his grip.

His eyes sparked with thwarted anger. But he controlled himself, and actually smiled, with a toothy, gold-capped grin and a slight nod in apology.

Fighting to keep her professionalism, she began, "Your letter said you wanted a security system, Colonel Fahrrad. But you're already working with another company—"

"My predecessor's choice, sweeting. I wish to make my own alliances."

That actually made sense, but the endearment grated. She tried again. "Fitzwater doesn't do hardware, though. We specialize in database design and implementation."

"I am not worried about hardware, sweeting. Or anything hard." His slow, sensual grin sent frissons of unease up her spine.

If he hadn't been a potential client—scratch that, a potential *international* client, deeply desired by the president of the company—she'd have walked out. As it was, she asked politely, "What do you want the security system for? Your government headquarters?"

"For the entire country."

"Wh-what?" Surprise drove the word from her lips. "The technology for securing a bank or building exists, but a whole country...? Wouldn't your military be a better bet?"

"Middle Yemen is too small and too poor, sweeting. But *you* have exactly what I need." Again that oily grin.

Actual alarm goosed Skyler to her feet. She suppressed a shudder to slide him the welcome folder. "Tell you what. Have your people send us the specs, and we'll get you a quote. My card's in the pocket. Thank you for your time.

I'll have someone show you out." She scrambled out of there and hoped never to see Fahrrad again.

Two days later, as she left work late, she was kidnapped.

Four men came out of the blue and plucked her right off the Boston sidewalk. Shock stunned her long enough for them to slide her toward the open back door of a black sedan. *If they get me in there, I may never return.* The dark maw disturbed her enough that she began to struggle. She wriggled loose and ran back toward the building but only got three steps before they caught her. Freaked, she did the first thing she thought of—she chucked her messenger bag into the nearest bush. She hoped someone would find it and know she was in trouble.

They stuffed her in the car. One held a out blindfold—and a gun. He didn't say a word, but the muzzle spoke for him quite clearly. She put the blindfold on.

Without sight, she got a skewed sense of time and place. Car ride. Being hustled through open space up a set of stairs. Sensation of intense speed and dropping stomach. Airplane? The drone of engine went on and on. With each passing moment her body got colder, and her mind floated farther away.

The riffle of cards. Her kidnappers broke their silence over what sounded like a card game. She didn't recognize any of the words, though.

Except one—Fahrrad.

That sent her stomach into shut-down mode.

Two stops. Three times she smelled food. Somewhere between twenty and thirty hours later, a door *shooshed* open, and she was pushed onto her wobbling legs into a wall of heat.

Her whole body went from ice to ash, no thawing in between. Trembling badly, she stumbled down clanging stairs onto tarmac so gooey it stuck to her shoes as she tried to walk. The air smelled of sand and spices and was so hot it hurt to breathe.

In the small, sane corner of her mind where she huddled, she remembered the saying "It's not the heat, it's the humidity."

Her lungs burning from the inside out, she thought, *No, it's definitely the heat.*

They removed her blindfold in a dank, sweltering room. Bed, small table, attached bath…it looked like a run-down hotel room.

One of the men shoved a dark blotch at her. But she only stared at it, hollow inside. Terror must've burned her out.

The goon shook the thing at her and spat some angry-sounding words. The blotch resolved as her eyes adjusted to a red teddy, mostly lace and air. Familiar.

Like the one she'd bought for her wedding night.

The guy shook the teddy again then pointed at her—with a gun.

In the hollow of her chest, anger sparked. She'd been harassed, kidnapped, threatened, and now was being rudely forced to wear an article of clothing she'd sworn never to put on for a man again.

The spark of emotion saved her from breaking down. She fanned her anger and felt a modicum of control return to her limbs. *Damn straight. I'm not gonna let a dictator with a bad hat and his goons get me down.*

Snatching the teddy, she stalked into the room's bathroom, a closet-with-toilet. As she changed, she searched the tiny room. The cabinet behind the mirror yielded a handful of bobby pins that she stuck into her hair—might come in handy for picking a lock, if she knew how to pick a lock. Still, doing something, anything, made her feel better, more in control.

She needed that feeling when she came out and they burned her own clothes.

"Hey, I might need those," she protested.

One had enough English to answer, "Not with the colonel." But they all leered in the international language of *yuck*.

She needed an escape plan.

First chance I get, I'm getting out of here.

As plans went, it was short on details. But her ears perked when one of the kidnappers patted his growling stomach. The wiry bilingual leader nodded, pointed at her, and barked a command at the smallest kidnapper, a thin youth barely past pimples. The youth scowled as the leader and the other two swaggered out.

Going out for dinner to celebrate, no doubt, leaving Scowly behind to guard her.

She gauged the kid's physique. Stringy but underfed. She probably outweighed him by ten pounds and had at least a couple inches on him.

She could take him. All she had to do was judge her moment.

Then Scowly cut considering eyes to her, licking his chops in a way that made her shudder. *Oh, no.* She crossed her arms over her breasts and mentally promised him dismemberment if he tried. *I'll fight. You may win, but not before I take thirty-five cents of your best hamburger.*

He growled but picked up a magazine.

Pressing a hand to her breastbone, she was surprised to feel her heart thudding hard and fast. That wouldn't help. She coached herself. *Deep breath in, press stress out.* Wait for the right moment.

She fisted hands and waited. And waited. She was ready to scream when her captor pointed to her and barked a word, probably "Stay," because he went into the bathroom and shut the door.

Yes. While he was relieving himself, she quietly let herself out.

She found herself in a narrow, airless corridor lined by doors. Definitely a hotel or boarding house. To her right, the corridor ended in a wall. To her left, it ended in a door.

Picking the door direction, heart pounding, she ran.

The door opened to a narrow, airless stairwell, hot as a chimney. Wood stairs. If anything had told her she wasn't in the USA anymore, Toto, those rickety wooden stairs were it. She crept down, panting heat like sandpaper, trying not to get splinters in her bare feet.

A switchback flight emptied into a well with *two* doors. The one before her probably led to another dank corridor. Swallowing dry, hot air, she chose the one behind.

It opened onto a lobby. Her heart soared. A lobby meant an exit, people, maybe even a police force. She took a couple steps into the room. Wall cubbies were stuffed with mail. A couple rickety chairs sat on cracked linoleum.

The door shut behind her, revealing a large curled-up orange triangle in the corner. Modern sculpture? She stopped for a moment, trying to calm her frightened panting, and stared at the bizarre art sitting mid-dirt.

The outside door banged open. The three kidnappers returned just then, bearing bags wafting spicy odors. Carryout.

Heart nearly exploding from her chest, she scoured the room for a place to hide, but the rickety furniture wouldn't conceal a praying mantis, much less her.

She spun and took to the stairs.

Adrenaline rocketed her up a half-flight before the searing heat leached all the strength from her. Legs stuttering, she forced herself to trot up the second half-flight to the original floor, ears straining for shouts of discovery and a slammed door below.

Nothing.

Passing the landing, a stitch grabbed her ribs as she started up the next half flight, slowing her to a limping walk.

This was not good. Her mind screamed at her to run, but her body screamed at her to slow down, rest. The hours of sitting, the terror, the killing heat, had eaten away most of her strength, and that panicked run had drained what was left.

Palm on the wall, she stopped mid-flight to bend over, panting. "I am strong," she told herself firmly. "I work out. I am reasonably healthy. And above all, I am *not* panicking..."

A shout from downstairs made her heart skip.

She started leaping steps two at a time. Cracked plaster walls flew by. She tried to remember her pep talk.

Not panicking. So what if kidnappers are chasing me? It's no worse than Phil hounding me for his TPS reports. An absurd image of her boss, his spindly arms toting a gun Rambo-style as he demanded his reports, distracted her from the growing stitch in her side. But the pain grew until she thought she had a burst appendix.

Pausing on the third floor landing, she held her cramped side, puffing breath. "I am strong," she coached herself. "I work out. *But not in hundred-degree heat.* "Definitely reconsidering...the all...Cheez Curlz diet."

Bam-bam.

Skyler froze, all her muscles clenched as she strained to identify the sound.

Thudding, rhythmic. Feet, hitting the stairs below. Damn it, her opportunity to escape, blown sky-high. Well, what did she expect, with her elaborate plan consisting of R, U, and N?

Hiding place. Panic goosed her to leap up stairs to the fourth floor landing.

Where the stairs ran out.

"Fry my motherboard." She scanned the small space. A ladder hung from the wall, and a hatch perforated the ceiling. Grabbing the ladder, she nearly beaned herself pulling it down. Lug the ladder into position, climb it with her trembling limbs, all before the kidnappers caught her?

Not happening.

She spun and ran back down the stairs. She'd made the second floor landing—just as the door flew open.

Throwing herself behind it with raised hands, she suffered a whack to her shielding forearms. As the door swung closed, she saw the legs of two kidnappers running up the stairs. Heads indicated two were running down.

Arms smarting, stomach churning, she followed the legs as the lesser of two evils. They turned past the third floor, continuing up. She followed cautiously. Peeked around the switch just in time to see one pair of feet disappear through the fourth-floor door—while the other stood guard.

Searching top to bottom while the other pair searched bottom to top? And they'd meet like a pair of clapping hands in the middle, trapping her.

Still, what choice did she have? She tiptoed back to the third floor landing. Panting, she cracked the door.

A dungeon corridor stretched before her, even danker than the second floor. It appeared carpeted in a sluggish river of blood and walled with a corpse's teeth.

She blinked. Her eyes adjusted to the low watt bulbs, and the hallway resolved to a dirty floor with a ratty red runner and chewed plaster walls picketed by narrow wooden doors. None of the teeth—er, doors—shouted, "Hide here."

Fighting to control her thudding heart and trembling limbs, she slid through the door into the hallway. Her mind clicked through and discarded possibilities as fast as a multicore processor. Open closed doors, possibly meet more goons.

Run back downstairs, *definitely* meet the kidnappers.

If only this were a computer game. A save game would be nice about now. Or a pause button. Why didn't life have a pause? Then she could try each of those doors, restoring each time one opened to a monster.

But no. If she screwed up, it'd be *Game Over*. Her stomach knotted.

Shouting. Footsteps on the stairs pounded down. She glanced back at the stairwell door, her throat tightening.

Hide. Didn't matter what might be behind the room doors, she definitely knew what was flying toward her in the stairwell. With a deep breath for courage, she scurried to the first door on the left and cranked the yellowed glass knob.

Locked.

"Smack me with a Dell." Rattling the knob did no good, nor did kicking the door, which, since her feet were bare, stung her toes. She hopped around, trying to bring the pain under control, remembered *Game Over,* and hobbled across the narrow hallway to grab a second door knob. She turned and pushed.

It gave.

She half-ran, half-fell into the room, slamming the door closed behind her, her chest heaving with relief.

Hiding place. Skyler scanned the room—and froze.

Standing mid-room was a giant.

Half-naked. Sun-bronzed chest. Very, very male.

And staring at her with eyes so blue they were pure cobalt fire.

Chapter Two

The big man might've been friendly, but Skyler couldn't be sure because her brains were getting rattled from her heart pounding so hard. She felt like a deer trapped in cobalt headlights.

She swallowed hard. Maybe she could still escape. She spun to the door.

The doorknob was turning.

Fear spiked. She was caught, her time run out.

Hands, big and warm, urged her toward the bed. As the door opened, the man eased her onto the mattress.

At the last minute he flung himself on top of her.

Her breath went out in a whoosh. He was heavy, all muscle, and this close not quite a giant but definitely a cut above king-size. His body completely covered hers. A computer game battle tank, the dumb muscle.

Cobalt eyes seized her attention. She sucked in air. Acrid heat was replaced with a shock of male tang.

His speed numbed her. Somehow, he'd deciphered what was going on, and was hiding her the only way he could. In plain sight. She could only lay there as he twisted her telltale strawberry hair behind her head and, as the door slammed open, pressed his lips to hers.

Definitely too smart for the dumb-muscle meme went through her head in the last instant she could actually think.

His lips parted and began to move.

Heat. Power. So very male. As his lips caressed hers, as his minty breath mingled with, then replaced hers, her fear evaporated. Her stomach unknotted and her blood began to fizz, as if the pumping adrenaline had been replaced with champagne.

She wrapped arms around his neck and kissed him back.

With a growl of approval, his tongue came out to play, teasing. She tasted the masculine tang of desire and opened her own mouth for more.

A pair of feet shuffled inside the room.

The man lifted his mouth to turn his head. A little moan of disappointment bubbled up in her.

"What the hell! Can't a man have any privacy?"

His voice rumbled against her, like a bass speaker vibrating on her chest. Her belly shivered in answering pleasure.

"I seek a criminal fugitive."

Acid speared her stomach, abruptly replacing the pleasure. That was the lead kidnapper. She could only hope her rescuer's massive shoulders hid her from his view.

But calling *her* a criminal? She bristled. *They* were the criminals.

Her rescuer's growl crescendoed. "Can't you see I'm busy? Out."

"But she—"

"Get out," the big man roared. "Get out, before I throw you out!"

"I...yes. My pardon." Feet shuffled away, and the door clicked shut.

Wow. He'd gotten rid of the kidnapper so easily. His steely resolve had almost a physical impact, as if he'd blown away the kidnapper by a turbo-diesel of sheer personal force. Awe lifted her.

Although, maybe the leader had only gone to get reinforcements. She chilled.

The man leaped up to lock the door.

His absence increased her chill. She sat up, wrapping arms around herself.

He strode to a rickety chest of drawers and echoed her doubts. "He's gone to get more. They'll try to break in. We need to leave."

"Right." She tried to get up, to get to the door, but her legs wouldn't hold her.

Then he dragged the dresser in front of the door, blocking it.

Confusion tightened her brow. "What are you doing? I thought we were leaving."

He spun to slash a sharp, assessing gaze at her. "We are. You'll need something a bit more, ah, practical, to wear." He slid open one of the drawers, pulled a dark bundle out, and offered it to her.

She started to reach for it, but her muscles, too tense for too long, spasmed. She started trembling uncontrollably.

I can't lose it yet.

But she *was* losing it, shivering, her eyes watering, exhausted by the rollercoaster of the last couple days. Red-hot fury, hollow-chested horror, heart-pounding escape, vein-freezing near-recapture. *And that soul-branding kiss.* Now, sitting here, shivering in the thin lace of the teddy she'd been packaged in while this powerful man filled the room...it was the last straw. She retracted her arm to scrub at her face.

He moved closer, his gaze piercing.

She was suddenly aware the lace left nothing to the imagination but the deepest colors of her blush. She suspected her kidnappers hadn't touched her because their boss wanted her in pristine condition. This tank didn't have those constraints.

He sat next to her, and she had to work not to roll into him; he was like the gravity well of Jupiter, making her feel even more helpless. She didn't like the feeling and scrabbled back.

But he only leaned his elbows on his knees, putting their eyes almost level. He shook the bundle out before him. It turned out to be a huge black T-shirt.

"What's wrong?" Casually he cocked his head. "Black not your color?"

Skyler blinked. A joke? The tank was *joking?*

Cry me a chipset. Maybe she really was in a computer game, and he wasn't the dumb muscle, but the gentle giant you didn't want to push too far. Or the paladin whose moral code (and underwear) was tighter than an Iron Maiden but who regularly rescued a couple damsels in distress before breakfast.

Or maybe she was going nuts. Maybe the last two days of forced plane rides, muzzle-prompted hotel accommodation, and slimy dictators had made all the bits and bytes of her brain go bad.

She said the only thing she could. "Black fits nicely with the mood. Thank you." Plucking the shirt from his hand, she noted her arm no longer trembled; well, not until she brushed fingers against his smooth, bronzed skin. Her body, tight and tingly from his kiss, began to shake at that.

She'd managed to keep herself together before, only to lose her composure from a man's touch?

Not in this century. Angry with herself, she yanked the shirt from his grip with more force than necessary. "Who are you, anyway?"

"The guy who's going to get you out of here." The big man stood to stride back to the dresser.

The bed sprang up a good six inches, almost catapulting her into standing, too. "Enigmatic, yet unhelpful." She floundered her way into the voluminous folds of the shirt, getting lost once. The tee fell, ungainly, halfway to her knees. "Really, though. Who are you? What are you doing here, and why are you helping me?" And her biggest concern, unvoiced. *Do you know Colonel Fahrrad...?*

He slashed a cobalt glance over one huge shoulder. "Do you trust me?"

Without knowing the first thing about you? What kind of stupid question is that? Considering he'd just saved her from recapture, though, she only said, "I'll trust you until you give me reason not to."

"Fair enough. Then save your questions until we're safe. That hair of yours is a problem."

"I have bobby pins. I could pin it up." She began to extract the stolen pins.

"Not enough." Tapping one long finger against the dent in his chin, he considered her from beside the bureau. With a sudden, resolute nod, he slung open a drawer and grabbed another T-shirt, hefting the bundle in his hand. "Last one. Wrap it around your head." He threw the shirt to her.

She snared it midair, bent, and turbaned her hair with the shirt. "Last one? Then what are you going to wear?" Hearing no answer, she straightened, tucking and tightening the excess material around her head, using the hairpins to anchor the tee to her hair.

He gathered a rope around his flat waist, muscles jumping in his arms and chest, distracting her for a moment. *If this is an adventure, he's not a truck, he's a pirate.* He certainly looked like one as he tucked in the ends of the rope and she saw a metallic flash at the waistband of his black silk pants—a knife. She swallowed excess moisture, almost having to work to remember her situation was dangerous and real.

Briskly, he strode toward her. "Come on. We don't have much time."

The only way out was the door, which was blocked. She backed away, wondering what he thought he was doing.

His arms came around her. Apparently, he thought he was picking her up. Actually, he did it easily, sweeping her up as he strode to the open window, where he set her on her feet. Her swooping stomach followed a moment later.

But before she could do more than blurt, "What...?" he clapped her to his side with one brawny arm.

"Hang on."

Holding her tight, he swung them both out the window, into the night.

Skyler squeaked as she dangled from the man's arm like a toddler. She faced the building, determinedly *not* looking down. Third story, after all. Dusty rose bricks filled her sight, maybe painted maybe earthen. Her feet batted air. Definitely an unsettling feeling.

She toed for the window ledge, her nape crawling, but couldn't quite find it. Maybe a glance would be okay.

Mistake.

Below her feet—*far* below—feeble lights illuminated a narrow cobbled alley or passage. Her stomach fell out her feet and she jerked her head up as she scrabbled for a handhold on his bare shoulders.

Looking up was better. Gray concrete, the roof's ledge, cut the indigo sky just a few feet above her. If she could get a good solid boost, she might be able to reach it. "Could you raise me a little...?" She trailed off, perplexed, as she saw him brace his feet against the wall and felt his muscles bunch.

Realization dawned—he planned to jump. *But to where?* Too late, she scanned frantically for a nearby fire escape or stair landing or any flat surface less than five feet away.

He sprang. Sailed over and *down...*

Her stomach *shooped* as she sailed through the air with a suddenness that made her clutch for a handful of brawn. He hit a fire escape with a clang, jarring her, snapping her jaw into her skull and nearly throwing her from his grasp.

She scrambled to find purchase on a naked torso that seemed to be built from silk-covered rocks as she whispered fervent prayers that he would find a shirt or grow chest hair or *anything* to hang onto.

"Stop squirming." He hoisted her over his shoulder, sack-of-potatoes style.

Her temper flared in the millisecond of time before she slammed into his boulder of a shoulder, hard enough to drive the air from her lungs. Her teeth rattled together, the only thing that cut off her venting every name in the book. She drew breath to scream her frustration, only to have the air knocked repeatedly from her as he jumped up the stairs of a fire escape across the narrow alley.

The alley into which her captors tumbled out below.

"It's them," she hissed. Or rather, hiss-whumped, flopping on his shoulder.

He didn't seem to hear her, still springing up steps.

She curled to get closer to his ear, her awkward position straining muscles she hadn't ever used. "Those guys who captured me," she said a little louder. "Four of them, down there in the alley. Do you hear me?"

He still didn't answer. The men below were milling around, searching. If any of them looked up...

"Hey, you, steroid Santa. We're going to be seen!" She kicked at the truck a bit for emphasis.

"Only if you keep chattering." He swung her up over the concrete ledge onto a flat roof, leaped up beside her, then turned and squatted behind the ledge, pushing her into the same position.

She scraped hands and knees on rough concrete, hissing her pain. Beside her, the blockhead bruiser was just as bare of foot and limb but didn't seem bothered in the least, reinforcing her notion that he was an iron-skinned tank in disguise.

His blue gaze was narrow as lasers on the ground below. As her sharp stings eased, she cautiously poked her head over the ledge to look, too.

From here, she could still quite clearly see the men below, arguing and pointing in all directions.

"What now?" she whispered as another man stepped into the alleyway and began issuing a stream of orders. She realized from her research into Fahrrad that, if this was Middle Yemen, the kidnapper was probably either speaking the local dialect of Midyemeni, or some Slavic language.

Had it only been three days ago that she'd been researching in the cool comfort of her own office? Damn it, it made her even angrier that she'd gone along with Phil like a good little trouper.

"Stop growling," he murmured. Flustered, face prickling, she did.

Below, the group split, some to the street and some to the back of the building.

Her rescuer rose to a crouch. "If we're quiet, we should be able to escape undetected."

"Yes, but where are we...going?" she finished to his rapidly retreating back. "Wonderful," she muttered. "When I want to walk, he treats me like a sack of potatoes. But a gravel filled roof? Gone." She took a tentative, barefoot step onto the roof proper, and realized Webster's definition of pain didn't really do it justice.

"Excuse me," she called hoarsely. She waved after his distant form, appealingly muscular only until she stepped on the next sharp stone. "Oh, yoo-hoo!" Tears came to her eyes as she took another step. "Quietly, he says. Fine. I'll scream very quietly." As she inched over the coarse gravel, she jollied herself on. "You can do it. C'mon, you live through Phil's code reviews, you can live through this."

Nearing the other side, she caught the flick of a rope with the corner of her eye. Her gaze rose in surprise, and in that moment of distraction, she stepped on a sharp-edged stone. Stifling a shriek, her foot recoiled automatically, throwing her off balance. She stutter-stepped trying to recover, trod heavily on a rock like an ice pick, yipped, and went down with a clatter. Stones dug into her flesh like full-body nuggies, and a groan escaped her throat.

Shouts from the alley and the pounding of feet coming closer wasn't the best news she'd had all day.

Long fingers wrapped around her upper arms and a strong grip pulled her upright. Her gaze smacked straight into a blazing blue glare. She swallowed hard. He opened his mouth, and she was sure he was going to carve her into hamburger. Prepared herself for it.

"How much do you weigh?"

"Wh-what?" She blinked.

"Your yelling made me miss my throw to the next building."

"I didn't yell—"

"Then your shrieking called your friends' attention to us."

"I certainly didn't shriek." She drew herself to her full height, putting her eyes level with the notch between his winging collar bones, but she virtuously ignored the naked, masculine muscles below. Mostly.

"We need to get off this roof immediately, which means I'll have to jump, carrying you."

Now she'd yell and shriek. "I don't think..."

She dribbled off as he pulled in a bushel of air through his nose. She tried not to see how much his already massive chest expanded.

"So tell me, and be honest. How much do you weigh?"

"Well..." Normally, one hundred fifteen pounds. But no clothes, two days with no food, maybe one-thirteen, and the run up the stairs counted for something, maybe one twelve. A lot of minutiae, but she came from a long line of engineers and knew in her bones that even the least detail could be important. Speaking of detail, there were these two lunking T-shirts, though she had no idea what they weighed. Have to make it an explicit assumption. "One hundred twelve pounds without the T-shirts. So, how far away *is* the next—"

"Hold that thought." He snared her by the waist and started running.

I'll never finish a sentence again without flying through the air. Her stomach spiraled, giddy or terrified, she wasn't sure.

As he built up speed, he ordered, "Hang on."

"To what?" she retorted, but it was too late. He hit the edge of the roof and jumped. The concrete edge abruptly receded.

For a moment, Skyler saw nothing but empty space in all directions. Her stomach tried to escape out her throat. It was like dropping off the last stair only to realize there was one left, except in this case there were four stories of missing steps. Her arms wrapped around his neck in utter terror.

She'd decided there was no next building after all when they slammed into the side of it. Dazed, her head lolled back. She saw his hand, tendons white, gripping the crumbling roof ledge.

Fingers slipping.

"Climb onto my back." His commanding tone pierced the ringing in her head.

Semi-concussed, dangling in space, and he wanted her to move?

Still, she tried. She released the death-grip she had on his shoulders—and slipped down a couple inches on his slick torso.

"Damn it, I can't help you. You have to do it."

Her arms trembled, muscles quivering as clanging rang below, announcing her kidnappers had started clambering up this building's fire escape.

Slowly she twisted around his body, trying desperately not to fall, stomach permanently kinking her throat. Her arms went fiery from the strain. Stinging also began to register, from a half-dozen little cuts, surprising her. Not so surprising was the start of a mass of dull throbbing of bruises blooming all over her body. Slamming into buildings would do that.

She slipped twice more, but gradually she clambered onto his massive shoulders. She wrapped trembling arms around his neck just as four Middle Yemeni madmen crested the other side of the roof.

Despite her probably choking grip, with both hands free, her powerful paladin pulled them over the ledge almost easily.

Only to drop her again at the excited shout, coming from a kidnapper jumping off the fire escape onto the roof.

Fortunately this time she splayed onto an asphalt surface. *Moving uptown.* She gave brief thanks that it was evening and the blacktop had cooled from near a hundred degrees Fahrenheit to something nearer eighty.

A sharp smack and the sound of a body hitting the tar brought her head up. Two more kidnappers had come over the top. She scrambled to hands and knees.

But the first lay on the roof, out cold.

As she rose to her feet, her big rescuer made a graceful leap, kick, turn, and thrust, all fluid and flawless, felling the two smaller men. This particular tank had hidden talents, as fast as he was strong. He waited a moment for the last kidnapper to reach the roof. When no more came, he peered cautiously over the edge of the fire escape.

"Damn." He came at her in a dead run. "He's gone to get reinforcements. We'd better move."

"Don't you ever stop to...no, *wait.*"

He scooped her up and bundled her into one brawny arm as easily as if she was a sack of kitty litter—as sexy, too.

She clung to him as he swung over the side onto the fire escape and leaped down the metal stairs in great, stomach-dropping bounds, three or four at a time. Hugging his naked, muscled shoulders, she hid her face in his neck. Breathing in brought his scent. Warm, masculine, it was skin and sweat and a hint of spice. Okay, it was a little sexy.

He hit the street and ran, easily, still carrying her with her face buried in his neck. The warmth of his body eased the sting from her cuts and the aches from her bruises. Her lids drifted closed, and she breathed deep, savoring his masculine scent.

Shouting abruptly snapped her gaze up. They'd come nearly three blocks from the dusty pink building, and a half dozen men in fatigues poured around the corner into the street behind them. These new ones wore some kind of army uniforms, khaki and leather. The guns were the same, though.

The shouting was Russian or Midyemeni, but Skyler didn't have to know the language to translate, "There they are!"

"Damn." The big man spun to his right. "Running isn't cutting it. We have to find some other way to lose them."

Skyler found herself unceremoniously dumped into a darkened doorway. Her pale skin seemed to glow in the moonlit night. "It's me. Even with my hair covered, I stand out." They'd need a miracle to get them out of this alive—or a sacrifice. She gulped. "You should leave me." Heart pounding, she peered around the corner.

"Leave you?" He gave her a brief almost-smile. "What kind of rescue would it be if I left the damsel behind?"

She gaped at him. Did he *know* she'd classed him as the tank? "I'm not the damsel, I'm the plucky heroine, or at least the saucy sidekick—"

"Hold that thought."

One of the soldiers had unslung his rifle. The tank ran out of the doorway and she thought he was letting her sacrifice herself after all

But he wasn't running away—he was charging *toward* the soldiers. Skyler's heart leaped into her throat. *Is he insane?*

The big guy rocketed toward the soldier, so fast that, before the soldier could aim the gun, her paladin rammed into him, shoving him into two of his buddies, and in turn four more. Soldiers dropped like dominoes.

Tank? Big, fast, and mean. But *her* tank.

Then the big man wheeled and all that power dived straight for where she stood in the doorway. She squeaked and cringed back. She was surprised not to get a set of cracked ribs as the wall of muscle plowed into her.

Is he trying to smash me flat...?"

The tattoo of machine gun fire dropped understanding into her. He'd dived for cover. She started to peer out, but he jerked her back.

"Two dozen more are coming. Unless we can find a way out of here, we have as long as it takes them to cover three blocks to live."

Chapter Three

"Move." The big man motioned Skyler into the corner of the doorway. She made herself as small as she could as he reared back—then slammed his massive shoulder into the old wood door.

Creak. But the door didn't give.

Skyler hugged herself. The soldiers' running steps were getting closer. What was wrong with Fahrrad that he'd employ goons like this to come after one little programmer? Although, considering the dictator's oily leer and the teddy under this lunking T-shirt, Fahrrad probably wasn't interested in her programming skills.

Her rescuer launched a tremendous lunge at the door. The wood and metal creaked loudly, and she could almost see it bow inward, but it still didn't break.

His face tightened, and he slapped his palm against the old wood. "Damn."

"We're d-d...?" She couldn't say the word, and substituted, "Done for?"

"Or worse. Wait, what's that?"

She heard it then, too, the roar of a truck racing up the narrow street toward them.

He started grinning like a demon. "Come on." Grabbing her by the wrist, he tugged her into motion.

Seeing as their lives hung in the balance, she generously decided to postpone making an issue of his continued caveman tactics. Instead, she stumbled along after him, concentrating on blocking the pain so she could keep up with his long-legged stride without tripping. She noted with consternation that his feet, though also bare, were not giving him any trouble on the uneven surface of the street. Hers were sore and sticky from both tar and bloody cuts, and she'd have given up her daily diet soda pops for a pair of shoes or even a nice smooth, paved road. Well, a day or two of privation anyway.

Behind them rang the clap of boots, almost drowning out her breath rasping in her ears. She cut a quick glance behind her.

The horde of men in quasi-military uniforms were nearly on them.

But behind *them,* roaring down the street, came a delivery-size truck—piloted by a guy who must've stolen it the way he barreled along.

"Ah, the quintessential truck driver." Her hulking benefactor kept running while the soldiers, becoming aware of the impending danger, hesitated. The tank grinned back at the oncoming truck. "Even if they had speed limits here in Misr, drivers would ignore them."

Misr. The name of the capital city confirmed she was in Middle Yemen.

Her rescuer was right, though. The truck plowed almost gleefully into the formation of soldiers. They had to leap out of its way or be annihilated, like a bowling ball scattering pins or grasshoppers fleeing a lawn mower.

But they'd regroup quickly. Once the demented truck passed her, the men would have a clear shot.

That would have to wait. The delivery vehicle now barreled down on *them*. She tensed muscles to do her own lawn-mower leap.

But her paladin grabbed her arm. "This is our chance." He yanked.

Not away from the truck. *Toward* it.

Paladin? She meant brute. Idiot bruiser. Barbaric psychopath.

"Are you nuts? We'll be killed!"

"Possibly. But if we stick around here, the probabilities go up exponentially."

Holding her tight, he jumped onto the side of the truck as the large vehicle careened down the street, slamming them both into metal sheeting.

"*Oof.*" Scathing words tumbled in Skyler's brain, but splatting like a bug insured none of them left her mouth for lack of breath.

Cursing and wailing rose from behind as she scrabbled to find purchase on two inches of running board, clinging hard with her bare toes. The tank guided her hands to small metal handles riveted to the side of the truck, which appeared to have been installed exactly for that purpose, to give people the ability to hitch a ride.

The truck took a corner, and the G forces tried to pull her stomach out of her ribcage.

Hitch a ride? Who the heck would do something so insane *on purpose?* She clutched the small handholds with a death-grip and flung a glare at her "rescuer."

The man hung next to her, his hair blown artfully by the wild speed, his eyes sparkling, and his grin almost rakish. *Programmers on a pogo stick.* Here she was, barely clinging as a madman driver tore up the narrow streets of Middle Yemen, and *this* guy posed like an ad out of *GQ*.

Skyler reached out a foot to kick him in his complacency, but the wind caught her leg and threw her off balance. Her toes slipped; her grip was torn from the handholds.

She fell.

Something hard hit her—*oof*—throwing her into a roll, and kept her rolling as she hit ground.

Eventually she landed sprawled on her stomach. When the world stopped spinning, she took an experimental breath. Lungs okay. She checked herself mentally. Head—attached. Arms—present, and, after a half-hearted waggle, all her fingers seemed to work. Stomach—trying to evacuate, but that was to be expected.

Dazed, she looked down.

Cobalt eyes stared up at her with an expression of mild disgust.

She lay on the tank as if he were a mattress. She wasn't as injured as she expected because the hard thing hitting her was *him*, a lot less hard than the pavement would have been. He'd apparently jumped as she fell, and pulled her into the concussion-absorbing roll that saved her life. Even now his strong arms were protectively tight around her.

She'd have been a lot more grateful if it wasn't for that disgusted look on his handsome face.

She wriggled loose of his arms and rolled off him, hitting the rocky ground with an, "Ow." She'd have more bruises out of this. Even now, purple flowers were starting to blossom on her legs and arms. Stupid translucent skin.

Beyond her, he rose gracefully to his feet to stand, nonchalant, against the night sky. His hands were open on his hips, and his legs spread and stable, like dual trunks of some great tree. The few scratches he had only added to his aura of potent masculinity. Her heart started hammering, and somehow, she didn't think it was from running. Damn, he was big.

Slowly, so he wouldn't see how she trembled, she rose.

He moved aside and pointed. Behind him, stars twinkled in the sweltering heat, glittering off the gentle swell of black sea.

"Is that a port?" she said. "Is that where we're going?"

"That's where *you* are going." The man took two strides, bent, and shouldered her.

"Wait!" She tried to kick him, but missed by several inches of now wished-for height. "Put me down. I can walk. Just put me down!"

He did eventually put her down, in the dimly lit hold of a large ocean freighter. "This ship is bound for Boston. You should be able to get home from there."

"How do you know that? Who *are* you?" Relief warred with confusion in her gut. "Aren't you coming?"

"No." True to enigmatic form, he only answered the last question. "Kul is on board. He'll take care of you."

What had she expected, a romantic rescue capped by a cruise filled with mad, passionate lovemaking? Not from a truck who carted her around like a bag of kitty litter or a sack of potatoes or *any* grocery store item. Grudgingly, she added, "Thank you." *I think.* "You saved my life."

"Probably," he agreed.

No false modesty for him; very Han Solo. She smiled ruefully, admitting to herself that she kind of liked it. "Where is this Kul?"

"Here in the cargo hold. Stay in the hold with him until the ship is under way, then go to the captain. Kul will help you out with him. He'll see you to safety. Use my name." He swung through the hatch.

"Wait!" Damn it. She had to remember, for a tank, he really moved fast. "What *is* your name?"

He barely glanced back over his broad shoulder. "Cliff."

"Ha. Cliff, Rock, Hulk. I get it. What's your real name?"

But he was gone.

*　　*　　*

"Cliff. Simply lucking fuvely. *'Hello, captain. Yes, I know I haven't booked a passage and you don't know me from Adam, but, hey, it's okay. Cliff said so.'*" Her arms crossed over her chest, Skyler leaned against a wooden crate, one amid jumble of metal containers and wooden crates in the dim hold stacked like a giant child's blocks. "That's sure to get me the red carpet treatment. Cliff!"

If he could be trusted—and grudgingly, instinctively, she knew he could—two days of terror were almost over. She rolled her shoulders. What had her life come to, that her freedom depended on a man she'd met—had *kissed*—an hour ago?

The weight of his body on hers, his hand, tangled in her hair, his mouth, sweet on hers, his tongue...

"Hello, young lady." The pleasant baritone voice came from her right. She whirled, ready to fight or flee.

A slim, middle-aged man faced her. "Please, miss. Come with me. Cliff has arranged for—"

"Are you Kul?" She tugged at the hem of the T-shirt, glad both its length and the dim lighting covered her blush. But excitement quickly overrode any fear or embarrassment. Now, maybe she would learn something about her rescuer. "You know Cliff?"

"I am indeed Kulinahr. And it was Cliff who brought me here. But please, we must—"

"Prince Kulinahr? The ruler of Middle Yemen?" She'd read about him during her research. She'd liked everything she read about the man.

The prince gave a short bow. "No longer ruler, I'm afraid. But alive, at least for the moment. We must hurry and hide. All ships leaving Misr are searched before clearing the harbor. Come, Cliff has made arrangements."

Kulinahr led her between crates, bales, and bags to a van-sized wood container marked with stencils "SAND SAMPLES - DO NOT DROP." One side was open. "Quickly. Come in and help me close the crate."

She ducked inside. Together, they swung the side of the container closed.

Darkness dropped over her. She heard Kulinahr fumble in the close air. Suddenly a small, battery powered lantern, sitting in one corner of the enclosure, illuminated the cramped confines.

Grim, tired lines etched the former ruler's unshaven face, lines that weren't in his official photographs. His suit was dusty and torn on one side.

Kulinahr picked up the lantern and ran it along the bottom edge where they had closed the crate. With a small sigh of satisfaction, he set the lantern down, and pulled hard on a thin, white cord snaking from the same corner the lantern had occupied.

A pungent smell crept through the crate. "Pepper." He straightened. "Fahrrad uses dogs in his clearance searches, ostensibly to search for drugs. Pepper will block their sense of smell for days, yet it's harmless."

"And Cliff managed to arrange for all this? How? When?"

"In the week since my country was taken…well, I will explain after we've left the harbor. But right now, we must be silent."

Skyler sat carefully on the rough wood of the crate's floor. Kulinahr sat opposite her and turned out the light.

She breathed carefully in the pepper-filled dark, trying to relax. Being on a ship inside a crate was just one more bizarre occurrence. She'd have some story to tell when she arrived back home. After she got home… Well, she couldn't really think past that. She closed her eyes and leaned back. Gradually, she became aware of her body. Her stomach twinged, her feet were sore, her body ached, and her leg was falling asleep.

Couldn't do anything about food or aches, but she could relieve the pressure on her leg. She shifted—and pain stabbed her bottom. "Ouch!"

"What has happened?"

"I've got a splinter in my…my…well, you know."

"Oh." A rustle, steps, and then Kulinahr touched her shoulder. "Here. Sit on my jacket."

Skyler reached out. Her fingers met rich silk fabric. "Wow. Nice coat. Are you sure? I mean, this seems pretty expensive."

"Yes, I'm sure. This suit will never receive another U.N. delegation, but I think it should continue a useful life. Now, quiet, please."

Taking the jacket, she arranged it into a seat pad, folded her legs into a half-lotus, and opened herself to her environment. Dim shouts of dock workers—she now wondered how Cliff had managed a route to the hold that avoided all their eyes—punctuated the muted clank and grumble of machinery, as if the outside was wrapped in cotton. Just over the threshold of her hearing was the incessant rush and slap of water.

A low thrumming of engines began under her. Her spirits lifted. They'd soon leave the harbor, headed home.

Then a series of sharper clanks and bangs made her suck in a breath. The start of the police inspections.

She held her breath automatically until her chest felt about to explode. Mindful of sound in this muffled darkness, she exhaled very slowly. As heavy boots on metal stairs mixed with shouts of men and pants and yelps of dogs, she barely breathed.

The clangs and yelps advanced and receded as the teams went back and forth between stacks of cargo. It seemed it would never end, but when, gradually, the sounds receded and then vanished, Skyler let out a gush of air. They were gone. She reached out a hand to touch Kulinahr, opening her mouth to speak...

A dog barked—right next to her.

She startled so hard she felt like she left her skin behind.

Boots clomped up to the crate. She sat trembling, eyes so wide she could feel the stir of air cool them. Snuffling at the edge of the crate was followed by a bark that sounded like, "Here!" More dogs came closer, whining and snuffling in their eagerness. She clamped her lower lip with her teeth and tried to make herself as small and quiet as possible.

Tickle. Skyler was balled so tight at first she didn't know where the urge came from. *Tickle.* Her throat pricked. The tickle built in throat and nose until her eyes watered, and she was certain she was going to cough. She swallowed several times in an effort to keep her body under control.

Suddenly, a dog sneezed. Another snorted. Several more wheezed and yipped. The dogs had run into the pepper and sniffed full noses. She rasped out a quiet cough in the confusion.

An officer shouted orders. Boots pounded and then clanged as the police hustled the dogs topside.

She started to unfold from her place, until Kulinahr's warning touch held her still.

Tramping returned. Then silence.

Crack! Skyler jumped. A resounding series of bangs and cracks followed, getting closer. The police were apparently hitting crates and containers, trying to scare any stowaways out of hiding.

They know we're here.

Her heart rat-a-tatted in her chest like a snare drum.

Several sets of feet marched closer—and stopped right outside her crate. Skyler's heart raced, her breathing so shallow and quick that air rasped like sandpaper. Kulinahr gripped her wrist, she thought in order to caution her to be quiet.

The crate tipped like a carnival ride.

Her world shifted under her, tilting crazily onto an edge, sending her tumbling along the side. But Kulinahr must've grabbed a handhold because she stopped short of bashing into the other end, his hand tight on her wrist, holding on with all his strength.

The crate dropped back on the deck with an explosive thud.

Kulinahr let go. She landed on her hands and knees. Gasping silently like a fish, she waited. Not moving a muscle. Not when the banging retreated, not when it stopped altogether, not even when she heard the boots clang back up the stairs. She remained frozen until, at last, she felt the ship move under her.

Gingerly, she edged into a corner. Now she knew how a deer felt during hunting season. Hiding in the woods, never able to show their snouts. Sneaking out only to eat. Her stomach picked that moment to growl.

Kulinahr's low voice sounded in her ear. "I believe they are gone. Normally I would advise prudence, to wait until we leave territorial waters to present ourselves."

Skyler nodded, then remembered he couldn't see her. "But...?" She sure hoped there was a "but". Her churning stomach was starting to make a nuisance of itself.

"But in this case, I believe it would be in our best interests for the captain of this vessel to know we are here sooner rather than later."

Scraping noises were followed by a couple metallic clacks. A pinhole of light beamed in about two feet up one wall. The prince's head disrupted the beam, and Skyler realized he was peering out a knee-high peephole. Whatever he saw or didn't see must have reassured him, because a moment later he opened the crate. Skyler creaked back to her feet. Snagging the prince's jacket, she followed him out.

"Here's your coat." She held it out to him, surprised when her arm trembled.

He took it, only to settle it over her shoulders. "Why don't you keep it for now?"

"Grandma always said to refuse an offer at least twice to know if it's serious. But in this case, thanks."

Smiling briefly, he started off.

She tried to follow. The floor, or deck or whatever, lurched under her. Concentrating, she managed to keep her feet but walking was weird for a while, and not just because her soles stung. "What was all that with the dogs?"

"Fahrrad evidently knows I was still in the country." Threading through the wooden crates and larger metal shipping containers in the hold, he muttered a phrase in Midyemeni. "I believe those were his special police. They are deadly. It is well Cliff planned this escape, for I think Fahrrad has spies among even my most loyal militia. They would have discovered us had we shifted in that crate."

"We're lucky you found that handhold then."

"Luck was not involved. The strap I held on to is not standard equipment for a crate; not on the inside, at any rate."

And how lucky was it that she'd run into the one guy...tank...man who had an escape planned from Fahrrad's men?

Or was luck not involved with that, either?

Cliff. Lightning in a crisis, rescuer extraordinaire. He'd saved her life, but he'd also treated her like kitty litter, and slightly stupid kitty litter at that. Had he known she was in trouble and come looking for her? If so, how had he known she'd be there, at that boarding house?

Had her messenger bag breadcrumb actually worked?

Somehow, of all the fantastic things that had happened, that was the least believable to her.

While she was musing, Kulinahr had reached a set of stairs and was halfway up. She sprinted to catch him.

She worked out regularly and was in decent enough shape, but by the time she overtook him, she was panting. The last few years sitting in front of a laptop screen with diet sodas and popcorn must've been more taxing on her than she'd thought.

Not to mention swinging through the air like Tarzan and Jane.

She clamped down on that thought. *Not thinking about Tarzan and his smooth chest and flat waist and muscled arms. Not at all.*

So of course the first words out of her mouth were, "What do you know about Cliff?" Mentally, she facepalmed.

Kulinahr reached the upper door. "He would make a most formidable enemy." He grunted it open and helped her through.

"Yeah." She found herself in a spare, metal corridor. Kulinahr paused to orient himself. While he did, she shifted her arms into his coat's sleeves then unwrapped the T-shirt from her head. Or rather, untangled it. The lunking thing seemed to have mated with her hair, probably why she hadn't lost it during the Cirque du Soleil that was their escape. The bobby pins had poked holes through the material and twisted in her tresses until the only way she could free herself was to tear out a couple hunks of hair, wincing with the eye-watering pain.

The prince decided on a direction and strode off with confidence. *Must've been a great leader.*

Scalp smarting, she followed. As she walked, she tried to take her mind off her stinging scalp and feet by folding the T-shirt. The voluminous cloth refused to stay in any orderly kind of shape. When Kulinahr stopped for a moment to take stock, she shook the tee out to try again— and felt something.

Small, flat and hard. Embedded in the material. Carefully, she moved her fingertips along the edges. It felt square. The prince took off again, waving at her to follow. She lurched into a trot after him, still poking at the shirt, trying to find some way to extract the object by feel. No openings. Methodically, she turned the shirt inside out and tried again, bumping occasionally into the walls in her distraction.

This time, she found a small storm flap pocket.

Poking gingerly, she got the impression of plastic. She started to withdraw the object, then had second thoughts. What if she took it out and lost it? She ran her finger over the edges, noting a notch and what felt like tiny metal threads.

It felt like a small computer board, but not any she'd encountered before. Puzzled, she was about to draw it out anyway when a gravely Popeye voice boomed out in the enclosed metal space.

"Hey. Hey you!"

Popeye the Grizzly Bear? The big, deep voice froze both Skyler and Kulinahr.

The sailor stepped into view with a snarled, "Stowaways! What are you doing here?"

Chapter Four

At the big rasping voice crying "Stowaways", Skyler tucked the shirt with its odd computer board under her arm and prepared to fight.

But the grizzled sailor, wearing some kind of coverall, was far from a lumbering bear. As the wiry mariner trotted up, she was surprised to see that he barely cleared the prince's shoulders.

Kulinahr spoke to him in a low voice and when the sailor started nodding, Skyler relaxed.

The sailor took off. Waving her to come along, Kulinahr followed. She trotted after.

The seaman led them through a dizzying number of tight passages and up and down enough ladders to qualify as a kid's playland. Her stomach growled at least three times. She opened her mouth to ask Kulinahr where they were going and how long they'd be lost in this maze but realized ruefully it would sound like a kid on a car ride. *Are we there yet?*

Finally, the seaman knocked on a door, got a booming "Come in."

This time she knew the booming voice was because of all the metal rooms. But again she was surprised when the seaman opened the door to a large man seated behind a desk, his florid face contrasting vividly with his short-sleeved epaulet-shouldered white shirt.

The captain stood in welcome. "Prince Kulinahr. Captain Fletcher, at your service."

Kulinahr led the way in. Fletcher's Boston accent sounded like home, and Skyler followed eagerly, shushing her sore feet through ankle-deep carpeting. Her eyes were dazzled by rich walnut paneling and stuffed, studded leather furniture, her ears by the hushed quality, dampening even the pervasive slapping water—but overriding that all was the scent of shrimp and tangy seafood sauce.

Skyler's mouth prickled.

The captain plucked a delicate pink shrimp from a tray clipped to his desk as he sat. He still hadn't seen her. "Sit, sit." He waved at a pair of overstuffed chairs opposite the desk, busy dipping the shrimp into shiny red sauce then through his ruddy lips.

Her stomach growled yet again, trying to gnaw its way through her backbone.

The captain's gaze snapped up. "Two of you?"

Skyler couldn't really hear him over the demands of her stomach. While she'd only vaguely missed eating the previous two days, in the last two minutes, she'd become ravenous. Pavlov's dogs had nothing on her. *Ring the shrimp, and she salivates.*

Kulinahr sat in one of the chairs. She slid her nearly naked behind into the other and found herself cuddled by a cloud.

"I was told one passenger." The captain's eyes cut to her and narrowed, his expression hardening.

She swallowed a lump. His accent sounded like home, but that glare said she was nowhere near safe. "I-I was kidnapped. Cliff rescued me. He said you'd know him."

"Cliff?" The florid man's eyes narrowed to slits on her, and she thought he was going to lock her in the brig to sweat the truth out of her. Instead, he leaned back, narrow gaze still considering her as he swirled a pink shrimp into red sauce, popped it into his mouth, and chewed. Her mouth flooded. Torture-by-shrimp, far more effective than simple nail-pulling. Flicking a bit of sauce from his bristling mustache, he mused, "Lots of people named Cliff."

At that, Skyler's taut nerves, and her temper, snapped. "How many look like a tank?"

Kulinahr glanced at her, eyebrows high, then laughed.

"That does sound like him," the captain admitted, dunking another pink shrimp into the sauce, releasing the sting of horseradish into the air. He bit off the end with relish. "But still. Tell me your story. How did you get here?"

Apparently Cliff's name wasn't the universal passkey he thought it was. Concerned the captain would turn them over to the authorities—to Fahrrad—if she said the wrong thing, she glanced at Kulinahr.

Her panic must've shown in her eyes because he suggested, "Shall I begin?"

She nodded.

"That madman, Fahrrad." The prince's jaw clenched. "I trusted him. I believed him. I made him my guest!"

Sympathy swamping her, she set her own hunger aside to lay a comforting hand on his arm. "He bamboozled all of us."

Thanks sparkled in his dark eyes. "Middle Yemen is a small, peaceful country. But men calling themselves freedom fighters began to terrorize my people with bombings, kidnappings, acts of horrible violence right on the streets of Misr. My citizen militia was overtaxed. I needed help. Fahrrad played on my desperation."

"And that's how you met Cliff?" Hunger of a different kind rose in Skyler. Now maybe she'd find out more about her mysterious rescuer. This would be just like Cliff, a hero swooping in to save a small, defenseless woman...er, country, against an evil dictator.

"No, no. Fahrrad came to me. He had a reputation for dealing smartly with terrorists, and I gave him entry. I should have known...he had planted his own men to disrupt my country. To *cause* me to turn to him. I played right into his hands."

"Why did he want your country?" the captain asked. "Oil?"

"Ah, no. As it turns out, we have small but rich deposits in this century's version of oil—rare earth elements."

Skyler sucked in a breath. "Vital to computers and batteries."

"And until now, mostly found in China, yes. I knew that was a possibility, of course. But I thought, what harm could he do? Even in his home country, he's considered a dinosaur—he'd roll back perestroika, if he could. My people would never accept him." Kulinahr fell silent, his gaze fixed on some point deep within.

Compassion warmed her, and a spark of admiration. He'd led his people to peace and prosperity in just a few decades. *He's a modern day ruler, yet put him in a galabiyya and keffiyeh and he could have come straight out of a book on the ancient patriarchs. The more things change...*

As her mind turned, her gaze wandered the small chamber, alighting on a table-sized globe—and beside it, a table bearing a second tray of shrimp, bowing in a circle to a cup of glistening sauce. A golden aura appeared behind the shrimp ring; she swore she heard a heavenly choir sing, "Ah!"

Before she even knew it, she'd risen and nonchalantly traipsed over.

"I hired Fahrrad to help us keep guard while our security system was designed and built."

Security system? Skyler's ears pricked and her heartbeat picked up. Fahrrad wanted one, too.

"We are small and locked in by much larger countries. Technology, not manpower, must be our salvation. A defense net may not have worked for a nation as large as your United States, but for us, it is feasible. Ah, to release my people for peaceful pursuits... Well, you can see the advantages."

"Country-wide defense? Code name Star Wars?" Captain Fletcher winked.

"Ah, no. Pizza Pie, actually. But it is brilliant, a marvel of advanced technology."

A glance showed the captain deeply engrossed by the sheikh's narration. One hand casually turning the globe, Skyler reached out with the other toward the shrimp, and...

"Ms. Jones," the captain boomed. "What are you doing?"

She nearly shrieked. Smiling past her skyrocketed heart rate, she said, "Just looking at your globe. Lovely. Was it hard to bolt to the floor?" Babbling, all the while keeping an eye on the shrimp. They were winking at her. She swallowed. "So, um, Prince Kulinahr. Is that how you finally met Cliff, escaping Fahrrad?"

He had turned in his chair, his gaze on her perplexed. "No, I met him before. Cliff was why I hired the colonel. Cliff was constructing the defense system. Even better, he wanted to build the manufacturing plant in my country. In one stroke, we'd double our protection and our revenue. Bonus, I would get a smart house."

"Cliff is a *businessman*?" Skyler's mouth fell open. "But...but I thought he was an international spy or something."

Kulinahr's cheeks folded in a smile. "He has some rather, ah, unusual skill sets. He warned me that Fahrrad intended to overthrow me. But the security system would not be ready for four or five months—and that was after he solved some sort of staffing problem—and I needed protection immediately. Alas, I chose the madman. But it was my country's security versus my own. I would make the same decision again."

"But if Cliff knew Fahrrad was plotting against you, why didn't he do something?"

"He did. He saved my life."

"Yeah, but couldn't he have done something about Fahrrad?" Skyler shifted uncomfortably beside the shrimp. The dictator's chilling smile, his reaching for her hair, his goons snatching her off the street, featured in all her nightmares and would for years to come.

The prince spread earnest hands. "You don't understand how much of a risk Cliff took saving my life. Fahrrad and his personal guard are ruthless. Murder is an acceptable political tool to him."

"Oh." Skyler read the steep price of the bloody coup in the sheen of Kulinahr's eyes, and her heart went out to him. "I'm so sorry."

"Thank you." He blinked and a tear trickled down his cheek. He dashed it away. "If not for the bravery of my personal servant and, of course, Cliff, I would not have made it out of the palace alive."

The captain frowned. "But the coup was over a week ago."

"The madman's search was intense, ruthless. He knew my people would rally around me and swept the country again and again. I only survived by hiding in the desert highland, constantly on the move."

The tang of seafood sauce wafted more insistently into Skyler's nose and awareness. Swallowing saliva only brought into contrast how empty her stomach was. Sidling in front of the shrimp, she casually reached behind her. "So, um, Prince Kulinahr. What will you do now?" She'd hide a few pieces in the voluminous folds of the T-shirt. A handful would hide nicely. Or two. Maybe even three. For once, she was glad of the tank's size.

"I hope to find support among governments friendly to me in the past. Or if not support, then at least refuge."

"Mmm." Gradually, so gently, her fingers wrapped around a tail...

"Now you, Ms. Jones." The captain's voice was like a cannon shot.

She dropped the shrimp. Cursed. "Yes?"

"How did you end up on board?"

She opened her mouth to say, "I don't know." But that would sound lame. No way she wanted to get in trouble with the man who held their freedom in his hands.

Again Kulinahr came to the rescue. "I can answer that. Cliff came early for me this evening. He'd had to move the schedule up because he'd heard about a Mr. Jones who'd been kidnapped and was off to look for him."

"*Mr.* Jones?" Skyler rolled her eyes. That, if anything, made Cliff's being a businessman real. No way a super duper spy would get such basic information wrong. Shaking her head to herself, she felt behind her for the shrimp she'd dropped.

"How long until the protection grid goes up?" the captain asked.

"Wait, what?" Skyler stopped searching, shocked. "Cliff is *going through with the deal?*"

Kulinahr shrugged. "He is a businessman. Since he cannot do business with me, he will do business with the current leader—and probably turn a better profit. Fahrrad does not know how to bargain." His tone was touched with scorn.

"But...but there are more important things than the bottom line!" Indignation on the prince's behalf pushed any hunger or fear of the captain away. *And here I thought Cliff was a hero.*

The prince loosely lifted a hand, palm up. "I'm not ungrateful. I owe Cliff my life. And the jobs he brings my people will help them prosper, no matter who governs them." To Fletcher he added, "The protection grid will be ready by the end of the year. After which, Fahrrad will be immune to attack."

Skyler came back to her chair, touching the sheik's arm in sympathy as she sank down in the seat. "Can't you convince the U.N. to help before then, or Congress or someone? Anyone...?"

"I hope so. But I am in exile." He gave her a gentle, remorseful smile. "The world at large may have more on its mind than one tiny country."

The idea of Fahrrad winning over this gentle, honorable man made her want to weep. "You said your people will still follow you. Maybe you could raise an army?"

"I will not put my people in jeopardy simply to regain my position. Besides, by the time I could get any viable forces gathered, well...the grid will be active."

The sour tang in her mouth wasn't hunger. "Because of *Cliff*."

"Ms. Jones, a word of advice." Fletcher turned his gaze on her and scowled, bushy eyebrows like low thunderheads. "Don't mention his name to anyone. In fact, forget you ever met him."

"Why?" More to the point, *how?*

"He shuns publicity. If you attempt to identify him in connection with your rescue, he will deny it."

"Right. I won't talk about him on Twitface."

"Not just social media. Do not mention him to the press, the police, or the government. Especially not the government. Do not cross him on this."

What? The captain made Cliff sound like a criminal. *Here I thought Cliff was a hero, idiot that I am. Perfect men only exist in fairy tales.* Inside, she was crumpling. She'd allowed herself to get carried away with daydreams.

Reality sucked.

"And now, my guests," boomed the captain, "I will ring for a late dinner. In the meantime, please help yourself to those delicious shrimps." He waved his hand at the tray beside the globe.

"Right." Skyler jumped up, crossed the room in a single bound, and began to stuff shrimps in her mouth. "Mmm, good." She licked her fingers. "When you ring for more food, could I have a glass of water? And a napkin? And maybe some pants?"

*   *   *

The secure phone rang loudly in the empty office, clanging five times before the blond man ran, cursing, through the doorway. He caught it on the sixth ring. "I didn't expect you to call." He was panting a little, though he was mid-thirties and in top shape. He chalked it up to the stress his boss was putting him under.

The voice at the other end was wry. "I didn't expect to call. Something's come up."

"Not more bad news, I hope."

There was silence. He wondered how many satellites were bouncing the signal as he waited patiently. Finally the other voice came again. "Good news, rather. I've solved that problem we had in staffing."

The blond straightened in surprise. "That was quick."

Another pause, less lengthy. "I know. But it's right."

"If you say so. One less thing to worry about, at least. Do you want me to make arrangements?"

"No. I'll take care of it myself."

Hanging up, he grinned. He'd heard *personal interest* in his perpetually lonely boss's voice, which actually meant *two* less things to worry about.

Chapter Five

While still on the ship, Skyler phoned her boss Phil and demanded three things. "A week's paid vacation with pay when I arrive home, and a security system installed in my apartment—paid for by the company."

"Okay," Phil said quickly. "And the third thing?"

She frowned. Phil had agreed too fast. But maybe that was because he knew what was coming. She geared herself up for an argument.

"Third—Fahrrad off the client list.

"Already done," her boss said with a speed that was slightly unnerving.

Frown deepening, Skyler hung up. Her stomach rolled unpleasantly, and not all of it was seasickness.

Phil always had an angle. Something would be waiting for her at the end of her week off, something unpleasant.

*   *   *

She was on the ship for three days when Kulinahr announced he'd gotten a flight for them to Boston. They debarked at a Mediterranean port, were badged by dark-suited men through customs, boarded a commercial 747, and she thought she was home free.

But after takeoff, the polite yet insistent gentlemen with the official dark suits took her into an empty lounge where they questioned her in great detail for nearly the whole flight. By the time the suits realized she didn't know anything and dropped her back in her seat, she felt more exhausted than in the whole two days of her abduction.

Then the plane landed and she was home.

Thanks to her bright red hair, the moment Skyler stepped off the plane in the United States, the press crowded around her. Kulinahr gave her a sympathetic, better-you-than-me look and used her ambush to slip away.

Coward.

True to her word, she didn't mention Cliff, despite the reporters shouting endless questions at her. "Did you experience Stockholm Syndrome? *I was only captured a couple days.* "Tell us about your feelings when you realized you were to be sold like an animal." *I was never up for sale. Do your research next time.* She nearly belted the overenthusiastic newshound who actually asked, "What would you have felt like if you had been killed by these terrorists?"

A few circuits short of a motherboard, but the press was emphatically better than the official suits. More showed up and she cringed until they dropped her off at her apartment. She didn't ask them how they knew where she lived. She only wished they'd been half as Johnny-on-the-spot finding her in Middle Yemen.

Then Cliff might not have had the chance to make such a big impact.

Outside the door of her apartment, she reached for her hip where her bag normally hung and stopped, momentarily flummoxed without her purse. Buzzing the super produced an extra key.

Finally home, she dumped the borrowed sack with T-shirts and teddy on her bed, stripped off the coverall Captain Fletcher's petty officer had scrounged up, and took a steaming shower. Then another, so cold her teeth chattered. Then another hot one, scrubbing until she scrubbed skin off.

Finally, during a fourth shower, the phone rang, her friend Tess.

"Oh my God. Skyler. Are you okay?"

Yes, she started to say. But somehow it came out as a long, blubbery cry.

"Sweetie, don't move. I'm coming over."

The hot water hadn't even run out before Tess showed up at her door—with three bottles of wine.

Skyler, wrapped in a towel, let her in.

Tess immediately enveloped her in a strong hug.

"Stop," she protested weakly. "You're getting wet."

"And I'm going to get wetter. Shut up and cry."

With a sigh, Skyler gave in and did. When she wound down, Tess released her.

"Now." Tess gave her a gentle push toward her bedroom. "Go get in your softest PJs. I'll pour while you do."

Skyler took her time. Now came the hard part. Tess would want to hear the full story. She returned to two glasses of wine, the first bottle nearby for refills and the second uncorked and ready to go.

"Sit," Tess commanded. "Drink."

Sliding onto the couch beside her friend, Skyler lifted her glass, needing two hands because her hands shook. "I'm not sure I'm ready to talk about it."

"Then I'll talk. We found your messenger bag."

As Tess paused to sip at her wine, Skyler threw back her entire glass. She barely heard Tess continue.

"We put the pieces together and got hold of the state department."

"Thanks." The alcohol's heat hit Skyler's belly, buoying her into a place where she could be calmer about the whole terrifying episode. "State put out an alert."

Casually, Tess poured her a refill. "So what happened?"

Skyler tested her memories, founded them slightly numbed. Still horrific, but less painful. "He kept wanting to touch my hair." She shuddered.

"Fahrrad? Ugh."

"Yeah." She picked up her glass and drained it again. Her hand, reaching for the wine bottle, shook. One bottle of wine was gone before she was able to tell her friend the whole story. "The kidnappers came running, so I ran, too." And began the flight which had brought her to that tank of a man. To Cliff.

Remembering his big, strong body, his competent rescue, the tightness in her chest eased. He'd saved her as dramatically as any graphic novel hero. Well, except for the lugging-her-around-like-kitty-litter part. That was more Deadpool than Captain America. But still.

Then he'd turned out to be a businessman.

"Yikes." Tess pressed a hand to her breastbone. "My heart is hammering. How are you not a wreck?"

Skyler poured a glass from the second bottle. "This helps. You, me, the wine. Also, I'm having a security system installed here."

"Isn't that expensive?"

"Cash is courtesy of a short, sharp discussion with our beloved company. They'll pay for it in full—apparently legal stuff comes from a different pot in the General Ledger than salary. I'm also buying pepper spray and training to use it. I got a week off to put the incident behind me."

"Just a week?"

"That's a luxury. I'll spend the whole next month playing catch up while Phil crabs about my dive in production."

It took all of the second bottle to brave showing Tess the teddy. Even now, safe, at home, tears leaked from her eyes.

Tess paled. "Why'd you keep it?"

"I don't know." Skyler's heart beat harder, but the alcohol dulled it into a throb. She clenched her eyes briefly, and the tears threaded hot down her cheeks. "To show my strength over adversity? It's not working."

"I know what'll get it out of your system." Tess drew her to her feet and led her to the kitchen, where she turned on the gas burner. "If you would do the honors?"

Skyler stared blankly at the flames until she realized what her friend wanted her to do.

An internal *yes* burned through her in reply. She opened a drawer and grabbed a pair of tongs as she pointed to a cabinet. "Get a big bowl of water in case I screw this up."

"You won't."

"You're right. I won't." Seizing the straps with the tongs, she held the red wisp over the flames until the bottom caught fire.

She burned the whole damned thing.

As the last bit went up, she plunged the tongs into the bowl. "That felt *good*."

Tess smiled. "You look better. Almost your own plucky self again."

"Thanks." She took the bowl, set it aside, and gave her friend a strong hug.

Once Tess had gone, Skyler dumped the rest of the sack on her bed.

Time to deal with the huge black T-shirts.

They didn't fold any easier. She laid one flat on her spread, managing not to think about the man who'd given it to her, and carefully folded it. It was easier with the cloth laid flat.

Then she picked up the second shirt—which was inside out.

It took her a moment to remember her explorations on the ship, and two whole minutes to find the small storm flap pocket, thanks to the wine.

When she finally pulled out the tiny flat square, she could only stare at it. Pins ran along both sides like rows of shark's teeth. Like an old-fashioned chip set, although there was something about its underside that looked strange, a glossy, wobbly sort of feel that was almost like a bank card holograph.

A retail anti-theft device for the T-shirts? If so, it hadn't done any good because that tank of a man had boosted at least two of the voluminous suckers.

Like he'd boosted her. *Cliff, carrying her in his big, strong arms, her face cradled in the nook of his shoulder, breathing his masculine tang*...she found her nose buried in black cloth.

She practically ran to her closet to stuff the shirts into her laundry hamper. Reopened it and poked the black material under the coverall. Then, just to be thorough, she grabbed her towels from the bathroom and stuffed them on top.

*   *   *

The week off was eaten up putting her life back in order—talking to the police, follow-ups with all the alphabet agencies, arranging for home security, and sitting through sessions on PTSD.

She was almost glad to go back to work.

Walking into Fitzwater Software and Consulting, Tess jumped up and swept her into a hug. "You ready for this?"

Acres of stress eased from Skyler's neck and back. She returned Tess's hug. "More than. Can't wait to lose myself in friends and work."

"Speaking of work." Tess released her to point.

Phil Westerby barreled down the hallway toward her. "Skyler, there you are."

Her boss, who'd given into her demands far too easily. She cringed.

Sure enough, he snared her arm. "Come with me." He dragged her toward his office.

"Welcome home, Skyler," she said acidly. "Nice tan." She supposed this was better than being flung like a sack of potatoes.

"You never tan," Phil said. "But I'm glad you're back safe. Now enough small talk. You have a new assignment. Urgent."

Skyler's temper spiked. The last "new and urgent" assignment had gotten her kidnapped. To keep her anger from making her do something stupid, she took a deep breath and tried to convince herself it was just business.

Nope. Still pissed.

Entering Phil's office, she opened her mouth to yell.

"Shut the door if you're going to shriek at me." Phil hurried to his big-assed chair behind his desk and power-sat.

"Shriek?" She slammed the door shut behind her. "I never shriek. I discuss logically."

"Loudly."

"Fine. When, in the name of all the gods of logic, do you think I'd have time for a new account? I didn't have room before, and unless you've suspended the laws of time and space, I don't have room now."

"Make room."

"I think you'd try to make us work twenty-six/ten if you could suspend the laws of time and space." Bless his money-grubbing soul, Phil would be more than happy if she took on another client. But there were only so many fires she could juggle. "No."

"Skyler, you're my top programmer-analyst. I need you on this assignment."

"Nice flattery. Still no."

"This isn't a debate." Phil thumped a file folder on the desk between them. "Sit."

That wasn't good. The thump was a signal. If he raised an eyebrow, the doo was deep.

Sure enough, he raised one brow—he trimmed his eyebrows but there was always one that went Shawshank-Redemption less than an hour after arriving at work. It made the brow-raise extra scary.

Agitated though she was, Skyler sat. The brow lowered, and she let out a relieved breath.

He pushed the folder toward her. "Have you heard of the Hawkesclyffe Computer Company?"

"Sir Humphrey Hawkesclyffe." She was surprised to see EYES ONLY written on it. "Computer genius. HCC is his hardware firm."

"Fortune 500." Phil removed his glasses, and started polishing them, slowly and deliberately. "But if his latest chip is even close to rumored specs"—he leaned forward and tapped his glasses pointedly on his desk blotter—"HCC will take over the industry."

Curious, she opened the folder. Pages of specs greeted her, all watermarked *Top Secret*. "This is about the HCCpi supercomputer?" Stunned, her gaze rose to Phil's.

"Based on the ultra-secret HCC *pi* chip." He made a small noise and perched his glasses on his nose. "Think about it, Skyler. A roomful of racks reduced to a single, cabinet-sized box. The HCCpi's speed will double the fastest supercomputer in petaflops per second on the Linpack benchmark. Perfect for everything from artificial intelligence to information security."

What was it with security? Fahrrad, Kulinahr, Phil, even herself...it seemed like everyone was going mad for security. "What's your point?"

"InfoSec is hot right now. Sure, if Hawkesclyffe sells wide, he'll make his second billion. But if he breaks into the security market? He'll be a one-percenter."

"So the rich get richer."

"Not just the rich—not if Fitzwater management and productivity software is bundled with each HCCpi. We'll make billions too."

"You mean Jerry Fitzwater will. Until I'm vested, *I* get squat." She knew Phil had agreed to her demands too fast. He might as well have said, *"I'll get rid of Fahrrad because we have a new, richer client who wants the same thing. And your week off meant I could sandbag you into taking this client when you returned today."*

She threw waving hands in the air. "Give this urgent assignment to Mel Pinlow. He's always belly aching that he can do everything better than me."

"Can't." Phil smiled like a shark. "He asked specifically for you."

Surprise lit her body. "Mel?"

"No, Skyler. Sir Humphrey Hawkesclyffe."

That pumped shock into her veins. "*What?* He asked for *me?*"

"By name. Now, Sir Humphrey has a reputation as brilliant egocentric—and is incredibly hard to please. But we want to please him, don't we?"

Palming her forehead, Skyler groaned. She supposed geniuses only had to be nice to their loan officers, not their vendors. Sir Humphrey asked for her, so he'd get her. She pictured Hawkesclyffe as Sir Alec Guiness, slender, white-haired, and using The Force on Phil. *These are not the programmers you are looking for.* She dropped her hand. "Why me? Why not you, or Alice, or any of a dozen people higher on the org chart?"

Phil shrugged. "Don't know, don't care. He wants you, he gets you. So, you'll be at the client intro meeting in two hours. And your temper won't. Utterly professional." He paused and his eyes narrowed at her, his boss's glare. His eyebrows waggled like a threatening finger. "Got it?"

She clenched her lids against her irritation. The little cog named Skyler might've been kidnapped and overseas and come back forever changed, but when it got home it was slapped back on the same spindle in the same big machine. "Utterly professional. Got it."

Returning to her desk, she did her best to lose herself in her work. *Sorry I missed the meeting, Phil. I lost track of time.*

Just before one p.m., her phone vibrated an alarm. She pulled it out, saw the group calendar alert pulsing on the screen, and glared. Punching it off with one stiff finger, she rose to her feet and stuffed the phone in her pocket. While she loved tech, it occasionally bit her in the behind.

She marched herself to the conference room. Remembered Phil's words. *"You'll be there. Your temper won't."*

Utterly professional. That had bit her in the behind too.

The last time she'd pushed through this heavy oak door, Fahrrad had been waiting for her. She told herself today couldn't be worse than that.

But because of the last time, before she entered, she paused to take a deep breath then pushed it out, picturing she was pushing her frustration with it.

It took three of those before she realized she wasn't getting any calmer. She'd have to go in and hope for the best.

Time to meet Sir Silverhair. She shoved through the door to the boardroom.

Chapter Six

The conference room was already filled, half the people seated at the table, the other half still standing and chatting.

Tess gave her a big smile and waved. Skyler managed a mechanical wave back as she had an attack of déjà vu the size of Mount McKinley.

Or the size of a cliff.

A man stood listening to Phil, but his cobalt gaze cut through the length of the entire room, eclipsing every other person there, to snare hers.

Those eyes burned with the same blue fire as the last time they met...as when they'd kissed.

Cliff.

He smiled slightly, as if he'd seen her remember it. As if he remembered it too, especially the kiss.

Her whole face heated as if she'd gone up in flames, and she knew she'd turned a betraying bright red. *Stupid translucent complexion.*

Blindly, she pulled out a chair and set her materials on the glossy cherry surface of the conference table. But instead of sitting, she leaned knuckles against the table, trying to collect herself. When she thought she heard Phil move toward her, she straightened to see him, grateful for the distraction.

Just about where Phil's eyes would be, she met a subdued gray silk tie subdividing a pristine white-shirt continent. Cliff certainly was not half-naked this time. His dark suit was exquisitely tailored, fitting his large frame perfectly. No padding; she remembered the breadth of those shoulders and power of that chest.

Steady, lady.

Skyler took a deep breath—and stopped mid-inhale with a rattle. Naked, he smelled of skin and sweat and spicy male. Civilization did nothing to tame that, only added a faint layer of expensive cologne and the rich smell of good cloth. Bottle it up and it could be sold as InstaSex.

Her legs trembled, dumping her into the chair.

"Hello." He pulled out the chair next to hers. The sight of his well-manicured nails and artistic fingers, slender but strong, startled her. Why hadn't she noticed those hands before?

Dimly, she was aware of Phil introducing them as Cliff sat.

"Skyler Jones, may I present the founder and CEO of the Hawkesclyffe Computer Company, and inventor of the HCCpi series and digital/analog *pi* chip, Sir Humphrey Hawkesclyffe."

Her hand flew to her throat. *This* man was Humphrey Hawkesclyffe? How could a Humphrey be a Cliff—? Hawkesclyffe...oh, no. Cliff, as in *Clyffe*.

Sweet exploding stars, she should have been ready for this. After all, Prince Kulinahr had told her Cliff was a businessman. Insanely, what passed through her mind at that moment was wondering why a Sir Humphrey didn't have a British accent.

"We've met. Ms. Jones." He held out his hand, the one she'd been staring at.

Even through her shock, she grabbed the offered hand—professionally. She could do it in her sleep, thanks to her ex-fiancé. Firm but not tight, one-two-three-release.

One-two-three... But "release" short-circuited when his fingers closed around hers, his hand big, hot, and engulfing.

Tingles shivered up her spine. Warm, wonderful shivers rippled through her belly. Her heart pumped faster, and where she sat was getting tingly.

Darn it. She'd managed to write off the impact of his touch, body, scent, as an overactive imagination, a tired, scared woman, and a warm man.

There went that excuse.

She forced a reply. "It's good to see you again, Mr. Hawkes*clyffe*, under improved circumstances."

"It depends on your perspective, Ms. Jones. I found our last encounter—stimulating." He finally released her hand with a slight, lingering caress that nearly made her shiver into little pieces of lust. His lips twitched.

"Stimulating?" Phil's eyes gleamed. "How stimulating?"

Irritation cut through Skyler's flustered feelings. *The conniving so-and-so. Phil thinks he's got a lever to make me take the account.* "An exaggeration." She smiled sweetly at the suited-up tank. "I was under the impression you found our meeting rather routine, Mr. Hawkesclyffe."

"Please, Ms. Jones. I told you last time we met—call me Cliff."

Phil perked up at that like a dog at a bone convention.

Sweet circuits on a stick, this would never do. "I'm sorry, Mr. Hawkesclyffe. You would have to call me Skyler before I could possibly—"

"Skyler, of course."

Grr. He was playing her and her nerves like a toy piano. Plink, plink, plink. "Phil, don't you want to take Mr. Hawkesclyffe—er, Cliff—to meet our president? Jerry's at the podium, and if you hurry, you can catch him before the meeting starts."

"We've met," Cliff said smoothly.

"They've met." Phil nodded. "So you two have fun." His *gotcha* smile curled higher into aggravatingly smug as he strolled away.

Skyler fumed. If she ever broke into the payroll system, someone was so getting a decimal point moved the wrong way on his paycheck. "Phil said you asked for me specifically?" She lowered her voice and spat, "Why the hell would you do that?"

"Because of how I feel about you."

What? Skyler straightened with surprise. Sure, he'd delivered that searing kiss, but otherwise he'd treated her like a sack of potatoes. "Which is?"

"You are the person for the job. I will have no other."

"Ah. The job." She tried not to let her disappointment show. "What a fine compliment Mr.—ah—Cliff." Well, what did she expect? Kulinahr had told her flatly that Cliff was a businessman.

Kulinahr. How sad and tired he'd looked on the ship. She had a sudden urge to take Cliff by the shoulders and give him a good shaking—if she could reach his shoulders. If she could shake a tank.

She scowled at him. "I don't think you're aware of how I feel about you."

"I'm afraid I am."

"Y-you are?"

Under the full impact of his penetrating gaze, her blood heated faster than sugar in a microwave. She had to resist an urge to fan herself.

Mentally, it was hard to connect this Savile-Row savant with the raw, savage man who'd swept her off her feet, but physically they caused far too similar yearnings.

Does he know...? She cleared her throat. "And how do I feel, exactly?"

"You think I deceived you. You're angry. I had my reasons, but they'd have taken too long to explain at the time—and they'd take too long now, so I offered Fitzwater a sizable amount of cash, contingent on you taking this job."

Damn it, Sir Humphrey is after my brain, not my body.

"Your president promised to double your salary."

She blinked, hearing that. Jerry Fitzwater had been known to cut his own kid's allowance for not trimming the grass around the garden after mowing two acres of lawn, yet Cliff talked him into doubling her...*double*?

"If that's not enough, I'll add a hefty bonus. And I'm a bit more generous than your president." He smiled slightly.

Her heart sped up at the white teeth and crinkles augmenting sparkling cobalt eyes. Good Gates, what that smile did to her innards should have been illegal. It certainly was incendiary. She shifted in her chair and swallowed a couple times. "Why? I'm good, but for that kind of money, so are a lot of other people."

"It takes some time to explain, and I'm afraid the meeting is about to begin. I would prefer to discuss this later—perhaps over dinner?"

"D-dinner?" An intimate dinner with a man whose very gaze could trigger spontaneous Skyler combustion?

Yikes. Dinner with the big hero *might* have been one of her fantasies in the past week. But she had to remember Kulinahr. Cliff was a businessman, not a hero. "Let me check my schedule." She pulled out her smart phone and pretended to find an appointment on her calendar. *Thanks for the invitation, but I have a conflict.* Easy way out, saving face for both parties.

"Tonight? Thanks for the invitation—"

"Great. I'll pick you up about six."

Skyler's startled gaze flew up to Cliff's. His cobalt eyes sparkled straight along her optic nerves to light up her brain with pleasure, momentarily making language beyond her. "But dinner...I wasn't..."

"We'll go to Rusterman's."

The most expensive restaurant around. Flustered, she started, "Yes, okay, but—"

"Ladies and gentlemen." Jerry Fitzwater rapped on the podium at the end of the table. "Have a seat so we can get this meeting underway."

A whump announced the chair on her other side being filled. A waft of cheap tobacco and sweat soured by a shirt on its second day announced her nemesis Mel Pinlow was filling it. Naturally.

She thought of "Mirror, Mirror," an episode in the original *Star Trek* show where the crew of the Enterprise is swapped with their evil twins. If ever there were an anti-Skyler, it would be Mel.

Mel was always after her projects, her clients. He measured success, not by the projects he completed or clients he satisfied, but by how overworked he was—which he would then turn around and use as an excuse to get *her* to do his work for him because "Skyler isn't nearly as overbooked as *I* am." And Phil would agree.

Squirming, she thought sitting between Cliff and Mel was like being between the sun and Neptune...or better yet, the downgraded Pluto.

Jerry Fitzwater rapped again for attention. "Today begins a historic occasion and an historic collaboration..."

Jerry's secretary typed rapidly, probably capturing his speech word for word, but Skyler couldn't concentrate because of Cliff, despite sitting raptly attentive beside her, was distracting her with just breathing. His warmth caressed her body, his scent invaded her being, his very presence seemed to tug at her.

How had he done it? How had he, despite her best intentions, cornered her into going to dinner with him against her wishes?

She sighed.

All right. Truthfully, it wasn't against her wishes. But it would be a bad mistake. Getting involved with a man like Cliff, who could leave an instantaneous impression on her that blotted out years of other men, but who'd never consider her anything but good business...no, that was trouble she didn't need.

She'd have to say no to dinner. Something deep inside rebelled, but she had to say no to both herself and him.

She nerved herself to turn toward him. To tap his muscular arm...and just say no. *Going to say no. Going to do it now.* She turned toward him, to whisper her regrets.

And nearly fell into his empty chair as he rose to take the podium.

Three strides, accompanied by enthusiastic applause—most enthusiastic from Tess and the other women, Skyler noticed with a sour pang—brought him to the head of the table, a position which seemed to be made just for him. He removed the podium and stood comfortably surveying the group.

"A historic occasion? Perhaps. With the speed that new information is coming to us, I'll settle for being on the cutting edge of technology. Or, as some prefer, the bleeding edge."

He stopped and, one by one, met the eyes of each person around the table. His penetrating cobalt gaze seemed to assess everything: their reactions, their mood, even their expectations.

Reaching Skyler, the blue of his eyes blazed until she squirmed in her chair.

He smiled slightly and went on. "You are all familiar with digital technology, like a light switch. You are also familiar with analog technology, like a light dimmer. The HCC *pi* Digital-Analog Logic Encoding chip combines both of these technologies in a single chip. Simple but effective."

"Like a quantum chip?" Mel asked. Skyler was surprised that he'd asked a really good question, but he spoiled it by grinning around the table. *See how smart I am?*

Cliff only raised a brow. "Better, actually. A regular chip exists in two states, on or off. A quantum chip has those states plus both states at once, plus the entangled state. Now I won't get into a phenomenon even Einstein called spooky—" he grinned, "—but *pi* technology increases even quantum encoding to an *infinite* number of states."

The whole table looked impressed.

"Digital-Analog Logic Encoding." Jerry's secretary paused typing. "The DALE chip?"

Cliff smiled. "We're going with HCCpi. We also takes advantage of new alloys for cooler processing, allowing us to shrink each chip to the size of a helix of DNA. And we've incorporated the latest advancements in laser data transmission."

Skyler was impressed in spite of herself—until she caught everyone around the table nodding. Looked like a ring of smiling bobbleheads.

So different from Prince Kulinahr's sad face. *"Cliff is a businessman. Since he cannot do business with me, he will do business with the current leader—and probably turn a better profit."*

The HCCpi was perfect for security—Cliff might be working with Fahrrad. And now he wanted to drag Fitzwater into it? She wanted to clunk her head against the boardroom table when that thought occurred to her.

Professional, Skyler. Go with the flow. She practically heard her boss's reprimand.

She glanced again at the smiling, nodding heads. Well, crap. There was loyal, and then there was lemming.

She cleared her throat. "That's hardware. We're software."

Phil glared at her.

She glared back. She was just asking the tank—*excuse me,* Sir *Tank*—reasonable questions in an utterly professional way. "As Fitzwater is a software firm, how do we fit in?" Okay, maybe a bit of a challenge, though couched in professional words.

Cliff only nodded, as if he'd expected her question. Had the gall to say, "Glad you asked, Ms. Jones." He gazed around the table. "I refuse to hobble the HCCpi with decrepit software. I want a team of creative, driven people, not afraid to take chances, make changes, or strike out into completely uncharted territory." He spread his fine hands out, encompassing the group at the table. "I'm here to select that team."

Despite herself, excitement rose in her breast. *Pick me.*

Then heads nodded and murmurs of agreement went around the table. There were even a few shining faces.

He had them eating out of his hand, and almost had her there, too.

Downing their medicine like good little employees. *Going with the flow.*

She had questions. Why was he here? Why had he asked for *her? Is he really working with that blood-soaked dictator, Fahrrad?*

For Kulinahr. Skyler cleared her throat again. "HCC already employs the best machine and assembly language people in the world. You don't need more software engineers."

"Don't be stupid, Skyler." Mel smiled snidely. "Sir Humphrey has the best, but he wants more of the best. Which is why he wants *us.*"

Skyler's internal temperature soared. Her ex-fiancé had hammered the rules of business into her. *Ron's Rule Number One: never tell a client he* doesn't *need you.* Guilt at breaking the rule, anger at still feeling guilty about her ex, irritation at Mel's brown-nosing, his sneering at her as he scented a corporate kill—it all boiled inside her, making her reckless.

She spat point-blank, "Are you working with Boris Fahrrad?"

"Not at present," Cliff said smoothly, without missing a beat. "No."

Skyler felt like the rug had been pulled out from under her. Poised to deliver a scathing lecture, she deflated.

He went on, "And to answer your other question, Ms. Jones, my own people will handle the basic machine code and operating system. But *you* will design apps to capture the hearts of the users. Intuitive solutions to let their minds soar."

"See, Skyler? Sir Humphrey has everything under control." Mel's voice was like a buzz saw. Under his breath he added, "Stop making trouble, sweetheart. You're way out of your league."

Sweetheart. It reminded her of Fahrrad's harassing *sweeting.* She turned her sudden appalled anger on Mel, whispering furiously, "Just because I don't snap out, 'yes, sir' when something doesn't make sense?" Louder, she said, "I still don't understand. Why can't Hawkesclyffe Computer people do the apps?"

"Because Sir Humphrey has chosen us," Mel jumped in gleefully. "The *rest* of us are *honored* that you have placed your confidence in us, sir." He smiled sickeningly at Cliff. "We will do our *very* best to deserve that confidence."

Gag me with a thumb drive. "But none of this makes sense—"

"We will discuss this, Ms. Jones—later." Cliff's eyes were blue agates.

The dinner date.

Emotions crashed inside her. Cliff's hard gaze, her fear that he was working with the hated dictator Fahrrad, her embarrassment finding he wasn't and she was wrong. All pitted against a hot, fluttery tumbling in her belly that had nothing to do with professionalism and everything to do with the power in his gaze and remembering the last time he'd demonstrated his mastery.

Emotions crashed and stalled. Her mouth stayed open, but nothing more came out.

"The end user is the reason for our existence. We must give them no less than our very best."

Wrestling loose of her churning feelings, Skyler burst out, "Well, *Sir Humphrey*, if you want the best, you will obviously be going with Daniel, our top designer, Alice, our senior project leader, and the alpha and beta programming teams."

"Obviously."

His reply threw her off. Had he suddenly become agreeable? "And naturally, the only person experienced enough to coordinate with your genius hardware team and us is Phil."

"Ah, no."

He hadn't become agreeable. Aggravating, but also almost reassuring. "Then who's in charge of us?"

"Phil will be."

"But I thought you said—"

"He'll run the Fitzwater teams. But the coordinator, the person in charge of the entire project, both my people and yours, is you.

"You're running the show, Skyler Lynn Jones."

Chapter Seven

"I...*what?*" Skyler stared at Cliff. She'd heard his words, but they made no sense. She'd managed projects in her time, but nothing close to the billion-dollar development this one was.

A joke. It was the only thing that made sense, that he was getting even for her interrupting. She answered in kind. "Oh, yeah, I'm doing all the work? And what will you be doing?"

"I'll be managing *you.* I think that's work enough."

Laughter filled the room.

"Funny." Fiery emotions jolted her to her feet. "But it's gone too far—"

"Exactly the personnel you ordered, Mr. Hawkesclyffe." Jerry Fitzwater flashed a suppressive glare at her, then with a little cough and a flourish, brought out pages of a contract. "Er, ah—as you requested. Project leaders, designers, senior and application programmers, and one top level management—ah, that's you, Skyler." He smiled a little weakly at her, which she acidly attributed to the doubled salary he'd be shelling out.

And then the enormous truth sank in. Her knees folded, and she sat, open-mouthed, staring at Cliff going over the ream of paper with Jerry Fitzwater.

He really meant it. She was going to run this project.

But it made no sense.

Around her, people were talking and shaking hands. Mel Pinlow glared nastily at her. No one saw the total illogic of what Cliff was doing.

As the meeting broke up, she tried talking to her boss, Phil, about it. "You do realize this means you'll be working *for* me, instead of the other way around."

"Hawkesclyffe wants it that way." Phil shrugged. "It'll make us money either way."

Tess stopped beside Skyler on her way out. "Congratulations." She was beaming so hard Skyler's eyes hurt. "It's about time you got a good assignment."

"You too?" She gaped at her best friend. "This isn't a *good* assignment in any sense of the word. I'll be responsible for all our people, and an unknown number of Hawkesclyffe's."

"And working closely with Mr. Magnificent. *Rowr*." Her gaze lingered on Cliff, who was handing a pen to a slightly green Fitzwater.

"The worst part of all!" When Tess's shocked eyes flew to her, she grimaced and reined herself in. "Stop drooling for one second and see this objectively, please? He controlled every aspect of this meeting with either honey or a big stick. And look at him haggle with Fitzwater. Working with Hawkesclyffe won't be easy."

"No, he looks pretty hard to me." Her friend's eyebrows rose suggestively.

"*Arrgh*. Stop that." Skyler said it both to Tess and her rapidly rising pulse. "My experience managing was a six-person team and a hundred thousand budget." An involuntary cringe hit her, remembering how *that* had turned out. "A barrel of chimps and chump change compared to this."

"So? It's the same, just bigger."

"On what planet? Complexity *explodes* with the size. A small system, a small problem, a midsize system, a huge headache, a big system, fecking impossible. Forget it." She sprang to her feet. "I can't do this, and I'm going to tell Mr. Know-it-all over there, just see if I don't!"

"Skyler, wait." Tess held out a restraining hand.

But Skyler stomped past her friend to Cliff's side. Waited, fuming, for him to finish up with Fitzwater.

"Well, she's talked herself into her own mediocrity again," she heard Tess say mildly to Phil.

Skyler shot her friend a glare over her shoulder and mouthed, *I can hear you.*

Tess just gave her a big grin and a thumbs up.

Phil smiled. "I don't think Sir Humphrey's going to let her get away with it, though."

"You think he can get it through her thick skull that she can't ignore her own talents?"

Skyler glared. *Can. Hear. You.*

Tess waved pleasantly. Even the hairy eyeball didn't have an effect. Friends were such a pain.

Phil chuckled. "If anyone can."

Skyler turned pointedly back to where Jerry initialed pages. Cliff's attention was focused completely on Fitzwater but to her seemed Cliff was deliberately ignoring her.

Jerry stopped and pointed. "Do you really need two QA teams?"

"Yes." Cliff spoke reasonably but firmly, as if to a recalcitrant child. "Quality software implies using Quality Assurance, yes?" When Fitzwater grudgingly nodded, he went on. "Well, my projects use a check and balance of two QA teams."

Skyler saw her opportunity. "You can substitute one for my position."

"Ms. Jones," Cliff's gaze cut to her. He spoke mildly, but the way his eyes gleamed unnerved her. "I said we would discuss this later. We *will* discuss this *later*."

Clients who threw fits to get their own way were annoying. Clients who used guile and reason? They were why shotguns were invented. She glared at him. "There's plenty of time now—"

"Later means later. Mr. Fitzwater just initialed the page confirming your position."

As if the ink sealed her fate, her bubble of righteous indignation deflated beneath her.

Was she doomed to manage this behemoth?

Her stomach turned fitfully. Managing a big project, budget, and a team, many of whom also happened to be friends?

Been there, done that.

Failed miserably.

As Skyler slunk out of the conference room; Tess waylaid her, grabbing her arm and dragging her into the ladies' restroom.

"Skyler Jones, Project Leader—it's an a-fricking-mazing opportunity. So." She began to slap stall doors open. Empty. Empty. Empty. "Why don't you want it?"

"I really don't want to talk about it—"

"Does this look like my sympathy face?" Tess pointed at her frown with extra scowl sauce. "You don't get to dodge on this."

"Fine." Skyler gave her friend a sprinkling of glower in return. "I've been a project manager before. Didn't suit me."

"You're a project manager now. Suits you just fine."

"Code manager." Skyler sighed. "Not people."

"*Pfft*. I've seen you work with people. You glow. I like how you manage people. You don't waggle your finger at them—you help them be their best. Add in hunky Mr. Hawkesclyffe, and this is the perfect opportunity."

"I *can't*." A sudden flush of nausea turned Skyler away.

"*What?* Skyler, what the heck is going on?" Tess's scowl appeared in the mirror behind her, concerned now. "Tell me."

"I-I had a friend." Skyler dropped her head. "At my first job. A good friend. We were part of a creative, tight-knit bunch of young people. Didn't hurt that we got paid well." She chuffed a humorless laugh.

"So, like here—except for the young part?"

That made her smile. "Yeah. And the Mel Pinlow part." She fell silent, pensive.

"The friend?" Tess prompted. When Skyler croaked the name, Tess leaned closer. "Sorry, couldn't hear that. Sounded like 'my Nissan.'"

With a small smile and a shake of the head, Skyler turned from the sink, met Tess's eyes, and said clearly, "Elissa."

Tess frowned, eyes twitching as if searching her memory. "I met her, didn't I? Tall, brunette hair down to her hips, favors cowboy boots, pipeleg jeans, and hugs?"

"That's Elissa. She introduced me to bar shots and line dancing." Skyler's smile faded. "But when the job needed to get done, no one stayed later or worked harder. I met her my second day, when I joined a project team. With her. And Ron."

"Your *ex?* Yikes. I hope this isn't going where I think it is."

"No, no." Skyler managed a wan smile. "Yes, Ron test-drove other women, but Elissa wasn't his type. He couldn't stand her, said she was all drama. I'm afraid I didn't try to change his mind much."

"Why?"

"He seemed so...smart. At least, he always had an answer, and I was nothing but questions in those days. He was the kind of guy people follow instinctively because he has all the trappings of a leader—tall, handsome, a sharp dresser, and decisive. His goal was to run his own company by thirty and retire at fifty. When he said Elissa was too emotional, I just believed him. He knew what he wanted and went after it—including me. After six months, he presented me with a pearl and diamond engagement ring."

"Fast."

"Decisive."

"We'll agree to disagree. Was Elissa jealous?"

"Not...exactly." Worms of doubt seemed to tangle in Skyler's stomach.

"What then? Exactly?"

Skyler sighed again. "Ron took an active interest in my career. At the time, I thought he was being helpful. When I got a promotion, to project manager, he brought me books with titles like *Top Down Management—Being Hard But*

Fair and *The Stick, Not the Carrot: Why Workers Don't Want To Work.*"

"Yikes."

"He'd say, 'Professionalism, Skyler. That's the key to success.' Then he'd poke a finger to my breastbone and say, 'No emotions in the workplace *ever*, especially the touchy-feely crap.' According to him and all the books he gave me, business only cared about getting results. Bottom line *über alles*. Ron would say 'A manager doesn't motivate, he spurs.'"

"Double yikes with a side of crap."

"Maybe, but he seemed to have it all down. So I tried to do what he said, though I was never dictatorial enough for him. Never hardline enough. Never good enough." To Skyler's embarrassment, she hiccupped a sob.

Tess's arm came around her shoulders.

It let her remember the worst. *Taking their relationship to the next level. Physical intimacy. Kissing ardently. Taking Ron's hand and putting it on her aching breast.*

Ron saying, "Needy women's needs. The preliminaries are boring, Sky. Let's skip to the good part." Him putting his hand between her thighs.

Her stifling her irritation. Her feeling of being used.

Him saying, "This is why I love you. You understand a man's needs."

Her, proud but ultimately unfulfilled. Telling herself feeling exploited was an overreaction.

Needy women's needs.

Skyler sighed and cast back to the thread of her story. "When I became manager, even workers who'd been friends—grumbled. Production fell off. I kept trying Ron's way, even...even when I had to reprimand Elissa."

"Oh, Skyler." Her friend's arm tightened, the simple, potent show of solidarity giving her the courage to go on.

"Elissa tried to tell me Ron was a heartless bastard, but he was my fiancé, the man I'd spend the rest of my life with. I thought she was jealous. With Ron's encouragement I started using the Stick far more than the Carrot. Even teams I'd worked with smoothly before...disintegrated. Elissa and I... she grew distant. Then cold. Then she was gone for good."

"I'm sorry," Tess said.

Her heart thudded painfully. "It left a hole in me. I tried to fill some of it with Ron by snuggling closer, but he didn't *want* to get closer. He criticized and scolded, not just my management, but me and our relationship. We argued more and more until he broke off our engagement. He wouldn't even try to reconcile. Didn't want honest talk, which he called touchy-feely crap. That wasn't *professional*."

"I'm beginning to hate that word."

"Well, he had a point. When we brought our bickering into the office, the team suffered. Upper management was disappointed in my performance and froze me out. I didn't get any more promotions, only the worst of projects, and was stuck in a management position I hated and wasn't good at. My life felt barren and my career tanked. Professionalism was all I had left, so I sucked up my emotions and dealt. Frankly, when you called me about this job at Fitzwater, it felt like heaven, being a blessed bottom-of-the-pack programmer again."

"So that's why you don't want to lead this project?"

"I hated management, Tess. I hated what it did to me, making me sharp and critical. I hated what it did to my relations, my friendships. Now Cliff wants me to do it again? No way in hell."

Though she was raw and hurting from remembering Ron, Skyler cared about her job and tried to be professional. So instead of hiding in the restroom, she opened the door and started for her desk.

Only for Mel Pinlow to waylay her in the hall.

His scowl told her he blamed his spleen on her. Because she'd gotten what he thought he deserved? She braced herself for a bitter tirade.

Sure enough, Mel sneered, "Nice going, Ms. Executive. You've certainly proven how easy you are to work with. You're really going to get on Sir Humphrey's good side with your *winning* attitude—and Jerry Fitzwater's, too."

Skyler kept walking. "Mel, I'm not in the mood for it."

"Moody? What's the matter, sweetheart? PMS got you pissy?"

She thought about yanking her screwdriver out of her purse and excavating him a new one. Decided she didn't want to dig in that morass. "Being female has nothing to do with what kind of job I can do."

He laughed, a kind of wheezy, choked sound. "Oh, that's funny. Hawkesclyffe is enormously rich and powerful. He can open doors you've never dreamed of, for the whole company—all you have to do is cooperate. But you're too pissy and stubborn to just say yes."

She stopped. "Cliff didn't get where he is today by drowning himself in yes-men."

"*Cliff?*" Mel smirked. "Maybe you can get back in Cliffy's good graces after all. Saying yes is not such a bad idea for a girl in your position." He winked slyly at her. "Or rather, a girl in the right *position* might get him to say yes."

Anger suffused her. *Mel's face remodeling is courtesy of Skyler's Fist Design.* Barely restraining herself, she gave him a smile that was all clenched teeth. "Mel, don't you have packing to do?"

"No." For one second the scowl turned inward, so hot and mean she actually flinched. "I'm not going."

"I'm sorry—"

"No, you're not," he snarled.

"Of course I am," she protested. But it was weak. "Well, then, you must have work to do."

"That, yes. And so do you." With one final leer, he swaggered away—then twisted with a flat hand which he turned palm up, mouthing *"on your back."*

Fists clenching, she took one step toward him. Reminded herself he'd be devastated, not working on this plum project.

He turned his back and stalked away.

Briefly she wondered why he'd been cut from Cliff's team. Maybe because Mel skated on the edge of sexual harassment with all the female employees, though he seemed to have a special soft spot for her. Rotted out with acid.

Spinning, she kicked into motion toward Phil's office, her heels clicking sharply on the tile floor.

I've got to get out of here before I hurt someone.

She stuck her head into Phil's office. "I'm going home to pack."

"Good." He didn't even look up. "Get that temper of yours under control."

"I don't have a temper—"

"So that you can sincerely apologize to Mr. Hawkesclyffe." His head came up then, gaze narrow. "Hopefully, you won't have to grovel too much."

She gaped. "*Me,* apologize to him? What did *I* do wrong?" Tess, Mel, and now Phil, throwing *that man* up as if he was perfectly wonderful? Oh sure, Cliff was rich and successful and blazingly handsome. So? Did that make him perfect?

Yes. Purr-fectly attractive.

She grimaced. Stupid hormones.

"It's not a question of right or wrong, Skyler." Phil shrugged. "It's a question of who's client. Mr. Hawkesclyffe is, so he's the boss, now."

"Oh, well, that's different. Sir Humphrey is the *boss.*" Her blood pressure rose, and it hadn't been all that low to begin with, not with Cliff's cutting her off, Mel's triumphant smile afterward...

Maybe Mel was right. Maybe Cliff did want yes-men.

A girl in the right position. I mean really.

"I'll see to it that I lower my professional standards for *him.*" She whirled and stalked away.

"More like lower your personal guard," he muttered.

"I didn't hear that!"

Skyler stomped to her desk, grabbed her purse, and marched out the door. Anger drove her to slam into her car and tear out of the parking lot.

She was halfway home before she realized she hadn't canceled the dinner date.

She grimaced at the windshield. What time had Cliff said he would pick her up, about six? Although, after her arguing, he'd cancel. Guys didn't like women who challenged them; big alpha men who were used to running the show wouldn't stand for it.

She caught sight of the scenic route exit. Grated nerves—at Cliff, at herself, at everyone—sent her careening across three lanes to make it, only habit making her check her blind spot first.

Stomping the brakes at the end of the offramp, she blew out air. Rolled her shoulders. This route would take her longer.

It was also the route she took when she wanted to work out a particularly knotty problem.

But there was no problem here. Oh, no, Cliff was not a problem.

Sure he wasn't.

Signaling, she turned onto the country road. It'd serve the big lug right if he listened to yes-Mel. Pinlow was cruising for an early change of careers; his last few performance reviews were pretty pitiful. Not to mention a bad rep for throwing tantrums whenever his plans were foiled by reality...

Which didn't apply to her, right? She hadn't thrown a tantrum. She had voiced reasonable doubt.

Uncertainty crept in.

She drove slower now. Cliff would never be uncertain. Completely in control of reality, he'd never be moved by any tantrum, let alone throw one.

Maybe Mel and Cliff weren't so much alike after all.

"Ha. Wouldn't that be convenient? Cliff could still be my knight in shining armor, champion of the little people, doer of good deeds. Well, face it, Skyler Lynn. He's not. He's a corporate dweeb, just like Mel Pinlow. A corporate overlord dweeb, but a dweeb."

A horn beeped behind her. A driver signaling annoyance with her. Lost in her thoughts, she'd let her speed drop under the limit. She feathered the accelerator to go faster.

Drive now. Think about Cliff later.

The car behind her—a really nice red roadster—sped up with her. Which was okay, until she was going ten miles over the limit and he—that obnoxious height and mass behind the tinted windshield on the driver's side had to be male—was *still* crowding her. She felt her temper begin to rise.

And was immediately ashamed. Her temper was how she'd gotten in this mess.

Then the sports car dropped back to a decent following distance and she felt even more foolish.

To drown her inner doubts, she clicked on her audio system. Her music system picked rock from the sixties. Humming along, she tried to remember the words. *Cool town, evening in the city...* She'd really lost her cool. Mel was probably right; Cliff wasn't going to hire her now. *Not after I proved how easy I was to work with,* she thought with biting sarcasm. *How accommodating.*

Will I even have a job after that stunning perform-ance?

She drove on instinct, keeping only the barest amount of concentration on the road. The rest of her mind wandered through a kaleidoscope of Cliff, anger, regret, Cliff, embarrassment, fear, Cliff.

Somehow, always coming back to Cliff. As if he was the meat in the stew of her psyche, though she barely knew him.

Though a dinner date would help with that.

But Cliff didn't even know where she lived. How could he pick her up for dinner?

Besides, she didn't have anything to wear. Briefly, she considered shopping—for a dress so stunning it would set him back on his heels...

"Damn it." Back to Cliff, *again.* She resisted the urge to bonk her forehead on the steering wheel.

Not a dinner date. A business dinner. Unless, like Ron, it developed into more...but she and Cliff would never get that far because she'd probably screwed up the contract.

She rolled eyes at herself. First Cliff was like Mel, then he was Ron. Who was he, really? Why did he seem to behave like James Bond one minute and Darth Vader the next? And why couldn't she keep him out of her mind?

Another sharp beep from the car behind her cut through her absorption. She winced. Driving with half her mind, she was probably going two miles per hour. She braced herself for the deserved finger the driver would shoot her as he passed.

He didn't pass.

Chapter Eight

Skyler checked her speed. She was actually going five miles per hour over the posted limit.

Another beep. Who the heck was that? She flashed an irritated glare into the rearview mirror.

The same sleek, red car rode her bumper.

"Back off buddy," she called out to the undefined hulk of a driver. "I've got a machine gun, and I know how to use it." Since she didn't have her window open, of course the driver didn't hear her, but she felt better.

Stupid sports car.

Why didn't he pass? She nudged her gas pedal slightly and opened up some space.

The red car immediately closed the gap.

"You want to race?" With a grim smile, she nudged the gas again, just to make sure.

The sports car driver not only closed the gap, he crowded her unmercifully.

Skyler's blood started pounding in her ears. She forgot work, forgot Mel, forgot even Cliff. Her attention zeroed in on the car behind her and the road in front. "You want a race, buddy? You got it."

She floored it.

Tess had said her car fit her personality perfectly. Skyler didn't know about that, but she took inordinate pleasure in the innocent family sedan with the super-charged V-8 engine. The fact that she'd tuned it herself to racing specs? Simply because she enjoyed bringing things to their fullest potential. Not because she ever raced.

Although sometimes, it was nice to have the extra power, to give someone a surprise. Like now.

She accelerated sharply up the two lane road, hugging the curves like spandex on a belly dancer.

The rush of speed thrilled through her. Okay, honestly, she loved going fast, loved the way it made her blood burn pure and oxygen smell sweet.

Competition only made it better.

She smiled. The blaze of adrenaline had consumed her anger. She glanced into her rearview mirror for more happy news, sure to see nothing but open road.

He was still there.

Her jaw dropped open. He'd stuck to her tail like glue, not so easy when she was taking curves at ten m.p.h. over the speed limit.

Shutting her mouth, she zipped around another at fifteen over. He not only kept up with her, he actually cut the corner tighter.

Miserable suckbag showoff.

Ahead of her loomed a large, slow-moving truck about to enter a blind curve. An evil thought floated into her brain, one she'd never try in a hundred years were it not for another beep from the sports car goosing her adrenaline.

She knew this road intimately, knew to a quarter inch where the passing and no passing zones were.

Time to lose Mr. Sportscar Showoff.

Downshifting, she darted out around the truck and floored it. The car roared around the tractor-trailer at the last possible safe instant. Immediately she cut over and braked to take the sharp curve. *Showed him.*

The low-slung, red rocketship of an auto jetted past her, directly into the curve.

Her jaw dropped as the wind of his passing buffeted her car. Poor Mr. Sportscar Showoff. He was pavement pate for sure. She moved her foot to the cover brake, to pull over and call 911.

But the car, gripping the corner like Velcro, slid in front of her, brake lights flaring.

Relief lit her. Yeah, she'd been irritated at him, but she'd never want to see anyone hurt. With her anger burned away, she even saw that he was almost admirable, a worthy adversary

Now that the red car was no longer crowding her tail, she settled back to a more sedate speed. Mr. Sporty was fine, he'd zip away, and the road ahead of her would be clear. All was right again in her world. Well, except for Cliff.

She found herself crawling up the red car's bumper.

The jackass was still braking.

"What do you think you're doing?" she screeched at her windshield. "You topped a hundred to pass me! You nearly killed yourself for the privilege of going faster than me, *so get going.*"

She waved her arms at the idiot, trying to make direct mental contact so he would know exactly what she thought of him. For one moment, she wished she really had a shotgun. Or a gun turret atop her sedan. With a laser cannon.

Abruptly, the sports car pulled to the side of the road. Spurred by her renewed temper, she jerked off the road, too, pulling in ahead of him. Jamming the car into reverse, she backed, spitting gravel to where the vehicle idled. She threw open her door, which was nearly taken off by the irate truck driver as he blasted past. Her swearing was swept away in the whirlwind of the truck's passing.

Slamming her door shut, she marched, teeth clenched, to give the parked driver a part of his education he had sorely missed.

"Where did you learn to drive, you dipwad?" she shouted at the tinted windshield. "Why did you pass, and then slow down? I could have hit you. I *should* have and watched that fancy car shatter in a million pieces. Of all the stupid, overbearing..."

The words caught in her throat as the door opened, and a long, trousered leg emerged, followed by lean hips, massive chest, and broad shoulders.

With that familiar body, she didn't need to see the owner's face.

She looked anyway.

Cliff's cobalt eyes cut into her with the force of lasers. Her anger drained, leaving her feeling limp and small. After everything else, she wondered almost idly how finely he was going to carve her.

"Are you trying to kill yourself? You can't get out of dinner that way. And, might I mention, Jerry and I signed the contract, so you can start packing. Now, would you prefer to drive home sanely, or would you like to come with me?"

She blinked, glanced at the red wet-dream on wheels— not a mere sports car, but a 250K+ supercar—then met his gaze. "In your ride?"

"Yes." Despite his still-obvious irritation, the corner of his mouth quirked. "Does that interest you?"

"Can I drive?"

The other corner quirked. "Maybe later."

"Well..." On the one hand, she didn't want to step into what, from her past relationships, was an obvious sand trap.

On the other, it was equally obvious she wasn't getting out of dinner. And there was the lure of that sweet ride.

"What about my car?"

"I'll have my personal assistant pick it up. Coming with me?"

Her feet lifted, as if they'd float her into the car without conscious thought. "I can drive later?"

"You're persistent." He grinned. "I like that. Yes."

Yes. She only barely stopped herself from chugging a fist in triumph. *Okay feet, now walk professionally.* She started for her car to gather her things. "Mel calls it stubbornness."

"I lived for a while in Missouri. Stubbornness isn't a bad thing."

Her feet floated a little more at that despite everything.

When she returned, he helped her into the passenger seat, then ran around the hood to his side. Even wearing more than a pair of loose pants, he ran easily.

I'm admiring his form, his athleticism. Not thinking about him in loose pants and nothing else. Really.

Sliding behind the wheel of the idling car, he moved smoothly into traffic. He drove quite competently, his long fingers sure on the wheel. It mesmerized her, the play of muscles and tendons in his capable hands.

Then she remembered she hadn't given him directions to her place.

"Turn at the next intersection."

"I know. Your address was in your files."

Her jaw dropped. "You memorized my address?"

"I have an eidetic memory."

"Figures." Stunningly handsome, brilliant in his field, and a perfect memory? No wonder he seemed like a hero. Sure, he was annoying the way he'd wormed his way into her life and charmed all the people in her office.

The fizzing in her blood didn't seem to care.

It was impressed, not just by the car she'd give her entire meager savings to own and his presence as big and broad as his linebacker's shoulders. But by something indefinable, yet as potent as his warm scent and how assuredly he'd swung her to safety, clasped to his strong, bare chest.

She stifled a groan. Now, her dreams would not only include his muscular body but his immaculately tailored suits and fast car.

He shot her a glance. *And those blue, blue eyes...* They'd look spectacular up on the big screen. Although, just because he wore a gorgeous skin didn't mean a saint lived underneath.

Please don't let this end like Ron.

A seed of pain lodged in her heart. Ron's rejection had left her miserable. Cliff was so much more man, she was certain if she ever fell for him, the end would be even worse.

One step at a time. Survive dinner with him tonight, worry about the rest of her life later.

She pulled her professionalism on like a protective cloak. No emotional crap. *Keep your head up, keep your eyes open, and cover your ass. And your heart.*

"We're here," Cliff said.

She looked up. While she'd been arguing with herself, they'd reached her apartment.

"As long as we met up early, why don't we have dinner right away? I'll move the reservations while you change."

"Sure." Sooner started, sooner done.

Or longer time together, a hopeful little inner voice said.

She ignored it.

Inside her apartment, Skyler rummaged in her closet for an outfit, not too provocative.

But stunning. Definitely should be stunning.

Canvas slacks? Too casual. Pleated skirt? Too schoolmarm. Spandex minidress? Too bed-me.

Men have it lucky, she decided. *They can wear the same suit to work and out. Besides not having to change, they save money to buy golf clubs, or whatever guy things they buy.* Women needed suits for work and dresses for nice dinners and good jeans for casual clubs plus matching jewelry and makeup and shoes and purses for each. What a racket.

Should be making notes for my stock broker. Buy shares in clothes designers, makeup manufacturers, and purse factories.

Just about to chuck it all and go in her business attire, she saw her jade dress hanging in the closet. She'd bought the gorgeous dress for Elissa's wedding and, disinvited after the management debacle, hadn't ever worn it. Elegant, conservative lines swirled to drape gracefully along her curves, and it showed just enough skin to be interesting.

Professional skin, though.

She took it out and held it against herself. Donning the dress for dinner with Cliff might just associate more pain with it, but its beauty practically demanded she wear it. She laid it on the bed, shimmied into a new pair of silky pantyhose, misted herself with her favorite scent, and slid into the dress. Then she pulled her hair out of its no-nonsense work barrette, brushed it into soft waves, and spritzed it in place. She considered a pair of heels in the closet, but they made her back hurt, so instead, she slipped her feet into a glossy pair of black slides. Hopefully she wouldn't be underdressed for dinner with a "Sir."

A cold drink of water refreshed her and made her almost believe she could survive another encounter with brawny action hero Cliff, and maybe even filthy rich computer magnate Sir Humphrey. She snatched up her purse and left the apartment, coaching herself as she hurried out.

This is a business dinner. Keep it matter-of-fact. We're just two professionals exchanging information over a meal.

Although maybe they could talk about how he'd heard about a Mr. Jones in Middle Yemen who had been kidnapped. If Tess had told the state department, how had Cliff found out? Third hand, overheard, or was there a deeper connection? Possibilities tumbling in her head, Skyler stepped outside.

Cliff lounged against his car, suit coat off, deep in the latest issue of a specialty hardware magazine, every line of his elegant, muscular body on display.

Desire blasted through her—and an inner truth. She hadn't worn her beautiful dress to a conservative business meeting. Deep down, she thought this was a date. Suddenly she wished hotly she'd worn the sky-high heels.

Then he glanced up, saw her, and smiled appreciatively.

Her body did a little shimmy. She sauntered to him, savoring the warmth in his gaze. *Maybe it's not the dress he appreciates, but what's underneath.* The thought that he saw and admired her, not her package, sent a thrill through her.

He opened the passenger door for her. She slid into the car, determined to keep that warmth in his gaze, determined to have learned from her mistakes with Ron. Determined to keep her temper under control, to exude professionalism. All right, sexy professionalism.

Determined to be perfect this time.

On the half-hour's drive to Rusterman's, a restaurant Skyler had never been to but had heard was pretty swank, she had time to worry she was overdressed or underdressed. So when the hand-hewn logs of the outside façade and rustic, pine-plank tables on a large deck overlooking a lake came into view, she relaxed.

Until she got inside.

A hushed, old-European style entryway greeted her. Thick red carpet, flocked wallpaper, and gold-veined white marble were complemented by antique gold fixtures, rich ruby linens, and glossy wood. Ornate and high-toned, not rustic and homey, the inside cranked her nerves tight.

Worse for her stomach acid were the diners sitting elegantly straight at the beautiful tables, model-thin women draped in the latest fashion creations, and men in perfectly tailored suits reeking of old money.

Then the maître d'hôtel greeted Cliff by name. "Of course we have your table ready, Sir Humphrey." He showed them directly to one of the best tables in the place.

Sir Humphrey, wearing his own hand-tailored perfection, fit right in.

Any confidence Skyler had had leaked from her like a deflating balloon, leaving her cold and shaky. *Should have gone out and bought something new and stunning.*

Chapter Nine

Skyler was already feeling cold and out-of-place when Cliff pulled out a chair for her and stood behind it.

Oh no. Not this. The times Ron had tried to hold her chair for her, she'd landed on her butt on the floor.

She grinned, nudged out the next chair over, and plopped herself into it.

The maître d's eyebrows winged high, but Cliff simply took the seat he'd offered instead. The moment he did, the wine steward came. At his elegant ease, Cliff spent about ten minutes discussing the finer points of the selections on the list with the steward, all of which were probably a couple Franklins a bottle. No raspberry beer for her tonight.

The instant the wine steward left, the waiter arrived. He explained the menu for the evening—in French. Cliff handled that with a composure she certainly wouldn't have managed with her one semester. She did get in a *merci beaucoup,* but other than that was satisfied to nod pleasantly. *So much for Ms. Perfection,* she thought ruefully. She'd wanted to kick or kiss the Cliff who rescued her. But Sir Humphrey? She might as well get used to feeling like she had braids, braces, and skinned knees around him.

A plate of appetizers, stuffed mushrooms, came immediately. While Skyler tried to eat the things without their skittering off her plate, at least three people found excuses to drop by and chat.

"Oh, darling, I've known Sir Humphrey for years!" a large woman, dripping with diamonds, exclaimed. She pronounced "years" with two syllables, yee-ahz. Then there was the white-haired gentleman, Mr. Harrison—the quintessential Brit Sir Hawkesclyffe *should* have been. Skyler rather liked his soft British accent as he talked about his wife, who was apparently involved in community projects back home.

The third person she didn't like at all. Professionally, that was. Because the woman distracted Cliff from their informative, *professional* meeting, not because of the blonde's incredible beauty. Not *at all* because of how she waved her décolletage in front of him as if she was displaying Mount Everest. Of course it didn't bother Skyler *at all* that Cliff didn't seem to mind—why should it? It was none of her business who he wanted to scale. Right?

Right.

Skyler unwadded her napkin from her clenched fingers as the woman swayed back to her own table. Had she worried about a professional dinner giving way to an intimate one? With all the visitors, she needn't have. People weren't here to eat or enjoy each other's company but to *be seen* by the in-crowd.

Cliff waved the waiter back to the table. *As if we haven't had enough visitors,* Skyler thought acidly. She was about to excuse herself and walk home, almost thirty miles, but she'd need all of them to work off her temper.

Then Cliff casually held out a hundred dollar bill to the waiter and said, "Do you have anything a little more secluded?"

After sliding a glance at her, the waiter gave Cliff a private smile. "Of course, sir."

Meaning the server thought this was an intimate dinner after all.

Skyler blushed, suddenly eager to put him—and her happily burbling hormones—straight. "We have business."

"Of course, miss." The waiter's smile grew even more suggestive.

Right—that hadn't sounded any better. *Sure* they had business. Her dress just *oozed* business. With a sigh, she shut up and stood.

"This way please, sir, miss."

Cliff picked up their drinks and stood too, waiting for her to follow the waiter first. As she cut in behind the server, she tried very hard not to think of the big man just behind her, though she felt his heat. Certainly not trying to sway like Ms. Mount McKinley.

Well, maybe a little.

The waiter led them to a small room with a single table. Cliff set down the drinks and pulled a chair out for her.

Fry my motherboard. The best she could hope for was to sit first and scoot awkwardly as he bump-bump-bumped the chair into place. One time, Ron had scraped the thing over her foot. So much for not embarrassing herself.

But as she bent knees, Cliff smoothly pushed the chair forward, and her behind hit cushion just as the seat reached optimal position.

Perfect.

Butterfly wings tickled her tummy. She'd never meshed so perfectly with someone else in her life. Not even working with her team, where they knew each others' minds so well, words were often unnecessary.

Cliff took the chair across from her. His eyes sparkled over the candle between them, and he smiled again, that warm, wonderful smile.

He raised his glass and toasted, "To teamwork."

Talk about mind-reading. Unnerved, she took her glass, too, but only mumbled some inanity before taking a deep gulp.

Alcohol buzzed her palate. She quickly put the glass down and glanced at him. Despite a server flitting about filling water glasses, Cliff's cobalt gaze was steady on her. As though she was the only person in the room.

Or the only woman who'd ever been created, and created just for him.

She pushed aside the warm tingle of appreciation that trilled through her, telling herself she'd noticed that about him at the office, his ability to concentrate completely on a single person or thing.

But it still made her feel absolutely special.

His attention shifted downward, to her mouth, her chin, the thin gold chain at her neck, and finally lingered on the gentle curves of her breasts. Her heart thudded in her ears. When his gaze rose to hers, his smile became warmer, intimate.

The clank of china signaled the soup course. The whole time the waiter served their steaming soup, refilled their wine and water glasses, and cleaned a few odds and ends from the table, Cliff didn't release her gaze.

Then they were alone, and he took her hand.

"You look beautiful tonight."

"And professional. Right?" The butterflies in her belly fluttered giddily as his long, bronzed fingers warmed hers.

Artistic fingers, yes, but quite strong. She remembered his using them to pull their combined weight over a rooftop's edge.

"Professional. Certainly." He leisurely traced his index finger along the tops of her fingers. "I can see these elegant hands on the keyboard, tapping out programming code just as elegant." By the time he traced the back of her hand, the stroke seemed, like cat's fur, to build up the charge on her skin. Her butterflies went soaring.

His lids lifted, his blue gaze gleaming in the semidarkness.

She swallowed, hard.

A small, intimate smile teased his lips as, achingly slow, he pressed a gentle kiss to the tips of her fingers. The warmth of his lips, his breath, pulled a groan from her throat.

Holding her wrist in his big hand, he turned her palm up. "I can see this slapping down on Phil Westerby's desk in emphasis—professional emphasis—as you demand better testing procedures."

She was so aroused by his simple touch that when he skimmed his finger along the inside of her hand, she trembled in response, her breathing turning ragged, her heart hammering. She'd never known palms were so sensitive.

But hers was, at least to him. Like electricity racing through a wire, his touch lit points of fire in her elbow, her breasts, and set off a churning need in her belly. Hot arousal, yet he had touched nothing other than her hand.

Still holding her palm up, he again kissed the tips of her fingers, but this time his breath billowed warm on the sensitive pads. She trembled to have those hot lips kissing the arch of her neck, his teeth nibbling her earlobe. Or his mouth pressing against the curve of her breast, teeth gently nipping their ripe peaks...

The click of the room's door made her snatch her hand away. A waiter glided into the room to refill already full water glasses. Cheeks hot, she grabbed her spoon and ladled soup into her mouth. It had cooled enough that she didn't burn herself, but she was so unnerved she probably wouldn't have noticed.

The waiter left. Skyler cut a glance at Cliff as she swallowed, creamy stock with bits of mushroom and rice signaling she should actually try to taste the next bite.

He sat relaxed, toying with his wine glass, not embarrassed in the least.

But he must've seen *she* was, because he sat straight, suddenly all business. "I promised you an explanation of your position on the HCCpi project. Would you care to hear it now?"

She hesitated. Was his choice of her professional or personal? She wasn't sure if she wanted to hear him say either.

Then she cursed herself for being a coward. "Yes, I want to hear about it. And I also want to know more about the project itself."

He picked up his own spoon and elegantly dipped soup. "I've made it my main business to get, and keep, the best talent in the IT industry. Not easy. These people do not grow on trees, despite management believing job titles make people interchangeable."

Skyler dipped her own soup, trying to copy his refined manners. "That's an enlightened view."

"Thank you. I now have five thousand employees world-wide, each of whom is an expert, if not a genius, in their own way."

"Then why do you need Fitzwater?" Skyler paused eating. She was genuinely baffled. "We're smart, not geniuses."

"I was missing one key position. How's your soup?" He spooned his own. The sight of his fine lips working, the bliss on his face, sent frissons through her.

"Good." She hurried to shovel the rest of her soup in her face, wincing mentally at her inability to stay focused on professional *or* refined with this man. She almost longed for a return to the tank, carting her around like a sack.

Then the bits of carrot, onion and mushroom slid along her taste buds. "The soup is delicious." She lost herself for a moment in the simple pleasure of eating.

She'd finished her soup just as a pair of men glided into the room. One gathered their bowls. The other, resplendent in white chef's attire, trundled a cart tableside.

The main dish was something that had to be finished with great flourish, dousing it with alcohol and turning it into a three-alarm fire right beside the table.

She was starting to feel pretty overwhelmed by it all.

After the flames had been doused with liquid and the smell of brandy and beef was driving her nuts, more waiters brought out dinner plates, and the chef slid thick steaks onto them. "Steak Diane."

A server set the plate before her. She stared down at a gorgeous brown steak smothered in mushrooms and glistening sauce. Definitely overwhelmed, but hunger topped it. She tucked into the steak, groaning as the tangy, tender beef seemed to melt in her mouth.

"Good?" Cliff said. The server set a plate before him.

"Good doesn't do it justice." Swallowing, she cut another piece as all the staff quietly disappeared, although the chef wore a pleased smile on his face. To Cliff, she said, "What key position?"

"I like your persistence." He grinned. "Geniuses are like cats. They work on what they want, when they want. I need someone to make them pull together."

"A leader?" She forked up beef.

"An inspiration."

Her chewing slowed, and she frowned at him. She managed to swallow before saying, "That's you. Head genius."

Cutting a precise cube, he paused. "I may be head cat, but in a herd of cats that's still a mess. Look, I'm not conceited enough to think I'm best at everything. I don't have the talent to make them work together, so I find him. Or in this case, her."

Her hands, suddenly nerveless, sank to the table. "I don't want to be head cat."

"More cat whisperer. Skyler, Jerry gave me your references. You perform your work well—"

"Programming. Not management."

"Hear me out. In each case, while you were at a company, the department you were in operated more smoothly. And after you left, the company's profits took a nosedive. Do you know what that tells me?"

"That I'm a good-luck charm? You don't have to pay me big bucks to be ornamental."

He forked up a square of beef. Chewed thoughtfully. "Do you like working with your team at Fitzwater?"

A new angle? Cautiously, she replied, "They're great people. Fun, bright, always ready with a joke."

"And you mesh well?"

"Sure. Sometimes so well we can almost read each other's minds." She took another bite of her very expensive steak, admitting to herself it might be a little better than McHamburger's.

"And your previous companies?"

"We almost always got along. I've been really lucky."

"Skyler, I have never worked on a team like that."

Surprise hit her, and sadness for him. "Well, you're a genius. Naturally, you can't expect people to keep up with you."

He stabbed his baked potato almost savagely. "Oh, they keep up—or they would if they ran in the same direction. But no, my geniuses go off on their own, down rat holes. They duplicate each other's efforts rather than taking the time to talk. It's stupid redundancy on the part of some supposedly smart people."

"I'm not a manager," she insisted.

"You're something rarer." He hit her with the full intensity of his cobalt stare. "You're a *unifier*."

"But—"

"Skyler." His fork dropped with a loud clatter, almost as if he'd thrown it. "I want you to gel my team. And I want you to have the position that deserves."

She frowned. "*Gel*—that's when a bunch of individuals come together into a cohesive whole. But Cliff, it's luck that makes synergy happen."

"Is it?"

Skyler shook her head, not knowing what to think but uncomfortable about the whole topic. Spooning sour cream onto her potato, she ventured, "Tell me about the project."

"Apple Pie." He sat back with his wine glass, gaze shuttered now. "Artificial intelligence–driven security system."

"Security?" She sucked in a breath.

"For banks and such. Using the full capabilities of the HCCpi, Apple Pie programming will not only identify and combat known cyberattacks, it will actively develop resistance."

"Like human immunity? That's brilliant."

"Could be. If my people would just stop arguing." His gaze leveled on her.

She winced. She knew what that gaze meant—installing her as the genius whisperer.

And what was wrong with that? She chewed on both steak and the idea, washing it down with a sip of peppery wine. Dang, that was definitely better than McGargles.

But the wine washed away her cobwebs too. "Look, Cliff, I have to be honest with you..." She shifted uncomfortably. She'd barely admitted this to herself, much less a man she'd known for a few scattered hours. "I was a manager once. It didn't go well. I wasn't..." Thinking of Ron didn't bring dancing butterflies in her stomach but acid-spewing dragons. Her throat constricted, she forced out a whispered, "Professional. If I fail—"

"Then you fail." He shrugged, as if no big deal. "We all do. It's usually forgotten in the next success. I don't think you will, but if it happens, we sit down, we examine it, and we learn how to do it better the next time."

Next time? *We* sit down? Not *you blew it* and hurled accusations?

Hope rose inside her, but tangled with stark, painful memories into confusion. He couldn't mean what she thought he did. She grabbed her water goblet to cover her confusion, grabbed the wine instead. The unexpected gulp of alcohol made her cough up her lungs. He half-rose to come help her, but the thought of his big hand caressing, not her hand, but her whole *back* made her shudder like an unbalanced washer's spin cycle *thump thump thump* and she waved him down. Between coughs she managed, "How would you know? I can't imagine you failing at anything."

"Don't be fooled by what I am right now. Life's most valuable lessons are often won through pain and failure." He picked up his fork and waved the tines at her plate. "How's your potato?"

With her emotions roiling, she dipped a fork into the puffy explosion inside her own foil, expecting pulpy ash. But as she tasted a bit, she was amazed at the soft moist mix of perfectly baked potato, butter, and sour cream with just the hint of chive, dusted by paprika.

"Good." She swallowed, followed the forkful with a sip of wine, and her dragons surprisingly mellowed. "Thanks, by the way."

"For what, hiring you, the dinner, driving you here, or stopping you from a crack-up on the road?"

She glowered. "For rescuing me in Middle Yemen."

To her surprise, the taut skin on his high cheekbones darkened. "It was nothing, I assure you. Simply in the right place at the right time."

"With a line to the state department," she guessed shrewdly.

A beat, then he shrugged. "I'd heard a rumor, is all." But he'd stilled before the shrug, sure sign of a hit.

Then, quite determinedly, he turned the conversation to general topics, delivering amusing anecdotes from a local comic convention, and the dinner passed in an unexpected—at least to Skyler—mood of camaraderie.

The rich food was filling, and, mindful of the stylishly thin, rich blonde in the general dining room, she put her fork down early.

She tried to skip dessert. "Just coffee. No cream, no sugar."

But Cliff ordered the chocolate and almond butter torte for himself, then the moment it came cut a slab off and offered it to her. It would've been rude not to try the decadent dessert, and she ended up eating half.

She'd planned to pay for her portion of the bill, but he wouldn't let her. As he scribbled in a tip she grabbed a peek, saw the bottom line had almost as many digits as her weekly paycheck, and decided maybe this once it'd be okay to let the billionaire cover it. Maybe he didn't have school loans like mortgages.

The drive back was silent. Skyler mulled over the things Cliff had told her, and he was apparently content to let her.

When he pulled the car up in front of her apartment building, she felt a little awkward. Should she give him a firm client-to-vendor handshake or a friendly hug? *Or a sizzling hot kiss to repay him for that hand foreplay...* She was leaning toward the handshake—her body voting loudly for the kiss—when Cliff opened her car door and stood ready to hand her up.

The warm shock of that little bit of chivalry short-circuited her brain. Taking his offered hand, she found the whole process of rising from the low-slung car much easier than had she tried it on her own. Taking her elbow, he guided her up the walk, and the heat and strength of his fingers reminded her compellingly of his caress in the restaurant but also his tight grip in Middle Yemen, pulling their nearly naked bodies together.

Embers stirred inside her, shooting into little flames as they mounted the stoop outside the apartment building.

He stopped; still connected by his hand on her arm, she stopped, too. Towering over her, he filled the space around her, his heat and scent permeating the very air she breathed. Her heart began to thud dully in her ears.

It felt safest to stare at his shirtfront, so she did. "Well, thank you for a lovely dinner—"

"Which you hardly ate," he said.

"I had half your dessert. And, well, we had a nice conversation," she added lamely.

"Yes. You and my tie are having a very nice conversation now."

She could tell him the truth—that his very nearness inhibited anything close to brain activity on her part, but how professional was that? What kind of team leader admitted that she was trembling with need from the simple touch of her boss?

And then those long, strong fingers slid under her chin, tips urging her to look up. The gentle pressure excited her even more.

She clamped down on that, pronto. He wasn't trying to be romantic. He just wanted to talk to *her* instead of the top of her head.

Giving in to his fingers, she allowed them to tilt her head back, revealing his face to her. He gazed down at her, their bodies so close, their height difference was very apparent.

The butterflies were back.

In the shadows of the night, Skyler couldn't quite see his expression. Was he expecting her to say something about the job or give him a good night? How very awkward. His fingers, warm on her chin, were starting to raise delightful goose bumps. She breathed in, to say goodnight, and got a noseful of his fresh, spicy, masculine scent.

Her mouth closed on the words. She hadn't dated since Ron, half-afraid her disappointment would rebound on a new man. Afraid Ron had left her too scarred.

Now, as Cliff's fingertips slid with tantalizing slowness from her chin down her neck, she shivered in delighted response. He caressed her throat, his other arm curling around her waist. His grip firmed. Any ghost of Ron went *poof.*

Anticipation furled in her belly.

He pulled her against him, suit coat rustling slightly as his fingers slid around her neck to burrow into the hair on the back of her head.

She shuddered. Her lips automatically parted, in eager reaction.

Bending, he kissed her softly.

Chapter Ten

The press of Cliff's masculine lips, his warm, sweet breath, sent Skyler's heart hammering overtime. Her blood caught fire as her body rose and opened to him, freely and with joy.

As if it was a signal, his smooth, silky glide across her lips changed, his mouth opening as his tongue came out to play, gently teasing the seam of her lips.

She wanted to open her mouth to him but tried to tell herself not to take it too fast. This man was dangerous. Not only could he make or break her chances in the industry, he could devastate her fragile, scarred heart.

Her body didn't want to listen to any of that. Her arms wound tightly around his neck in return, and her lips parted, urging him to kiss her harder, deeper.

He responded.

With one powerful arm, he shifted her to lay suspended in his embrace like that night high above the Middle Yemen alley. Though her feet were on the stoop, she couldn't feel them touching.

She groaned very softly, but he heard her. He answered with a slide of both hands along her ribs, pulling her breathlessly close. And then he claim her mouth fully with his own, exploring her gently but thoroughly. Oh, he was good.

Her body rejoiced. She pressed against the great length of him, feeling each hard button on his coat imprint her torso as she tangled her fingers in his thick hair, trembling beyond her control. She pressed into his muscular thighs, urging him wordlessly to ask to come with her into her apartment building. Into her apartment. Into more.

"Cliff..." *Come in. Come in now before I drag you in.*

Ron's voice whispered in her brain. *I didn't leave you scarred. I left you desperate.*

Desperate. Her whole being flinched.

Wedging her hands between her and Cliff, she flattened palms against his brick wall of a chest and pushed. He released her immediately.

So fast it was less like letting her go and more like dropping a hot match.

She cringed. Avoiding his gaze, not wanting to see his anger, she muttered, "Uh, thanks for a wonderful evening, Mr. Hawkesclyffe. I look forward to doing business with you." Grabbing his hand, she quickly pumped it, then threw open the outer door and escaped into the safety of her building foyer.

No one was in the entryway to see her so she fled like a scampering bunny to her apartment.

She unlocked her own door with a shaking key and hurled herself inside.

Back flat against her apartment door, she covered her face with her hands. Sweet blue screen of death. She only had two rules these days. Number One: avoid romance in the business setting. Number Two: never take a management position. Both led to hell.

Yet with Cliff, she'd tripped merrily down both paths.

The door thudded against her back. Her heart leaped into her throat.

Cliff.

He hadn't really bashed the door, only knocked. But he'd entered her building and there was only the thin plank of her apartment door between them. It felt more harrowing than it was.

No, she wasn't scared. It was simply that her determination was going to be tested a little sooner than she thought.

Right.

"Skyler. I want to come in. Open the door."

Not by the hairs of my chinny-chin-chin. "Uh...Cliff, I can't, uh...the phone rang, and, yes, it's my mother. My mother's on the phone, and she's calling long distance, and—"

"Don't lie to me. I promise I won't try anything. Just open the door."

Not try anything?

Her cheeks heated. Wasn't he *supposed* to be so captivated by her beauty that he couldn't keep his hands off her, despite being angry? She felt strangely disappointed—and highly embarrassed by her disappointment.

The door. She should open it. While Cliff struck her as being patient when he needed to be, she also knew him to be a man of action.

She took a deep breath, turned, and opened the door. He stood on the threshold, arms crossed over his chest.

"I'd like my brass board back."

"I don't have your…" A brass board was an engineering prototype. The T-shirt, its hidden pocket, the strange flat board—it really was a computer board.

Was *that* why he had taken her to dinner, then kissed her so wonderfully? To make her pliable enough to easily recover the brass board?

Maybe not, but one thing was clear. He wasn't going to let any personal awkwardness get in the way of his business. *A businessman, first, last and always.*

She huffed a disgruntled breath, using the excuse to harden the battling feelings inside her. "Come in. I'll get it."

He crossed the sill, his sheer size and presence making her skitter back. But he didn't come any farther, just filled her apartment building entryway, crunching anger in his jaw, legs spread—and arms crossed.

Equal parts aggressive and *defensive*, as if she'd hurt *him*. Strange. She'd never imagined a tank could be injured in any way, but that was definitely a flicker of pain in his eyes. Shame seized her neck and kicked her down the hallway to her bedroom door where she scurried inside to get his T-shirts and board.

Though she'd never expected to see him again, she'd washed the shirts. Now she was glad she had. She pressed her nose briefly to the voluminous cloth. Any lingering scent of him was overlaid by April-fresh chemicals. The brass board was on her dresser where she'd stared at it several times, wondering. About what it really was, of course, but also simply daydreaming about the man who'd possessed it. Now she knew. It held a prototype computer chip built by a genius in the field. If it was the *pi*, worth billions. No wonder he'd sought her out.

Returning to the door, she handed him both shirts, laying the board on top. "Your *pi* prototype."

"Thank you." His tone was clipped and formal, and for the first time, sharpened with the edge of a British accent.

"You're welcome," she replied, equally formal. But he'd confirmed it was the billion-dollar chip. "You're lucky I still had it. Kind of lackadaisical treatment for something so important."

"The production model's built. This one's obsolete. Frankly, I'd forgotten I had it until my PA asked for it." He turned to leave.

She started closing the door, then stopped. "You know, I'd have given the prototype back if you'd just asked. You didn't have to go through all..." She waved her hand vaguely at her mouth, letting some of her own hurt and anger through. "...that."

Cliff had turned back and now stared at her. "For your information, if all I wanted was the brass board from you, I could have simply taken it." He turned heel and strode out.

Dashing to her front window, which looked out onto the street, she was in time to see him get into the red sports car.

She watched him roar away, disappearing around the corner a good twenty miles over the speed limit. Shaking, she leaned her forehead against the pane.

"...I could have simply taken it."

Yes, for a man of Cliff's abilities, she supposed that was true.

Skyler went to bed at the usual time but she lay awake for hours thinking about that encounter. About him.

"If all I wanted was the brass board..."

So, what else did he want?

And then, sometime in the small hours of the morning, a different play hit her.

"If all I wanted was the brass board from you..."

From *you.*

What else did he want—from her?

*   *   *

After her restless night, Skyler woke hazy, grumpy, dopey, and four other dwarfs. She climbed out of bed only to see, draped over the chair where she'd tossed it last night, her lovely jade dress.

Her sour stomach became an acid ache.

Cliff. Loving, sexy. Angry, hurt. By her.

Mel Pinlow, with his notions of sexuality formed in the nineteen-fifties, would have labeled her a tease. She wasn't, but Cliff *was* a guy. A guy she'd kissed like she was sucking a chocolate shake then suddenly pushed away.

What was he to think?

She clasped her elbows momentarily, then resolutely strode to the chair and picked up the jade outfit to put it away.

Sliding the dress into a gap between her business suits, she stroked the fine material and sighed. That kiss. Even if he'd overstated the fact, *"I could have simply taken it,"* that kiss on her stoop was too intense to have been intended simply to soften her up.

At some level, he was interested in her.

Her hand wandered to her lips, her tummy fluttered in memory. She'd *never* fired up like that when Ron kissed her—although, in all fairness, she'd never given herself so totally to Ron's touch as she had to Cliff's.

Then again, her ex had always seemed to hold back slightly, too. Cliff had jumped into the conflagration with her.

Until she'd pushed him away. Then he'd gone cold.

Her lips chilled. Her fingers trembled over them. Jerking her hand away, she turned resolutely from the closet.

Her normally automatic morning routine became fragmented, jumbled. She brushed her teeth twice and forgot to comb her hair. She nicked herself three times shaving her legs and bled through two sets of pantyhose before putting on skin glue and a pair of slacks. Both her toast and her coffee were burnt.

She left for work, not just late, but screaming late.

Bursting out of her apartment, she was halfway to the underground garage before she remembered—she'd left her car at the side of the freeway.

Cliff said his PA would pick it up, but how, when she had the keys? Would he even bother now, after she'd given him the brush-off?

She hadn't thought of her sedan once, after the man had roared into her life. Halfheartedly, she pushed the button on her car's keyfob. Poor thing, lost, alone, abandoned. The fob chirped...and a lock clicked.

Skyler twitched in surprise. Someone else's car was keyed to her fob? She trotted toward the click.

Where her car waited in her usual spot.

She blinked in surprise. *How...?* She spun around so fast her hair flew like a pinwheel. No sexy tank, no slump-shouldered PA. Slightly spooked, she gave the car a once-over. Nothing looked out of place, and her messenger bag rested sedately in the back where she'd left it, so she got in a drove to work.

Half-expecting a red car to appear out of nowhere, she drove several miles before she remembered most of her team was home packing today for whichever HCC installation Sir Humphrey had in mind.

Well, after last night it was a near certainty she was off that project. An even fifty-fifty she'd even kept her job. She continued on to Fitzwater. Bracing herself as she entered for any big, half-naked men who might jump out of a doorway to kiss her. None did.

Her tummy butterflies folded their wings and slunk away.

She'd just stowed her purse and messenger bag when her phone dinged. A quick glance showed a text message from Jerry Fitzwater himself, calling an afternoon meeting of the employees assigned to the HCC project.

Not her, she was sure. The severance paperwork probably hadn't been processed yet. Jerry might not know Cliff had canned her.

But no canceling messages showed up in the intervening hours, so when two p.m. came, she crept into the conference room.

No suit-coated trucks lay in wait.

Her cheeks heated at her own behavior.

Thick manila envelopes marked with the HCC logo ringed the table. "Okay, folks," Jerry began as she took a seat. "We have our marching orders. The team is working onsite at Hawkesclyffe's facilities near Rockleigh. The address and directions are in the packet on the table in front of each of you. Apartments will be provided. Work starts tomorrow afternoon, so if you haven't finish packing and getting your affairs in order, you have the rest of the day."

Skyler cringed at the word, *affair*. She'd had a good chance at a very sexy man.

Shot down the toilet last night.

Half-heartedly, certain Cliff was too efficient and energetic not to have adjusted the paperwork to exclude her by now, she flipped open the letter-size manila envelope. The team roster was on top. She scrunched her eyes, not wanting to see her name gone. *Coward.* She opened her eyes and scanned the list from the bottom up. As she went and her name didn't appear, her stomach soured...and then, at the top, there it was.

A miracle. Her name was still on as project head. The whole day brightened. Maybe she hadn't angered him as much as she'd thought.

Once home, mistake or not, she packed. She coached herself as she folded and placed. *Maybe a mistake, but if not—got the job, do the job. Utterly professional.* If Cliff— no, better start thinking of him as Mr. Hawkesclyffe—if he stuck with the ridiculous idea of her heading the team, Tess and Phil would help her do the job to the best of her ability.

She actually began to get excited. Together, they'd make the thing work. Even if she totally bombed, just working for HCC was a once-in-a-lifetime opportunity. The HCCpi, ripping fast but cheap, had vast possibilities for making the world a better place. She'd be part of helping to make that happen.

*   *   *

The next morning, Wednesday, Skyler rolled her suitcases, messenger bag, and laptop bag downstairs to the garage only to see her parking space was empty.

She had just enough time to freak before a gun-metal gray Mercedes purred into the lot. Even though the car wasn't familiar, she felt a prickle of recognition on her neck.

Ramping up to a cramp as the Merc parked in *her* spot.

The window rolled down. It was Cliff, naturally. He nodded without smiling. "Good morning."

Oh yeah. She'd pushed him away. Despite that, the idiot butterflies in her stomach started fluttering like they were ribbon dancing, making her snap out, "Where's my car?"

She set down her luggage as he got out, his body longer and leggier than she remembered.

"All right, skipping the pleasantries. My PA took your sedan to corporate headquarters so I can drive you. I'll brief you about the company on the way up."

"But how did you get my key?"

Color stained his high cheekbones. "Yes, sorry about that. I was sort of on a deadline, and I'd forgotten to ask Monday, so I hacked your onboard computer."

"You *what?*"

He held up placating hands. "I know I should have asked, but you didn't seem quite in the mood for me to show up again. Did I mention that deadline is really tight?" He grinned hopefully at her.

The boyish charm on those chiseled lips was irresistible. Or maybe the man himself was, to her. "Fine. I forgive you."

"Whew. Thanks." He popped the trunk of his car and came over to grab her cases, lifting them all easily to heft into his trunk.

She didn't know if she was more riled or impressed that he was able to hack her car's computer. "You could have phoned to ask."

"I know." He winced and gave her a quick, sheepish grin. "Old habits. I should have asked, and I'm sorry. I'll do better next time."

Next time? She frowned. "Where's your red greased lightning?"

"With that trunk?" He closed the lid. "I thought you might have more than a box of tissues."

"Ah." Skyler slid into the passenger seat, spirits lifting that he seemed to have gotten over Monday. Although she was a little miffed at his highhandedness with her car. But not a lot. When she poked at it, she realized she was bubbling that he'd done it because he wanted to spend time with her.

To discuss the project. He wanted her, but only for her mind.

That soured her mood, which surprised her. *I'd rather he wanted me for my body?*

No. I'd rather he just wanted me, *period.*

Wait, what?

Palming her forehead, she burrowed deeper into the buttery leather of the seat as if she could hide from her own thoughts. Business affairs were trouble and Cliff, specifically, was a whole truckload of trouble.

She did not need that kind of trouble.

"Skyler?"

Dropping her hand revealed the man himself, twisted toward her in the driver's seat, apparently watching her this whole time.

Warning drilled her. He was scary-perceptive. She straightened in her seat and thought professional thoughts. "So brief me."

"Right." He started the engine and smoothly reversed out of the space then drove off.

Well, that sucked. She'd expected a "What's wrong?" or even "What are you thinking?" She scowled. His cool patience was sexy, but didn't he ever lose that cool, even a little?

Like when we kissed...?

She opened her mouth to ask, *"Did you want to talk about the other night?"*

But he said first, "So, to bring you up to speed on the situation you're stepping into."

She closed her mouth.

He kept up a constant monologue on the state of affairs at HCC—who she'd meet, including a team called the Black-Armband Test Team, what their background was, how she might deal with them. He also gave her information on the company itself, how it had started, where it was going.

The only thing he didn't talk about in connection with Hawkesclyffe Computer was himself.

Skyler finally broke in. "You've told me how to work with your people. But how do I work with you?"

That started him on another monologue about how he wouldn't be there, business trips and all, since the company had facilities in fourteen countries—and then excruciating detail about each of those operations. Not including Middle Yemen, she noted hopefully. It added more weight to his "not at present" working with Colonel Fahrrad. Kulinahr must've been wrong.

"The Apple Pie project will provide three-sixty security for institutions of all sorts, but the initial version is targeted at banks."

"Right." She sat there, pleased with herself. Professional, cooperative.

Then he added, "Although, it would be advantageous to build our chip manufacturing plant in Middle Yemen, if that should come about."

Her heart plummeted.

He seemed not to notice. "Good for both our countries. We'd have an independent source of components, and they'd get much-needed income—"

"Is that wise?" She shut suddenly stinging eyes and clenched her fists to keep her voice from shaking.

"What do you mean?" An edge hardened his voice.

She chose her next words carefully. Fighting with the boss on day one wasn't professional or cooperative. "Well...the country isn't stable."

"The leader's an ass," he ground out. "Doesn't mean the people should be penalized—"

"You said you weren't working with Fahrrad!" She cut him off, Ron's corporate no-no number two.

Sure enough, he scowled and shook his head impatiently. "I'm not. But if things go the way I think they will, it will be to the country's advantage to bring me in."

"Don't you remember that bastard kidnapped me?"

"Of course I remember. And while I'm sorry for what you went through—"

"He's not to be trusted," she overrode him again. "He'll take the money and run, don't doubt it. And further-more—"

"Furthermore," Cliff raised his voice slightly and added that powerful edge to it, "he is a potential client. Though I appreciate your recent experiences, I don't think you're particularly in a position to criticize."

"*Really?* What position *am* I in?" Her voice rose in defensive anger. "Don't forget how he abducted me, or what he was going to do with me. I think that puts me in a *good* position to criticize plenty."

"I don't care if you call him a broken-balled bastard, as long as you don't do it to his face. This is *business* we're talking about, not a personal vendetta."

Business. Of course it was.

His jaw was clenching like a nutcracker's, but so was hers. Silence reigned for miles.

Then, almost grudgingly, he added, "And you don't know enough about the situation to criticize my decisions."

She gaped. "Don't you realize this man thinks Joe Stalin is the last of the real men, and that Boris is a pale imitation? Why did you help Prince Kulinahr, if you're only going to stab him in the back by working with Fahrrad?"

"Enough." Cliff's face hardened into a mask. "There are more people who depend on my business acumen than just me. We won't talk any more about it."

She snapped her gaze straight at the front windshield. *Oh, we won't, huh? Just wait until we get to your offices, where my car is. We'll see how much there is to say when I can drive out of there.*

Quit.

Go home.

Lose the opportunity to be in on a project that could change the face of computing, and maybe the world.

Her angrily thudding heart slowed. Doubt crept in. She eyed Cliff cautiously, without moving her head. He sat ramrod straight, his jaw set like iron.

Misgivings washed through her. She was right, wasn't she? He was allowing himself to be corrupted by the lure of the almighty dollar.

Wasn't he?

As the minutes and miles passed, her temper cooled. Maybe...just maybe he had a point. If it wasn't for the almighty dollar, she wouldn't have food or a car or a place to live. Multiply that by all of HCC's employees...maybe she was being naïve.

Maybe she and her high-minded attitudes didn't belong in the business setting; feelings didn't belong at work.

Hold onto your Hades' thermostats, maybe Ron was right?

The more she thought about it, the more she could see Cliff's point of view. Thousands of people counted on him for their livelihood. How did they and all their families weigh against one small country and one lonely, deposed ruler?

The idea saddened her. Her shoulders collapsed and her nose prickled with tears.

Deliberately, she tried to remember the positive. Cliff had at least saved Kulinahr's life. Thank goodness the tank had been in Middle Yemen to rescue the prince. Thank goodness the tank had been in Middle Yemen to rescue her.

And then she thought—if Cliff had been in Middle Yemen only to rescue the prince and her, why hadn't he left with them?

Chapter Eleven

Cliff exited the highway into a rural residential area. Skyler barely noticed the scattering of warm, tidy subdivisions alternating with fertile fields and heavily wooded tracts.

"So I asked but I'm not sure I got a straight answer." Now wasn't the right time, but she was already feeling awkward, why add not this? "That night in Middle Yemen. Your being at the hotel. Was that luck?"

"In a way. The embassy mentioned an American pro-grammer had been kidnapped and there was a strong possibility you were taken by Fahrrad's crew. So I was looking for you. But I was only at the hotel to gather information—although I did check in under an alias, just as a precaution."

"And after you rescued the prince and me...why didn't you return with us?"

His face blanked. A beat before he answered. In that moment she feared the worst.

"I'm not going to pretend to misunderstand you. No, I didn't stay to romance Fahrrad."

She let out a breath she hadn't even known she'd been holding. "So what were you doing?"

He slowed, and his competent hands turned the wheel onto a small, privately marked lane. Large, arching trees lined a black asphalt road, like the center aisle of a wedding chapel.

"Kul and I had a contract for the countrywide security system, Pizza Pie. We'd gotten to the point where I was looking for strategic partners, and I'd identified Fitzwater Consulting as a possible. I shared that with Kul." He paused, and went on almost hesitantly. "I was concerned Fahrrad might have gotten hold of the paperwork. I was checking to see if I was the reason you were kidnapped. But the system was wiped, the files burned. Fahrrad found Fitzwater on his own. Ah. We're here."

Suddenly, the tree-lined lane gave way to a parking lot surrounded by small ponds. Across a footbridge spanning a burbling brook lay the corporate headquarters for Hawkesclyffe Computers.

Her breath went out in amazement. Even from here, it was the most beautiful building she had ever seen. Two stories in some places, one-story in most, the structure blended with the flowers, trees, and green lawn as if it had grown there. People walked, alone and in groups, down garden-like paths. No one hurried, yet the air seemed full of quiet excitement and purpose.

Cliff pulled the sedan into an unmarked spot near the bridge. She took a deep breath. Let it out, slowly. All of the tension of the past hours left with it. Here, in this place, she felt oddly at peace, and smiled.

Tess emerged from the building, waving.

As Skyler got out of the car, her smile grew, and she waved back. Her head automatically swiveled to Cliff, to share her happiness with him.

He was stoically transferring her suitcases from the Mercedes to her sedan. He'd parked next to her car, and she hadn't even noticed. Their argument—no, her yelling—came back to her in a rush of hot embarrassment. She rounded the hood toward him to offer an apology, but Tess rushed up and caught her in a hug.

"Skyler, you're going to love it here." Tess grabbed one of Skyler's hands and started pulling her toward the building. "This is what we've always talked about for our team. You've got to see the size of the offices."

As her friend shepherded her away from the man who was so frustrating, yet who'd made it all possible, she glanced back.

Cliff managed a wan version of his smile. "Go on. Get used to the place. We'll talk later."

Hope rose in her chest. After the fiasco with Ron, she'd worked her way to the conclusion that open communication was what had been missing. Open communications were key to long-term relationships, both business and personal.

She'd been handed a second chance to make one or the other—or both—happen with Cliff.

Her step was jaunty as she entered HCC headquarters and paused to breathe in. Two stories of glass atrium soared above her. The central reception desk was surrounded by casual meeting areas and relaxed seating intertwined with roses, burbling water, and gorgeous art.

Tess took her on a tour. Well, more aptly, her friend dragged her here, then there, then to the next thing, exclaiming every time, "You've got to see this!"

Greenery abounded, potted plants and trees and flowers. On the other side of the atrium was a big pool.

Gold flashed. Skyler peered in to see hand-sized goldfish—before Tess dragged her away again.

The offices were quiet, well-spaced, and well lit. Everywhere she turned, there seemed to be a window, and the roof was dotted with skylights. Plants hung discreetly in corners or lined cabinet tops.

The people here were fully charged, too. Apparently, those outside weren't on break; work went on wherever people wanted, outside or in. Skyler's excitement built at every new thing she saw in the facility, from the company gym to the subsidized gourmet cafeteria.

Finally Tess said, "I saved the best for last. *Our* office space."

"How good can it be?" Skyler asked as her friend dragged her along. "We're the vendor...good grief." Her jaw dropped entering a sweeping wing of offices every bit as big and nice as those she had already safaried through.

"And wait until you see *your* office!" Tess grinned in excitement. "It's back this way."

Skyler managed to get her jaw retracted just in time for it to fall splat onto the floor. Not really, but it was a near thing because *her* office was the size of a conference room. *Her* desk was an aircraft carrier.

Then she got the real shocker. *Her* personal assistant walked in carrying a steaming cup of coffee.

"For you." The handsome, mid-thirties blond man held the cup out to her with a smile. "Cliff says you like it without cream or sugar."

Beside her, Tess gasped; her friend's dating radar was pinging off the scale, but the only thing Skyler could think was that Cliff remembered how she ordered her coffee at the restaurant. She basked in that a moment, a smile playing on her lips.

"Ms. Jones?"

She realized from the man's raised brow she had waited too long, and took the coffee from him. "Thank you...?"

"I'm John Cavanaugh. And before you ask, I type ninety words a minute."

"I'm Skyler," she responded in kind, "and I type seventy-five words a minute." At John's smile, she put the cup on the aircraft carrier and held out her hand. "Pleased to meet you."

He shook with a firm clasp, one she returned easily.

From there, the day sped by with intros and getting grounded. She was winding the day up in the big office—her office, and her jaw still gaped a little at the thought. She pushed it shut absently with one finger. Wouldn't want Cliff to catch her drooling.

The thought of him made her wonder where he was. She felt better now, more in control of herself. Maybe she could even face him without making an idiot out of herself. With all the employee-centric touches here, she'd been totally wrong about his being in it for the cash—and she'd never been so glad to be wrong.

She buzzed John. "How do I contact Mr. Hawkes-clyffe?"

Her new assistant's voice came through the phone. "Cliff? He left for England an hour ago. He'll be gone three months."

"*What?*" Her heart contracted painfully. "But..." But he'd said they'd talk later.

He'd also said he was on a tight schedule.

Gone, without even a goodbye.

Chapter Twelve

Skyler's chest felt like a block of ice. She and Cliff had argued, and now he was gone.

Echoes of Ron stung her eyes. Most every one of their arguments went like this, too. They'd quarrel in hot anger; she'd cool down and want to talk; he'd avoid her. The last, worst time, she'd called his office to apologize, to try to work things out.

He'd left work for the day—leaving her ring with his secretary.

The secretary had been the one to break the bad news to her then, too. Ron hadn't even had the decency to handle breaking off their engagement himself.

She blinked back moisture as her chest started to heave of its own volition.

"Skyler?" John's voice came again. "Cliff didn't want to disturb your getting introduced to everyone. He left you a message, though. Do you want me to read it? It's short."

Her stomach plummeted. *He regrets to inform you it's not going to work out...*

But her corporate mask came up automatically. *Thank you, Ron.* "Y-yes. Yes, of course."

"It says, 'Develop Apple Pie system for banking network, not Pizza Pie countrywide defense.' Does that make sense to you? He left the project docs and his itinerary with me. We can go over them tomorrow. "

A weight lifted in Skyler's chest. "Develop for banking." He'd heard her after all. He was telling her she wasn't working on Fahrrad's defense network. Maybe he had some heart after all.

Maybe this isn't Ron all over again.

Then John said, "Oh, and he had a box for you. I'll bring it in."

Her heart plummeted again. *Ron's secretary, pointedly bringing in the empty ring box. "He wants it back."*

The door opened and John handed her a box...that had the picture of a smart phone on it. "Cliff said if you're going to be alpha geek around here, you need the latest tech."

As she opened the box, confusion gave way to delight. A slim phone nestled in heat-form packaging. Extracting it, her hand nearly floated away. It was light as a feather. "This is cool." Her smart phone was nice, but this one, flat as a credit card, fit perfectly in her hand. She touched the screen as John left. The phone responded instantly with a bright, readable display of icons over a wallpaper of the HCC building, the picture quality so good it felt like she'd see birds flying through any minute.

Settling herself behind her desk, she started acquainting herself with the project documents Cliff had left, glancing every so often at the phone, and smiling.

At the end of the day she left with Tess. All the assigned apartments were in the same complex a few miles from the HCC campus. While not as humongous or spectacular as her office, her apartment was just as lovely, with a view of a river park across the street. And surprisingly, nobody had to share.

They were being treated less like contractors and more like cherished working partners. Skyler couldn't help a glow of belonging. Optimism lightened her outlook, and the fight took on less and less importance.

She knew she'd hear from Cliff the moment he landed in England.

Two days passed without word, then a week, then several. At first she didn't think anything of it. She was busy coming up to speed on all aspects of the HCCpi project, hardware, Apple Pie software, and the most important, the peopleware.

Then Jerry Fitzwater called yelling at her about the weekly project report forms. Cliff might not be about the bottom line, but Jerry needed the reports pronto so he could bill his new very best client. Grinding her teeth, she logged onto the Fitzwater system only to get a headache trying to make the forms function properly. She finally had to ask HCC operations to poke a hole in the HCC firewall. That and a couple aspirin relieved the headache.

But she was surrounded by reminders of Cliff everywhere—including the fact that John had been the PA Cliff had talked about. Bad, in that she felt John's first loyalty was to Cliff and every questionable decision she made would be reported back to him.

But good, because, as Cliff's personal assistant, John knew far more about the business than anyone else. She leaned on him heavily for just about everything, except gelling the team. Sure enough, Cliff was right; she seemed to be a natural. John said as much in their morning stand-up meeting.

"Belva told me you can stay here as long as you want. That's a great compliment, coming from her. Oh, by the way, I got an email from Cliff."

"Finally." She had written him several times, trying to keep her tone as professional and impersonal as possible. "Did he answer all my questions?"

"Ah, no. Actually, he probably hasn't gotten your mail yet."

"It's *email.*" Skyler tapped her foot impatiently. "Do bits and bytes move slower overseas?"

"Ha. No, of course not. But you saw his itinerary. I'd imagine he barely has time to read the critical stuff. That's assuming he can get a hot spot for Wi-Fi or 4G."

"He was supposed to be in Greece for five days last week. You're telling me they don't have Wi-Fi?" She pulled John's phone from his hand and read Cliff's email. "Dear John: I just remembered you need to ask Skyler to follow up with OS Dev about the compiler designs before the end of the month, blah-blah-blah..." She handed the phone back. "He can ask about stuff that's already in development, but not answer my questions? What's really going on?"

Her PA grinned and shrugged his shoulders slightly. "Sometimes Cliff gets a project in his teeth and doesn't like to be interrupted."

"By an *email*? Maybe incessant phone calls would break his concentration, but a few emails—"

"Maybe you should contact OS Dev about the compilers before you forget."

"Don't try to sidetrack me." She paced the room, tapping her arm with one agitated finger. "The least he could do is answer my questions. I thought this project was important. I thought..." *I thought* I *was important.* She stopped abruptly at the sting of pain at the thought. Whether it was the impact of his original rescue, the searing memory of his two kisses, or the fact that she was working daily in his company with his PA, Skyler couldn't forget Cliff. Though apparently the opposite wasn't true. Ego-wrecking, but she'd have thought he'd at least remember she was head of the most important project HCC ever tackled, as good as *running his fricking company.*

"Now, Skyler, it's not what you think."

That placating tone of voice, designed to calm hysterical women and overheated project heads, made her grit her teeth. *Professionalism.* Shoving emotions deep inside, she put on her best corporate mask.

"You're absolutely right," she said, so sweetly she gave herself a sugar high. *Yetch.* "I'm running this show. I don't really need Cliff to make my decisions. Back to our agenda. What's next?"

*   *   *

The secure phone line rang late that night. John answered it in one ring. "Yes?" His voice was private, muted.

"Green light," Cliff said. "Pizza Pie is a go."

"Good." John paused, unsure of how to say the next thing.

The other man must've sensed his unease because he said, "You have a problem?"

"Maybe." He lowered his voice to a whisper. "I think *she* suspects something."

A soft curse came through the line. It echoed eerily on the weak connection. "It can't be helped. Do what you can to throw her off."

Exasperation made John bark, "You're kidding. Look, she's smart and determined. If she knew what was going on—"

"No."

"But she might be able to help—"

"I said no. I won't get her involved that way. It's too dangerous."

John suppressed an eye roll. And this was why his boss was perennially lonely. The spy who never spoke his name on the phone also never let anyone close enough to the real man to form a real relationship.

"So, what do you want me to do?"

"Misdirect her, rattle her, give her a different puzzle to gnaw at, I don't care, but distract her, however you have to."

"Seduce her?" he asked bitterly.

A crackling silence filled the line. Then a barked, "I said distract her, not disrespect her."

Well, well. John's good humor abruptly returned. "I'll do what I can."

"I'll take care of it when I get back." A breath like a sigh.

"Of course."

He hung up quietly, and sat back in his chair, shaking his head.

This won't be easy. But it will certainly be entertaining.

Chapter Thirteen

After another week with no communications from Cliff, with the majority of the project under her belt and running smoothly, Skyler had room to worry.

She decided to pump John for information. But to make the information pumping as casual as possible, she took him to a working dinner at Alfresco's, the restaurant where HCC took all their vendors and clients.

"So, how long have you worked with Cliff?" she asked him in a suitably blasé tone as their entrees arrived.

John laughed, and winked gently at her. "I thought that might be the reason for all this."

"What are you talking about?" She ignored her hot cheeks. "I invited you to dinner to thank you for your help. No other reason."

Digging into his lasagna, he answered her with a raised brow.

Busted.

She forked up her own mushroom and spinach ravioli, dripping chive butter sauce, but barely tasted it.

John chewed appreciatively, swallowed, and gave her a gentle smile. "I've worked closely with you for almost seven weeks now. I worked for Cliff for seven years before that. I know how easily women are attracted to him."

Yikes. She was not only obvious, she was as common as clay. Gut churning, she set down her fork.

"In fact, one of my unofficial jobs is to sidetrack female affections before they can interfere with business."

Oh, stars above. Interfere with business. She'd cut her own heart out before she'd let her stupid emotions do that.

He cut off another wedge of lasagna, his gaze dropping to his work. "Not that that applies to you."

"I should hope not. I'm simply naturally curious about the man who's given me such a great *business* opportunity. I just thought it might make a good *business* topic for dinner."

He gave a laugh, as if he saw through her pitiful excuses. "I only meant I'd never be able to sidetrack you."

"Ha." She bit off a sizzling retort, seeing another way in. "You met Cliff seven years ago? How?"

Instead of answering, John grinned around a forkful of lasagna, strings of gooey cheese running like ski lift cables to the plate. "You're just like him, you know."

"What? What do you mean by that?"

"Well, look. Normally I wouldn't talk about it, but..." He cast a glance around. They were the only occupied table in their corner of the room. "Cliff told me about rescuing you in Middle Yemen, so you have some idea he's not just a regular CEO."

With a cool nod, she took her fork and began to eat again, but inside she was bubbling excitement. Was Cliff a super-secret spy after all?

"Cliff and I met as civilians seven years ago. We tell everyone that like it was the first time. But we'd met before. See, I'm ex-military. About ten years ago, I was on duty in London, part of a covert joint task force. Cliff has dual citizenship, his dad US military, and his mum a blue-blooded English lady, daughter of a baron, I think...anyway, Cliff lived there at the time.

"He was an electronics wunderkind even then. He invented a nanogate black bugging device the Brits used to spy with. Stopped enemy terrorist attempts without a single drop of blood being shed."

"That was Cliff?" Skyler had dropped all pretense of eating and simply leaned forward, eyes and ears wide to catch every syllable. "I remember reading about it. A marvel at the time. Easy to hide, almost impossible to discover because it was tiny, and the case was built from invisibility metamaterial."

"Yeah, a miracle. But I bet you didn't read about the FUBAR when it was first used. Cliff's design was solid but the lowest bid built it. The first time it was installed in a terrorists' camp, it crapped out. He felt personally responsible and went in to fix it."

"He went *into* a terrorist camp to fix it?"

John nodded. "Scrawny as a bean-pole then, and he'd never done anything more active than lifting a physics text. He spent two weeks learning self-defense with martial arts experts and training with the best undercover agents in England, and darned if he didn't pull it off. Earned himself a KBE for that—Knight of the British Empire."

That was the heroic Cliff of her romantic dreams, not the practical businessman. The juxtaposition stung her. "How did you get involved?"

He forked up the last bit of lasagna, chewed and swallowed, then sat back with a contented sigh. "I'd been filing requisitions for this kid's equipment, took one look at his record, and I knew he'd be toast without a lot of help.

I was the one who insisted on his training and coached him in martial arts myself. He was so impressed, he asked me to keep training him after."

"You done with that, hon?" The waitstaff pointed at John's empty plate, whisking it up when he nodded. She turned to Skyler.

"I'll need a box."

"You got it. Dessert menus?"

John didn't even hesitate. "Hot fudge sundae for me. You should try one, Skyler. They have the best hot fudge in the city."

"I'm kinda full, but..." It wasn't as if any sexy tanks would be asking her weight in the next day or so. "Sure. Make it two." She waited until the waitstaff had gone, then went back to the topic under the pretense of *professional* interest. "So, when Cliff started his computer company—"

"I was the first one he hired. In the beginning, he paid me with pizza and beer. Now, I have part share in the business. Since his mum died, I think I'm closer to Cliff than anyone." John took a sip of his drink, then smiled. "Which is great. I get the fallout of lovesick women." He winked again.

Skyler contained an embarrassed shudder. She was not, by anyone's definition, lovesick. She was successfully running one of the biggest development operations of her life, not mooning after the man who'd left her in charge. Not lovesick at all. "Why did Cliff pick Fitzwater to come onto the HCCpi project? Do you know?"

"Sure." John shrugged. "I was in on the investigation from the start."

"Investigation?"

"You don't think Cliff hires people blind, do you? He doesn't do anything without a great deal of thought and research, and believe me, he checked into Fitzwater and each employee's background as thoroughly as the FBI. Or maybe more so. The Brits taught him quite a bit."

I just bet. She remembered the night in Middle Yemen.

The waitstaff returned with their sundaes. John dug into his with a passion she had only seen on some of the hotter soap operas.

Skyler picked up her spoon as she considered the tulip glass in front of her. Glossy fudge melted rivulets in the snowy ice cream. She took a tentative spoonful.

The ice cream was cool and sweet, the fudge thick, warm, and rich. Both ran deliciously down her throat. She closed her eyes and savored. Dipped another taste, savoring again. Each bite was better than the last.

She surfaced from her sundae high halfway through the tulip glass. John had already finished his. He wiped his mouth on his paper napkin.

Then he hit her with, "But the reason Cliff picked Fitzwater? That was you."

Her spoon clunked onto the table. She was gaping at him, her brain whirling. "*Me?*"

"Yes."

Me. I was the linchpin.

Then why is he ignoring me?

"He needed someone to meld the team, and we had narrowed it down to three people. Then, right after he put you and the prince on the boat, suddenly you were it. He had to have you." John's eyebrow raised in an unspoken question. "You happen to know why?"

She mulled it over. What about that episode had convinced him she was management material? Her artful escape planning?

Yeah, sure.

The lacy teddy?

With Ms. McKinley to scale? She thought of the beautiful woman at the restaurant and decided that wasn't it, either.

"I don't know. Damsel in distress doesn't strike me as a sure-hire line on a resume."

"Oh, of course." John tossed his spoon in his empty tulip glass. "Cliff doesn't trust easily. But if he works with a person under pressure, well, he says he can tell more about a person in five minutes of a crisis than in five years of day-to-day business." He leaned back. "I've been meaning to talk to you about something."

We need to talk was never good. Anxiety splashed into her. About lovesick women? About Middle Yemen business? About her not cutting it in the rarefied climes of the corporate corner office?

"The project is going very well. You really don't need to put in these eighteen hour days any more. You have people working for you, following your lead." He put a hand on hers. "Relax, Skyler. You're doing a great job."

"Oh. That wasn't what I expected." The waves of anxiety ebbed but didn't completely disappear. "Cliff could do better, I'm sure."

John made a noise like *pfft*. "He's a great leader, but *you* get down in the trenches beside us. I like that." He sat forward, eying his tulip glass. Taking the spoon, he scraped industriously at the film of fudge in the glass. "He might've thought of relaxing the dress code on Fridays. But you broke it with blue jeans and sandals every day. My banker dad was scandalized, but I love it." He licked the spoon. "I'm working better because I'm more relaxed. You did that. Cliff would never have come up with the idea."

"Sure he would have. He's a genius, after all."

"Hardware genius. Personally, I think he's part machine. He drives himself like one. For all that he is a great guy, sometimes he treats his people the same way."

"I wouldn't know," she said pointedly. "I haven't worked with him. He ran away before I could."

"And people who refuse to think?" John continued as if she hadn't spoken. "You know, the ones who recite what they learned in school, but never know why? He's constantly prodding people mentally, and they resent it."

Skyler sighed. "If you're trying to tell me something, just spit it out."

"You just have to know how to handle him. When he irritates me, I simply grin." He demonstrated, mouth curving in that easy smile she now knew so well. "That annoys him."

She laughed. "Ah, the intricate dance that is male bonding."

"Exactly."

The two sounded like brothers, constantly trading punches but rock solid underneath. In many ways, she felt that close to John, too, and all the people on the HCCpi project, as if they were family. As though she belonged.

And Cliff?

Don't be silly. That's purely professional.

*   *   *

The next day, as Skyler dried her hands under the jet stream in the lavatory, she found herself thinking about Cliff yet again, and shook her head ruefully. She'd only been in the man's actual presence a handful of hours. But his impact on her, even in those few hours...

"I have to stop thinking about him."

153

A dreamy sigh made her jerk in surprise.

"He *is* handsome, isn't he?" Tess washed her hands at the next sink.

Skyler realized she must have said the words out loud and winced. "Um, yes?"

Tess gave her a guilty glance. "Of course, you get first dibs. Since he's your PA."

Skyler turned to Tess with a grin. "You have a crush on *John*?"

"Crush?" Tess's cheeks reddened. "That's such an adolescent term."

The blush looked cute on her friend, and Skyler's own grin widened. "What would you call it?"

Tess popped the button on the hand drier and shouted over the roar, "I have a purely adult appreciation of his masculine appeal."

Which only made Skyler grin harder. "Of course," she shouted back.

Tess cast a sidelong glance at her, and stifled a return grin.

All those lovesick castoffs from Cliff. Skyler wondered what John would do, given a woman attracted, not to Cliff, but to him. She waited until her friend's drier finished and said in a normal tone, "Does he know?"

"No." Tess dug in her purse for a slim lipstick and twirled it up. "I've sort of been waiting for the right time." She slicked on a coat.

Skyler could sympathize with that. Only for Cliff, either zipping her places in cars, trucks, or boats, or zipping himself out of the country, the right time was never. Not that she had any feelings for the man other than an appreciation of his masculine appeal...*wow*. She didn't believe that any more coming from her own brain.

"John's all yours," she said aloud. "Although, as long as I've known you, you've never been afraid of coming straight to the point. Why haven't you just told him?"

Tess stopped mid-swipe and turned to her, surprise clear on her face. "This isn't business, this is *romance*. And John is special. Maybe even the right-one-special. Failure is so much more, well, personal."

The word echoed in Skyler's head. *Personal.* That explained the roiling in her gut and mind, even months later. Cliff had kissed her silly, argued stridently with her, then run off. To her, it felt personal. If it had just been about the job, maybe running off wouldn't have felt so much like desertion.

Her friend went back to slicking her lips in the mirror. "Anyway, John doesn't even notice me, with all those women he has around him all the time. I guess I'll just wait until he's old and ugly and needs me."

"Tess, don't be ridiculous. You're a wonderful person. If John can't see that, can't see *you*, then he doesn't deserve you."

"Yeah, that's what my mother always said, too. I have personality, I don't need looks. *Bull hockey.* If I'm so wonderful, why isn't John crawling all over *me*?"

Skyler opened her mouth. Closed it and shook her head. This was too near to her feelings about Cliff for her to offer any perspective. "Sometimes guys are shizzola."

"You can say that again."

*   *   *

"John. What the hell is this?" Skyler slapped the expenditure printout on John's desk. It was Friday, almost two weeks after their dinner.

He *tsked.* "Such language, boss."

"Don't try to side-track me, *Mr.* Cavanaugh."

"Uh-oh. I've become a Mister. This must be serious. If you call me John Jensen Cavanaugh like my mother, I'm scooting."

Skyler's lips twitched in spite of herself. But this was too important. "Just look at this phone log!" She stabbed at items with her taut finger as she spoke. "Saudi Arabia, one minute. Yemen, another minute. Jerusalem, fifty-five seconds. Not regular long-distance rates, but charges that suggest heavy-duty scrambling. And worst—Middle Yemen, two minutes."

"How did you find this?"

"Going over the quarterly budget. Some anomalies caught my attention and you were busy, so I asked Belva to dump the phone log. Don't try to distract me."

"Like distracting a runaway train," he muttered. When she glared he smiled with bright innocence.

But those call locations, combined with Cliff being out of the country, only added up one way to her.

He was working with Fahrrad.

She asked one pointed question and steeled herself for the answer. "Who's charging these phone calls?"

"Dunno. Maybe some kid who stumbled onto our one-eight-hundred number?"

"A kid with a jet?"

"Skyler, Skyler." John *tsked.* "You're doing great at your job, but you are overworked. Leave all this detail work to me. It's only a few bucks, after all. You shouldn't be worrying about it."

"Don't patronize me." She slapped the report.

His eyebrows rose.

Fists clenching, she turned to stare out John's large window without really seeing the beautiful landscape. A couple deep breaths kept her from putting her fist through the plate glass. When she turned back, she was calmer, but her hands remained balled. "This is Cliff, isn't it?"

"No," he said, too quickly. "Cliff doesn't call while traveling. Never has. Besides, we have no reason to think Cliff is in Middle Yemen."

Except for the fact that he's a businessman and Fahrrad is big profit. But though her gut was screaming at her that this was Cliff showing up in the worst possible way, she knew she could be wrong. Jumping to conclusions.

"Fine. Then I want you to check on these calls and find out exactly what they are—and exactly who is making them." She jabbed at the report on the desk. "Because when Sir Humphrey comes back, I don't want there to be a single line item he can criticize me on." She leaned her fists onto his desk and stared him in the eye. "Understand?"

John sighed in exasperation. "Cliff doesn't think like that, Skyler. If he chose you, he won't be breathing down your neck. He trusts you to do the job."

Unsaid was the '*as you should trust us,*' but she heard it loud and clear. Choking back a sarcastic retort, she merely said, "I guess I don't know him as well as you do."

"But you know me." John spread his hands in a gesture of appeal. "And I say Cliff won't second-guess your decisions."

"Really?" She spun into pacing. "I've made design changes in the implementation, John, critical changes. And some of the policies I've instituted are considered downright heresy in other companies."

"He'll approve. Skyler, if you won't trust Cliff, trust me."

She spun back to him, her anger deflating as suddenly as it had come. "I do trust you, John." *And, more fool me, I trust Cliff.*

Snatching up the phone logs, she strode back into her office before he could hear those unspoken words, too.

*   *   *

The secure phone rang.

John started forward in the chair. It was earlier in the evening than usual. He reached for the phone, knowing he'd fudged a bit when he'd spoken with Skyler. Cliff the businessman never called in while traveling, but Cliff the spy did. And though Cliff trusted her with his business and the livelihood of his thousands of employees, he hadn't seen fit to trust her with everything.

John chuffed a sigh. All things in their own time. He answered. "Yes?"

"It's me."

No duh. "Is there trouble?"

"Some. The key personnel were evacuated during the instability crisis. I'm having to train new ones from the ground up."

"How does that impact the schedule?"

There was some static, and he had to ask the question again.

Finally the reply was clear. "Not good. I estimate we're at least a week behind. How's it going there?"

"We're right on schedule." John paused. His boss would not like the next bit. "She knows about the phone calls. I'm pretty sure she knows what you're doing. I caught her checking into Omega team. If she sees what they're doing, and worse, says something to the wrong people—"

"Damn it. She'll jeopardize the mission."

Look, if we bring her in on it, we can buy some time."

A burst of static obscured the reply on the other end. When he could hear again Cliff was saying, "Pull the Omega team from the Pizza Pie coding. Tell her it's Apple Pie all the way. I'll do the rest."

"I'm not sure that'll satisfy her."

What sounded like a growl came over the line. "I'll take care of *her* when I get back."

The connection was almost immediately severed.

John sat back in the chair with a grin. He couldn't wait for the show.

Chapter Fourteen

"Why is this report so vague?" Monday morning, Skyler stalked into John's office and plopped her laptop in front of him. She had the weekly team reports file open to a page with a single line on it that read, "Made progress."

John glanced at the screen in a way that she almost thought he'd known what she was going to show him before she'd brought it in. Her nerves, already tight, rankled.

"Oh, this? This is just the Basement Bombers."

"Don't call them names."

Blond brows rose. "That's what they call themselves. They had their pick of airy offices but holed up in the farthest, darkest corner of the basement. They like it down there, like being on their own. They hate reports, they're constantly hiding from management, and they're essentially unsupervisable, but they do their jobs if you know how to talk to them. I'll take care of it."

"No. This is why Cliff hired me. I'll take care of it." She picked up her laptop, slapped it shut, stuck it under her arm, and marched off.

"Skyler, wait. There's no need. I can find out what you need to know."

"Yes, you can." She spun in the doorway. "But will you?" She glared at him, vindicated when he winced. "Tell me the truth."

"Skyler, I'll be as honest as I can. What's your concern?"

She stalked back to his desk, putting menace in each step. "My concern is that I tried VPNing into their computers but was unable to connect. My concern is that a team of programmers is working on code I can't see. My concern is not that this team is unsupervised, but rather that they're working on Pizza Pie."

She'd used the code name Kulinahr and Cliff had given test John, expecting him to pretend ignorance. But to her surprise, he nodded.

"That was their original assignment. But it's changed, Skyler. I told you, we're just doing Apple Pie now."

Implying they'd worked on Pizza Pie only when the prince was still in power. But she didn't buy it. "Then you won't mind if I check, will you?"

Before John could stop her, she marched off.

Skyler stalked into the basement and was about to stalk into the Bombers' group office when she had a better idea.

Standing just outside the closed door, she pitched her voice to carry. "Did you see there's cake in the cafeteria?" The company chef normally made only healthy alternatives, but he'd produce a killer birthday cake on occasion. "Better get some before it's gone." She dashed around the corner and was rewarded a moment later with the click of a door opening and the scuff of feet heading upstairs.

She sneaked into the Bombers' office and took a quick look at the cornermost desk, where a laptop was open to a lock screen.

But she had the admin password.

The lock screen cleared to the company's proprietary visual coding environment, open to whatever the Bomber programmer had been working on.

She flipped from visual mode to code mode, scanning the modules—and she saw only Apple Pie. She tried another laptop. More Apple Pie. The third, same. The fourth and fifth.

Nothing but Apple Pie.

Her spirits rose. Cliff might have returned to Middle Yemen for any number of reasons, but the most important thing was, neither he nor John had lied to her.

She was working on Apple Pie. Just Apple Pie.

Smiling broadly, she skipped upstairs on light feet. So many times John had said trust Cliff. Having proof, now she could, and she wanted to reward him.

She'd make this project the best Apple Pie ever.

*   *   *

It was late that evening when John's secure phone rang. "Yes?"

"Delay the shipment." The voice on the other end, far from its usual wry tone, sounded weary.

"That's not good."

"No. We've had delays and a couple setbacks. We're three weeks behind now."

"Three weeks?"

"Can't be helped. You?"

John gave a laugh, but he felt no humor. "Something put nitrous in her engine. She's brought a new meaning to the word efficient. We're two weeks ahead."

A tight silence from the other end. Then, "You have to stall her."

"You want her to get suspicious again? We scrubbed Omega team barely in time. Why can't you stall expectations there?"

A breath of air, like a sigh. "I'm uneasy."

"Something wrong?"

"No. Maybe. When I tried to delay, the client knew I was lying. He quoted chapter and verse of exactly how far the project is along."

"That's not good."

"No. But I have an idea. I'll keep you updated."

"Yeah. Sooner, rather than later, okay?"

"When I can." The call ended.

John got up from his chair, rubbing his neck. He hoped everything would work out on schedule, but not for the first time, he had his doubts.

Chapter Fifteen

The next day, Skyler was refereeing a squabble between the Basement Bombers and the Black-Armband Test Team. She was developing a headache and beginning to see what Cliff meant about herding cats, when a text came through on her cell phone.

Normally she wouldn't have taken it mid-meeting, but desperation prompted her to look.

It was from John. "Call 4 U. Office. Cd Y." *Call for you, code yellow.* Which meant high importance. Office meant she couldn't just pop it onto her headset.

She rose, already texting confirmation. "Excuse me. I need to take a phone call."

Hurrying into John's outer office, she saw him on the line. He nodded her through as he said into his headset, "I'm transferring you to her now."

In her office, she picked up her handset. "This is Skyler."

"Skyler? This is Kulinahr."

"Prince Kulinahr, how lovely to hear from you! How did you know I was here?"

"I didn't. I was calling Cliff."

That soured her pleasure. "He's off globe-trotting. I haven't heard from him in months."

Boo hoo, Cliff doesn't call.

Only means he trusts me to get the job done.

And in the end, doing a good job was the only thing that was important, right?

"But Mr. Cavanaugh told me you might be able to help me."

"I'll do what I can. Although I'm no international spy or even billionaire businessman with helpful government ties. Only a lowly computer tech."

"If you are willing to help, that is more than I have gotten elsewhere." A sigh came over the phone. "Friends do not always turn out to be friends when one is no longer in power."

She winced. "You contacted the government friends who'd supported you before?"

"Yes. I did not get the best of responses."

"I'm sorry to hear that."

He must be disappointed with how often business came before friendship.

"If I regain my throne, I will see people differently. I will not be so naïve. Ah, well, I guess deep down I really didn't expect anything else." He sounded older, tired.

"Isn't *anyone* helping?"

"Yes, there is." Kulinahr's voice brightened a bit. "One person."

"That's all?" Skyler frowned. "How much can one person do?"

"Quite a bit, actually, if they are smart and resourceful. Which, tangentially, is why I called. I have a question."

"Okay, shoot."

"You are acquainted with computer-controlled security technology?"

What was déjà vu called the fourth time around, déjà *vier?* "I'm on a security project right now."

"Wonderful. Well, I have been thinking about the system Cliff had planned for me for my country. And thinking about what happened to me, it occurred to me that it's all very well for a system to resist attacks from the outside. But what about attacks from the *inside?*"

She sat forward. "Wow. That's a good point." She turned the Apple Pie design over in her mind. The system was firewalled and moated to the hilt, but if a process was already on the inside...? Definitely something she needed to discuss with the teams.

Kulinahr was still talking. "I think that's especially important if what Cliff told me about the system still holds—that it rewrites itself to adapt to realtime situations. How will it know it is not writing in modifications based on embracing malicious code?"

Skyler found herself puzzled. The prince would think about attack from the inside because of the coup. But how would he know to apply it to adaptive systems? "Well, we're only doing bank security, not countrywide."

"I know, but still. If some day HCC does provide computer-based defense for my nation, I would like it to be as safe as possible."

"Of course."

Kulinahr's relief was palpable. "Thank you very much, Skyler. I will not forget your friendship. I only wish I could do more for you in return."

"I didn't really do anything. Besides, you already did plenty for me. I honestly think that captain would have thrown me off the ship if not for you."

The prince laughed. "Well, then perhaps we are even."

After a few pleasantries, Kulinahr said goodbye and hung up.

Feeling guilty she hadn't been able to do more for the prince, Skyler canceled the rest of her meetings and met with her top-level teams that afternoon and the next day, to make sure they'd designed and implemented inside system defenses as part of Apple Pie.

As she added the information to her weekly report for processing at Fitzwater, she wondered again at the prince's unexpected computer savvy.

But then John came in with a stack of end-of-month reports, and a few minutes later the Bombers Black-Armband Team came squabbling into her office, and her day moved on.

*   *   *

The secure phone rang in the middle of Sunday night. John woke instantly and grabbed it. Calls outside normal contact times were never good news. "What's wrong?"

"It's confirmed," Cliff replied. "There's a leak."

"*What?*"

"On Monday I asked our friend to...suggest information to the person at the top."

"Me?"

"No, *her.*"

His boss's voice more caressed the pronoun than barked it.

"Oh. And?"

"That information showed up in the client's mouth today."

"Damn."

"When I asked him where he got the information, he admitted he knew exactly what we were doing. Boasted, actually. Said he wouldn't have been very good secret police if he didn't have his sources. Then he admitted he's been following our progress since July."

John swore again. "Just after the Fitzwater team came onboard? That's it, then. It probably wasn't intentional, but she must've talked."

"No. I don't know who the leak is, but it's not her."

"It's got to be. Starting in July, and our friend only gave the information to her? Or maybe it was intentional. She's angry with you, after all. Given the timing, it's *got* to be her—"

"*No.*" A crackling silence. "I'll never believe she'd betray us. There's got to be another explanation."

John took a measured breath. "Like?"

"Like she put it in her report."

"Which is completely *internal*—" When he heard his boss suck breath to argue, he said quickly, "Fine. What are you going to do?"

"The only thing I can. I'm coming back."

Oh, not good. "Now? With the project there already late?"

"Do I have a choice? I started the balls rolling. They'll roll by themselves for a while. I hope. Doesn't matter. The leak originates there, so I must return to find it. Plug it. Fix damages."

"Right." Releasing his breath, John got out his laptop. "I'll get things ready here."

*   *   *

It was a warm morning the last Monday in August when Skyler strode through John's office to hers, mind on the week's schedule. She muttered a distracted, "'Morning."

"Skyler, wait."

John's tone caught her attention. "What?"

"Cliff called in from Moscow. He's spending a days in Paris, and then returning."

"Returning where?" Jerusalem? London?

"Here."

"Here." Here, as in the United States...Here as in *HCC*? "But he's a month early!"

"No, you're a month ahead of schedule. You're doing such a great job, he wanted to come give you thanks himself."

Panic kicked her mind into overdrive. "Assuming he agrees with everything I've done, and doesn't see it and want to raze it and start from scratch."

"Skyler—"

"Just get my managers into the board room asap, okay?"

With an audible sigh, he lifted his phone receiver. "Fifteen minutes soon enough?"

"Make it ten."

He sighed again.

She ran into her office, dropped off her purse, scooped up all the files and her laptop, and ran to the boardroom. Thanks to John's efficiency, her managers started flooding in almost immediately, surprise and curiosity on their faces. When John walked in with the last manager, she nodded at him to shut the door and began.

"I'll need all the records of the project thus far. Not just the weekly progress reports you've been giving me. This is for the boss. Color graphs. New data flow diagrams. Phil, I'll need the updated app list. Include complete explanations for the mods we've made. Roy." She named the accounting head. "Get me the latest cost analysis, with percent complete, dollars expended, the works." She paced at the head of the meeting table, pointing at people as she talked. "Belva, I want a compilation of the production workup we did on the chip. Make sure you write up that little shipping problem we had—"

"He's not big on formality, Skyler." Belva had been with Hawkesclyffe computers for three years. "The weeklies you get are the most regimented we've gotten in years. He'll take an oral report from you."

"Oral?" A zing caromed through her middle. Last time she'd gotten "oral" with Cliff, it had begun in heaven and ended in disaster.

Ruthlessly, she crushed the memory. She was so busy crushing that she almost missed the concerned glance between Tess and Belva.

"I think Skyler needs to lighten up." Her friend pulled out a rubber band and stretched it over her thumb.

"Put that away." Cheeks hot, Skyler glanced at the other managers at the table. She and Tess had met as second-shift clerks at an insurance company during college. They'd used rubber-band fights to unwind or pass the time then. They'd even had one or two at Fitzwater. Great fun and a good way to burn off the stress of working fourteen-hour days. But she and Tess were at a different level now. Rubber bands were definitely *not* professional.

"Hey, let me see that." John reached over to take Tess's rubber band, and Skyler could have died. Then he said, "Nice. Thick enough that you could decapitate someone with it."

And he shot it directly at her.

It happened so fast she could only stare at the thing as it came at her, hitting her in the chest. "Ow."

"You can't do that to my friend." Tess jumped to her feet with another small, thin band already cocked. She fired.

The band bounced off John's nose. "Ow?"

Skyler laughed. She'd probably be fired for it, but the expression on his face was worth it.

"Here." Belva passed a thick rubber band to John.

"Payback." He aimed at Tess—but just as he was about to release, Belva banked a stinger off his ear. He jerked, the band flopping off to the side. "Hey! Traitor."

Suddenly, the air was full of rubber bands. Somehow, Tess had passed a box to every person in the room, and there was a free-for-all. The only one not shooting was Phil, who scooted his chair back to hide behind the six-foot tall potted palm. Roy joined him, not to cower, but to use the palm (and Phil) as cover to rain terror on the rest of the room. Until Belva, holding the white-board before her like a shield, advanced to his fortress. Dropping it, she shot him down.

Tess slid under the table and sprang up from time to time to make a strategic shot on someone's rear end.

Skyler had never laughed so hard in her life.

John and Tess were dominating the scene at one point when they partnered, back-to-back, and got everyone else in the room to scatter. Then, partnership forsaken, they turned and shot at each other.

"Okay, okay." Skyler raised a hand in surrender as tears of laughter cascaded down her face. "Point made. Let's go get ice cream."

"Chocolate fudge, here we come," Tess crowed.

They piled into two cars, Skyler driving one. It felt like college again, with the freedom and friendship, and despite her metabolism being closer to thirty than twenty, she joined in when everyone ordered the biggest chocolate fudge sundaes on the menu. After that they went out drinking, and then to a local movie theater to see a cult classic that Skyler had seen as a junior. She still remembered the lines, mostly, and shouted them in a good-natured but ragged unison with the rest.

Completely relaxed as she headed home, she marveled at how close they had all become in such a short time. And how they could distract her from...instantly she tensed up.

Cliff was coming.

Chapter Sixteen

Wednesday, Skyler woke in a panic. She leaped into the shower, grabbed the clothes she'd laid out for today—professional blouse and solid charcoal skirt suit pressed to within an inch of its life—and burned a layer of rubber off her tires getting to the office.

Once there, she sat at her desk and tried to work, but couldn't concentrate. Nerves swarmed her stomach like insects, so badly she was nauseous.

Cliff was due any minute now, and though she had received constant reassurances from everyone, she remembered too clearly their disagreements at Fitzwater's offices, the road-rage race, Cliff's cold anger after their first kiss, and fighting over Fahrrad in the car on the way up here. He could cut through her every defense like a plus-five saber.

Then the good memories filtered in. His hands, competent on the steering wheel as he drove her to a lovely dinner. His seating her at the table, their meshing with ease. His ability to kiss her senseless.

Her nerves began to untangle.

As long as she kept everything professional, she'd be okay. She just had to remember not to do the things that set off the bad feelings. Not race him, not fight with him, not kiss him.

Not ask him point-blank if he was still dealing with Fahrrad.

She sprang to her feet and kicked into pacing.

Although, what would she do if he was? Throw a tantrum? Fight him? Quit? Even if she believed Cliff when he said she was the best there was for this job, she'd seen the people he socialized with, met the people he worked with. It wouldn't be hard to replace her with someone almost as good, plus smarter and more beautiful to boot.

Why would Cliff want to keep her if she made trouble? Ron hadn't, and she'd been trying to please him.

And if she tried to please Cliff?

She stilled, her whole body on the cusp of *oh, yes, please,* when John brought in a stack of correspondence to sign.

Trying to win love through job performance? She shook her head at herself. What kind of idiot was she?

John must've seen her fretting because he gave her shoulder a quick comforting squeeze. She smiled her thanks, but as he released her to drop the letters on her desk, she glanced out her office window for the fifteenth time that hour.

She expected either the Mercedes or the coupe, so the big, shiny pickup truck pulling into the lot surprised her. Still, she felt the now-familiar prickle on her neck.

Cliff had yet *another* car?

Well of course he does. Rich boy, emphasis on boy. *Toys don't change, only their price tag.*

Sure enough, he swung out of the truck with a graceful leap. In stark contrast to his usual business suit and definitely not the black silk of Middle Yemen, he wore blue jeans and a crisp cotton shirt rolled up at the sleeves.

As he strode past the cars in the lot, dwarfing them, Skyler recalled how big he was, how heroic, and her tummy butterflies danced. She slapped a hand over her stomach. Stupid insects. He crossed the parking lot with his ground-eating stride to disappear from her view, into the building.

She turned to see John exiting her office. She opened her mouth to call him back for moral support. But when he glanced back, he only smiled gently and walked out. She'd have to brave the storm herself.

Almost literally, Cliff blew into her office like brisk spring showers. *Forgot how big he was next to cars? How about how big he is compared to* me?

"John tells me you've been working too hard, so we'll debrief offsite."

"Thanks," she shouted at the traitorous John.

"You're welcome," floated cheerily back.

With a sigh of exasperation, she returned her attention to the big man standing beside her, heating one side of her like a fireplace. "You and me and who else?"

"You and me is enough. And to be sure there are no interruptions..." He held out a hand. "Your phone? You still have the smart phone I gave you, right?"

"Of course I have it." She kept it on her always because *he* had given it to her. Not that she'd *ever* tell him that. She reached into the suit coat pocket and pulled it out.

"Good." He took the thin phone and shut it off.

"Hey." *Partners communicate.*

Then he grabbed her hand.

A shock streaked up her arm like a bolt of lightning. His hand engulfed hers, skin warm enough to cause a whole weather system to build inside her. The stomach dancers were going insane.

Cliff didn't seem to see the effect he was having on her as he towed her out the door and dragged her through reception. She would have to have a word with him about his caveman tactics—but at least he hadn't thrown her over his shoulder. Progress, right?

Skyler saw Tess and Belva gaping. She made frantic signals for them to rescue her, but they only waved *buh-bye* as Cliff pulled her across the French tile and out the front door.

As he towed her across the footbridge, she had to concentrate to keep him from pulling her arm out of its socket. Not really, but her arm tingled with excitement at holding hands with him, and her gut was tightening with anticipation just being with him.

She forgot to be worried she might have to report; she wondered instead if he would kiss her.

Idiot.

Yeah. But maybe kissed *idiot?*

Cliff loaded her into the passenger compartment of the truck and packed his long frame into the other side. Deftly, he swung the gear stick into reverse, and backed out of the parking lot so fast the tires squealed. Skyler squealed, too.

With a grin, he threw the truck into first and spun onto the main road, heading in the opposite direction from the way she took home.

Heading away from civilization.

"Where are we going?" she shouted over the engine.

He just shook his head and pushed the shifter up into second. The muscular vehicle roared to full life when he lifted it into third.

The road was made for this. As they flew through increasingly rural countryside, the wind blew her hair around her face and brought her the sweet scent of newly mown hay.

Tension, worry, doubt faded away.

He muscled the truck into a turn onto a wooded road. The scent of hay gave way to the tang of pine. The flash of a red-winged blackbird flying among needled branches caught her eye.

Cliff slowed and downshifted to ease onto a wooden bridge that crossed a small stream. Negotiating the bridge, he turned right onto a dirt road. Out her window, the stream burbled parallel to the road, the water merrily tripping along. A few moments later, he pulled into a clearing, and stopped.

Skyler threw open the truck door and breathed in the sweet scent of grassy green meadow and sunlight, wildflowers, water, and pine. "Oh, it's gorgeous." She leaped down, excitement giving her feet wings. "Where are we?"

He slid out his side and strode quickly around the front to stand beside her. She turned to see his cobalt gaze, intense on her, almost hungry. Excitement tangled in her stomach—she'd forgotten how fascinating those eyes were.

He reached for the lapels of her suit coat. Slowly, he eased the coat off her shoulders. Gravity helped him take it from her body.

Then he grinned, lost the starved-wolf look, tossed the coat back inside the cab, and went to the bed of the truck.

"We are in a park." Nonchalantly, he gathered a blanket from the bed then strode to a clear, flat spot of grass where he spread the blanket on the ground. Birds chirped in a nearby tree and butterflies flit past.

"Yeah, the rampant nature tipped me off." Had she imagined that hungry gaze as he eased off her coat? "What park, and why?"

"My park. For a picnic." He went back to the truck bed then heaved a huge basket from it onto the grass.

"Wow. Nice."

"Nicer if you relax."

"Okay." She sat on the blanket, kicked off her shoes and wiggled her toes. Amazing. For the first time in months, she felt at her ease with this big man. Maybe it had to do with her getting the job done. Maybe it was the beautiful setting, so much like a family picnic from her childhood.

But just maybe it was the man himself. He seemed freer here, unfettered by the trappings of a business environment.

And he looks really hot in those jeans.

That's not professional.

Relaxing. Don't care.

Throwing back the lid of the hamper, he drew forth an amazing assortment of food and drink. Imported cheeses and crackers on a plate. Fresh peaches and kiwi, and huge, red strawberries.

She plucked up one of the plump berries, dunked it in some sour cream, coated it with dark brown sugar, and ate it with relish. The blend of tart and sweet was perfection. "Mmm. Thanks. I wouldn't have thought about taking an hour out to picnic. This is really nice."

"I'm all about simple but effective." He rummaged in the basket, muttering. Then, triumphantly, he pulled out a corkscrew.

She laughed. "Don't you need to have a bottle of wine to go with that corkscrew?"

He grimaced, and began rummaging again. Soon enough, the wine surfaced, and he beamed expectantly at her.

She laughed again. "Isn't it too early in the day for wine?"

"I'm still on London time. It's five p.m. there. Skyler, after all my traveling, I need a drink, and I don't want to drink alone. Please?"

"You said please! All right, pour us some of that wine, and let me toast your return."

"And I'll toast your successfully leading the project." He smiled.

As soon as both glasses were full, she clanked hers gently against his. "To teamwork."

"Teamwork."

She took a professional sipped.

Cliff drained his in two gulps. "Drink up."

"I am drinking." Skyler attempted another professional sip, but he tilted the bottom of her glass and it was drink or drown. She polished off the glass, then waggled it at him sternly, only to have him pluck it from her hand for a refill. The surprise made her laugh, only it came out suspiciously like a giggle. She caught herself, and crossed her arms in mock severity. "What're you trying to do, get me drunk?"

"Not drunk, drunk. But John said a glass or two is how you relax."

Her mouth dropped open. "Blabbermouth. See if I give him a raise after this."

"Don't worry. I've already done it." He handed her the filled glass.

"I'm surrounded by troublemakers. What else did John tell you?"

"Not much I didn't already know. He said you were a terrific boss, and the people at the company love working with you. I see our project is ahead of schedule and right on budget. Good job."

Good job. When she was halfway to being in love with him? *What did I expect, poetry? Kisses?* She took a big swig. "Thanks. Anything else?" *Nothing about love-sick women? Nothing about your sidekick side-tracking my affections before they interfere with business?*

Was this romantic setting all just *good business?*

Somehow, in her agitation, her glass was empty again.

"He mentioned you have better taste than I do in restaurants." Cliff poured a refill.

"John? That's easy." She snorted, then cut it off in horror. She *never* snorted. "Your John is a chocolate-fudge-aholic. Your fancy-shmancy restaurants never have decent chocolate fudge. You've kept my glass full, but yours is empty. Keep up, Hawkesclyffe."

He grinned. "So, this is what it takes to get you to relax." As she attempted to sip, he reached for the bottle.

Their arms collided and she ended up with wine splashing her face and going up her nose. She started coughing.

"Oh damn, sorry...sorry." He snatched up a napkin and tried to wipe her face. The flimsy paper soaked up the liquid and promptly disintegrated in his big hands, leaving him with a mass of sticky paper pulp. It made her laugh in between coughs, and he started laughing too, making the wiping process even more of a mess.

When she finally quit coughing, and their laughter wound down, she lifted her heels from the blanket to spin, wobbling a bit, on her butt, turning her back to him. "You're dangerous," she lectured at the trees. "First you try to drown me, then you laugh. What if I needed CPR? You'd be laughing too hard."

"CPR is for when your heart stops. You mean mouth-to-mouth." Gentle fingers alit, flower-petal light, on her chin, urging her to turn her head toward him.

Her heart stopped, or at least time seemed to stand still, on the cusp of something beautiful.

*　　*　　*

At that moment his stomach rumbled. He laughed. "I guess I really am still on London time."

It broke the moment, and she told herself she was glad. Yet, as he sat on the blanket and dug into the food, someplace deep inside her warmed. Seeing him eat brought her pleasure. Seeing him smile brought her pleasure.

Heck, seeing him *breathe* brought her pleasure.

She realized she was far too vulnerable to this man— who was her boss. Or at the very best, her business partner. Business partners belonged in the boardroom and lovers belonged in the bedroom, and the two should *never* cross.

Although, if they could...

No. Not with him. Hadn't John said Cliff avoided the lovesick women? She watched him make a sandwich as big as her head then demolish it.

Yeah. Lovesick my ass.

This might even all be a ploy. Corporate gamesmanship. He knew she was pissed at him for dropping everything in her lap then taking off without a word. He was acting all sweet to get her pliable. Damn him for bringing her out here, making her want things he couldn't ultimately give her.

She stoked her resistance. "Kulinahr called while you were gone. Do you know that of all his so-called friends, only one person has the guts to help him? After all the good he's done for his country, he only has one ally? That's criminal."

"It's not all that unusual." He licked mayonnaise off his fingers. "You want me to make you a sandwich?"

She was pretty sure if she ate his size sandwich, she'd explode. "Thanks, but I'm still pretty full from breakfast." She nibbled another strawberry. They were tasty. "Why do you say it's not unusual?"

"Before, he had the clout of a head of state. Now, he's only a person."

"*Only* a person?" Acid tinged her voice, matching the anger that dumped in her blood. "Since when has that become such a lowly occupation?"

"I didn't say that. I merely meant—"

"What? That heads of state, no matter how ruthless, are more important that individuals? That a leader's actions can never be questioned, like some kind of god? Isn't that how we got Stalin and Pol Pot and their ilk?"

His tone went cool. "If we are to discuss this instead of relaxing, kindly do not interrupt me. Especially do not assume to divine my meaning. Unless you're a mind-reader, now."

"Heavens, no," she bit out with mock amazement. "I'm not a godly head of state."

"This isn't about Kulinahr." Frowning, he leaned closer, gaze searching hers. "What's really eating at you?"

She poked her forehead. "Can't you tell?"

"Skyler, I'm sorry for that mind-reading crack. Can we get into this later? It's been a long two months." As he spoke, he bent closer to her until his breath heated her lips, tickling the delicate flesh in a most delicious way. Just a little closer and his mouth would touch hers... "I'd rather make love to you than fight."

Make love...?

All the breath left her body. Before she could even start to make sense of that, her libido revved up, indicating very loudly its desire to fully cooperate. Like on that steamy night in Middle Yemen, when his big body, bare-chested and hot, pressed her into the mattress, his mouth sweet and questing...

Staring up into his eyes, she managed to finally suck in air, trying to cool skin that was suddenly superheated, trying to remember past lessons learned. *He's using my body, my needs, against me.*

Her body didn't care.

Ah hell. With him, *she* didn't care.

Chapter Seventeen

Skyler slid her fingers into Cliff's hair. When he didn't move beyond watching her with dilating pupils and flared nostrils, she brought her face slowly closer to his—and gave him a short, sweet kiss.

He tasted of wine and heat and fresh clean male. Her heart pulsed faster and she kissed him again. Her eyes drifted shut as she pressed light kisses to his firm lips.

With a soft groan, he brushed his lips against hers in return.

She savored the feel of his mouth, the heat, the movement, the sensation of silky skin against her sensitive lips. Her blood began to fizz, and when she slit her lids, she saw his eyes closed in bliss, lashes dark against his skin.

Her eyes slid shut again, and she gave herself over to sensation.

His tongue played at the seam of her mouth. She parted her lips in anticipation. With a sigh, he delved inside, softly exploring. Her fingers tightened in his hair, and now his hands came around her face to hold her in return.

"You're so sweet, Skyler." He kissed her deeper, tongue thrusting flames into her mouth. "So warm and soft." He backed off to nibble gently on her lower lip, then nipped down her chin until he nuzzled the delicate flesh of her neck.

His warm breath, the gentle caress of his lips triggered urgency in her blood. Her heart beat faster, her belly fluttered with need, and her breasts tightened and filled with tingly anticipation.

She arched her needy breasts toward him.

"Ah, yes." One big palm left her face to caress down her arm—and slide forward to cup her breast.

The heat seared her. She pressed into the oven of his hand. Like an invitation, that brought his other hand down to join in, cupping then kneading her breasts in tandem.

And then, gently, deliberately, he plucked her nipples.

Arousal zinged through her, sharp, sudden urgency. "Oh, more." She hissed the words. "More, please. More."

His head bent, and as he plucked again, he nipped the delicate flesh of her neck. Bright need jangled through her. She moaned. If he should nip like that on the tips of her breasts, she was sure she'd disintegrate.

"So sweet," he murmured, his breath billowing warm on her skin. "I want to make sweet love to you."

Make sweet love. The words resonated through her flesh into her deepest cells. Releasing his hair to wrap her arms around his neck, she rose to her knees, with a half-formed idea of pressing her throbbing, needy self against his lap, hoping he was ready for making love, not some day or hours from now, but right now.

She was awkward about it, catching her knee on her discarded shoe and falling against him. It reminded her abruptly that the last time she'd had sex was with Ron. That he'd called it it *making love,* too, after they fought.

Only it wasn't love-making, it was *using,* Ron using her body against her to win the fight.

But, oh, how Cliff used it.

Laughing, Cliff caught her as she fell and used his great strength to sweep her legs out from under her, settling her sitting crosswise on his lap. He slid a big hand into her blouse, under her bra.

Directly onto her private skin.

Her breast tightened joyfully, her skin burned in triumphant response. Intuitively, she knew she had about two seconds before losing herself to Cliff's expert hands and mouth.

But thoughts of Ron had confused her. She didn't want to stop Cliff—she burned too hot now for that—but instinct told her to slow this down. Cool her all-too ready libido.

To give herself time, she groped for her half-full glass of wine, found it, and haphazardly chucked it, to give herself an excuse to ask for more.

She accidentally chucked it into his face.

Cliff released her with a torrent of sputtering. She tumbled off his lap. His hair, face, and shirt were glistening with a sheen of red.

"I-I'm sorry." She hadn't meant to get violent. She'd just wanted an excuse to slow him down.

Instead, she'd drenched him.

Guys didn't like to be contradicted. Mel Pinlow got angry simply when he was shown up. Ron, Mel, Phil, they *really* didn't like to be humiliated, say by being doused with a glass of wine.

Big alpha guys? She expected Cliff to be coldly enraged. She expected him to cut into her with his words, to chop her into pieces small enough for Skyler-salad sandwiches.

Look on the bright side. Cold anger cools things down. Right? Ha.

She didn't feel like laughing.

But as Cliff stared at her, his expression wasn't angry. It was intense. She was confused for a moment, until she got a good look at his eyes.

His fine mind was working overtime, synapses rapidly firing.

Panic set in. From past experience, he'd figure out what was really happening. Figure out she'd done it because she was scared, figure out she was scared because she was responding to him not just physically but emotionally—figure out she was vulnerable.

That would go one of two ways: he'd use it against her or he'd spurn her.

She had just seconds before that intense intellect of his would figure it out.

Immediate distraction was in order. Again, she did the first thing she thought of, the thing that had been uppermost in her mind since she'd tossed the wine to stop it.

She placed her palm behind his neck and pulled him in to a searing kiss. Talk about a Freudian slip. Subconscious wish-fulfillment, but once started she didn't want to be doing anything else.

Still, she had a half-second to think *I'm an idiot* before he reacted like a starving man.

His mouth closed hard on hers, his arms wrapped around her, and he eased her back onto the blanket, coming down on top of her, covering her with his body, as he had that hot night in Middle Yemen.

His lips made magic against hers.

She moaned and arched up against him, forgetting business, forgetting Ron, forgetting lines that should never be crossed. Reveling in *response*. Response to the hard, powerful body above, commanding her to yield and open herself to him. His teeth nipped at her lips until they parted, and he thrust his tongue deeply into her mouth.

And she opened wider, wanting *more*. She'd wondered too long if he even remembered she existed to ignore this solid proof. Questions could wait; for right now, she'd take the physical connection. Wrapping her arms around as much of him as she could, she held on like she'd never let go. Wanting to kiss forever. Wanting urgently to make love.

Still wanting *more*. Wanting a connection beyond the physical.

Wanting him to fall in love with her, as she was falling in love with him.

Oh, God. Has it gone that far?

And how pathetic was she, how starved for love, that she felt so attuned to him just from a heroic rescue, a romantic dinner, and a picnic?

And three soul-searing kisses.

Skyler didn't realize she was crying until he sat her up, away from him. Without his body pressed into hers, even the sunny day felt cold.

"What...what's wrong?" She ground her fist into her eyes, because she knew what was wrong. Her redhead's complexion meant her emotions broadcast out into the world for anyone to see—not just anger, she wore her heart on her sleeve, too. He'd seen the tiny bleeding heart on her sleeve.

And Cliff avoided love-sick women.

She blinked wet eyes. In less than five minutes, she'd blown it. She'd proved it was impossible for her to fit into his high-powered, strings-free-sex lifestyle. Showed she was too emotional to manage his world-class company.

His gaze burned into her, seeming to follow her every thought. He had the strangest expression on his face, confirming she'd wrecked everything.

Trembling, despite everything, she yearned to dive into his arms for comfort.

Career suicide. Still, she wanted his comfort so badly she nearly succumbed.

Instead she reached deep, to the emotional armor forged from the fire of Ron, and pulled on her corporate mask.

It should have been easy. All she had to do was pretend she didn't care, that her heart was invulnerable. Yes, that was it. All she had to do was pretend she wasn't in love with Cliff.

She burst into fresh tears.

"Skyler, sweetheart. You're exhausted." He took her wet cheeks in his big hands. "John told me you were working too hard, but I thought he was overstating it. You need a vacation. Take it. Company-paid. Take a week—no *two* weeks, and go to New York shopping, or the Florida beaches, or the French Riviera..."

"No, no..." She'd begun to moan it almost immediately, each new word skewering her with despair. She hoped this time might be different. Thought *he* was different.

But here he was, trying to *get rid of her*. Oh, it was couched in the nicest of terms, but this confirmed he considered her an embarrassment. She had proved she couldn't play the corporate game.

Her armor had failed her—with him, it seemed full of holes. Her emotional closets had failed her—if only she could be as smooth about this as he was.

She called on the only thing she had left to save her.

Anger. If he really wanted to get rid of her, she was going to make him work for it.

Swiping her eyes, she ground out, "Shopping? Nice. But not how I relax."

"No?" He sat back, a guarded expression on his face.

"No." *Beat this, Mr. Hawkesclyffe.* "I'm a programmer. I find coding very restful."

She glared into his blue gaze, saw him absorb the words. Check, Sir Humphrey.

Then, incredibly, he smiled. "Hey, that's how I relax, too. Tell you what. Let's take this food somewhere we can be comfortable." He started gathering up the picnic things, talking as he worked. "You need to get away from the front line for a while, and to be honest, I could use a break from the heat, too."

Confusion broke through her anger as she watched him lift the packed basket and stand. "You do?"

"Yes." He dumped the basket in the truck then returned to offer his hand. She automatically put hers in his, embarrassed when her palm squished unappealingly. But he only gripped firmly as he pulled her to her feet. Plucking up the blanket, he led her, still by the hand, to the truck, where he opened the door for her. "The low-level interfaces are all designed, but the coding's not finished. Between the two of us, we could get them knocked out by Friday next."

"What are you saying?"

"You, me, and a hot processor." He threw the blanket over one arm to cup her face in both hands. Again, he didn't seem to be bothered by her wet cheeks. "A Skyler-and-Cliff programming vacation extravaganza. I'll reserve us a small conference room for the whole two weeks." He gave her a big smack on the lips then urged her up into the truck.

She found herself being belted in, head whirling, wondering what she had gotten herself into.

He clicked the door shut then slid into the driver's side, practically bubbling with enthusiasm. "It'll be fun to be mucking about in the code again. Another great idea, Skyler!"

As he started the truck and took off, she blinked in stunned surprise. Being obstinate had not only *not* gotten her kicked out, she was now going to work one-on-one with the man who made her forget her own name?

Check mate, Skyler Lynn.

*   *   *

The evening of his friend's return, John sat companionably with a bubbling Cliff in their favorite restaurant's private room.

He grinned at his friend's animation. Cliff wasn't quite as giddy as if he and Skyler had hit a home run—if the pair had crossed *that* threshold, he sure wouldn't be here—but definitely more upbeat than he'd been in months.

Which meant there was a chance Cliff had finally come clean. Casually amid the flow of excitement, John inserted, "So have you told her what you were doing in Middle Yemen yet?"

Abruptly, his friend scowled. "No."

Like a spigot, the burble of words cut off with that no. But John knew how to pry.

"Well, I can see why. She scares the crap out of me, too."

Cliff shook his head. "I can't tell her the full story until I've secured the leak—"

"I thought you'd never believe it's her?"

"It isn't her." The other's eyes narrowed and his words turned distinctly growly. "But anything I say to anybody could get back to the client. So I can't tell her the full story."

"Part of the story?"

"Well...problem is, I'm not sure how she'll take it."

John raised both brows. "Is it important?"

"Important? I don't know." Cliff studied his hands clasped loosely in his lap. Then his head came up, his gaze direct and intense. "Yes, it's important. No, it's vital."

"Vital, hmm?" John hid a smile. "Why?"

His friend sagged. "I don't know."

John kept his knowing smile firmly tucked away.

Chapter Eighteen

Skyler slapped her tablet's Bluetooth keyboard in disgust. "This miserable piece of junk is *never* going to work. The code simply won't execute, no matter how I beg!"

Cliff glanced up from his laptop. "Beg, Skyler? I didn't know you spelled the word 'beg', much less used it." He tossed his mouse and kicked back. The mouse knocked into Skyler's, sending hers rocketing off the table. He looked around as if to say, *"Now, how did that happen?"*

It was three days into their "vacation." In those three days, no mention had been made of the disastrous picnic. Skyler had donned her most effective corporate mask, and Cliff seemed relieved. Or at least he was cheerful. But as they worked together, her mask skewed then slipped. He was just so damned personable when he put his mind to it.

One thing to be happy about—the code they were writing was pure Apple Pie. John had told her the truth.

An electronic crackle was followed by John's voice. "Anyone left in the building, please call oh-oh-two. Anyone still here, call oh-oh-two."

"The all-call?" Skyler frowned. The last person to leave set the building alarm, but checked first that no one else was still working. "How late is it?"

Cliff sighed and checked the clock on his screen. "Nearly eleven. Eleven p.m., on a Saturday night. Once John leaves, we'll be the only people in the building. Even operations has turned over to the offsite watch." He pulled out his phone. "Call John."

As his phone rang, Skyler dug a hand through her hair and turned back to her keyboard, hooked up with her tablet. "Oh, my goodness. I've got to get the rest of this code checked tonight. Gonna be another all-nighter for me." She hadn't been able to sleep the last couple nights, anyway. Every time she drifted off she had dreams. Cliff kissing her neck, her mouth, palming her breasts, plucking her nipples...

"Again?"

Which was what she moaned in her dreams. *Again. More.*

"It's me," he said into his phone. "We're still here. I'll set the alarm when I leave. Good night." He ended the call.

She only figured out what he meant when he rose and clapped his laptop closed. "I can't have you getting burned out on me. I hereby issue an executive decree that you accompany me to the company gym. I'll meet you there in about ten."

"Cliff, I don't think—"

"Part of the problem. We're too *fuzzy* to think." He reached over and punched her tablet's sleep button. "Nine minutes, now." He strode out.

Skyler stared, incredulous, at his departing back. *Wow, tight butt.* She swore, leaped to her feet and scampered after him. When she reached the hallway, he was already gone.

Swearing a longer string, she headed for the company gym. Though she'd had a complete tour of the compact but well-provisioned workout area when she first came, she only used the track, stairstepper, and treadmill, avoiding the unfamiliar free weights and more complicated machinery.

She stood outside the gym, vacillating. While she was sick to death of code that wouldn't work, did she really want to spend a hot and sweaty hour with mounds-of-muscle Cliff?

Well. Put that way, the answer was obvious.

Skyler had workout clothes stuffed into a kit locker, bits and pieces worn more for comfort than style. She squeaked out of the cramped locker room on moth-eaten runners, her breasts smooshed in a new tank top, her bottom wobbling in baggy yoga pants. She felt both undressed—because she'd taken her sports bra home to wash and had forgotten to bring it back, and she was relying on the tightness of the tank's spandex to keep her breasts confined—and dowdy, because the ancient pants drooped like a hound-dog's face. It was worse because the moment she entered she was bombarded by the inspirational posters tacked up around the room—skin-tight compression capris on sports models. *Their buns are already so tight, if you fell against one you'd chip a tooth.* She was certain she looked ridiculous.

Glancing around, she saw one of the room's televisions yakking silently to itself—sound was available by connecting a Bluetooth headset—before she spotted Cliff moving gracefully through the first exercises in some sort of martial art.

Hoh-lee crap. Muscles slid smoothly under glossy, bronzed skin. Skyler stared. Those were the same movements he'd used that night in the sweltering heat of Middle Yemen. Moves that had been devastating for their opponents.

Her stomach tingled. The effect was devastating on her, too.

He glided fluidly from one position to the next, seemingly effortless, but a light sheen of perspiration marked the actual exertion involved.

He doesn't sweat; he only perspires.

Cliff finished the exercise with a slow rotation of his torso. His back rippled under the thin tank he wore. A tide of lust rose in her, heating her face, making her heart pound, and tightening her nipples, making them poke out visibly from the tight spandex.

Which was of course when Cliff turned and saw her.

She quickly clamped down on her body's reaction and pretended to be studying the poster beyond him. Hopefully he'd think the nipples were because the room was a little chilly.

"Skyler, there you are." He strode over, smiling in welcome. "Have you gotten the spiel?"

"Um, John showed me the gym, but I never had time to use anything but the stairstepper and treadmill." Which sounded better than her being intimidated by a few machines.

"Never too late. I'm proof of that. I'd better explain the operations to you, in case we use the other equipment. You wouldn't believe the hassle our insurance carrier gives us about such things."

Skyler nodded politely as he pointed out the stations of the universal weight machines in the center of the room, the free weight stations, treadmills, and other cardio machines. "Of course, you know how to use a running track." Cliff pointed to the three lanes circling the room.

"Yes. Yes, it's all coming back to me now." She let a hint of acid into her voice. "I think I'll start with a little stretching."

Skyler marched to a *barre* mounted on the wall. She was slightly irritated that Cliff's simply *exercising* could cause her so much wretchedness. Not fair.

Unless she could hand that wretchedness back to him.

She reached back into the attic of her memory for the year of ballet she took to overcome a young girl's coltish awkwardness.

I'll show him what stretching can do, she thought with a trace of malice.

Moving through the first series of exercises she learned so long ago, she stole a glance at Cliff.

He wasn't even looking.

She fumed. Beginning the second set, she set her heel on the *barre* and stretched, feeling tendons pop.

And snuck another peek.

Still nothing.

He might at least appreciate the effort. Phooey.

She switched legs, bending to her knee and sneaking a peek under her leg at Cliff. Was he really that rapt over selecting the weight for the bench press? Or was he *pretending* that he wasn't looking? A trickle of sweat—*I sweat, he perspires. I thought I was a lady. Double phooey!*—down her spine told her she was warmed up enough to tackle the cardio machines.

Cliff glanced up, for all the world as if just noticing her presence. "I'm ready. You?"

"Yup. Think I'll hit the stairstepper then do a short round of weights."

"That sounds like a good combination. Mind if I tag along?"

"Not at all." And then the imp of her redheaded forebears made her add, "If you think you can stand the pace."

He only raised a single brow, but she knew the challenge had been heard.

They mounted their side-by-side machines at the same time, the *boop* as they hit their computer reset buttons nearly simultaneous. Cliff craned a look as she entered one-one-six into the keypad.

"I thought you weighed one-twelve," he remarked.

"Who asked you to peek?" Skyler let a touch more acid bleed into her tone. "It's the last three days. I've been working my tail off for you; who has time to diet with Overseer Cliff around?"

"Have you *really* been working that tail off?" he said with an air of innocence. She could almost see him mentally putting on a (tarnished) halo.

"Never mind my tail. Let's get going." Exasperation mingled with a tingly realization that he'd almost certainly been watching her warm-up.

The stair machines beeped almost simultaneously, and they began treading on the pedals, quickly gaining a steady rhythm. She craned a peek at his readout. He'd picked the Herculean heavy-training level routine.

"Macho creep," she muttered to herself. "I'll show this bucket of testosterone how it's done." She re-entered her training routine to match his.

"Hey, watch it." He frowned at her readout. "Let's not overdo this, either. Nobody profits if you get injured."

"This? This is my normal, take-it-easy workout pace," she replied with a curl of lip.

"Your funeral," he grunted as he stepped up his pace.

She matched him, then took quick inventory of her body. Knees beginning to complain. Breath becoming shorter. Thighs tightening up. She told her body to relax. But after five more minutes, her breath was more gulping oxygen in response to demands made on her legs, and she had to summon all her redhead's stubbornness to keep going.

Beside her, Cliff purred like a Porsche in its element.

"Tired, yet?" he asked.

"Not a...bit of it," she gasped out, surreptitiously moving her workout level down a couple notches. There was ultra competitive, and then there was just death wish.

Beside her, Cliff was still going at Captain America levels. His muscles writhed as he hunched his shoulders like a huge bear. He put his head down between his shoulders and began charging like a linebacker, pushing the stair machine beyond its programming. Meanwhile Skyler's legs were on fire and her arms like lead from gripping the rails. She edged the workout back another notch, then another, and still felt like every cell in her body was screaming at her *for the love of all that is holy, woman, stop.* She eased the routine back one more notch and put her face up, straining to at least finish the workout.

Minutes ticked away as she churned out steps, every iota of her competitive nature focused on, not winning, but simply keeping from dropping into a trembling pile of muscle noodles on the floor.

Only the insistent beeping of the timer penetrated her curtain of sweat as the routine ended. She stopped, her whole body trembling as she rode the pedals down. Her fingers were permanently fused to the rails.

Cliff stopped too, panting hoarsely. He tottered off, obviously having pushed himself to the max, yet he still had enough left over to stop at the room's refrigerator and grab a couple bottles of water on his tottering way to the bench nearby. He sat with his head down, gulping great quantities of air. She braved balancing on her legs to get at the water. She wobbled to the bench and plopped down beside him, mopping at her brow and feebly brushing her hair out of her face.

"Well, *that* was certainly fun." He handed her a bottle, his breath already coming a little more normally.

"Exhilarating. Wouldn't have missed it for anything," she ground out. She snatched the bottle, blessedly cool, and tried to twist the top off. Her fingers had no strength. It took her three tries before she cracked it open and took a drink of pure bliss.

But as her heart rate slowed, she realized it *had* been fun. That even sitting next to him slowly dying from rasping breath and a ribs-rattling pounding heart was fun. Breathing in his masculine tang, staring at the sheen of exertion on his skin, wanting to *lick* it...

Crap. Ron had never affected her this way.

She and Ron...yes, they'd had fun, at least to start with. She'd enjoyed going to movies with him, and out to bars, and the usual things done on dates.

But Cliff, well, he was different. Or not him, but *them*. She'd enjoyed the *stuff* she did with Ron. She enjoyed simply *being* with Cliff, whether they were talking shop, or competing, or eating together or...or doing physical things.

She sighed. If only she could be the model corporate lover. If only she didn't *really* care.

"Well." He stood and stretched. Muscles sprang into relief, hard against the damp singlet.

She sucked in a breath at all that gorgeousness. She felt cheated, being so close and yet not being able to touch.

I could touch.

His body, sure. If she wanted to ignore everything she'd learned from Ron. But touching the real man, the real Cliff, was something else.

He relaxed from the stretch and smiled at her. "I'm tired enough to sleep now. You?"

She smiled back and nodded. "And then some."

"Let's take a walk around the track to cool down, and then how about I drive you home?"

Without thought, she replied, "No need. I have my car here."

"Oh. Right, I don't know what I was thinking. Well, let's get going." He started for the track.

She followed, frowning. Had she imagined the disappointment in his voice?

Too late, she wondered if that had been an offer.

They talked about inconsequential things as they sauntered around the track. After dressing, he walked her to her car, which he'd never done before. But when Skyler raised questioning eyebrows at him, he only said, "It's later than usual. I want to make sure you get off okay."

"I'll be fine, Cliff."

"Sure." He paused. "Do you want me to follow you home?"

Was this another offer? But his head was angled such that the parking lot lights cast a shadow over his face. She couldn't be certain. Professional was the best bet.

"I'm fine. See you tomorrow?"

"Right. Tomorrow, then." He was still standing there in the shadow when she pulled out of the lot.

*   *   *

The phone jangled John out of a deep sleep. Military training ensured he woke immediately but years on the civilian clock meant he didn't wake completely. He opened one eye and blearily took in the time. Two o'clock, as in a.m. He picked up the phone, grunting as his muscles stretched. "Hello?"

"It's me."

He grunted again. "What's the matter?"

"I just got a call from Middle Yemen. Our client is getting antsy. As in, threatening to torture my assistants unless they install the new protection grid and bring it online."

John swore. This was not good news. "Are we ready with the shadow project?"

"No."

"Can we delay, then?"

"Our client is aware that Apple Pie is nearly complete. Unless I want to pull the chip factory and start fresh, I've got to find the leak and plug it."

"We both went over HCC with a fine-tooth comb. We're clean." John rolled onto his back and ran one hand through rumpled hair. "Could we sabotage Apple Pie, then, to set it back?"

There was a long silence at the other end.

"You still haven't told her."

"No."

"You'll have to."

"In time. Now is not the right time."

"Why not?"

There was a short silence. "She's beginning to trust me. When I'm sure of her reaction, then I'll tell her."

"I think you're making a mistake."

Cliff's sigh sounded empty and alone over the phone. "Maybe. But I can't take the chance. I'm close to tracing the leak. Say—did you open that pinhole in our firewall?"

"The pinhole? Yes. We needed it so Fitzwater personnel could communicate with their home office…" He saw where his boss was leading. "Damn."

"Ah. Yes. That's the last puzzle piece. I know who the leak is, and why."

"Simple industrial espionage?"

"Cash is never simple. Once the leak is taken care of, I'll be able to start fixing things."

"And you'll tell her what's really going on?"

A silence. "Yes. Eventually. Probably. If there's a good opportunity."

John shook his head as he hung up. Organizing the second, shadow project was going too slowly. About the only thing on track was the project they did not want to complete.

He did not get back to sleep that night.

Chapter Nineteen

The next Wednesday just after one p.m., Skyler sat side by side with Cliff at the conference table of their snug little vacation meeting room, unwrapping her lunch. Food tasted better, the day was brighter, and she was the happiest she'd ever been.

Then she saw something that leaped out like a pimple on the big, flat-panel monitor before them, split to show her tablet screen on one side, his laptop on the other.

"Wait." She set the sandwich down and picked up her pencil, using it to point at first her side, then his. "This is basically the same chunk of code, used twice. I think we should pull it into its own object."

"Then each of us call it? Simple but effective. I like it."

She and Cliff had been working and exercising together every day for a week, including the long Labor Day weekend. The coding of Apple Pie was nearly complete. But that wasn't what made her happy.

Cliff did.

She'd never enjoyed herself so much, though she'd never let the man responsible know.

They'd shared a handful of cozy lunches now, as well as work camaraderie. A tiny part of her was disappointed they'd never extended it past dinner...to breakfast. But it was a tiny part.

Besides, their two weeks weren't quite over yet.

Now, he leaned over her, warm and companionable, and dragged his finger across the dualed tablet's screen to highlight a section of code. Yellow highlighting followed his finger, making the text spring into relief on the big monitor.

"If we pull this line, and this and this..." Drag, drag. "I think we'll have essentially what we need." He grabbed his tuna salad on whole wheat with sprouts and ranch dressing, and bit off the edge.

Skyler chewed on the top of her pencil. "What constructor?"

Cliff reached across her to pick up her sandwich, also a tuna with sprouts, and waved it under her nose. "You should eat this instead of the eraser. More nutritional value."

She patted her tummy. "Too many fudge sundaes are starting to take their toll."

"Really?" He brightened. "Can I have it then?"

"You're worse than my dad's dog. Oh, okay," she conceded when he started to pout theatrically. "You can have half. The design calls for almost the same sort of thing to be done here"—she clicked her pencil to stylus and was about to use it to poke the text on his laptop when it flipped to screen saver. "Darn. Can you wake up your machine?"

"Mmm?"

She glanced up from the screen. He had half her sandwich in both hands and was busy chewing.

"Fine, I'll wake it. She moved his soda, mostly down to ice, to poke the enter key. It woke, revealing a lock screen with the cursor pulsing slowing in the password field.

"You'll have to enter your password."

"Right." He popped the last bit of sandwich in his mouth and reached out to touch the keyboard—managing to swipe tuna and mayo on the first key he touched. "Oh, hey, can you enter it? It's PEPPERONI."

"Pepperoni?" Even as she echoed him, incredulous, she was typing letters. "Not some bizarre combination of symbols and numbers that's utterly unhackable? A food item?" She finished with a shake of the head. "Well, it's you. Of course it's a food item. All right, this code does almost the same thing." She poked a string of text. "Should we combine functionality?"

"You're playing devil's advocate again, right? I thought we'd decided to limit objects to one function each."

"Yeah, just testing. Can I have your brownie?"

"Skyler Lynn. You won't eat your sandwich because it's too fattening, but you *will* eat two brownies?"

"I was just thinking of you, Cliff, and your boyish figure." She smiled sweetly.

"No."

"Can I have your peach then?"

"Half." He sliced it awkwardly with a plastic fork.

"Watch it!" Skyler wiped peach juice off the screen. "Have some respect. You paid at least a couple hundred bucks for this monitor. Grunt coding, we're only worth $80 an hour."

"We're actually free right now. Well, except for the cost of lunches."

"And dinner most of last week. And, if we work as late tonight as last night, dinner, this week, too."

"Mmm. Chinese? Italian? Sushi?"

"What's wrong with pizza?"

"The pizza place in town?" Cliff made a face. "The cook thought a cardboard circle was a crust and made it into a sausage special."

Skyler had heard the story from John, too. "Well, it's not like it got to the table."

"Because it caught fire in the oven."

"Okay, what about The Pizza Place? They make a divine stuffed spinach with pine nuts."

Cliff's eyes lit up. "And that terrific double cheese garlic bread?"

"Yep. But not until you write this object."

"Easy." He attended to the keyboard in front of him, and after a few minutes of tapping, grinned at her. "All done."

"Not again." She groaned. "That's the third time!"

"You haven't tested it yet."

"It'll work. They all work. It isn't fair, you know."

He polished his fingernails on his shirt, admired them for a moment, and then smiled wickedly. "Fastest coder in the West."

"You really missed your calling. You shouldn't be heading up a multibillion, multinational corporation. You should be a dweeb programmer."

"Compliments will get you nowhere. I'm still waiting for the constructor and destructor routines."

She pulled her Bluetooth keyboard closer and got cracking. Two minutes later, she looked up expectantly.

He was just polishing off her brownie.

"Hey!"

"I'm doing you a favor. Your girlish figure, you know. Drink your soda, and let me check your code."

"Don't you dare comment on the indenting."

"Speaking of comments, where are they?"

She blushed. "Uh, it's self-documenting?"

He crossed his arms and tapped one stern finger on his biceps.

"Would you believe I was going to go back and put the comments in?"

He shook his head slowly.

"Uh, well, you see…" She nudged his drained soda off the edge of the table. It fell to the floor with a clack of ice. "Oh, gosh, Cliff. Clumsy me. Could you clean that up?" While he was distracted, Skyler gleefully commented the hell out of the code.

As he picked up the last ice cube, he gazed at the screen suspiciously. "This wasn't commented before."

"Of course it was," she said with mock indignation. "You're having delusions—probably brought on by a guilt complex developed from stealing my brownie."

He leaped up, grabbing her half-full soda and held it threateningly over her. "Yeah? Well, in about a second, you're going to have de*lug*ions."

She laughed. "No, no, please!" She wiped the tears from her eyes. "That soda's half my day's salary. Don't waste it!"

He gazed at the cup in his hand as if seeing it for the first time. "You're right." He placed it, reverently, on the table. "And the equivalent of two lines of code from you."

"Why, you…you…" About to rip out a really good one, Skyler caught Cliff's dimple peeking out. Her taunting repertoire suddenly evaporated. "Oh, yeah?" she sneered.

"Snappy." With a full flash of dimple, Cliff sat, pulled her keyboard over, and ran the test. They'd lighted early on using his laptop to show the test protocol, hers to run it.

Skyler sighed. That man could make code jump through hoops, roll over, and beg. Was there anything he couldn't do?

Moments later, his dimple disappeared into a scowl. "Hey, Skyler. The form's not working right. See, when I type in a value, it's supposed to bop over to the validation object to check it. But it seems to bypass validation."

Well hip-hip-hooray, he isn't perfect.

She scanned the code, not reading it so much as *feeling* for wrongness.

Sure enough, the problem jumped out at her. She stabbed the line with her finger and crowed, "Here. See? You have greater than. It's supposed to be greater than *or* equal to. And," she stared more intently, "this is *your* coding!"

"Even geniuses make typos." He affected a shrug. "I guess it's a good thing we're working together."

"You *guess* it's a good thing?" She landed fists on hips and stared, probably a lot more impact had she not been sitting, but she was having too much fun. "It would've taken you ten minutes to find that bug. Ten minutes. At least. And you just *guess* it's a good thing that we're working together?"

"Okay, okay. Here. Have a sip of soda."

Suspiciously, she took a drink.

"Hey, not so much!" He pulled the cup away. "Okay, now you're paid."

She kicked him in the leg. The agile creep leaped nimbly out of the way. How did he move that much mass that fast?

Grumbling, she pulled over the keyboard and corrected the code. After recompiling and testing, she moved on to the next module. Cliff was right with her. The programming was coming so easily, it felt like code and objects flowed from her fingertips. After she completed each part, she lifted her fingers from the keyboard. Cliff, in a synchronous, fluid motion, slid the keyboard in front of him and executed the test. They synched perfectly.

They'd just gotten through two of the final three modules when the PA system clacked and the air opened to John's voice.

"Anyone still in the building, call oh-oh-two."

Cliff took out his phone. "Nine o'clock already? Well, I tend to forget about time when I get wrapped up in a project. Especially if I'm enjoying it."

He's enjoying our time together, too. Heart light, she listened to him talk to John, expecting another workout.

Instead, Cliff said, "Give us five minutes to clean up before you set the alarm, okay? Thanks."

"Oh." Disappointment speared her. "We're not working out?"

"Are you kidding? With my mouth set on double cheese garlic bread?" He'd already cleared the table and was halfway out the door. "It's pizza time!"

Pizza. It reminded her of Pizza Pie, the code that, at no time during their time together, had he gotten anywhere near. Cliff told John they were doing pure Apple Pie, bank security only, and now as they wrapped up the project, she had proof he meant it.

So Skyler shrugged, smiled, and disconnected. "Pizza, the perfect overtime pay."

On their way out of the building, Skyler's phone chimed. She stopped in the soft, warm September night, and pulled her phone from her jeans pocket.

Cliff smiled. "Glad you like the phone I gave you."

"Someone has to be alpha geek." She blushed. She didn't tell him she kept it close because he'd given it to her.

"Voicemail?"

"Yes. I'll put it on speaker." She pushed the loudspeaker icon and played the message.

Tess's voice chirped, "Hey Skyler, you'll never guess what I just heard on the office grapevine. Not that I ever spread rumors, you understand." She chuckled evilly. "Since I got this directly from Jerry, I consider it fact, not rumor."

Skyler was more hungry than interested in Jerry right then. But Cliff seemed to be listening, so she let it play.

"Mel Pinlow got canned today. Not only did he screw up another big job, His AssHoliness got a sexual discrimination suit filed against him. But that's not the worst. Or *best*."

"Oh dear." Skyler felt sorry for Mel and hated to see bad things happen to anybody, but she wasn't totally surprised. *Time wounds all heals.* Without Tess and Phil there to cover for him, his true character had been revealed.

"Get this—he was selling company secrets to an overseas client. Design specs, code, you name it."

"Industrial espionage? *Mel?*" Skyler felt her jaw drop.

"And when I thought about the number of times he cut into *you* about *your* professional conduct..." Tess laughed. "Well, I thought you'd like to hear."

"Poor Mel." Skyler ended the call and put away her phone.

"You feel sorry for that jerk after how he treated *you?*" Cliff's nostrils were flared as if he wanted to punch something.

She gaped at him. "You're angry about that?"

"Darn right I'm angry. Why do you think I didn't pick him up for this project in the first place? I'd have fired him long before now, or at least put him in rehab training. No, I'd have fired him for being nasty to you."

Flabbergasted, she remembered thinking, long ago, that Cliff and Mel were like-minded peas in a pod. The sudden gulf between her image of Cliff and the reality of him slapped her like a laptop to the face. How had she missed this decisive manager, this supportive friend?

Although, in her defense, she was confused by all the different Cliffs she'd met. The sweet lover at the picnic. The sophisticated diner ordering in French. The powerful president and CEO of a multibillion dollar company, and of course, in Middle Yemen, her night in shining armor—or black silk pants. She blushed.

All those Cliffs...if she had been a computer system, she would have had a system overload/abort transaction message about now. So many different facets.

What do you know about Cliff?

Kulinahr, reaching the upper door of the ship, answering her. "He would make a most formidable enemy."

She had to remember, not all of Cliff's facets were necessarily friendly to her.

"Skyler?" He was eying her strangely.

Oh yes, here was another Cliff, the astute human being. *Say something*, if only to sidetrack that magnificent brain. "I don't like to see anyone get fired, although in this case, I supposed it's for the best. Maybe Mel will learn something from it."

"I doubt it. Egos like that seldom learn from experience."

This she could parry. "Oh? How did *you* learn so much, then?"

"Ha." He smiled cryptically. "Practice." He strode away, heading for yet another strange car.

"What does that even mean?" She ran to catch up. "Hey, let's use my car this time, okay?"

"Want me to drive?" He took her elbow and steered her toward her sedan.

"My car. I'll drive." Skyler popped the locks, watched him fold his long frame into the car, fanned herself, then slid behind the steering wheel. Her faithful sedan started up on the first crank, and she pulled smoothly out of the parking lot. "Besides, you still haven't let me drive your red coupe."

"I will." Cliff amused himself by futzing with the stereo for a while. After he had rejected half a dozen or so stations, she took pity on him and showed him the presets. He hit the first one, liked it, and settled back.

She smiled, a bit ruefully, to herself. Since the episode in the park, Cliff had been the perfect gentleman. Gradually, her feeling of awkwardness around him had subsided. She enjoyed Cliff's company and felt more and more comfortable with him. Every day she found more things they had in common.

They were getting closer every day.

Which was bad. She was trying to achieve a good *professional* relationship, not fall in love.

Not just because of her experience with Ron. As they put the finishing touches on Apple Pie, she began to realize the project would be over soon. She'd return home to Boston.

When that time came, she wanted to be able to walk away with no regrets, no hurt on either side.

Even that brought an ache to her chest. Skyler clenched her eyes briefly.

"Skyler? What's wrong?"

Cutting a glance at him, she found his cobalt gaze laser-keen on her.

God, why does he have to be so perceptive?

When the Deity didn't answer her, she made an attempt at sidetracking. "So, do you think John will ever notice Tess as more than a friend?"

Cliff hummed. "Tess and John? Really? Tess is interested in John?"

She'd said it to distract him, but perked up as she realized how brilliant that particular conversational overture was. Close to her own truth without revealing her feelings, she might find out his thoughts on the matter without unmasking. "Yes."

"Why hasn't she said anything to him?"

"She's afraid to. John's so attractive, he must have scores of women after him..." Lovesick, one and all. "I'm pretty sure Tess doesn't want to embarrass herself."

"John has scores of women after him—who aren't Tess. He'd jump at the chance to date her. He hasn't asked *her* out because he says she always seems so aloof."

Okay, that wasn't like her own situation. She'd never been aloof in Cliff's arms.

"I'm surprised you haven't mentioned this to him. You're close friends."

"We're friends, sure." She and John had shared laughs, drinks, even sundaes. But... "But never...intimate... friends." Immediately, she wanted to knock her head into the wheel. Why had she found it necessary to say *that?* Face heating, she cut a glance at him.

Cliff's eyebrow had gone up. "I know. John would have warned me if you were lovers."

And now her face was burning. "Great. So glad we had this little chat." Did men share everything? Was nothing sacred from locker-room discussions?

But once she made the final turn and the first spicy breeze floated through the window, baked crust and tomatoes and melted mozzarella, annoyance and doubt melted, too, in anticipation of a good dinner. She always felt better on a full stomach.

Skyler parked, leaped out of her car, and hurried toward the restaurant. Cliff's reply, something about non-competition, was lost to her as she flung open the door. The tang of pepper and oregano nearly knocked her off her feet. She left him to plug the parking meter and beckoned to the hostess.

"Your usual table, Skyler?"

Another reason she felt better. This was a regular haunt, a safe place to talk and relax after a long, hard day's work. She smiled. "Yes."

Cliff entered just in time to receive a lingering once-over from the hostess. Then they were led to a secluded booth with a window view of the river.

A college-aged waiter zoomed up as they seated themselves. "Stuffed spinach pizza and diet cola?"

Cliff rolled his eyes. Before he could snark, Skyler added, "And two orders of cheese garlic bread, Terry."

When the waiter had gone, Cliff waved at the walls. "This is the real reason you've gained weight, isn't it? Trying to blame those innocent hot fudge sundaes. *Tsk, tsk.*" He shook his head slowly.

She primly unfolded her paper napkin and placed it on her lap. "Nonsense. The crust is whole wheat, spinach is a marvelous source of several vitamins and minerals, and cheese is a basic food in the milk group."

"And diet soda?"

"That's an essential component of a very necessary food group."

"Which is...?"

"The diet food group. So I can eat more hot fudge sundaes."

"And brownies."

"Ha. Fat lot of them I get with *you* around."

"You had one just yesterday."

"We ordered *four*. I thought I'd save one for later, but you gobbled them up so fast, the one I did manage to grab, I nearly got my fingers bitten off."

The waiter zoomed back and slid a loaf of spicy-smelling bread in front of each of them.

Cliff ate all of his, then sat, gaze wistfully following Skyler's second slice on its way to her mouth. After a few minutes of puppy-dog eyes, she swallowed carefully. "Would you like some of mine?"

"Only if you're sure."

"I'm sur—" She wasn't really surprised to see the rest of her loaf disappear. "How do you survive on *l'haute* cuisine when you entertain clients?"

"I don't." He washed down the bread with a full glass of water. "I have a cook who raised seven sons. She feeds me after I've been out."

"You're going to go home and eat after this?"

"No, of course not." He grinned and pressed his fingers into the crumbs of bread on her plate, then licked his fingers. "There is, however, a chocolate cake in the refrigerator at my house, calling softly to me."

"Really? Are you sure that's not my brownie, singing from your stomach?"

He raised one eyebrow. "I can see you're going to be stubborn over this."

She raised one brow in imitation of his. "I prefer 'tenacious.'"

"Hmm." He tapped his empty glass thoughtfully, then picked up the pitcher and poured them both more water. As the ice cracked, and not looking at her, he said, "Maybe you'd like to try some."

"Some what?"

"Chocolate cake. Hannah makes it with semisweet bakers chocolate and cream cheese and fresh eggs and, well, it's really good."

"You mean...you're inviting me to your house?"

Cliff's gaze came up then, eyes blue and clear, intent.

"Yes."

Chapter Twenty

"You're inviting me to your *house*." Skyler knew she was echoing the same question, but she couldn't quite believe she'd heard his answer right through the sudden pounding of her blood in her ears.

Cliff nodded. "No strings attached, of course."

"No strings?" Skyler shook her head. No strings, with her heart already throwing out tether lines? "Impossible."

He smiled ruefully. "I don't blame you, after the way I behaved the last time."

"No, that's not it." She flushed, feeling slightly guilty. It was the first time he had mentioned the picnic, and now he was taking full blame for the incident? Sweet man, impossible man... "Yes, okay. I'd love to come."

A smile spread clear across his face, lighting his eyes. "Thanks."

"For what, gobbling cake?"

"For giving me another chance. So, which do you like better, coding or managing?"

She wondered at his sudden shift in topics, but said, "I like them both, I guess. I like working with your people a lot." Especially him.

But that was about all she thought professional and proper to say, so she then attempted to shift the focus from herself. "What about you? Which do you like better?"

"I like them both, too, I guess," he said, mimicking her overly bright tone. "Good grief, Skyler, I get more on the real you from John than I do from you. I thought we were finally getting on. What's the problem?" His eyes narrowed. "Are you afraid of me?"

That bull's-eye knocked the air out of her. Lucky guess, or was he really that sharp? Mentally gasping, she fenced, "You think I'm afraid of you just because you own the company and control my job?"

"Let's not start that again."

His sharp tone made hers rise as well. "Well, aside from the fact my boss thinks you walk on water and your influence could keep me from ever finding another job if I ever crossed you, no, I can't think of any reason to be afraid of you." *Let's not mention crushing my heart.*

Sitting back with crossed arms, he glowered. "If you must go there, might I point out it would be a phenomenal waste of time for me to rescue you from Middle Yemen then go to great lengths to employ you, if I didn't believe in you?"

Words stuck in her throat. Fortunately the waiter zoomed in with the pizza. He set the steaming hot pie between them, then whipped out a metal server and dug it under one precut slice.

Cliff waved the waiter off, and served the pizza himself.

As he slid a thick wedge on her plate she found her voice.

"Why did you rescue me?"

"I was in the area and you needed rescuing." He raised an eyebrow at her. Some of his irritation seemed to have cooled. "I told you about it."

"Yes, but did you know?"

He slid a wedge onto his own plate. "Mmm. Smells great." He picked it up and bit off half the slice. "Tastes even better. Did I know what?"

Skyler watched him chew. "Had you already picked me for this job? Is that why you rescued me?" she asked finally.

"You mean to hold it over you? Other way around, actually." He finished the slice. "I'd narrowed things down to three resumes, including S. Jones, although I wasn't sure the S. Jones who'd been kidnapped was the same as the resume, until I met you."

"At the office?"

"No, at the hotel."

She blushed, remembering it. But wait... "I didn't tell you my name then."

"People at the embassy said Mr. Jones had been kidnapped, and could I do recon for Mr. Jones? Apparently I wasn't the only one confused on that point. Then I saw you, and the matter was cleared up immediately. Definitely female. Seeing you in a crisis, well. That's when I decided you'd be perfect for the job. You were magnificent. I knew you were perfect for me."

"You mean for gelling the team?"

"That too." His gaze met and held hers, his mouth crooked up on one side in a very sexy smile, and for a moment she couldn't breathe.

She glanced briefly away. "I'm glad you were there. I don't think I could have escaped Middle Yemen, otherwise."

His smile quirked. "You didn't seem glad at the time."

"There were…other factors." Sexy, high-handed, half-naked factors. "So, um, about dessert…"

About to slide another slice onto his plate, his gaze rose abruptly. "If you don't want to come by any more, I'd understand—"

"No, actually, I'm done here. Since I want to save room." She pushed her plate away.

His eyes widened. "Oh. *Oh.*" He immediately dropped the slice back on the pan. "Check, please. *Check.*"

Silently, she walked ahead of him to her sedan, wondering what she'd find at his home. Whether he'd be professional…or not. The idea of his…not…excited her. And scared her. Unlocking the doors, she slid in, feeling him slide in beside her. The tension was starting to make her hyper-aware.

As she pulled away from the curb, she said, "Where to?"

"Drive toward the offices. I'll direct you from there."

She fell silent until they were almost to HCC, mulling over their little spat. Finally she said, "You know, I didn't mean it before, about being afraid of you. I'm not afraid of anyone just because they're in a position of authority. But, well, you're big, you know. I'd imagine most people would find you…intimidating."

He laughed. "Not so very long ago, you could have kicked sand in my face at the beach."

"I can't picture that." She was glad he wasn't angry any more.

"But it's true. I was a skinny kid. Tall, but gangly. No interest in sports whatsoever. Turn right here."

Skyler realized they were headed toward the park Cliff had taken her to for their picnic.

"In high school, we had jocks, nerds, and freaks. Jocks were brawn, nerds were brains, and freaks were artsy—and none of them crossed over into the realm of the other two. You're strong and creative. Somehow, I can't see you with broken glasses and a pocket computer."

"But I was. Nothing interested me except for electronic gismos."

Yet another side to this complex man. "I'd have liked to have known you then."

"Actually, probably not. I was a precocious string bean. Obviously, that didn't make me too popular with my peers."

"It must have delighted your parents."

"Mum just despaired of me ever making it in proper society."

"I'm sorry."

He shrugged. "It was a long time ago. Dad...well, I don't know what he would have thought. He was dead by then—probably why I never got into sports."

"Because he never threw a ball with you?"

"Because Dad's physical excellence just got him killed."

Her breath left her. She managed, "I'm so very sorry. May I ask...how?"

Cliff gave her a series of directions before continuing. "He was a career serviceman. He volunteered for every extra assignment that came along, which allowed Mum to live in the style to which she was accustomed, and got Dad out of the house. And since he kept himself in peak physical condition, he was always chosen for the highest-paid, and coincidentally most dangerous, assignments." He smiled thinly before going on.

"One day, he volunteered for a peace-keeping force in the Middle East. He and his commanding officer were taken hostage the day after he got there. Dad died helping the officer escape."

Like father, like son. "He was a hero, then." The directions had taken her into the park. She slowed, uncertain.

Cliff glanced up from his own thoughts. "Keep going straight."

She fed the car gas. The parkway, surprisingly, curved into a long driveway.

And at the end of the drive stood the most beautiful home she had ever seen.

"Welcome to the American homestead. A wedding gift from the grandparents. While Dad was still alive, we lived mostly in England. After Dad was gone, we began spending more time here. Mum wanted me to know my father's world, too."

Two stories in most places soared to five in a corner tower crowned by an observatory. The driveway continued past it to an apron of what appeared to be a garage, but had at least six doors.

Now she knew where all the different cars came from.

He directed her to park in front of a sweeping set of stairs. As she got out of the car, Cliff came around to take her hand.

"Ready?" He paused for a beat, his blue eyes searching her face.

Ready for what? Chocolate cake? Or igniting the fire that coursed through her blood, that had burned for him ever since his first soul-searing kiss?

Her words caught and tangled in her suddenly thick throat. She could only grab his hand tighter and nod.

With her hanging on with a death-grip, he mounted the steps, taking them slowly. She followed, holding on as he unlocked the solid cedar door, massive, but it swung open silently.

"My home." With a wave of his free hand, he urged her to cross the sill first.

It was like crossing into a different country, a different time. The cut stone floor rang under her heels; she was almost afraid to step on the beautiful, intricately woven carpets scattered around. Her way into the huge front hall was lit by chandeliers. A full suit of armor stood in one corner. On the walls hung oil portraits of men and women in clothes from earlier centuries.

She gazed around her in awe. "This is your home?"

"Mostly, it was my mother's." He led her through a vaulted archway into a high-ceilinged, airy corridor. "I keep a few rooms decorated as she preferred, in her memory."

"That's lovely." Skyler followed him past several rooms in various styles, finally finding herself in a very modern kitchen. "Your mother's?"

"The kitchen's all Hannah's, thank goodness. I loved Mum to pieces, but she had no interest in food and could barely pour cereal."

Arrowing to a small breakfast table for four, he pulled out a chair and handed her into it. While she sat he got a carton of milk from a large, gleaming refrigerator, two glasses, and a couple plates from a cupboard. Setting everything on the table, he asked her to pour. While she filled a glass with frosty-cold milk, he dug a large cake knife from a drawer and set it beside the plates. While she poured the second glass, he disappeared through a door, returning moments later with a large metal cake carrier, which he set on the table in front of her.

With a flourish, he drew off the top. "Ta-da!"

The cake revealed was well worth the fanfare. A wedge was already gone, revealing light, high layers separated by a third of an inch of fudgy frosting. As Cliff cut them each a big wedge, her mouth started watering, the scent of chocolate so rich it was painful, stinging both her nose and taste buds with anticipation. Finally, he seated himself, smiled at her, and waited.

Sensing he wanted her reaction, she sampled a small, moist corner of the cake. Sweet, achingly dark chocolate flavor hit her taste buds. Her eyes closed in bliss as she chewed with pleasure and swallowed. "Your Hannah is a culinary genius."

"Better than the brownies?" he teased.

"I don't know." Opening her eyes, she gave him her best narrowed glare. "We'll see how much cake I actually get to eat."

He laughed. "Actually, quite a bit. Hannah made two." He dug into his own piece, cutting off a third of it in one forkful.

Skyler opened her eyes fully in an amazed stare. "Were you really ever a skinny little kid?"

She was just bantering, but he sobered immediately. "Yeah. Childhood as a dork was rather painful."

He was silent after that, but she ached for him, for the small child he'd been. She tried to get him to talk more. "John said you didn't take up weight training until after college."

Shaking his head, he stirred and met her gaze squarely. "Yes, but it's misleading because I started college at sixteen, skipping through a bachelors and masters to graduate in three years. Being a bit of a loner, I didn't have much else to do."

She dropped her gaze to study her cake crumbs. "I guess, after you started working out, you had to make up for lost time."

He didn't pretend to misunderstand her. "Once I bulked up? Sure, I had a lot of offers of companionship, but some of the women offering were those whose rejections had been the cruelest."

"Ouch." Skyler was beginning to see a very different Cliff, one more like herself than she'd ever realized. "I wasn't terribly popular either. Used to be all I had to do was say some thing vaguely intelligent to scare off a prospective date. Then I thought I found a man who loved me for my mind...but it didn't work out."

He glanced up from his second piece of cake. "You know, I think that's the first thing you've said about yourself that I haven't had to drag out of you?"

She paused. "I guess you've always seemed so professional and perfect to me. It's hard to be one's own bungling self with someone who always does things just right."

"Me?" He snorted. "I'm far from perfect. You'd be amazed at how many screw-ups I've had. It's just that I always come back and try again, and again, until I do get it right."

"I knew it. You're stubborn, too."

"I prefer 'tenacious.'"

They laughed together at that. Cliff served her a second piece of cake, and helped himself to a third. Skyler cut into hers, and chewed slowly, considering. He wanted her to be more open. What could she reveal without revealing her heart? Something about her job? No, he knew about that. School? Hers was boring next to his. Family? She thought about that for a while. Her family seemed nothing like his.

His military hero father, dead when Cliff was still mostly a child, his mother soon after, probably neither of them understanding the technical streak in their son, perhaps not understanding their bookish, genius son at all.

She ventured, "Maybe I don't talk about myself because there's nothing much to say. I mean, our family made the Cleavers look like neighborhood trend-setters."

Cliff's face lit up. "Ah, a personal anecdote. So, yours was the typical American family? Two kids? Dog? Minivan?"

"The works. Mom was even stay-at-home, until my brother was in high school. Then she went back to work."

"What did she do?"

Skyler laughed. "Crossing-guard. She just retired last year. Dad retired three years ago. They go traveling now."

"That's how I'd like to do it. Raise the children in a secure, loving home, then send them out into the world—and when they're out, live it up."

"You're silly! It takes two decades to raise children. How much living it up do you think you're going to do at...er..."

"Fifty," Cliff quickly cut her off. "I'd only be fifty."

"Hey, me, too."

"I know. We were born the same year."

Skyler made an exasperated noise. "That's the real reason I don't tell you anything about myself. I don't need to. You already know it all."

"Not everything. You said your family was traditional. Are you?"

"I think it's important to give kids a safe home. And everyone needs love." She winced mentally at that. Even knights in tarnished armor? "But I think my parents are doing it the right way. You don't marry your family—you marry each other."

"So, when you're fifty, you're going to be painting the town red, too."

"Either that, or I'll go back to school. I've always been interested in art."

He raised a brow. "Why didn't you go into that before?"

"Well, I had to make a living." She smiled. "My parents weren't going to support me forever. And besides, they had my brother to pay for. I guess boys are more expensive than girls, with their cars and everything." She glanced sidelong at him, wondering if he was aware that having six cars was unusual.

Cliff squared his shoulders. "*Some* boys pay for their own 'cars and everything.'" He drank milk, then considered her. "Had you ever thought of marrying some rich guy and doing what you want to do now?"

"That doesn't sound fair. I mean, just because some poor slob has worked his tail off to make money shouldn't turn him into marriage meat."

A smile flirted with the corner of his mouth. "So you'll only marry someone who makes the same income you do?"

"That's not it." She found herself suddenly wanting to be serious. This was important to get right. More, this was important to get right *with him.* "I just think a person should put his or her fair share into a marriage. If I marry a rich guy, it shouldn't be to do what *I* want, it should be to do what *we* want. And vice-versa—if a woman makes more, the marriage should still be equal." She arched a challenging brow. "Maybe some guy should ride *my* coattails to success."

He appeared to consider that. "So you want a trophy husband?"

She dropped her fork. "Me, marry somebody for their *looks*?"

"Or for their prowess in bed." He cut a sidelong glance at her. "Or both."

Screwball. She got the sense that he was teasing her...mostly. Strangely, she thought a part of him also really wanted to know what she thought. So she answered in all seriousness, "Okay, me and a trophy hubby. Um, no."

"No? Seems like a no brainer. Gorgeous, good in bed...what's not to like?"

"Well, what if I lose my job? If he's married me for my money, he'll be gone. Or what if *I* marry him for sex, and he loses his—"

"Ouch. Okay. Point made." He crooked her a grin.

She smiled back. Even serious discussions were fun, with him. "I'd always worry that my trophy husband would meet someone who makes more money than I do. Or feel used. It's a relationship that spells disaster."

"That's pretty clear-sighted." Cliff speared up a last chunk of cake and chewed thoughtfully. "You'd be surprised at how many men can't see that clearly."

"Not really. To be honest with you, most men I've known haven't been able to see beyond the end of their...zipper."

That got a laugh out of him. A twinkle in his eye, he said, "Ah-hah! So you're a misanthrope. You don't want to marry at all."

Skyler shook her head vehemently. "Of course I want to marry, if it's the right person."

He pushed his plate aside and gestured with his fork. "All right, Skyler Jones. You don't want to marry for money. You don't want to marry just for sex. You don't want to marry only for children. Yet, you do want to marry. For what?"

For what indeed? For love? She pushed her own plate away with a sigh. Yes, love would be her reason to marry. But not love like Ron meant it. Not love that stopped at the bedroom and was forbidden outside the home. Her life stretched beyond that. No matter the corporate games she had learned to play, no matter how much she masked her feelings, they were there. Feelings at home, at work, dating.

She wanted a man to love at home and in the bedroom. But that was only part of her life. She wanted a man to love at play, at work, and all the in-between times, too. "I want to marry someone I can spend my entire life with. A friend."

He nodded. "I'd want it all. I would marry someone who was not only my friend, but someone I loved, too."

Someone I loved.

That resonated so strongly with her when he said it that she wondered if this man was the right one, the one she could love forever.

And if she could be the right woman for him.

Scary.

"Well, of course." Her voice sounded a little strange when she finally spoke. She had to work to iron the roiling emotions out of her words. "Everybody wants to have the perfect mate. But not many of us find perfection."

"No, that's not it." He put his fork down and leaned forward, cobalt eyes intent. "Perfection isn't what I'm after. I want love, which is a very human emotion—and human means far from perfect. You can't program love, after all. That would take the wonder, the delight out of it. I'm not searching for Ms. Perfect, or even Ms. Right. I want someone who's as human as I am, and especially, who's willing to try, like I am. To make mistakes and try again. Someone who would try to love me in return, and keep trying, for the rest of our lives."

She nearly drowned in the depth of his gaze. *I love you,* she nearly said.

But what if she did? Was he really asking for *her* commitment? Or was this simply a philosophical discussion she was taking too seriously?

How could he ask for a commitment like that from her without making his own?

Will he treat me like Ron?

She played it safe. "I think we all search for people to love us." Trite. She glanced away.

He sighed and sat back. "That's true. But I guess it's easier to take than to give."

She winced. "No question about that."

A clock in the hallway ticked away the seconds in the black silence of Skyler's head. Suddenly it struck the hour, jarring her from her thoughts. She looked up.

"Is it really midnight?"

"I'm afraid so."

"I'd better be getting home. I promised you I'd have that tracker module written, and, to be honest, I haven't even started it yet." She jumped up, dumped her dishes in the dishwasher and raced to the door.

Cliff didn't catch up until she got to her car. "Skyler."

She turned, her breath catching in her throat. At his size. At his nearness. At the chiseled perfection of his slightly parted lips.

His eyes were on her but unfocused, his gaze inward. The muscle in his jaw jumped, as if he was at war with himself. Finally he shook his head, the battle decided, though she didn't know if he'd won or lost. "Drive safe." He opened her car door and waited until she was inside to click it shut. He stood back and watched as she pulled away. He was still standing there, watching, when she drove out of sight.

Whatever the outcome of the internal battle he'd fought, whether he'd won or lost, she felt like *she* had lost.

Chapter Twenty-One

Thursday, Skyler and Cliff wrapped the final module for Apple Pie. Friday they played around with a hangman program while they waited for integration test results from the Black-Armband Test Team. Results didn't come in until after they'd returned from dinner.

On one hand, Skyler was excited. If the results came back favorable, she'd have successfully run a huge project. Oh, there were still final touches to the hardware and distribution side of things, a couple weeks of work, but the hardest part of the HCCpi project would be triumphantly wrapped.

On the other hand, it meant her time here was now ticking toward the end.

So when the email came, she opened it with mixed feelings.

But she read it with growing enthusiasm. "It says, 'Real-time cyberattack defense response is immediate and surgically precise. Immunization functions learn from attacks and accurately predict evolution of new strains. Whole system is robust. Apple Pie is airtight.' Airtight, Cliff. We did it!" She raised her hand for a high five.

He swept her into his strong arms for a hug.

Her body immediately dialed up to eleven. Success was an elixir in her blood that ignited into instant desire. She wanted to tear off her clothes, and his, and take him here on the meeting room table.

She was so shocked at her response, she broke from him awkwardly. He looked away as if he felt the same.

Then he turned to her with a quirked grin. "Want to celebrate by hitting the gym?"

"You got it."

Awkwardness disappeared as somehow a friendly workout on side-by-side stairsteppers turned into another competition.

Skyler admitted to herself it might have been her fault. But only to herself.

"I don't...know why...you do this," puffed Cliff.

Even if she had been in the mood for confession, she couldn't answer. Her lungs hurt too much.

But her spirits soared when she saw she was half a flight of stairs ahead of him, winning for a change—though she'd had to decrease the climb difficulty to zero, whereas he was working on level ten. Cheating, but totally worth it.

Then, in the last minutes of their routines, he made an awesome comeback.

She dug deep for every spare bit of energy, burning sheer willpower in the last seconds. Despite her strength and wind having improved with the daily workouts, she knew she would pay dearly for this in the morning.

The routine ended. Gasping her last breath, she glanced over at his machine. She'd done it. She'd gotten more stairs than him.

Legs wobbling like rubber bands, she stumbled off the machine to totter painfully toward a nearby bench. Every muscle was on fire, and her heart was pounding so hard it rattled her ribs.

So. Totally. Worth It.

He tottered behind her. They collapsed on the bench together.

A few deep breaths, and he managed to slow his breathing from freight train to nearly normal.

Cheaters. Never. Prosper.

Still worth it.

Cliff handed her a bottle of water, already open, then cracked a second and drank the whole thing. Closing it, he set it down and smiled. "Ready for another round?"

She whacked him, the palm of her hand making a satisfyingly loud *smack* against his muscular shoulder, but it stung. "Ow." She nursed her hand against her breasts.

"Serves you right." He smirked.

"Does not." Damn. She was going to *have* to work on her comebacks.

"Does, too." Cliff grinned wider and stretched his long legs out in front of him. "You know, CEO abuse is highly frowned upon in these here parts."

"Ha." She was finally getting her breath back. "CEO stands for Cliff's Ego's Obstinate."

"That's reaching a little." He flung his arms over the back of the bench, tilting his face up. Suddenly, his grin of savored effort became a rictus of pain. "Yeowch! Got a cramp in my shoulder. Does it hurt!"

Skyler set down her water and sprang to her feet. "Put your arm down, lean forward, and hold still." She scooted around the back of the bench. When he'd creaked and groaned his arm into place, she pressed fingers into his back between his shoulder blades, and slowly felt the vast acreage for the knotted muscle. "It's a good one." She located the offending tissue and began massaging. "Sit still, and we'll have you fixed up in no time."

Yikes. *Fixed up in no time*, how June Cleaver. Although, touching these lovely, warm, broad shoulders was soooo nice...

She mentally slapped herself. "This is your fault, you know. If you hadn't gone and made this a contest, you wouldn't have gotten a cramp. *What* a macho man."

"My fault?" His tone was aggrieved. "Who was pumping her steps like an overheated CPU?"

"You didn't have to try to pass me."

The knot in his shoulder began to ease under her fingers. She relaxed in response. With a will of their own, her hands began stroking his shoulders, straying to his chest. His lovely, oh-so-caress-able chest...*caress*? In a definitely not-caressing move, she dug her fingers savagely into his bulging triceps.

He yelped in agony. "I thought massage was supposed to *stop* it from hurting."

"Sorry." She let up a bit, not trusting herself to say anything more. Since she'd realized she was falling in love with him, she'd been especially careful to keep things light and frothy. If he even guessed she considered him marriage material...that was too damned close to lovesick. She worried he'd push her away, and she'd lose even their enjoyable friendship.

But it was hard with her growing emotions urging her to, if not make it a lasting relationship, at least take it to the next step, into the physical.

"All-call." John's voice came over the speaker system. "Anyone still in the building, please call extension oh-oh-two."

Task at hand.

Don't think about anything else, especially not that back. Keep those visions of masculine muscles out of your mind.

Hard, thick muscle roping miles-wide shoulders...

Okay, that didn't work. So think of something, anything else.

Like their competition...so much fun. No, like eating while they worked...meals shared, watching his sharp, white teeth bite into a sandwich, masculine lips moving...

Crap.

Okay, since that didn't work, pretend you're petting Dad's dog...

She found her strokes had unconsciously softened again. Cliff relaxed, his head lolling onto her middle. It felt right, there against her body. She sighed, gave up, and just enjoyed. She stroked his shoulders, neck and back, surveying the terrain and storing all the data for later retrieval.

He sighed in reply, tension seeming to flow out of him, his head heavy against her.

She cradled him between her arms as she continued to caress his upper shoulders. Gradually, the realization dawned—John would be gone by now. They were alone together.

And nobody would be in the building until dawn.

Skyler trailed a hand over Cliff's shoulder and onto his chest. As she did, he took her hand and brushed it with his lips. His breath warmed her skin, and the intimacy made her shiver. She leaned against him, wanting the feel of his body against hers.

If only she could be sure he felt the same about her. Or at least be sure he wanted the same thing she did.

Then he turned, looking up at her, his mouth opened to say something.

Their gazes met and locked, the air suddenly crackling with tension.

He managed, "Do you want...?"

He wanted the same thing she did. She said the word before she could chicken out.

"Yes."

"You and me...?"

"Oh, yes."

Now, after weeks of working and playing together, she wanted to do one more thing, the most important thing, together with him. She put aside her fears and misgivings to partner him wholeheartedly.

She bent and pressed her mouth to his.

With exquisite slowness his lips tasted hers in a kiss. At first tentative, the soft sliding of skin against skin, the barest tasting of breath. But each touch urged more, each taste primed a deeper one, until her lips parted in invitation and he thrust his tongue boldly into her mouth.

Her heart beat faster, began to clamor with excitement. When she rounded the bench, he stood and cradled her face to kiss her even deeper. She wound her arms tightly around his shoulders, fusing them together.

His breathing was strong and vital. She'd never known anything like it. How anyone could express their openness and desire through their breathing was a new revelation in communication. Her body molded to the hard planes of his body as she stroked his back. His palms were a warm cocoon for her cheeks and his fingers a brushing contact against her temples as they drank of each other.

No man had tasted as wonderful as Cliff. With a little moan, she thrust her tongue into his mouth in return. His hands glided from her face, down her back to her hips, tugging her into him. She reciprocated, letting her hands wander in an idyllic garden walk down his well-muscled back to his taut buttocks. His hands—oh, his clever hands—cupped her rear and massaged gently. Her legs grew weak and her pelvis flowed into molten lava.

"Skyler, sweetheart."

Cliff's arousal pressed insistently against her, and for the first time, she couldn't find any excuses, not that he wanted his brass board, that he was trying to butter her up for the job, or even that he was distracting her from a fight.

No, from the desire tensing every muscle of his body, from the hunger in his face, and most certainly from his hard arousal yearning into her, he wanted *her*.

She trembled with excitement. His kisses came hot and fluid over her mouth, increasing in fervor. Not only did he want her, but he wanted her now.

His hand slipped forward, rounding her thigh to brush just above her mound. Where he waited—until she writhed against him, letting him know he had permission.

His fingers slid into the junction of her thighs.

She hadn't had a man's hand there since Ron's. The sensation of heat and weight triggered a full-color recall of Ron's diving to the bull's-eye.

Old tapes sprang to life. Emotions drenched her, bypassing Cliff's gentle seduction to tug painfully on the scar tissue of memory.

Her broken engagement. The devastation of struggling to keep her career amid emotional turmoil. Confused, she pulled away from Cliff, feeling as though a part of herself was tearing away as she did.

"What's wrong?" he murmured.

Nothing? Everything? She couldn't tell, the present tangling with the past.

He pulled back to study her face. She had to say something.

Words battled in her head, but she didn't know which ones to use. Too much at stake, her tentative, new-found friendship with this amazing man.

Amid her roiling emotions, she just shook her head.

His body tensed beneath her hands, his cobalt gaze narrow, searching. "You want this. I can tell."

"Yes." She didn't lie to him. "I really want this...want *you,* but I-I've worked so hard to be professional. Too hard."

She released him and turned away. "I don't want to risk losing what we have now."

"I see." His tone was flat, all emotion ironed out.

She dared a glance back.

He glared at her with anger and disdain—underlined with the young, rejected boy's pain.

That hurt look lurking in his eyes made her want to shrivel into a worm. "Please understand. These office romances always turn out sour. Believe me. I know."

"How?"

"I just do."

"Fine." He turned away, anger and rejection in every line of his back.

Answering anger began to rebuild her corporate mask and the crumbling wall that protected her—until he shuddered.

A shudder of hurt, of sadness cracked the rigid tension of his big frame.

Her heart gave a thump of grief. She'd done that to him.

For him, then. She shoved aside her anger, her fear, and concentrated on him. Not for herself, not for whatever they might have together, as coworkers, friends, or something more. But for him, she had to bare the still-raw sores of her grievous past.

And hope he never used her vulnerability against her.

"At one time, I-I was engaged." She took a deep breath, the words hard to get out. But for him, for his suffering, she had to do it.

His head swiveled, just enough to show one ear and partial fan of long dark eyelash. He was listening. Still angry, still hurt, but listening.

Haltingly, fearfully, she told him about Ron.

It was one of the hardest things she'd ever done. The story was painful and private, hard enough to tell a best friend like Tess. Cliff could hurt her more, and she didn't know how he'd react. Would he stand with her through it? Despite it?

And damn it, with Cliff, it mattered whether he did or not. Because Cliff mattered. Her throat got thicker and thicker as she talked.

By the time she admitted, "Ron said...he said he loved me," she felt as if her whole body had swollen with pain and grief. With Cliff, she hadn't just told the story, she'd relived it. "He loved me...until he didn't."

Trembling, she fell silent.

Cliff's arms came warm around her shoulders. Skyler squeezed hot eyes shut.

But as he continued to hold her tight, something deep inside began to unwind.

Gently, Cliff said, "Sounds like he didn't really love you. Not like you deserved."

"He said the words." She shook her head. "But you're probably right. Every time we made love, his body said something else. I should've realized…it wasn't makeup sex, but sex used to shut me up."

"Bastard," Cliff snarled.

She curled in his arms, burying her face in his chest, in the scent of his still-damp tank. "I saw what I wanted to see. Ron always said, 'Sex is fun as a solo sport, but with a partner it's an adventure.' I believed him because I wanted that—I wanted a partner. Not just for sex, but for life. I thought I'd found that partner in Ron, a mate at work and home. I thought he wanted me that way, too."

"Sounds to me like he wanted, not you, but what you had earned—respect, and a firm foot on the management fast track. He didn't have what it took to get those, so he went for you instead." He stroked her hair. "He played to your desires."

"And I ate it up." She sighed. "Until, at work I became a harsh taskmaster, and a shrieking shrew at home. I felt…fragmented. I hardly knew myself anymore."

"He tried to remake you in his own broken image. I'm so sorry, Skyler."

He understands. Something tight in her eased. As Cliff's palm caressed her head, she finished. "After Ron left, I tried to put myself back together by investing everything in my career. I worked hard to get my self-respect back. Now, it's tied up in my job, and I can't lose it again. Cliff—if I go to bed with you and it doesn't work…" She heaved a watery breath. "I'll have lost my self-respect and my job. But there's more." She wanted to look at him, see how he was taking it, but couldn't risk it yet. "I'd lose your friendship. That's the worst of all."

"I understand. It's okay."

Hesitantly, she raised her gaze and finally looked at him.

His face was so compassionate, so loving, she did something she swore she'd never, ever do again. She broke down and cried. Really bawled this time.

It was terribly unprofessional. Ron would've sneered at her thin-skinned reaction, too girly to play in the big boys' sandbox.

But all Cliff did was rub her shoulders and murmur consoling words as she worked it out.

When she wound down to red eyes and sniffles, she laid her head against his chest. The steady, strong beat of his heart gave her the courage to say what needed to be said. "Crying is the absolute worst thing you can do in business."

"Ron said that?"

"Yes, but I believe it. It's unprofessional." She gave a watery laugh. "And here I've done it twice, in front of the CEO. I g-guess that proves I'm not cut out to be a manager."

"Ron's words, again."

She managed another laugh. "Yeah. He'd have insisted on my resignation on your desk first thing in the morning."

"Totally ignoring you've just successfully finished a billion-dollar project."

"It's not completely finished."

"Skyler." Cliff slid a finger under her chin and tipped her head to meet his gaze. "Maybe they'd think crying qualified for the boot at Stuffed Shirt Corp. But not here."

Skyler, gaze riveted to him, felt as if her heart was in her eyes.

"A real professional isn't perfect, and knows it. A real pro admits their flaws as needed, and then *does the job anyway*. That's *you*."

"Ron always said a pro needs to compartmentalize business and personal."

"Because he's an ass who bought into the uptight, anal-retentive style of professionalism that can't integrate different parts of life."

That made her laugh.

Cliff was all about integration. He blew down the walls between business and personal. Working for him was working *with* him; being friends brought her both a physical desire for him and a growing emotional *need*.

Brushing back a strand of hair from her face, he added, "Skyler, I'm not going to try to talk you into being my lover. That's not fair to you. But I do want you to understand my feelings on being professional yet human. Think about it."

She wiped her eyes. Being professional yet *human*. She'd have said something then, embarrassed herself by asking him if he did care about her, but he went on.

"I think we've done all the damage we can do here. Let's shower then get some food. I could eat a moose, hooves and all."

That brought some normalcy back. She decided now was definitely not the time to go into feelings. If he was hungry, she knew from experience that he wasn't going to be thinking of much else until he was fed.

"Second supper? Okay." She pried herself from the warm security of his arms and stood. Resolutely turned to head for the women's locker room, stopped, and asked without turning back, "Did you really mean that, about being professional yet human?"

"Hopefully, you know by now I mean what I say. C'mon, I'm hungry. If you make it fast, I'll even share my dessert."

"Well, how can I resist such a selfless offer?" She walked as sprightly as she could away from him, into the women's locker room.

Once she gained the safety of the closed door, she sank back against it, utterly miserable. She'd just told the best damn man she'd ever met that she didn't want to be his lover—when that was *all* she wanted to do.

She heard Cliff banging his locker; odd, she hadn't heard it when they came down here before. Maybe he really was angry but hadn't told her. She bit her lip and fought back tears again. *Cliff's not Ron.* He proved that just now, proved he cared about her. Sure, maybe he didn't want to be her one-and-only, but what was wrong with having at least part of him? *Carpe diem,* as Grandpa used to say. *Seize the day.*

The thought galvanized her. She straightened and went to the small locker.

What if she could do it? What if she could integrate work and play—and love? She'd told Cliff about Ron, she'd bawled in Cliff's arms, for heaven's sake, and she hadn't frightened him off.

Maybe she could take that scary next step.

What would it be like, being Cliff's lover? She pulled her tank off, imagining that his hands were doing it. She rolled it over her breasts, seeing his gaze riveted to her. She'd bought new sports leggings for him. Pushing the stretchy material over her hips, she bent, dreaming that she was exposing her most private areas for him.

A door banged. The sharp hiss of a shower next door told her she'd better get a move on. Now would not be the time to be late.

Skyler pulled off the rest of her clothes and hurried across the ceramic tile, her bare feet making little *pungs* on the floor in her impatience. She'd blown it for today, but there was always tomorrow, right?

Great, just put me in an antebellum gown on the steps of Tara.

She spun the shower dial. Water blasted out cold; she yipped and grabbed the knob to adjust it to less than arctic temperature.

"Gotcha, didn't it? Me too. I forgot about John's warning email."

Cliff's voice was *right on top of her.* Skyler jumped then scanned the stall. The section of wall above her was open between the two showers. "Cliff, is that you?"

"You were expecting maybe the Spanish Inquisition?"

"I didn't see John's email. Did it have something to do with the hole in the wall?"

"Yeah. The showers were acting up and John called the plumbers in. They opened the wall, peered in with lots of *hmms,* said something about water pressure and replacement pipes and coming back tomorrow. Time and a half, oh joy. Although these showers have always been a bit temperamental."

She'd just been dreaming about standing naked before him. Now she learned there was a big hole between the men's and women's showers? "You're sure you don't have a ladder over there? I mean, for the repair work and all?" Skyler stepped under the shower, wet her hair and began to shampoo, keeping one eye on the hole.

"Scout's honor, Skyler. But if it'll help, I'll be glad to talk to you. Or better yet, sing."

"Sweet Simon Cowell, not another bathroom *America's Got Talent.*"

He began to warble tentatively. "*Mi, mi, mi.* Ah, such good acoustics. I never could see why opera wasn't performed in the shower instead of a great drafty barn. Okay, now. *Vesti, Pagliacci.*" He swarmed up to the high note and cracked broadly. "Say, remind me to tell you how tenors *really* get the high ones."

Skyler sighed to herself. She could even live with his singing. She was an incredible dope. *Or he's an incredible man,* a little inner voice reminded.

She began to soap her body, trying unsuccessfully to avoid stimulating her overworked libido. Cliff began again, this time with something he called *Madama Butterfly*. He briefly sounded as though he was drowning.

"What did you do with all the money your mum gave you for singing lessons?" Skyler couldn't help but tease.

"Ha. Just listen to how high I can go." Cliff forced his voice like a rusted locomotive up the mountainside, creaking precariously as he gained altitude. Finally he goosed out something that sounded more like a shriek.

"Ouch!" A bar of soap had just hit her in the head.

"Hey, where'd my soap go?" he asked.

"Here, on my head," she called back. "I probably have a concussion. What were you doing, anyway?"

"Just putting a little oomph into it. I must have shot it through the gap in the wall." He laughed. "I bet I couldn't do that again in a zillion years."

Skyler picked up the bar from the floor. This was his soap. It smelled like him. She closed her eyes and filled her lungs with the scent. "Why don't you use the company body wash?"

"It takes too many pumps, and I never get a real lather. Hey, Skyler, just toss the bar back over to me."

She imagined herself to be the soap, gliding over each wonderful, strong curve of his body, secretly kissing every part of him.

"Okay, okay, I promise not to sing any more; just give me back my soap. Skyler?"

She took a long, ragged breath. It was time to stop playing games. With herself, with Cliff, with any time they might have left together. She took another breath to tell him. But her heart dropped dizzyingly into the pit of her stomach. Her throat dried, and she could barely speak.

"Skyler?"

Last chance.

"Why don't you come and get it?"

Chapter Twenty-Two

There was a stunned silence. Then Cliff's shower turned off.

A faint creak from his shower door. A few moments of breathless anticipation.

Her door opened behind her, cool air wafting in.

She turned in the shower, one arm crossing her, breast to shoulder, the other holding the soap out, as she tried to keep her hand from trembling. The steam boiled across the door and cleared.

Cliff filled the doorway, motionless, as though carved from rock. The powerful beauty of his naked body struck Skyler physically. Hair was plastered over his brow, tiny rivulets running down his jaw, neck, torso, trickling along his smooth tanned skin.

Their gazes met, and she saw for the first time how carefully he watched her, gauging her, as though he could see the warring emotions inside her.

Then he smiled.

Skyler's eyes dropped, and she found herself staring at the chest she had been caressing in the gym. She set aside the soap and reached, hypnotized, to touch the droplets forming on one broad pectoral, and as she did so, he stepped closer. Her gaze jerked up.

She stood breathless before him, a whisper separating them, gazing wonderingly at the open desire on his face. A heartbeat; two. He was waiting for her, making sure she was ready. She smiled her assent. He breathed a sigh like a prayer, took her in his arms, and pulled her flush with him.

The full contact electrified her.

He whispered her name. Cobalt twinkling from heavy eyelids, he slowly caressed her back with one hand while turning off the shower with the other.

She closed her eyes and breathed deeply of his clean, warm skin. Stretching against him, she savored the silky feel of him against her, roughened here and there by masculine hair.

He grazed a thumb along her cheek. Opening her eyes, she found him staring at her mouth with intense desire. Waiting again. Giving her a chance to change her mind.

Not happening. She ran her tongue along her lower lip then tilted her chin up.

With a groan, he lowered his head to kiss her.

Cliff took his time, kissing her quite thoroughly. She was dizzy when he lifted his lips, only to take her mouth again, deeper, longer. He explored every inch, tasting her breath, teasing her with his tongue, nipping with his teeth.

When she was panting and straining against him, he dropped his head to nibble her earlobe, his breath tickling her ear. A thrill ran down her spine to pool in her hips.

Only to splash into giddy glee when he swept her up from the floor into his arms.

Then, as if that display of strength wasn't enough, he curled her into one brawny arm.

Passion splashing through her, she seized his head in both hands and grabbed his mouth in a searing kiss.

He chuckled and with his free hand, began to explore her breast. Lightly, playfully. Circling the curve with hard fingertips. Cupping gently. Brushing a palm over her nipple, over and over, until it rose to a hard peak.

She gasped and arched into his teasing hand. Ron never took time like this. For him, two pulls on her nipple, and then it was time for the main action.

Skip to the good part.

She took Cliff's teasing hand and settled it between her thighs. Letting him know she understood, that it took longer for her to become fully aroused, that he might not be able to wait.

Letting him know she understood a man's needs.

"Not yet." He took his hand from between her thighs to grasp her hips, turning her in his embrace to wrap her legs around his waist. "I'm enjoying this too much."

His breath billowed against her sensitive neck. As her arms wrapped around his shoulders, he slowly licked and nibbled every tendon, every inch of her sensitive skin.

Her doubts shattered. Cliff seemed more than willing to go with the preliminaries, to make sure she was ready.

He nibbled his way to her breasts, licking one, then the other to taut fullness. One of his hands moved from her bottom to trace the curve of her spine, tickling the downy hair at the base. She never knew spines were so sensitive.

To make sure she was ready? Or to make sure she was beyond ready, frantic with need?

The slower Cliff went, the more aroused she became. Tension trailed his every nip, his every stroke. His sure touch erased memories of Ron completely.

Soon she wanted to go faster, harder, not to get past the preliminaries, but because she was on *fire*.

She arched into Cliff's mouth, tightening her legs around his waist—only to have him ease back. She tried again, to the same.

If she didn't get some pressure where she needed it in about ten seconds, she was going to self-combust.

Frustrated, she cried, "Down!"

"Your wish is my command." He released her to slide slowly, agonizingly, down his taut, muscular torso.

Stars, that slide was hot.

He smiled into her eyes. "More?"

"No," she panted. "Everything. Now."

He laughed. "Your wish is my command. But I'll need both hands free. This way."

Taking her hand, he led her out of her shower room into his locker room to where a thick exercise mat lay in one corner.

He spread a pair of towels on the cushion. Laying her down on the towels, he knelt one knee between her legs.

Then he stretched out above her. She wriggled, on fire, with all that luscious masculinity coming closer. Like a push up, chest and biceps bunched and swelled as he gradually lowered his weight toward her. Panting, she opened her mouth for a taste, but before she could lick or nibble anything, he slid his body down hers, his mouth finding her breast. Kissing, licking the curves, gradually circling higher...until his tongue touched the tip.

She gasped and arched. He wet the nipple, making it pucker, sending a tight, hot pang through her. She arched harder, wanting, needing him to suckle her, to feel the hot tug of that clever mouth.

"Not yet."

He kissed the other breast just as sweetly. Just as not-sucklingly. "Yet!" She grabbed his head, trying to pull him into satisfying her ache.

He only trailed small, gentle kisses down her torso, sliding his head from her trembling hands.

Reaching her belly, he stopped.

She sucked in a breath and held it.

He licked her abdomen, so lightly he barely brushed the hairs. She groaned, renewed breath with panting. As he shifted, gradually, downward, her panting became rasps and her heart beat heard.

Finally his kisses brought him to the place she throbbed for him. Tension nearly crippling her, she slid her legs open.

He skipped past to nibble her thigh. She groaned; he was stoking her need, building it up until she wanted to grab him, throw him on his back, and take *him*.

"Cliff, please," she gasped.

But he only switched to the other thigh, licking it, tracing a line from outer muscle to the sensitive flesh inside, hot breath making her quake.

"Enough!" She grabbed his head with both hands to stop his sensual torture. "In. Now."

She tried to pull him up her body, to make him give her the release she craved. He only smiled lazily at her and got up. Walked away.

She sat up like a jack-in-the-box to protest. Saw he was grabbing a foil packet from his wallet and lay back down. Anticipation furled in her belly like a hot, licking flame.

Sheathing himself in protection, he returned to her. He lowered himself over her in another push up, barely a breath between their bodies. Skyler swallowed heavily at the sight of the tension in his arms and chest. The zing of heavy need translated into immediate action. She scooted downward to put her hips beneath his—and raised her legs to trap him.

He captured both her wrists in return—with one hand. Slowly, he let some of his weight rest on her. And there, pulsing along the length of her belly, was the proof he wanted her as much as she wanted him, exciting her unbearably. She gazed into his face; his smile was still languid, but deep in his half-lidded eyes glittered powerful, raw desire.

A thrill rushed along her to the core. An answering urgency filled her.

Again he waited for her. Knowing he wanted her so badly but still cared first for her pleasure, she parted her lips, inviting him to kiss her.

He slowly leaned toward her until their breath mingled. Then, as if he could hold back no longer, he kissed her with desire as raw as she'd seen in his eyes. He released her wrists to slide a hand between them—and brush fire along her groove. She moaned. Setting up a steady, hard rhythm with his fingers, he burnished her until her fire burned so high it threatened to overwhelm her.

And at the cusp, he parted her thighs with one big hand and, with a sure, strong thrust, drove himself completely into her.

Shockwaves burst through her. She whimpered and clutched his brawny back as he began to thrust, with a concentration so total it consumed them both. She rose higher, need burning brighter. Curling her legs around his waist, she locked at the ankle, forcing him in even deeper. Wrapped completely in her body, he seemed to lose all rationality and began to pound into her with his total strength.

Loving it, she held onto him for dear life, Cliff her only anchor in the whirlwind of sensations gripping her. He was generating enough force and friction to really make her burst into flames. She felt him swell, and pause, release imminent, but still waiting...for her.

He cared for her, even in the extremes of his own passion. It pushed her over the edge.

She fell, shuddering, pulling him with her. Waves burst, on and on, for so very long. For forever.

Gradually, the waves slowed and ebbed. Echoes throbbed sweetly as a deep calm washed over her.

He slid onto the mat next to her, pulled her into his arms, and cuddled her to him, pillowing her head in the crook of his shoulder.

She blinked up with heavy eyelids. With a naturalness that would have surprised her another time, she curled up in his arms and fell asleep.

*　　*　　*

Skyler woke a short time later to Cliff's gentle kiss. She roused lazily, her eyes staying shut as she enjoyed the heat and silky feel of him.

His mouth left hers. "Hey, Skyler, I'm hungry. And this mat is getting hard."

She sighed. "You're a man of creature comforts, aren't you, Mr. Hawkesclyffe?" Grudgingly, she opened her eyes to his playful grin—and naked chest, so there was some recompense.

"I am, indeed." He chuckled. "You're one comfortable creature." He skittered away when she took a swat at him.

She laughed. "I've never seen you move like that."

"I'm well-versed in all the latest forms of movement. Sideways, backward, forward, in, out—"

"I thought you were hungry." When it occurred to her hunger wasn't always for food, her cheeks heated. "Second supper."

"Yes. Let's go out to eat. I'll pay."

"Well, since you eat all my food anyway, I suppose that's only fair."

His face fell pitifully.

"*Kidding.* You only eat most of it."

The grin returned. "Okay, then. Let's go!"

"Let's clean up and get dressed first, shall we?

Cliff drove her in his red coupe to a local twenty-four hour restaurant, where he ordered the biggest meal on the menu.

Skyler handed the server her menu. "Double it. I'll have everything he's having." When both men stared at her she said, "The best defense is a good offense. Since you eat half my food anyway, this way I'll get a decent meal."

The waiter just shook his head. "I'm obliged to ask— anyone for appetizers?"

Cliff grinned and ordered bread sticks and mozzarella balls as appetizers, and malts to drink. He demolished half the bread sticks and cheese balls in one minute. Skyler timed it.

She raised teasing brows. "You're losing your competitive speed."

"Can't help it, eating with you. Now, maybe if you challenged me more—"

"What, by hiding my food? By making it harder to identify?"

"How about by distracting me?" He waggled both brows.

Her face heated. Why could she only think of one way of distracting him? "I would, but that only makes you ravenous afterward." *Ravenous.* Much more and her face would go up in flames.

But Cliff reddened, too. Yay, she'd finally gotten him. Only fair, with the way he could wrap her around his little finger...or other parts of his anatomy. Her whole face fired.

He grabbed another two bread sticks. "Shall we change the subject? So, how many kids do you want?"

"Wait, *what?*" Her jaw slacked, and for a moment, she couldn't answer.

"Kids. You know, children. How many are you going to have?"

You, not *we*.

The panic eased and she considered the question. "I guess a lot depends on my spouse." She parroted something her mother always told her, "Kids take two parents, you know."

"I know." He waggled both brows.

Her whole body flushed hot. How did they get back on *that* topic? "I mean to *raise.*" Which, considering him a half-hour ago, wasn't any better of a word choice. "Well, there are great single parents. But me? I might try if I only had one child, but to handle more, I'd need a spouse. Maybe if he likes to work with children, we could have two or three."

"And a dog."

"And a house with a white picket fence. But, I'd need the husband first."

"Because it's expected?"

"No, because I don't think I'd enjoy taking care of all of that by myself. It's enough to get my dishes done every week."

"Every week! You dust muffin. My dishes get done daily."

"Yeah? How?"

He shrugged. "I use paper plates."

"Ah." She thought he'd have a housekeeper, but maybe Hannah was strictly a cook. "How many kids do you want?"

"I guess I could handle the single-dad thing with one, too," he said, suspiciously innocent-sounding, echoing her words. "Being an only child, though, I'd make a lot of mistakes. I'd like to be married, so my spouse could help me out. Then I could have two. I guess I could even handle three. Especially if we kept Hannah on to cook."

"I guess." There was that *we* again. She suddenly felt uncomfortable with the whole conversation. "It's supposed to rain tomorrow, you know."

He sighed almost inaudibly. "Cold front moving through, I expect."

Was that aimed at her? Luckily, their soup and salad arrived then, and Cliff was momentarily distracted. When he surfaced, Skyler was ready for him.

"Did you notice Tess today? She was walking around like she was on cloud nine. Didn't hear a word I said. I think she's gotten good news from someone special." She bounced in her seat, excited to share her secret.

He only sucked milkshake, nodding. Swallowing, he said, "Oh, yes, I'd mentioned our talk to John. I expect he asked her out."

Spoilsport. What good was an exciting secret if he knew it already? "Why didn't you tell me?"

"Sorry. I thought Tess would."

She stabbed her cherry tomato. "Tess was about as coherent as brain-damaged BASIC. The only thing that came out of her mouth was a bad rendition of 'Singin' in the Rain.' I have no idea what key she was in."

"Being in love does make one energetic."

"Only for certain things." She paused eating salad, her whole body heating. How had she gotten on *that* topic, again? She grabbed her malted and sucked some to cool down.

"Speaking of which." He waggled his brows, letting her know he was on *that* topic, too. "How about we go to my place after this? Much better showers."

"Is the mat any softer?"

He laughed. "Brace yourself. I have a real, live bed."

"I bet it's a water bed, you being a handsome bachelor, and all."

"Nope. Just a plain old bed. I had to argue forever with Mum just to upgrade my little twin to a queen size."

She finished her salad as Cliff vacuumed up any food that wasn't nailed down. As the waiter cleared their plates, Skyler could only think of one question. Once the server left, she said, delicately, "Should I bring my car or will you drive me home?"

He stopped stuffing another breadstick in his face to scowl at her. "I don't care what kind of reputation I have, Skyler. I'm not a playboy. If you come home with me, you're having breakfast with me."

"Oh? Do other women do that?"

"Hardly. Most women are just interested in my body or my money. I don't need that. I don't want that. And I certainly don't bring *that* home."

She blinked at him, impressed despite herself. "What *do* you need?"

His eyes bored into hers, blazing pure blue fire. "Someone to love me."

This time, she was braver. She opened her mouth to say, *I am that person.*

But the server zoomed up—and dropped Cliff's hot plate on him.

It hit his thighs. He leaped to his feet, yelping as scalding gravy seeped through his pants leg just above the knee. Exclaiming, the waiter patted his slacks with a napkin, to blot the gravy, although it would also prolong the skin's contact with the hot liquid. Cliff pushed him away. He closed his eyes, then, moments later said calmly, "Everything's fine."

"But sir, your slacks—"

"Please, don't trouble yourself. We'd like our check now."

The manager rushed to the table without being called. He apologized profusely. "It's on the house, sir. You and your wife's meal is on the house."

You and your wife?

Chapter Twenty-Three

As Skyler helped Cliff limp back to the red coupe, worry for his injury despite his assurances tangled with the manager's words. *Your wife.* It had sounded so natural, she'd hardly noticed at the time.

What if it were true? Cliff's ring on her hand, eating every dinner with him, waking up each morning with him...

"Skyler." He handed her the keys, his lips thinned and clamped together. "You'll have to drive."

That tossed any other thoughts out of her head. "You said you were okay!"

"I *am* okay. Except for the pain. It's excruciating."

"You should've said." She fussed getting him settled in the passenger seat. "We should have gotten that leg in cold water right away."

"It's all right. We're close to home. I have some first aid things there. You remember the way, right?"

Anything having to do with him, she remembered, but she just said, "Of course," and climbed into the driver's side.

Supercar, but older model. The beast had a clutch. She put her foot on both accelerator and clutch and attempted to start the engine.

The car roared to life so suddenly her feet leaped off both pedals. The engine coughed and died. Cliff muttered something about really being in pain now, but merely smiled at her when she glanced at him. She pushed in the clutch and tried again. His smile was thin, but she wasn't going to be picky while fighting with this miserable machine. She wished they'd taken her car, but she'd been floating in the afterglow of...

The engine hummed into life.

Surprised, but pretending not to be, Skyler pulled out into traffic. Cliff was strangely quiet. She found out the reason when they got to his bathroom, just off the master bedroom.

He grabbed a yellow and white tube of ointment from the closet. Closing the lid of the toilet, he dropped his trousers to sit.

Revealing a huge bright-red blotch marring his thigh.

"Oh, Cliff!"

He gritted his teeth and fumbled with a small tube. "Wait until I get this damn anesthetic ointment on. Then I can properly appreciate your sympathy."

She grabbed the tube away from him, twisted it open, and began smoothing ointment over the burn. "Just like my baby brother," she murmured.

Cliff glared, but it wasn't more than a moment before he sighed, closed his eyes, and relaxed against the tank. "That feels good."

"I know. You should have said something sooner. Why won't you ever let me help you?" She didn't just mean with the leg.

"Dunno." He cracked an eye open, studying her. He knew she meant more than the leg, too, because he admitted grudgingly, "Leftover paranoia? The only mission I did with a partner...first sign of danger the partner ran, leaving me worse off than if I'd done the mission solo."

"Ah." Skyler massaged. "I'd never do that, you know. Never leave you holding the bag."

"No." His voice was shaded with mild surprise. "You'd snarl and call me every name in the book, but you'd stick."

A warm glow settled in her. "You know, this burn is pretty nasty. Maybe I'd better take you to the emergency room."

Both eyes slit open, his gaze a narrow warning. "Not in the coupe."

"Phooey. Your car is not more important than your leg."

"The leg will heal. Besides, the pain is gone, thanks to that anesthetic. See? Perfectly numb." He pinched the reddened skin idly then spoiled it by wincing.

"Gone, I see. Well then, it's not because you're afraid of the doctor, is it?" She slipped an ointment-covered hand under the edge of his shorts.

He leaped up. "Now, Skyler, let's not be hasty." He edged toward the door.

"Burns need to be taken care of properly."

He stopped, a half-smile curving his mouth. "Would you take care of me? Properly?"

A towel rack held clean hand and bath towels, and a couple washcloths. She used a washcloth to wipe her hands clean of ointment then grabbed a hand towel. Turning on the cold tap, she glanced over her shoulder at him with a raised eyebrow. "Why, are you a burn?"

"A bad one." His eyes twinkled.

She soaked the hand towel in cold water then wrung it out with a mischievous smile. "Well, in that case, you'd better strip to the waist and put on a paper gown."

"Yes, Doctor."

Cliff slowly unbuttoned his shirt with his clever fingers and then drew the edges back from his chest. She was fascinated by the play of muscles. Removing it, he twisted and tossed it over a corner hamper. Turning threw his lean waist into relief. He stood straight, shoulders back, arms relaxed and ready, and pretended to look around.

"No paper gown, Doctor."

She swallowed. "Well. I guess you'll have to lie down on the examining table without it." She waved at the bed. "I'm a busy doctor you know. Don't have time to wait for restocking."

Dimple peeking out, he obliged, stretching his big frame completely out on the bed. Muscles bunched and stretched under his sleek skin as he folded his hands behind his head. She closed her eyes briefly as pure desire shimmered through her. Swallowing again, she opened her eyes and climbed onto the bed next to him. "This will be cold at first." She spread the hand towel over his burned thigh.

"Right—yikes!" He panted in reaction.

"I don't like that rapid respiration. I think I need to inspect your airways." She lowered her head toward his.

His breathing changed, less reaction, more anticipation.

Leaving the cool towel to do its work, she lowered her mouth onto the silk of his lips. He gently rubbed his mouth against hers. She licked his lower lip with the tip of her tongue, and he made a feral sound deep in his throat.

I did that. A thrill sparkled inside her.

"You're a good doctor. I'm already feeling better." He brushed another kiss to her mouth. "What else?"

"Next, I'll check your pulse." She kissed lightly down his jaw until she reached the smooth skin of his neck. Gently she nibbled his throat. He groaned. She traced the tip of her tongue down his neck to the great swell of his chest.

"Now, your heartbeat."

She placed her palm on one side of his chest, only half-covering his massive pectoral. She used her lips on the other, kissing his smooth, taut skin. When she reached his nipple, she tongued it as he had done to her, teasing it, loving it. His louder groan resonated inside her, lifting her own excitement.

"Respiration and pulse are healthy." She kissed the underside of his heavy chest. "Let's see about that abdomen."

With her hands clean of the anesthetic ointment, she felt free to explore the taut hillocks of his flat belly. She ran fingers along the dark ridge of hair, tracing it downward from his navel. Leaning forward, she brushed her lips against the hair. It tickled.

"Doctor," he whispered. "I think you're a bit overdressed for this examination."

"Why, so I am." She got off the bed. Remembering the lip-licking vision of his slowly emerging chest stripping his shirt, she took her time opening the buttons on hers, teasing him with a partial view of her cleavage, then turning to unhook her bra. She kicked off her shoes and socks then slid her jeans sensually down her hips, leaving only her panties. Nearly naked, she turned, arm across her breasts, eyelids lowered a bit shyly. She'd never played like this.

Cliff's gaze burned.

Relief poured through her, and an answering desire pooled hot in her belly. She lost the panties, climbed onto the bed, and kissed him. He lifted his head off the pillow and opened his mouth to her, but didn't use his hands. Drawn in by his heat, she wrapped her arms behind his head, pulled him to her, and explored inside his mouth with her tongue, her groin beginning to throb. Moving down, she kissed his neck and throat, then his gorgeous chest, tasting his skin, the scent of sandalwood soap and man and the heat of his body pushing her farther, faster, until the ache between her legs hammered at her.

She raised herself on her knees over him and nodded back toward his hips. "Those shorts are preventing a complete examination. Off."

"Yes, Doctor. Right away, Doctor." He slid his hands between them, curled his legs, and with a lithe yank, got naked. The towel tangled with the shorts and he gave a little wince at the scrape despite the anesthetic ointment.

"Oh, Cliff, I'm so sorry—"

"What about this, Doctor? I think it needs your full attention." When he laid flat again, the evidence of his desire for her was huge.

An answering desire rose and beat in her. Okay, he wanted this. She'd just have to be careful of his wound.

As he rolled protection on, she rewet the towel in the bathroom, wrung it out, and returned to gently lay it on his burn, noting the red wasn't so angry.

He groaned. She climbed back on the bed, his corrugated belly pumping faster with his excited breaths.

She was extra careful when she straddled his hips, making sure she wasn't touching his burn, easier because it was closer to his knee than his groin.

Cliff's hands were there immediately to help her, guiding her hips over and helping her fit him to her. Slowly, she settled him inside.

"*Skyler.*" His eyes clenched in pleasure. A thrill washed through her.

She set her own rhythm, delighted when he thrust upward in perfect sync. His eyes opened on her, and his gaze *burned*.

A moan escaped her lips. He grabbed her hips and began thrusting up into her, faster, harder. She gripped his huge shoulders, arching back as she rose toward the peak. His hand slid between her legs, and he caressed her.

She dissolved in pleasure. Her legs melted, and she sat down on him, sheathing him completely. When he hit bottom she gasped, her thighs clutching him.

He called her name again and shuddered his release into her. She trembled with him as pleasure coursed like cleansing fire through her veins.

The last shudders left her. Heart pounding in her ears, she relaxed onto his big body, careful of the towel-covered thigh.

Slowly, her breathing steadied. His had already slowed. Lulled by the gentle rise and fall of the chest under her, she slept.

The sun, streaming through the window, woke her. She lay on unfamiliar, luxurious sheets. Blinking around her, she saw a room that wasn't hers. For a moment, she was confused.

Cliff's scent, masculine and tangy, brought the present sharply into focus. A warm depression next to her said they'd slept the night here, together. She smiled to herself. They'd made love twice and sure enough she was here the next morning.

But where was *he?*

She got up to find him, dislodging a whiff of her own smell. Change of plans. Shower first, find Cliff after.

He stuck his head into the bathroom while she was soaping with silky body wash. "When you're ready, I have breakfast in the kitchen." He plunked a steaming cup beside the shower.

"Coffee? I'm in love," she called out after him as he left, half-hoping he hadn't heard.

Half-hoping he had.

She brought the empty cup down with her a short while later. He'd set out bowls, spoons and some milk. "I'm afraid Hannah has weekends off. We'll have to suffer with cold cereal."

She scanned the boxes in the cupboard. "Hey, look—Frooty-Os! My favorite!" She blushed. "Uh, I'll bet you're thinking I'm being a bit childish..."

"You mentioned you liked them as a kid." Cliff brought the box down calmly. "Would I have gone out and bought some if I thought it was childish?"

She stared at him with saucer eyes. "You bought breakfast cereal for me?" She wasn't sure if that was the sweetest thing she'd ever heard or the most egotistical. "Why, you, you smug, cocksure—"

"Would you rather have cold pizza and orange juice?" He opened the box and poured cereal and milk, giving her a quirked smile over his shoulder.

Skyler sat down and shut up. Conceited man, she thought. Conceited, wonderful man.

"So," Cliff said as he took the seat across from her. "Want to go shopping today?"

She munched cereal. "What about the project?"

"It's Saturday. The hard part's done. Let's take the day off. Better yet, let's take two days off."

Cocking her head, she considered it. A weekend off? Two whole days? "Huh. What would we do?"

"Have fun."

"What is this thing called 'fun'?"

He laughed. "It's what normal people do. I heard it increases endorphins and leads to better health."

"I'm all for endorphins." Excitement built in her. "I did want to visit the zoo. I heard it's the best around."

"It is. And there's a theme park just an hour away. We could spend a day at each."

The two of them, together, for two whole days. Nothing to do but spend time with each other. She didn't smile so much as feel her entire body lift, including the corners of her mouth. "Then let us experience the endorphin boost called 'fun'."

The day at the theme park was lovely. For all his sophistication, Cliff approached both rides and lines as a little boy at heart, with wide eyes, laughing in delight. She was amused when he tried every new food stand and was touched when he won her a plush teddy bear at the ring-toss.

They spent the night at his house again. A wonderful night, filled with talk and love-making—and a little sleep.

The next day, they spent at the zoo. Skyler felt as if they were a pair of teenagers, holding hands, oohing at the lions and laughing at the monkeys. He bought her ice cream and took her on the little train that ran through the grounds. In the reptile house, she amazed him with her extensive knowledge of snakes, acquired from many years living with a younger brother. On the way home, they stopped for pie and coffee, and talked about all sorts of things. The talk never seemed to run out. It amazed her how much they had in common.

Sunday night, she danced into his mansion. Everything seemed brighter. "Endorphins are good."

He laughed. "They are. Say, I have a breakfast meeting tomorrow with a prospective employee. Should I drop you off at work first? Or would you like to take the Ferrari?"

Her eyes opened wide. "You'd let me take your baby? Not just let me, you'd encourage it? You must be high."

"Endorphin rush?"

"Give him all the endorphins!"

*　　　*　　　*

The phone jangled John out of a deep sleep. He swore as he slapped the thing to his ear. "What?"

"Our client just called. He informed me I've been gone long enough. He's going to start executing personnel unless I'm on the next flight out." Cliff's tone was grim. "I need to get back to Middle Yemen, *now*."

John sat bolt upright. "You haven't finished preparations."

"With Pinlow gone, the leak is plugged. I've fixed most of what I need to here. You can take care of the rest of the fallout."

"And the Pizza Pie code?"

"Schedule me a flight, earliest possible. I'll use whatever time is left tonight to finish the extras of Pizza Pie—including the mods we discussed. Oh, you'll need to send Belva to that breakfast meeting."

"You'll tell Skyler what's going on?"

"She was kidnapped by that maniac, John. She went through enough pain and heartache. I'm not deliberately subjecting her to more. Once everything is straightened out."

John clenched his eyes. While his friend's heart was in the right place, this would not end well. "You really think that's best?"

"I really do."

"You're sure—?"

"Yes. If she knew everything, she'd only worry. I won't have that, do you hear me? I won't."

John replied the only way he could. "You're the boss."

The rest of John's night was filled with urgent preparations. He'd been losing sleep like crazy, but thank goodness, the military trained him for that, too.

Chapter Twenty-Four

Monday morning, Skyler woke to an empty bed. A mug of coffee waited on her side table. She showered, dressed, and came downstairs to find Cliff was already gone. But she remembered his breakfast meeting—and that he'd said she should use his Ferrari.

She drove herself happily to work.

Tess met Skyler outside her office. "John told me. Are you okay?" Her friend seemed hesitant.

"What are you talking about?" Skyler skimmed past John's empty desk to her own office and put her purse away, ignoring the sudden cloud edging of her happy mood. "Okay with what?"

"The boss leaving again."

"I haven't read the schedule for two weeks. I've been on 'vacation.'" Skyler smiled. And what a vacation.

"It wasn't on the schedule. I just wanted to make sure you were okay with it."

"Okay with...? Where is he going, Siberia?"

"No." Tess hesitated then blurted, "Middle Yemen."

Middle Yemen? Realization hit Skyler like a fist. "No, he can't." She covered her face with her hands.

Tess touched her shoulder. "Skyler, what's wrong?"

"Nothing. I...I just need a minute."

"If you want to talk—"

"Later. I'll call you." She dropped her hands to give Tess a sickly smile. "Really. I just want to be alone a few moments to regroup."

"Well...okay. But if you need me—"

"Thanks. You're the best."

Tess waited a moment more then shook her head and left the office, shutting the door quietly behind her.

Skyler sank into her chair and covered her face again, this time with a silent moan.

Cliff lied.

It felt like he'd stabbed her. As if this whole weekend had been to divert her attention from today's coming blow.

The timing was just too close. Apple Pie finished Friday, he leaves for Middle Yemen Monday? He'd planned for the security system to go to Fahrrad all along.

Profit meant more to him than anything, even personal integrity. Even betraying a friend.

Or a lover.

She tried to remember the little boy Cliff must have been, small, defenseless, misunderstood.

Or had he lied about that, too?

The vacation...how much of that had been real? The whole weekend spent together, when he'd talked with her, played with her, made love to her.

More camouflage?

She'd begun to hope...

She felt so stupid. Just because they had made love, just because she might be *in* love, didn't mean he was.

Here she'd thought she finally knew him, the real him. She didn't know him at all. Talk about compartmentalized.

This was the Cliff who'd run away for two months without explanation, the Cliff who dealt with Kulinahr as a *head of state* rather than a person.

Maybe that was only part of who Cliff was. But if there was any part of him that could negotiate with Fahrrad, she didn't know if she could live with that.

As she waited for Cliff to arrive at the office, her frayed emotions whispered to her with echoes of Ron. He was a cunning seducer, a conniving businessman. Once he touched her body, her head had been outvoted.

Cliff or Ron?

Does it matter?

The door flew open, startling her. Cliff strode in, smiling. "Skyler, there you are!"

She drank in the sight of him...fooled again. She mentally slapped herself. That damn self-assurance of his triggered all her feelings of professional inadequacy and personal vulnerability.

He'd *used* her.

He said, "I have to be away a few days, but when I get back—"

"How *could* you?" She jumped to her feet. "How could you even think I would condone your going to Middle Yemen after what happened to me there? How *dare* you?"

His face went pale, as though she had slapped his face. "Skyler, it's not what you think."

Ron could go pale on command too, trying to play on her sympathies. She hardened her heart. "Then what is it?"

"I...It's...damn." His expression was so twisted with pain, she felt herself softening despite her own hurt. Finally he said, "I can't tell you. I'd need to tell you everything, and I don't have enough time. Not to do it right." His gaze searched her face, looking for something.

"You can't tell me?" It came out shrill. She breathed hard. "Then let me guess. We've been working on Fahrrad's system all along, haven't we? On Pizza Pie?" She leaned forward on the desk. "You *know* what he's planning, Cliff. You know he'll use the money for upheaval and cruelty and suppression." She waited, holding her panting breath, for him to say *no, of course not.* Impossible words. He said nothing. She slapped the desk. "But you don't care, do you? All you can see is the profit, the bottom line. Well, here's the bottom line from me. Go. Get out! Good riddance." She was shooing him out of his own company, but at that moment, she couldn't care less.

He went to the door. But instead of stalking out, he closed it gently with himself on her side of it. He turned, standing in front of the closed door, arms crossed. "Please, don't jump to conclusions." His voice was very controlled. "Things happened out of order. I didn't tell you because, well, after everything you endured over there, I didn't want to distress you any more. Especially not on your vacation." A tiny smile softened his face, appealing to her. But she steeled herself to say nothing. He sighed and went on. "The bank version of the system is still viable—"

"*Not countrywide defense,* you said," she roared, overriding him. "Back when this all started, when you ran out the first time. You didn't deliver *that* message in person either. You leave the lovesick women to John."

A frown sprang up, and his eyes narrowed in a puzzled expression. He moved closer, cautiously. "Lovesick...? What do you mean by that?"

"Don't you dare." Panicking, she shored up her vulnerability with a hard offense. "Don't you dare try to change the subject. Middle Yemen, Cliff. That bastard Fahrrad."

He uncrossed his arms and held up both palms, like a truce. "Please, Skyler. It's not what you think. Trust me."

"Trust you?" She retreated behind her desk, where she stood, trembling. "Like I trusted you for the past three months? Like I trusted you this weekend?"

Like I trusted Ron?

"There's something behind this, isn't there?" That penetrating gaze of his sharpened. "More going on. I feel like I'm arguing against a black box. What's really bothering you?"

"I should have known." She blew past his shrewd guess, gathering steam. "I suspected from the beginning that the project was going to benefit Fahrrad. But you said no, that wasn't the case, and I worked to believe you. I saw signs of the worst, but either you or John downplayed everything, and I told myself I was overreacting. I wish I *never* worked on this project, never helped you stab Kulinahr in the back." Wished she'd never made love to Cliff—*no, gone to bed with him*—knowing it was going to hurt this much.

She pounded on the desk as if that could equalize the pain. "You can take Middle Yemen and stuff it. And you can take *us* and stuff it, too."

Cliff's gaze went stony, his big body stiff. "I'm sorry you don't trust me, but maybe you don't know me that well. I thought after this weekend..." He glanced away, and for a moment, his face softened. Then his lips tightened, and he turned back. "I still don't think you've told me what's really on your mind, but it doesn't matter. I have to go to Middle Yemen. It can't wait. When I get back, we can..."

His gaze flicked to her, vulnerable.

She let him see only her fury, hiding the pain.

His eyes hardened again. "Or maybe we can't. Goodbye, Skyler." He spun and threw open the door.

"No!" She screamed it. "You're not leaving me again."

Before he could march out, she ran in front of him and pushed furiously against his broad chest. She barely moved him, but he backed off under his own power.

"Again? What do you mean, not leaving you *again?*" Confusion flickered in the depths of his stony cobalt gaze.

"When I first came. We'd argued about Fahrrad on the drive here. But instead of talking it out, you left." For months. "You walked out on me that day and worse, you had your secretary lie to me. Rather than talk it over, *you left me.*" Her voice faltered, and the pain slipped out. "Like Ron." And then in a whisper, she added, "I told you."

"Skyler..." His voice was soft, broken. His fingers slid under her chin, to raise her eyes to his gaze.

She jerked away before he could. "Don't you dare, Mr. Hawkesclyffe. Don't you dare short circuit my reason with seduction." Her voice became strident; she couldn't help it.

His face paled. "No. Skyler, never that."

"Never? Then what was the picnic, when you wanted to make love rather than argue? Can you honestly say you don't want me to put up and shut up like a good little employee? That whatever I feel, the professional facade is always more important?"

"Did Ron treat you that way?" he asked hesitantly.

She forced a laugh. "What do you think?" Then she shrugged. "Go to Middle Yemen. But this time, I'm leaving, too. If you don't have to be responsible, neither do I."

He held his hands out in a pleading gesture. "Be responsible for what?"

She shook her head. "Don't worry about firing me. I quit."

"Skyler wait." He caught her face with cupped hands and stared deep into her eyes. "Would it help if...if I told you I'm falling in love with you?"

Her body went cold. "Ron told me he loved me. Every day. He sent me a dozen roses for every birthday and every Valentine's Day. Until I didn't do what he wanted. Then the ice was so cold it cut. What he really loved was his image of me, not me." She jerked her face from his hands, hurried back to the desk, and grabbed her purse while he stood there looking dumbfounded. "Well, I won't put myself through that again. So this is goodbye."

She strode past what was more a statue of a man than a man. Out of the office, out of the building, out of his life.

Chapter Twenty-Five

Her dignity carried her as far as her car, which was in the lot from Friday. Once inside her sedan with the door locked, she collapsed, crying. She'd really thought Cliff was different. Not that they would agree about everything, but that he would listen to her, and they'd work things out.

She grabbed a paper napkin from the glove box and wiped her wet cheeks, sitting there, crying like a boob. She should start the car and drive home. Home, where she had tissue and comfort food.

But some part of her wanted him to come after her, to at least make a stab at talking things through.

Except he didn't have time.

"No." She said it out loud, her voice cracking. "No more waiting for a hero who isn't a hero at all." She turned the key and started out.

Behind her, someone burst from the office at a dead run. She started to look in her rear view mirror...

But she didn't want to see. If it wasn't Cliff, her heart, already breaking, would crack in two.

She floored it and squealed out of there.

At her apartment, she dragged herself inside and cried a little, but nothing felt right. She made a cup of tea, boiling the water, extracting the teabag from its paper, dunking it into the hot water. She was still dunking it mindlessly when her cell phone rang. She jumped a mile.

The caller ID read "John".

She set it down in pain. Even John reminded her of Cliff. Instead of answering, she stalked into the bathroom to wash her face.

Twisting on the tap, she didn't wait for the water to heat up before scooping a handful and splashing her face. The cool liquid felt cold on her overheated flesh.

She leaned wet hands on the lip of the sink and stared at herself in the mirror. Red-rimmed eyes greeted her, and a soft puffy nose and lips.

What was wrong with her? She should be exultant. At last, she'd seen through a man before he could hurt her. Or hurt her too much. She had even walked out on him for a change. She should be triumphant.

Instead, she just felt tired.

The water was hot now. She scrubbed her smeared makeup off and rinsed but didn't feel any better. Face dripping, she found herself staring at the toilet. Remembered Cliff sitting on his, sighing in pleasure as she treated his burn. She remembered vaguely that he'd been saying something about his partner...that was it. *"First sign of danger the partner ran, leaving me worse off than if I'd done the mission solo."*

She'd told him she'd never leave him holding the bag. He'd answered, *"You'd snarl and call me every name in the book, but you'd stick."*

But she hadn't stuck. She'd left him.

Before he could leave me.

Didn't matter. Certainly she still was responsible enough to deal with whatever message John had left. Snatching a face towel, she blotted herself dry as she strode back into the living room and punched play. She listened with half an ear.

"I just thought I should tell you. There was an emergency in procurement." He'd sounded stressed. "And you weren't answering my pages here..."

She'd walked out on, not just the job, but John, too. She felt bad.

"So, anyway, I called Cliff to handle it. He wanted to go after you for some reason, but like I said, it was an emergency..."

Yes, that was it. She felt bad because she'd never not finished what she'd started. She'd have to go back to HCC.

"Anyway, after that, he left in a hurry, but then stomped back in here with all sorts of growled commands that I really didn't like...so I thought maybe whatever he needed to talk to you about was important. That maybe I shouldn't have stopped him, but of course I had to..."

The relief filling her was a surprise. She couldn't condone Cliff's going to Middle Yemen, of course, but she could finish the HCCpi project. Stay true to herself, to her need to do a good job to make the world a better place.

"I thought I'd better let you know what happened. Um, call me, okay?"

Deep inside, she knew the relief was really because that had been Cliff running into the parking lot. Running after her. John had delayed him, but in the end, he really had come after her. *Maybe he wanted to try to talk things out.* She nearly called Cliff, but changed her mind at the last minute and called John.

Better warm up in emotionally neutral territory, as it were.

He must've called someone after her, because it went to voicemail.

"This is John Cavanaugh, Mr. Hawkesclyffe's PA. I'm away from my desk, but..."

Shock made Skyler press end call. She knew John was Cliff's PA first, but hearing him say it made her *I quit* gut-wrenchingly real. Reluctantly, she redialed.

"John Cavanaugh."

It was him, live. And here, she'd steeled herself to leave a message. Now, she had to deal with him. "John, it's Skyler."

"Thank goodness." His voice was a bit strained. "Cliff is gone. I don't know if you heard my voicemail, but he snarled a few instructions and slammed out of here. He's halfway to Middle Yemen if he's still going at the same rate." He hesitated. "He said you quit."

"It's a long story. But I don't quit a job before it's finished." Besides, without Cliff there, it would be easier to return, right?

A sigh. "Am I glad to hear that. This project is too big to steer solo. And, except for Cliff, you're the only one with the whole thing in her head."

"I'll finish the HCCpi project with Apple Pie," she cautioned. "Bank security only. Another week, if we work really hard."

"Sure. You're in charge."

Right. I'm in charge.

She hung up the phone after saying goodbye to John. If she really was in charge, the next press release would read: *The Hawkesclyffe Computer Company announced in a surprise move today that they will no longer be doing business in Middle Yemen. Would the president of the firm please return at once?*

Sure, she was in charge.

*   *   *

Skyler went back to work Tuesday with Cliff's tacit blessing—all communications were handled through John, who must have told him she was still there, because no project managers showed up to take her place. In a way, it was more painful than if he had yanked the company away from her. Didn't he care she'd come back? Why hadn't he called, tried again to talk with her? She finally broke down and asked John for contact info, but he said Cliff was "in deep." When she asked what that meant, he hesitated, then said he was unreachable except in an emergency.

It's only an emergency of the heart.

She did her job, but inside, her stomach was a blizzard, and she walked around in a cold daze. She just couldn't shake the feeling of wrongness. Cliff was gone. Though she didn't want to, she missed him desperately.

Well, maybe she'd at last seen through a man before he could hurt her too much, but she still hadn't walked away soon enough.

That afternoon Skyler supervised packing the HCCpi prototype, Apple Pie software loaded up, for beta testing.

In Middle Yemen.

Now that there was no reason to hide it from her, John told her he'd helped Cliff set up the *pi* chip factory in Misr. Chipsets were already shipping to the computer production plant in New Jersey.

Next week, if the prototype performed up to spec in live testing, the HCCpi would go into mass production.

She supposed Cliff would load Pizza Pie when the prototype arrived. She wondered if the Basement Bombers had coded it in the two weeks she'd been on vacation or if Cliff had squeezed it into his evenings and wee hours of the morning. After all, he was a genius.

Skyler hated her own part in it, but at least she hadn't worked on Fahrrad's national defense net. Pizza Pie was all Cliff. Businessman genius Cliff.

Yet, she kept remembering him the way he had been at the park and at the zoo. Just a little boy, who had found a friend at last.

Skyler clutched the paperwork. The clerks sealing the boxes blurred in her vision.

One of the clerks looked up. "Boss? Something wrong?"

Professionalism, Skyler. "No. You're doing a great job." She breathed in a lungful of air to clear both her mind and her nose and smiled through her emotional pain. "Everything is great. I always get a little emotional seeing a project come together."

She turned away before the clerks could see her bravado for the lie it was.

*   *   *

Skyler mechanically went through the motions for the rest of the day, and the day after that, holding meetings here, negotiating contracts there. To most outward appearances, she was at the top of her form. She thought she was covering her numb heart perfectly.

Until, Wednesday night, Tess dragged her out for supper.

At the sundae parlor.

"Ice cream is best for what ails you, am I right?" Tess laid open the menu and pointed at the largest sundaes. "Pick one. I'm buying."

When the server came, Skyler tried to order a small scoop of ice cream.

Her best friend retorted, "Nice try. We'll both have the Pig Trough." As the server left, she leaned forward and nailed Skyler with a gaze as penetrating as Cliff's. "Now. What's wrong?"

"Nothing?" She tried a smile, felt it wobble. Realized she wasn't numb, but rather that she'd build a dam to hold back her tears. Worse, they'd accumulated behind the wall until it was nearly overflowing. Worst, Tess's warm concern was cracking the concrete.

"Bull-loney. You're *acting* as warm and efficient as always. But I can see behind that."

Skyler slid her gaze away from Tess's penetrating stare. "Are we here to nitpick or eat?" Pretending nonchalance, she played with her napkin-wrapped utensils.

"We're here to eat. But it's been ages since we've been able to talk together, just the two of us."

The server returned at that moment with two foot-long boats, manned by a rainbow of scoops of ice cream wearing cherry hats swimming in sauces from caramel to strawberry to hot fudge.

Skyler waited for the twinge of her salivary glands kicking in. Nothing. She just stared at the sugar feast in front of her, blinking, thinking she really was numb after all until she realized her eyes were wet. She shored up her emotional dam by tossing off, "Yeah, it has been a while since I've had a free second. You know how it is, working for a certified genius like Cliff. Never a dull moment.

Always on the go." She shot Tess a brief, brilliant, and definitely not weepy smile.

"How sparkly white your teeth are." Her friend dipped up glossy fudge, a sarcastic brow raised at her. "Really contrasts with your dull red eyes. I suppose you have some great times working for the certified genius, huh?"

She closed her annoyingly red eyes. Her whole body seemed tight and scratchy and tense. "Pretty nice, yeah."

"And the wall goes up. Skyler, I'm just concerned—"

"I do thank you for that. But I'm dealing with it in my own way. If you want to help me, let's just eat."

Tess blew a loud breath and for a moment Skyler thought she'd challenge her.

If she did, Skyler wasn't sure she wouldn't run out.

But instead Tess said, "All right. You know I'm here for you when you're ready. In the meantime... Well, I have a problem too. Not as bad as yours, whatever it is, but you're my best friend, and I need to talk. Is that okay?"

Skyler released a relieved sigh, her muscles relaxing. "Yes, of course. More than okay. It would take my mind off myself."

"Thanks." Tess smiled briefly. "You know John asked me out. We had a terrific time, and since then, we've gone out some more."

Skyler's heart warmed, something she wouldn't have thought possible an hour ago. "Good for you!"

"But frankly, I'm also worried. You know how office politics are. I'd hate for the harpies to make a mess of us. How do you suggest I play this one? And don't tell me not to get involved. I've got a feeling this guy's for keeps."

For keeps.

Skyler's heart squeezed in her chest. She breathed through it. Tess was happy, that was the main thing. "I knew something was up. Says right here in the rules 'Tess does not buy sundaes unless there's an ulterior motive.' So, how serious is it?"

"Serious enough for me to start exploring joint housekeeping."

"Awesome! Good thing Fitzwater got rid of Mel Pinlow. If he'd found out, he'd have made your life miserable."

"There are other Pinlows in the world."

"Unfortunately." She thought briefly of Ron, then more painfully of Cliff. She'd tried twice and gotten it wrong both times. What advice could she give her friend? "Know what I think? Your biggest problem isn't another Pinlow. It's you."

"Me?"

"You and John. Ron and I...where we went wrong was that we'd bring our fights into the office. Sunday's personal disagreement made its way into Monday's memo, and the rebuttal came in Tuesday's meeting disguised as a business problem."

"So what did you do?"

"Well, I told myself I'd never date a coworker again. I thought the solution was to completely separate my business and personal life."

Tess looked pained. "Please tell me that's not what you think now."

"It sure would be cleaner. But if you're as invested in your career as I am, or work with the man you adore like...like *you* do...well, I don't think people like us *can* separate our careers and home life without becoming slightly schizophrenic." She sighed.

"What can I do?"

"The only thing you can. Stay professional at the office. Of course, there is some disagreement as to what is *professional.*" Talking was helping. And there was at least one businessman in the world who'd taken her blubbering in stride. Who was to say there weren't more?

She wasn't out of the woods yet, but for the first time she thought she might, if not get over Cliff, at least get past him, eventually. Appetite nudged her to dip her spoon into chocolate-coated ice cream and sample.

"Isn't being professional 'dress for success,' a go-getter attitude, keep your feelings to yourself? You know, like Mr. Spock selling used cars."

Skyler smiled in spite of herself. "Someone told me recently a professional does the best she can with what she's dealt. If you're sick, tell the client 'I've got a cold, I feel miserable, but what can I do for you?'"

"What about dress for success and the rest?"

"A monkey in a suit is still a monkey. Don't get me wrong. The sizzle is as important as the steak. But you can't have a good sizzle without a good steak. You're the real professional, not your clothes. I guess the bottom line is...do your job like you've always done it, better, if you can. The only difference is you drive home together." She smiled at her friend.

Tess smiled back. Then her mouth pursed in thought. "But what about the rumor-mongers? I don't want people saying nasty things about John and me, especially if we have to work with them."

"Who cares about the Mels of this world?" An echo of anger shivered through her waning numbness. "Do you remember how Mel brown-nosed around Jerry Fitzwater then bad-mouthed him behind his back?"

"Not just Jerry." Tess shuddered.

"Nasty people say nasty things. Inevitable, so why worry? Fortunately, there's no one like Mel at HCC."

Briefly, Tess reached across the table to clasp her hands. "Thanks. I feel better." Her friend smiled.

Then Tess took her spoon and dipped up a cherry with a studied expression. "So what changed your mind?"

Skyler thought about Cliff. But cautiously, she said, "I haven't changed my mind about Ron."

"Then what happened to the mighty oath you swore never again to indulge in office romance? Now, you're saying it can be done. What changed your mind?"

"I'm more mature?" Skyler affected a shrug, though inside she was squirming.

Tess, of course, caught Skyler's evasion and glared. "Chicken."

Skyler winced. "I'm not Marty McFly, but that hurt."

"Buck-buck-buck-awk!"

"Friends are sooo annoying, especially the smart, persistent ones. Fine. Oh, this is not going to be easy." Still, she took the plunge. "Cliff changed my mind."

Tess rewarded her with a fierce grin. "I knew it! All those late nights and working lunches."

"Tess, I broke down crying in front of him. I thought I was history as far as the job was concerned." Memory assaulted Skyler, widening the crack in her emotional damn. She stuffed it closed with words, tumbling over each other. "Instead he told me the same things I'm telling you about professionalism. That a real professional isn't perfect because nobody is, but a real pro knows they're not perfect and admits it then does the job anyway. Professionals are humans, not asses who buy into the uptight, anal-retentive style of professionalism that can't integrate different parts of life—"

"Skyler honey." Tess grabbed her hands. "It's okay."

She realized that despite spouting a torrent of words, her dam had opened wide anyway, tears trickling down her cheeks. She pulled one hand from her friend's to snatch a napkin and wipe her face. "It isn't. We broke up."

"You and Cliff?" Tess's face paled, eyes wide. "But why? He's perfect for you. Smart, sensitive, and it's obvious he loves you to pieces."

"Tess, please. I can't accept his attitude of business at any cost, I simply *can't*. It's just too much like Ron. And doing business with that slime Fahrrad? I don't know how a man who is so smart can be so dumb."

A pause. "I'm so sorry, honey."

"I'm not." She *wasn't,* though her heart pounded painfully and her eyes kept leaking. She dashed them. "Better I found out now." She pushed away her sundae. "Can we go?"

"Of course." Tess called the server over and paid. She tried to get Skyler to take the rest of the day off, to go home with her and talk more, but Skyler refused.

Talking had opened the dam of her emotions, and it had hurt so much. How much worse would actually shattering the dam to pieces be? *She'd* go to pieces.

She couldn't handle that, not now. She went back to the office instead, and tried to work.

But she couldn't keep her mind on the simplest task. So, she got up and went to the gym.

Chapter Twenty-Six

The workout room reminded Skyler of Cliff, but at least it wasn't the men's locker room and its corner mat. That would have been intolerable. She climbed onto the stair machine and was slogging away on her second climb when John entered.

"Thought I might find you here."

"Why?" she puffed.

"Cliff does the same thing when he gets worked up. He works out. Hey, you're doing that wrong, you know."

She threw him a glare that, if she had been any less tired, would have wilted him. "Really? I didn't think you *could* do this wrong."

"Oh, sure. Stand straight, or you're not getting the maximum benefit." He headed for the stationary bicycle.

She straightened her posture, found herself worn out in five minutes, and stopped.

John, who had been warming up on the cycle, came over. "Great. Now, what weights do you do?"

She shrugged. "Oh, you know, the manly ones. Two hundred pound barbells and such."

"Okay, since this is your first time, let's start over here at the machines."

She got off the stepper and followed him, interest piqued despite herself.

He continued, "Free weights are more effective, but you need to have some strength built up first, or you might hurt yourself."

"Thanks, Arnold. What else?"

"Hey, I built Cliff's body, I can do yours."

"I don't want a body like his." *Yes, I do*, said her libido. She shushed it.

"What was that?" John glanced over his shoulder.

"I said, what is that thing there?"

"This machine is for your back muscles. We'll start with twenty pounds." As he fiddled with the stacked weights, she came over, sat, and took the handles. He nodded at her. "Okay, now pull smoothly behind you, and don't let the weights fall on the release. Good."

While she pulled weights, John kept up a steady stream of conversation. Skyler thought acidly that Tess must've sicced him on her, to distract her from Cliff. But, turnabout was fair play, so as long as he was talking, she figured she'd asked him casually about her friend.

"I heard you had a romantic dinner with Tess. Did they burn the pizza crust again?"

He just grinned. "I wouldn't have noticed."

"Wow. You have it bad." To think, she had been floating around like Tess a few short days ago. She pushed the weights savagely.

"Hey, take it easy. You don't build strength that way, you tear muscles."

John took her through machines for her biceps, triceps, pectorals, and muscles she couldn't even find, much less remember the names. When he finally called it quits, she felt like a colander full of spaghetti, she was trembling so hard.

"I think you'll do just fine. Remember, don't do weights tomorrow."

"I'll remember." Every time she sat down, she'd remember. Or try to stand. Or lift something. Or do *anything*.

But her mood had lightened for the second time since Cliff left. She laughed, a little rusty.

She actually felt better when the news banner flashed across all of the room's screens.

"Super-AI defense system goes live. Middle Yemen leader hailed as innovator, strong on security."

Skyler just stared a moment, before she ground out, "I just shipped that out yesterday!"

John winced. With a half-hearted shrug, he said, "Fahrrad forced our hand."

She turned around, mounted the treadmill, and did another half hour of furious running.

Pizza Pie was online.

*　　*　　*

It wasn't just her emotions making the work harder. John threw delay after delay at her. First the distribution company they'd contracted for the HCCpi hiked their prices, and John made her consider every other warehouse and carrier in the country before he miraculously renegotiated with their original company for almost the same rate. Then whatever had gone wrong with the water system in the locker room affected the whole company and John shut down the building for two whole days while he got the plumbers in to look at it. Miraculously quickly fixed when on Monday, she threatened to deal with the plumbers herself.

Almost as if he was doing it on purpose. He probably wasn't, but the result was the same. Her week-and-out expanded to at least another week or more.

By the end of the day Tuesday, exhausted from bleeding emotionally, even more exhausted from covering it up, she decided she needed to make a clean break.

She marched into John's office. "We were supposed to deliver the first HCCpi/Apple Pie system this week. That's been delayed for another week."

"At least," John inserted rapidly.

"Doesn't matter. You won't need me for the final details. I'm leaving Friday."

It was supposed to be a catharsis; instead, it felt flat.

Especially when John's face fell. "But you can't. Cliff won't be back yet. He wanted to talk with you—"

"Not happening." She crossed her arms and stoked her inner shields.

Completely undone when John said with warm sympathy, "He had to go, Skyler. You know he did."

"I know he *thought* he did."

"I'm sorry you feel that way, really I am." He spread his hands in a gesture of appeal. "But there are factors you don't know about."

"Wanna tell me what those factors are?"

John's gaze skidded away. "Cliff should be the one to tell you."

"Then I'm left to guess." She threw her arms into the air in exasperation. "Business. Bottom line. Profit."

John was already shaking his head. "Personal profit doesn't mean jack to Cliff. But the company...look, there's a lot wrapped up in this new HCCpi. The industry is ultracompetitive, you know that. New products, fresh upgrades arrive daily. But Cliff has only introduced one new model since the first line."

Her arms slowly lowered. "Just the one?"

"Yes. With market pressures crowding the price-point of current models until we're practically giving them away. He's milking the cash cows for all they're worth, but those cows are beginning to run dry. We need the HCCpi, which means we need the *pi* chip which means we need Middle Yemen to manufacture it cheap enough and fast enough to compete in the marketplace. The big boys are right behind us. They could snap up the slack any day; Cliff's breakthrough was as much serendipity as genius."

"I sympathize. But..." She shook her head. "Doesn't alter the fact he's dealing with Fahrrad. Didn't Tess tell you what happened to me, what happened to Kulinahr?"

"Yes." John sighed. "But you're two people. Hawkesclyffe Computers employs over five thousand worldwide. Cliff is ultimately responsible for those people's *livelihoods*. Without a profit, he can't do that. Add in the hundreds of new jobs for Middle Yemeni in the chip factory plus those mining and refining the rare earth elements... This was not an easy decision for him to make."

"I'm sorry." And she was. Her body felt like lead. "I understand and even applaud Cliff for making tough decisions. But *I* can't live with the choice he's made." She turned to go.

"Wait, Skyler. There's more to this. I can't tell you about it, but it may change your mind."

She didn't turn back. "I doubt it."

"Cliff is an honorable man, no matter what you may think. Will you agree to wait until he gets back before you leave? Hear him out, listen to his side of the story?"

"When he wouldn't listen to mine?" When he left anyway? When he hadn't called in the week plus since he'd gone?

"No."

She exited John's office and tried to stalk out of the building, but felt guilty for leaving before the project was completely finished.

It goaded her into turning around, stalking past John to shut herself in her office and work until nine.

Then, when her black mood hit bottom, she went to the gym. A mile running and a few minutes in the sauna refreshed her enough to head home.

By Thursday, John cautiously told her, "Your stamina has improved. That means your cardiovascular system is stronger."

"Pretty soon I'll even have muscles." She flexed biceps.

"Good job. The only person I've had respond faster is Cliff." He wiped his hands on a towel.

For the barest instant, her competitive streak rose. Then she remembered the last time she and Cliff had competed...or rather, all the times they'd pretended to compete, their play masquerading as battle. Love, which neither could acknowledge, wearing the mask of contest. It made her terribly sad.

She pushed the ache away, laying it at the feet of dehydration, grabbed her water bottle, and headed off for the sauna.

She'd finished all but some very small details, which Tess and John had promised they'd take care of. Her friend, of course, was staying.

Skyler was packing up over the weekend. She didn't have to be back at Fitzwater until Wednesday, but she planned on taking a few days off when she got home to relax.

I'll pack up and go home, and Sir Humphrey Hawkesclyffe in all his radiant glory will fade from my mind like a bad dream.

Sure he would.

*   *   *

On her last day, Skyler was puttering with some computer work at her desk, re-reviewing employee evaluation forms and aimless drilling down into the quarterly profit/loss statements.

She came across the petty-fund line item for the two weeks before Cliff had stormed out. Their programming vacation.

She blinked scratchy eyes. Although, even if she managed to rout Cliff from her mind, she'd still see reminders of him every day. The company appeared in the stock market columns, and the man himself was often quoted in the trades. With the arrival of the new computer and *pi* chip, HCC exposure would only increase.

Maybe she should find a new profession. Like stunt pilot. Armed forces? She laughed ruefully. The way John had trained her, they'd snap her right up.

Her throat felt thick and scratchy too. And she'd developed a heavy ache in her chest. A cold? Pneumonia?

She wanted to lie to herself but couldn't. Only if the cold was named Cliff.

With a sigh, she shut down her HCC laptop for the last time. John could take care of the rest. She felt like a stranger here. She shook her head, remembering it was only five months ago she stepped out of Cliff's sedan and felt like she was home at last.

Skyler walked slowly to the gym for a workout. There was really nothing much more for her to do. After beating her black mood into submission, she showered, dressed, then walked around the company to say goodbye to all her people. His people. Tess and John were cleaning up some detail offsite, so she was spared the hardest goodbyes of all. Besides, she'd see them around—though it would never be the same.

She dragged herself home...no, to her *apartment*. Boston was her home. She started packing, found herself too tired, got ready for bed, but couldn't sleep. So, she got out the tape and boxes, took the last bits of herself laying around the place and simply dumped them in. Each thing seemed to remind her of her friends. A rubber band. Goodbye, Tess. A small hand weight. Goodbye, John. A ticket stub from the zoo. She choked back a sob. Goodbye, Cliff.

She couldn't make herself drop the stub in. Instead, she set it on top of her clothes left out for tomorrow and went back to bed, crying herself to sleep.

*   *   *

John stalked around his office, glaring at the desk phone. He hadn't heard from Cliff all week. If it didn't ring today, he would have to nudge some of his most highly placed contacts.

It was extremely unusual not to hear *something*. Sure, his friend's disposition had been sour when he'd flown off, but now John wondered just how sour.

At midnight, he packed up his things to go home. He was worried, but Tess was waiting for him, and he couldn't delay any longer. Still, he hesitated. Maybe the phone would ring…

Brrring.

The timing was so unexpected, John almost didn't grab it. Shaking himself, he snatched up the handset. "Where the hell have you been? What's going on over there?"

There was static from the line, then Cliff's voice came, flat and weary. "It's time."

John's tirade died immediately. "I thought we were waiting until the client was feeling secure with the system."

"We were. He is. Too secure. He's wondering why I'm still here when everything's done. We're ready. Mostly."

"Personnel? Materials?" John tensed. The client was Fahrrad, and personnel and materials were their code words for loyalists to Prince Kulinahr and weapons to fight.

"In place."

He released a sigh. "The backdoor?" With Pizza Pie up and running, the only way to get the militia and their munitions into the palace—or even the country—was a backdoor Cliff was trying to crowbar into the system.

"Incomplete."

Relief fled. "Then it's hopeless. We'd have been better if you hadn't brought up that damned airtight system."

"I had to. He was paranoid. We needed him to feel secure. Besides, there's still a chance."

The fire of hope flared. "How?"

"I'd almost completed the backdoor. It'll work—if I trigger it manually. Stay with it until the plan is complete."

"Are you insane? He'll catch you."

"I'll pretend ignorance. He'll believe me."

"You hope," John said darkly.

"Doesn't matter what I hope." A weary sigh. "The window of opportunity is closing. It has to be now. Start the clock on your end."

"Are you *sure*—"

"No. But what else can I do?"

"You could get out. Let the chips fall where they will." John shook his head. As if his friend's sense of responsibility would let him. "You will get out as soon as you can, right?"

Thunder struck outside. Crackling obscured part of the reply. "...finish this myself." Then the line went dead.

John stared at the phone, gut churning. Then he took out a burner phone and punched in numbers. When the line picked up he said, "One hour."

Another number moved up the schedule on his transport, though the earliest the plane could be ready was five a.m.

John, with an airman's practicality, went home to get some rest before the worst of the storm hit.

*   *   *

Thunder woke Skyler from a restless sleep at four a.m. Peeking outside at the torrential rain, she sighed and dressed. She wandered through packed boxes and generic furnishings, flicking on the television on her way to the kitchen. Without her things, the place might as well have been a hotel suite, blank and without character.

Tabula rasa, just like her future. A clean slate, ready to be rewritten.

Unpacking her teapot, she'd just put the kettle on when a knock came at her apartment door. *What the...?* Who would visit so early? She peered through the peephole. John and Tess stood awkwardly in the hallway, sheepish and concerned.

Well, of course. The only folks who would visit so early were relatives or concerned best friends.

"May we come in?" asked John. "It's a little on the humid side out there."

She opened the door, forgetting the chain. The clonk-rattle as it hit the max of two inches made her say ruefully, "Just a minute. I'm not quite awake."

"Sorry we're so early,' Tess said. "John is going out of town, and he sort of insisted."

"Right." She closed the door, lost the chain and opened the door wide. She had a bad premonition about what was coming, and attempted to stave it off by acting like this four-a.m. visit was no big deal. "No problem. Want some tea? Let me turn down the babble box."

"Skyler—"

"Glad you guys stopped over before going out of town. Where are you going, John? No, never mind. It's probably someplace I don't want to know. Now about that tea—"

"Skyler." John's tone brooked no nonsense. "I know about you and Cliff breaking up."

Skyler rolled eyes at Tess. "Traitor." But she said it mildly. Tess shrugged sheepishly.

"I don't care," John said. "You're still the best boss we've had. And I feel the same about both of you."

"You love us both equally, huh?" She attempted to smile.

"No, I think you're both a pair of idiots."

That goosed a rusty laugh from her. "Don't beat around the bush, John. Why don't you come out and say what you really mean?"

"For smart executives, neither of you is being too smart personally. Yes, I'm off to Middle Yemen. But before I leave, I want to make sure you *don't.*"

Explained the early morning call. "John, I have to."

He exchanged a baffled look with Tess. She put a hand on his. He smiled warmly into her eyes.

In that moment, Skyler knew they would make it, that they'd be a couple for the rest of their lives. And her heart filled for her friend, then broke for herself.

John, for once, didn't catch her emotional state. "You need to talk this out. You have to see that. Why don't you want to talk this thing out with him?"

"Or with us," Tess put in.

"Because...because it's too late." Skyler stared at the tube, but her thoughts were turned inward. She barely registered the talking head, a map over his shoulder.

John frowned. "It's only too late if you leave."

"You should at least stay until Cliff gets back," Tess agreed.

Oh, she did *not* want to hear this. Or consider it. She focused on the television instead. Something about the country's outline caught her attention. It looked like—

"What's going on?" she murmured, picking up the remote to increase the volume. John opened his mouth to try again but she raised a palm as she thumbed the plus button. "That's Middle Yemen."

Startled, he turned toward the television.

"...are still unclear, but it appears that the countercoup was successful. Despite the Midyemeni AI defense system, Prince Kulinahr has entered the country and stormed the palace with a citizen militia. He has been confirmed as the legitimate leader of Middle Yemen by its Parliamentary Council in a unanimous vote. Colonel Boris Fahrrad, who had come to power earlier this year, has been declared a criminal."

"Damn," John said softly.

Skyler let out a whoop of joy and almost missed what came next.

"Breaking news... This footage has just been released, taken by a private party behind the palace."

A grainy video played. The palace hove into view. Phone footage from the way the picture walked around the back of the building

Suddenly a bound and blindfolded man was hustled out the back door.

The newscaster voiced over, "Sources say Sir Humphrey Hawkesclyffe, founder and owner of Hawkes-clyffe Computers, has been reported missing in the street fighting and confusion in Middle Yemen."

Chapter Twenty-Seven

Skyler stood there, heart in her throat, as the screen cut back to the newscaster.

"Sir Hawkesclyffe, frequently in the country for business, has been acknowledged by Kulinahr as a prime catalyst in this countercoup. The government of Middle Yemen has assured both the British and American ambassadors that Sir Hawkesclyffe's safety is a top priority, but refuse to confirm the identity of the captive in this video."

Skyler stared at the television, stunned. A memory surfaced, her conversation with Cliff on the long drive here, months ago.

"You said you weren't working with him!" She'd cut him off, a corporate no-no.

But he'd replied mildly, "I said I wasn't working with him at present. And I'm not. But if things go the way I think they will, it will be to the country's advantage to bring me in."

To the *country's* advantage, not Fahrrad's.

"Cliff's gone and put Kulinahr back in power!" Damn secretive alpha-male hero. Why couldn't he have told her?

Did he think her temper would've screwed things up...? *Well, duh.* "You realize what this means?"

"Yes," John growled. "I need to get over there, now."

She spun to him, the implications making her heart pound. "Good lord, you don't *think* that's Cliff in the video...you *know* it. Why aren't you over there already, helping him?"

"Not my fault." He bit the words off. "I had a ride scheduled in plenty of time to help, but Fahrrad forced Cliff's hand. The countercoup went off early." His phone rang, "The Star-Spangled Banner." "I need to get this." He pulled out his phone, thumbed it live and pressed it to his head. "Yes, Mr. Secretary? Yes sir. No sir, he had to stay with the computer system to hold the backdoor open." A pause as John's face went pale, then red. "Yes sir. I'll get there as soon as possible." He slid the phone away.

"What's wrong?" Skyler's heart was in her throat.

"Cliff hamstrung the security system so Kulinahr's forces could enter the city and palace without Fahrrad seeing. Looped camera feeds, false sensor data, and the like. Turns out he also changed the passwords so Fahrrad couldn't get back in."

"That's good, right?"

"Good for keeping Fahrrad out—but *bad* for finding Cliff. Without the system, we have no eyes on the city."

They couldn't find Cliff? It hit Skyler like a faceful of ice water. She forced herself to think past her horror. "He changed the server password or the Apple Pie master password? Or both?"

John blinked at her. "I don't know. But the pair of us can get there in under four hours in the modified Blackbird."

"You're Air Force?" Tess said.

"I'm a lot of things." He was still staring at Skyler.

"The *pair* of *us?*" Skyler's heart rate skyrocketed. "Why me?" she squeaked. The last time she'd been in Middle Yemen, it had been as a frightened captive.

"I forgot—*you* know the system. When Cliff hacked into Pizza Pie to disable the security grid, he had to stay onsite to do it."

"Which means he was a sitting duck for Fahrrad, I know."

"It also means that's the last place he was before he was taken." He paused, jaw working. Skyler could tell he was furious and scared for his friend, and barely holding the fury back. "Cliff isn't the type to idly stand by. If he was able, he'd have *left us a clue.*"

Hope seared her. "If he wasn't able?"

"Then our only way to find him is to hack back into our own system. Skyler, nobody knows Pizza Pie better than you."

"Apple Pie, and I only coded a few modules." Her voice shook.

"You personally reviewed all designs. At the time I thought it was overkill, but now you're the only person who can navigate the whole thing. Besides, I take off in less than half an hour. What other programmer can I get to go with me by then?"

Terror iced her veins. She wrapped arms around herself and stood there, trembling. She'd been Fahrrad's captive. Go back to Middle Yemen? No. Not her. Returning to the place she'd been helpless and a captive was the last thing in the world she wanted to do.

Fahrrad's captive—but Cliff rescued me.

Now Cliff was the captive. Who'd rescue him?

I'm the only one.

She was a civilian. John. John was the military man.

But John wasn't a programmer. He could hack the backdoor of a palace but not a computer.

Cliff needed *her*.

Determination blazed through her fear. "Right. Okay, unless you deleted my HCC credentials, I can download the system specs onto my phone on the way." She'd kept the alpha-geek smart phone Cliff had given her, telling herself it was because of its advanced tech. But really she knew she simply couldn't let go of the first present he'd given her. Now she fervently hoped it wasn't the last. "Let me grab a change of clothes and my passport and we'll go."

"There's my gal." Tess snared her for a fierce hug, one she returned as fiercely.

"Thank you," Skyler whispered into her friend's ear.

"For what?"

Her heart burst with emotion. "Everything."

With a final squeeze, Tess released her. "I'll hold down the fort here."

Skyler threw together a quick backpack of necessities plus things she could have used last time in Middle Yemen, like pepper spray and a headscarf. Leaving her keys with Tess, she stuffed her purse in the pack and followed John out the door.

He must've bought cars from the dealer next door to Cliff's. A two-seater Porsche was parked at the curb. John chirped it open as he sailed toward it.

She trotted after him then peeled off to slid into the passenger seat, settling her backpack on her lap. "So you were in contact with Cliff all along? If he knew where he was being taken, why didn't he call you?"

He lowered himself into the driver's seat and started the engine. "My guess? He didn't have time. He probably only had time to leave a clue somewhere on the system before they took him captive. Something they wouldn't find, or if they did find it, wouldn't understand."

"Oh." Skyler took out her smart phone and connected to the HCC server. She sure hoped she understood whatever genius clue Cliff had left. "So what was he doing the first time?"

John zipped out onto the street. "When?"

"Those two months. When I thought he was schmoozing Fahrrad." Connected, she navigated to secure team storage and considered which system schematics to download. She had an enormous storage card in her phone but even it was finite.

"Gathering loyalists. Trying to build the chip plant while delaying defense system activation. All while trying to maintain his cover as greedy playboy businessman."

Skyler paused in her work to shiver. Cliff was brave, risking his life, and maybe giving it up, to get Kulinahr into the palace.

She just hoped she could be half as brave.

"I should have trusted him, shouldn't I?"

He shot her a glance. "Actually, no."

That wasn't what she'd expected. "No?"

"No. If you'd trusted him, that would have meant he wasn't perfectly playing his part. That's the sort of thing that can get a spy killed."

Surprise made her nearly drop the phone. "He's a *spy*?"

"Well, more a covert-operations consultant these days. But yeah, spy."

"Wow. And you're his handler?"

"I'm his PA. Which is a lot more work, let me tell you."

Through everything, that made her smile. If John could treat this as situation normal, she'd try to, too. She began to pick and download information. "How long have you been planning to put Kulinahr back in power?"

"Since Fahrrad took the country. That was why Cliff continued to work with him. The businessman cover kept the spy close."

"I wish he'd trusted me with that information." She could've avoided a lot of heartache.

"*I* wanted to tell you." John shook his head. "I argued for it. Your knowing would've made everything much easier. But Cliff...well, let me tell you something about him. This information is private, but I think you've proven yourself safe." He raised a questioning brow.

"Of course. I'd never hurt him." She winced, remembering his stiff, hurt body at their last fight. "Well, not deliberately."

"Right. See, you're the right person. Cliff trusted the wrong person, once." He shook his head. "An old flame."

A knife of possessiveness stabbed her. "What happened?"

"She was a civilian, but she heard about Cliff's mission and wanted in. Of course, she was totally unprepared for reality."

She remembered Cliff saying, *"The only mission I did with a partner...first sign of danger the partner ran, leaving me worse off than if I'd done the mission solo."*

Doubt replaced Skyler's jealousy. This must be the same woman. Glancing out the window, she clutched the phone harder. *Am I going into a situation unasked, unprepared?*

"No. You're nothing like her."

Surprise snapped her head around to him. "Did you just answer my thoughts?"

He raised a brow. "It was pretty obvious some sort of doubt was going through your mind. And in answer, I *asked* you to accompany me, plus you're more than an expert in this particular field."

Reassurance eased her grip on the phone. "Was the mission dangerous?"

"Not really. But the moment things got tough, she folded like a cheap lawn chair, and that made it dangerous. She got out, Cliff got hurt. He hasn't really trusted anyone since."

Poor Cliff. For the first time in weeks, a surge of sympathy flooded out the anger and pain. "I'm surprised the military allowed a civilian on a mission."

"Not military. Although even now, I'm not sure what alphabet agency was behind it. Look, Skyler, the thing was supposed to be a simple two-person undercover surveillance job, Cliff and a partner posing as a married couple. Cliff's girlfriend wouldn't let him do it unless she played the wife. Mid-job she lost her nerve, and the whole thing blew up. And because this is Cliff we're talking about, it blew up in *his* face, not hers. Here we are."

Skyler cut a surprised glance out the window. Houses and businesses had given way to open spaces. John turned onto a gravel driveway, taxied the car to the edge of an unmarked airfield, crunched to a halt, cut the engine, and jumped out.

Skyler popped out on the other side. "Where are we—?"

"Don't ask." He led her into a hanger where a tall, burly man opened lockers on two pressure suits and helmets.

She stared in wonder. *I'm going up in space?*

Her phone rang. She pulled it out of her pocket and frowned at the readout. Something about the name Hannah sounded familiar.

John leaned over and saw the name. "Cliff's cook? You should take that. In case he contacted her." He grabbed his suit and handed her the other. "You can use speakerphone while Al helps you put your equipment on."

"Um, right." She dropped her backpack, took the suit and stared at it as she activated the call. The flight suit looked as complicated as a jet itself. It brought home like nothing else the kind of trip she was on.

"Was the mission dangerous?"

"Not really. But the moment things got tough, she folded like a cheap lawn chair."

"Ms. Jones?" A homey alto came from the speaker. Skyler shook herself. Cliff wasn't going to get hurt again because she couldn't handle a few tough conditions.

With the tall, burly man named Al to help her, she changed as she said, "Hi, Hannah. We've never met, but I'm Skyler Jones—"

"Yes, Ms. Jones, Cliff has talked a lot about you. A lot."

Embarrassment heated her cheeks. He'd really been excited about their relationship, excited enough to talk with his cook. Skyler felt a surge of shame.

Fold like a cheap lawn chair later. Job to do now.

She pushed her feelings away to get on with it. "How can I help you?"

She assumed Hannah had heard somehow about Cliff's danger, but it turned out the cook had other things on her mind.

"I heard from John that you're leaving, Ms. Jones."

"Please, call me Skyler."

"Skyler, I don't want to interfere, but you should know—Cliff hasn't done this since his dad, Colonel Hawkesclyffe, was killed. Over twenty years ago."

A shadow of unease made Skyler pause donning her suit. "I don't understand."

"Before Cliff left for Middle Yemen, he tore home because he'd forgotten his passport. So I made up a nice bag lunch for him, but he didn't take it. He said he wasn't hungry."

"He's never done that before?"

"Well, you know how he eats. But that's not what I meant. While he was upstairs, getting his passport—and he never, ever forgets anything, Skyler—that's when he did it."

The shadow darkened into full-blown fear. "Was he sick?"

"He was crying." Hannah's voice went dark with emotion.

Skyler's chest exploded with brutal cold. Cliff, that big bucket of testosterone, crying? "Wh-why?"

"I think you know why. He was miserable because you two fought. Ms. Jones, I'll say this simply—you need to stay until he gets home. Hear him out."

She wanted to weep. "Of course I'll stay." What else could she say?

Al tugged on her suit, obviously wanting to finish fastening it.

What else could she say? Nothing, unless Cliff was found...*until* Cliff was found. Then she'd apologize to him. But right now, she had a job to do. She turned to let Al check the suit. "Hannah, I need to ask. Has Cliff contacted you in the last twenty-four hours?"

When Hannah answered in the negative, Skyler felt as if her last hope had been cut off.

Job to do. A job that will help him come home, so I can apologize—hopefully for the rest of our lives.

She said goodbye, set the phone to vibrate, tucked it inside her pack, and finished dressing. John put her helmet on then led her to the plane.

Her transpo was total badass.

The modified Blackbird had tandem cockpits. Skyler's heart pumped faster in excitement as she took her place behind John. The bird smelled of space age fuel and had an instrument panel like a science fiction story.

But her heart also beat hard in fear. She was going to Middle Yemen. Where she'd been stripped and degraded. Where she'd nearly been enslaved and maybe worse.

Where Cliff had rescued her, and not the other way around.

So what? she chided herself. Han rescued Princess Leia in *Star Wars*, but two films later *she* rescued *him*. She had to remember that Cliff needed her to be strong. Not fold like a cheap lawn chair, not while there was hope.

But I'm no hero. Cliff had put Kulinahr back in power. *He* was a hero.

She was the opposite of a hero. She had hurt him. Made him weep, according to Hannah. Skyler's insides crumpled in regret. She was so flawed.

I'm not perfect. Why did I expect Cliff to be? Shame hunched her shoulders.

Not perfect. *Except being a perfectly matched pair.* Yearning and love tangled inside her. In not being perfect, he was perfect for her.

"I'm the biggest fool in history," she muttered. Shame, regret, yearning, and love, but most of all hope, exploded inside her—just as the plane took off, leaving her stomach behind.

They refueled mid-air soon after talking off, which she thought was odd but John seemed to find normal. Then, within minutes, the Blackbird was going so fast the clouds blurred. For the first half-hour, Skyler swiveled this way and that to see, sure her eyes must be big as moons. She'd finally gotten her heart to slow from hummingbird to bunny when John's voice crackled over the helmet's headset. She'd also forgotten he'd said the things were voice-activated. "I'm going to contact the state department and find out the latest intel. I'll pipe you in."

Skyler listened anxiously and was shocked when he connected straight with a Mister Secretary in the States and a Madam Ambassador in Middle Yemen.

Then she started giggling at herself. She was in a jet more like a spaceship than a plane, why be shocked at an international phone call?

"I'm upping your oxygen," John said to her. As a hiss began in her suit and her giggles subsided, he said, Madam Ambassador. What is going on over there? Have there been any ransom demands?"

"No, and frankly that worries me."

"An angry, insane ex-dictator has Cliff but hasn't demanded money? Yeah, have to say, that worries me too."

Skyler abruptly chilled.

John went on. "Is the colonel alone?"

"No. Fahrrad fought his way out with several squads of private mercenaries. But he's on the run, Captain Cavanaugh. He might have even fled the country."

"Or he might be plotting how to retake it. Hardcore military men with him, nothing to lose... Plus one of only two people who know the whole HCCpi system. We have to find Cliff as soon as possible. I'm bringing an expert with me. We'll be there before four, local time. If Cliff left any clue in the palace or on the HCCpi, we'll find it." John cut the connection.

Skyler heard something that she'd only heard once before in the unflappable PA's voice—fear. She waited a beat, her heart in her throat, then asked, "What did you leave out?"

"I don't want to worry you."

"I'm already worried. Tell me the worst."

A silence, while John checked his instruments. Finally he blew air. "Cliff engineered Fahrrad's downfall. The colonel took Cliff, but not for money. That leaves two reasons. The best is that he took Cliff to kill him."

"K-kill?" Her breath hissed in her helmet. Something inside her broke. She whispered, "Cliff's d-dead?"

"No, probably not yet." But before she could feel relieved, John went on. "But there's a worse possibility. The crazy bastard might think he can retake the country. If he does, he'll torture Cliff for the passwords and information on Pizza Pie's backdoor."

"Oh, no. Can Cliff...can he withstand that?" Meaning, did he have ways to distance himself from the pain.

"He's been trained, but that's not a good thing for him. He'll hold out longer, maybe long enough for Fahrrad to get really inventive."

Skyler felt sick.

"Cliff won't break easily, but he will break. That's why we need to find him. Not just to save him but to locate and neutralize Fahrrad."

She clutched her backpack. "But...Cliff has been in situations like this before, right? He knows what to do? How to escape, or at least how to get word out?"

"A month ago I would've said yes. But he's never been caught before." John paused, then hit her with, "Cliff has never *let* himself get caught before."

The implications smashed her with an iceberg of guilt. Their last fight...her storming out on him...he would have desperately needed to have his head on straight for this operation, but that furious flinging of hurtful words could easily have blown his concentration. Had it gotten him so upset he hadn't been able to escape?

Worse, had he been so upset he hadn't *wanted* to escape?

She tried to swallow, but her throat didn't work. *Oh, dear God, please let him be okay.*

Chapter Twenty-Eight

John must've pushed the Blackbird to its limits, because, refueling twice more in the four hours they were in the air, they landed in Middle Yemen shortly after three p.m. local time. As she climbed out of the cockpit, she was hit with a blast of heat. She wasn't sure how she felt, now that she was actually back. Afraid, but that was as much for Cliff as for herself.

Would she be able to do it? Would she be enough to save the man she loved?

"It's okay to be afraid," John said as he helped her off with her flight suit. "I am, too." She was glad for his assist. This morning she'd been in her apartment, angry with Cliff. Mere hours later she was in Middle Yemen and afraid for his life. She felt off-balance, out of kilter. It seemed everything was moving too fast.

After she and John got out of their flight suits, the American and British ambassadors were waiting for them in a sleek black sedan. John ushered Skyler inside and settled behind her.

She shifted on her seat, luxurious leather, but she couldn't enjoy it, worried about Cliff.

The sedan took off. The Middle Yemeni officer who drove it had taken Driver's Ed from someone in Hades. Skyler grabbed for a handhold and noted the ambassadors did the same.

The American ambassador cleared her throat before speaking. "Captain Cavanaugh, my official apologies for this state of affairs. As you know, our government was friendly to Prince Kulinahr, but as long as Colonel Fahrrad had the token backing of the Parliamentary Council and official control, we could do nothing."

Cliff had done something, but Skyler kept the words to herself.

John didn't. "Yeah, well, you left Cliff hanging out in the wind."

The ambassador coughed. "While Mr. Hawkesclyffe was ostensibly working on his own, he did keep his contacts in the state department abreast of his actions, and we aided him as we could. We knew he'd infiltrated the palace under cover of providing his security system. We knew he used that cover to to connect with Kulinahr's loyal militia and recruit new members."

John gave a curt nod.

The British ambassador said, "We were pleased to hear an overwhelming majority of the Middle Yemeni militia and citizenry was still loyal to the Prince."

"We did what we could." The American ambassador exchanged a glance with her British counterpart. "Our governments partnered to ease import restrictions to allow Cliff to arm that militia."

The British ambassador nodded. "Although, of course, it was Sir Humphrey's efforts which allowed the counter-coup to go off flawlessly."

Skyler's fingers fisted in her backpack. They made it sound like Cliff had merely assisted.

"Call it like it is." John glared at the ambassador. "*Sir Humphrey* risked his life, orchestrating that countercoup without real help from either of his governments."

Go, John.

The ambassadors exchanged uncomfortable looks. The British ambassador cleared his throat. "We will aid you however we can in finding Sir Humphrey."

The American ambassador said, "What's your plan?"

"We go to the palace, to the last place we know Cliff was free—the HCCpi. If he planted a clue to his whereabouts, that's the most likely place. In any event we'll try to break into the system, so we can use the citywide cameras to find him."

"Prince Kulinahr has experts working on that," the Ambassador objected. "They haven't even been able to get into the computer room. I understand they've been attempting to hack in via networked computers, but they haven't made any headway."

Skyler's heart rate skyrocketed. She knew from working with Cliff that he held the entire system plan in his big brain. Not even the government's top computer experts could crack it. What made her think she could?

"Skyler knows the system." John's voice and face was filled with confidence. "If anyone can get in, she can."

She took a deep breath and straightened in her seat. Didn't matter whether she could or not. She had to try.

The car screeched to a halt in front of the palace— where people were pouring out the doors.

The American ambassador frowned in confusion out her window. "What's going on?"

John pushed the car door open. "Let's find out."

John spearheaded their way through the mob. Skyler hugged her backpack and kept tight to him. Inside the palace, it was even more of an uproar.

Prince Kulinahr, dressed in fatigues, directed the militia himself. John said, "Your Highness. What's going on?"

The prince was pale, but his face was grimly determined. "The madman called. He threatened to turn the defensive armaments on *us*."

Skyler's heart rate rocketed.

"He has control of the AI?" the American ambassador asked.

"I do not think so. But he has Cliff. It is only a matter of time before even such a strong man breaks."

Terror made a thick lump in her throat.

"How long?" the British ambassador asked. "How long do we think Sir Humphrey can hold out?"

"Days? Hours? But it doesn't matter. I must give myself and the country up to Fahrrad in one hour or he will...well, best you listen to it from the madman's own mouth. General Adisa." Kulinahr waved in a tall, distinguished man. "Continue coordinating the search." To Skyler and the rest he said, "I have mustered every available soul to find Cliff, but I fear it is already too late. Come."

"We may be able to help with that," John said as he fell into step beside the prince. Skyler hurried after, followed by the ambassadors.

Kulinahr led them into a large office filled with heavy furniture—and animal head trophies.

Skyler nearly tripped at the sight.

"Fahrrad's idea of decorating." Kulinahr's visage was grim as he strode past the central desk, as large as an aircraft carrier, to a small conference table in the corner. "I would have gutted it and started over. Now...I don't know. Listen, please."

He pressed a button on what looked like a conference hub. His own voice came from the device.

"What do you want, Fahrrad?"

"What do I *want?*"

Skyler's heart beat harder hearing Fahrrad's oily tones again, dark now with anger.

The dictator went on. "I want what's best for Middle Yemen. Me."

"You think *you* are what's best for my country?" The prince's recorded voice was caustic.

"I know it. Middle Yemen sits like a fat sheep amid hungry wolves. It needs a strong, unifying leader to protect it, not a bunch of little people pulling in different directions."

"A leader who slaughters and kidnaps to get what he wants?"

"A leader who makes the hard decisions. Who doesn't take no for an answer. Who's *not afraid to lead.*" The colonel's voice rose in volume until he shouted the last. Chillingly, his next words were quite pleasant. "Thank you for the palace AI, by the way. I will enjoy turning it on you—if you do not surrender the country and yourself to me in one hour."

"Or else what, Fahrrad? We cannot get into the security system, and I think neither can you."

"Ah, but I have the system's maker. It is only a matter of time...and a few unnecessary body parts...before I will have full access." He laughed.

Skyler was sick. He meant to...Cliff's competent fingers...she swayed. "Oh, God."

John's hand cupped her shoulder, tightening reassuringly. "We won't let that happen. All right, here's what we're going to do." He turned to the rest, his tone decisive. Skyler saw how good he must have been in the military. "We have less than an hour. Let's unlock that security system. Worst case, we keep the madman from blowing us up. Best case, our boy has left us clues as to his whereabouts."

The American ambassador sighed, and she scrubbed her face with one hand, her hard-nosed image cracking a little. "We've been trying. The experts have been trying to break in for hours. That system is impregnable, and so is the computer room."

"Maybe. But Skyler's here now, and she's the next best thing to Cliff himself. Or better."

For the first time the prince managed a small smile. "Of course. I will take you to the nearest workstation—"

"I could try that," Skyler interrupted. "But with so little time, wouldn't it be better if we start right away at the main console?"

Kulinahr looked confused, until John said, "Your Highness, if we could see the computer room?"

"Ah, yes. Of course. Right this way." The prince strode out of the office.

Skyler's heart thumped her ribs as she trotted in his wake. John had done what he could, getting her here.

Now it was up to her.

She only hoped she was up to it.

The server room was behind a tall, reinforced metal door. Two uniformed men guarded it while three young people with the lean, hungry look of expert hackers, did complex-looking things to the pad beside the door.

Kulinahr said, "These three assisted Cliff most with the installation here, but they are loyal. They can answer your questions."

One of the boy whiz kids stepped back. "All known codes have been disabled. We tried everything from dusting for frequently-used keys to short-circuiting the wiring. Nothing works."

"Cliff might've jammed the whole mechanism," John said. "If he wanted to be absolutely certain Fahrrad couldn't get in."

Skyler frowned and asked Prince Kulinahr, "Is that door the only access?"

"I believe so. Tyler? "

The young man, Tyler—or what had sounded like Tyler to her—answered her. "The central computer room is impregnable, like a bomb shelter. There is the air system and two fiber optic cables connecting it to the outside world, but even those are failsafed. The door is the single point of access."

"Yes, but is the keypad the only way to unlock it?"

"Oh." The young man's frown cleared to a sheepish look. "*Oh*. No, there are also three electronic proximity key fobs, and one physical key. But the fobs are also disabled or locked out of the system, and we can't find the physical key."

Skyler's heart whooshed in her ears. Did that mean Cliff had hidden it? If he had, where? It could be anywhere.

No, wait. John said Cliff had stayed in the computer room because he had to physically be here to keep the system open to the countercoup. If he had been tied here, the key had to be nearby.

She scanned the hallway, trying to think like him. "What does the key look like?"

"Like a regular key, except chipped on the shank. Stainless steel, square bow."

She gazed at the door, trying to see it from Cliff's perspective. The handle and keyhole at her hip level, the top of the door high above, so high she couldn't reach it...and neither could Fahrrad, but *Cliff* could. "John." A hard beat of her heart goosed the name from her lips. "You're tall. Can you reach the top of the door?"

"Like this?" He touched the edge where the door fit snugly into the frame. "We can't wedge anything in like a jaws of life, if that's what you're thinking..."

She flicked her eyes up, over his hand. His gaze followed hers, his eyes widening as he got it. "The casing ledge." He stretched up and felt along the head casing, his whole body going rigid when he found the key. "Yes."

Tyler reddened. "We were focused on the tech."

"Understandable," Skyler said. "Unless you know Cliff likes things simple but effective."

John snatched the key down and used it. The sound of the lock clicking open freed something in Skyler's chest.

One down. Two to go.

She must've said it out loud because John frowned at her as he swung the door open. "Two? Don't we just have to break into the system?"

"Two parts to the system."

"The machines and the security code," Tyler said.

"Right." She hurried into the computer room as a guard stepped into the doorway to keep the door open.

Air poured down on racks of machines, chilling her already-cold body. She wrapped arms around herself and shivered, but she forced herself to walk the room and take stock. "You don't want Joe Sysadmin to have access to Pizza Pie when he maintains the servers, and you don't want Rambo Programmer to be able to lock up your machines."

In the time that it took her to explain, she'd found the rack with the security system, a workstation attached to it. She sat before the workstation. "Okay. Here's hoping he knew we'd be coming." She woke the monitor to the admin login.

"Why?"

"Because I only know one Cliff-password." She typed PEPPERONI.

The screen changed to a familiar desktop.

Triumph pumped her. She threw a fist in the air.

John crowed. "You did it!"

"I did half of it. Now I need to get into the security system admin." With a deep breath to slow her hammering heart, she clicked on the Pizza Pie icon, typed in PEPPERONI again...and nothing.

The triumph drained away. Her shoulders sagged.

"What's wrong?"

"Everything. That's the only password I know."

"What do we do now?"

"I'm not sure. We'll have to guess." Half-heartedly, she typed in a few things, French_Fries, Brownies, Mum. The negative buzzer each time ate into her already waning confidence. After a dozen tries, she stopped, her guts churning with fear and failure.

Her eyes unconsciously skimmed the computer screen desktop as behind her, worried voices murmured.

Suddenly her gaze was snagged by a small icon.

A frosted chocolate cake.

"Wait." It reminded her of the first time she'd been at Cliff's house. Hannah's chocolate cake.

She clicked on the icon. A simple text file came up, with a single line.

The woman I love.

Skyler's heart skipped a beat.

John leaned over her shoulder. "It's a clue?"

"I...yes." She took a deep breath, and another, her chest feeling too tingly and full. Then she clicked again on the Pizza Pie icon and at the login screen typed, SKYLER.

The system came up. Skyler blinked itchy, inexplicably wet eyes.

John smiled. "Now you can reset the system so we can see through the street cameras?"

Kulinahr came to stand over her other shoulder. "And keep the madman from training our own guns on us?"

"Yes, I think so." She brought up the camera modules one by one, scanning their code, not reading the lines so much as opening her awareness to the places it felt off.

The change jumped out at her on the third module. "This object. He commented out the camera feed access and wrote in input from saved video files."

"How did you find that so fast?" That was Tyler of the whiz kids.

"I just did." She shrugged, but his noticing felt good. "Okay, all we have to do is take out the new code, uncomment the old, and recompile the module. And we'd better reboot the system."

"No!" A shout from the hallway, what sounded like a young boy, distracted them all a moment. "I am to find the red-haired lady!"

There was scuffling outside the computer room and suddenly a boy in white shirt, khaki pants too short for him, and dusty sandals dodged between uniformed legs. One thin arm shot up, a wad of black in it. "Look, look."

"A bomb!" The uniformed man leaped for the child. The boy jagged to the side, and the guard landed on the floor, but he managed to clamp a hand around the child's ankle.

"Red-haired lady," the boy cried as he struggled against the man's grip. "Here!"

He threw the wad at her.

Fear made her flinch, but her subconscious told her to catch it.

She snagged black jersey cloth. A T-shirt.

"It's okay." Swallowing her heart out of her throat, Skyler unfolded the shirt, one of the big black T-shirts Cliff favored. She felt for the hidden inner pocket.

Jackpot.

"You think Cliff sent the boy?" John asked.

"With a clue to where he's being held, yes." She practically ripped the shirt, pulling the hard, flat square from its hiding place, and held it up with a grin.

"What is it?" the ambassador asked.

"The HCC *pi* prototype." Skyler turned the brass board over in her hands. Something—a flash in the wrong place or a slight irregularity in the feel—caught her attention.

She peered closer. One side of the board was defaced with several long scratches.

Destroying the chip.

If Cliff's clue had been in the onboard memory, it was gone now. She wanted to cry in pain and frustration.

So close. She was so close to saving him, and he'd even given her a clue, but it wasn't enough. If only she'd trusted him. If only they hadn't fought. Her throat thickened, her heart beating a heavy dirge of recrimination. She remembered the ease with which he had escaped with her that night months ago. If they hadn't fought, if she'd simply trusted him, he'd be free right now, laughing with her over some shared joke.

Instead of about to die.

How could he die? Why now, when they'd had so little time together? She'd had happiness and threw it away for want of a little trust.

She stared at the board again. The scratches. Three scratches, forming a warped triangle…what if the clue wasn't stored electronically? What if the *scratches* were Cliff's message?

Simple but effective.

The scratches, taken together, vaguely resembled the bizarre sculpture in the hotel where she'd been held prisoner. Elation burst in her blood.

"I think I know where he is!" She jumped to her feet.

"Where?" John barked.

"The hotel where I was held prisoner. It had a wilted triangle sculpture in the lobby. It sticks out like…like a cow in an art gallery. Cliff stayed at that hotel; he'd have seen it, too, and known it was memorable. I don't know the name of the hotel, but the outside is dusty rose in color, either brick or plaster or paint—"

"I know. It was on Cliff's private report to me." John thumbed through his phone and produced an address.

Skyler wanted to hug him. "Let's go!"

"You can't," the American ambassador protested. "If you're wrong, we need the cameras operational—"

"I can do that," Tyler said. "Change the code, do the recompile."

"Go." Kulinahr urged her toward the door with a gentle hand on her back. "We will finish things here, and send assistance, if it turns out you're correct. And we'll continue to search if you are not."

"Car?" John asked.

"Commandeer whatever you find."

John grabbed her arm and half dragged her outside.

The same sedan that brought them there still waited at the curb. John shouted the address at the driver, throwing open the back door for her. She slung her backpack onto the back seat and slid in behind it, John scooting in beside her.

He'd barely closed the door when the driver pulled out like a jet pilot. Skyler was thrown back into her seat. She grappled for a seat belt, finding it and losing it again as the driver kicked around a corner so fast it smashed her against the side.

"Hey!" John said. "Slow down—"

"No," Skyler said. "We'll live." Her blood absolutely burned to find Cliff and free him. Less than half an hour. "Go faster!"

Chapter Twenty-Nine

The officer drove even more maniacally. Skyler held onto whatever she could find, narrowly avoiding getting crushed in a particularly quick turn. If they didn't get to Cliff in time, it wouldn't be for this guy's lack of enthusiasm.

John held grimly to the seat with one hand, stabilizing her with the other. "Okay, one call and Kulinahr will send reinforcements, but we may not have the luxury of waiting for them. We need to make a plan. Skyler, tell me about the hotel's layout."

She told him as much as she could remember, including how Cliff had rescued her, skipping only the kiss that had started it all.

"Good." John's body slammed into the door on another tight turn. As they bumped their way down the main drag, dodging cars and people and animals, he began, "Here's what we need to do..."

When they arrived, the dusty pink of the building jumped out at her, painted bright orange by a wash of fear and the low, slanting sun.

She croaked, "That's it. Stop!"

"Not right in front," John said. "In case Fahrrad has men watching."

The officer squealed the cab around the corner. Before it even came to a stop, John threw open the car door and leaped out.

Memory crowded Skyler, the terror and helplessness triggered by her last time here. Automatically, she dug in her backpack for the headscarf she'd packed. She tied the thing tight around her tell-tale hair then after a moment's thought grabbed the pepper spray and her phone and jammed them into a pocket.

When she slid out, her legs buckled and she stumbled, catching herself against the side of the car. The need to find Cliff urged her to run for the hotel, but memory and fear chilled her muscles, and she trembled despite the heat.

"It's okay, Skyler." John squeezed her shoulder. "What you're feeling is natural. Breathe through the fear. Then use it to fight."

She breathed deep. "Right."

"Where's that fire escape?"

Another deep breath. *Gotta do this*. "This way." She led off, with each step pumping energy and strength into her muscles as she marched to the building across the alley from the hotel

At the foot of the fire escape, John made a tremendous leap to catch the bottom. He scrambled onto the platform then lowered the ladder so she could climb up.

She lurched up the ladder, heart racing.

The roof's gravel was much less painful with shoes. John was gauging the distance between buildings.

Looking to see if he could jump it.

Skyler's neck crawled. "Somehow, that seems a lot farther away in daylight."

John simply grinned. "I think I can do it. You go back down. I'll let you in."

"What if Fahrrad's inside?" Skyler couldn't help panting. "He'll have those goons."

"I'll subdue Fahrrad's mercenaries, then let you in." He put a hand on her shoulder. "You're feeling the same helplessness and fear as when you were last here, kidnapped. I get it. It's okay."

He really did understand. Something inside her relaxed. And in relaxing, she realized she wasn't off the hook. "Yeah, I'm scared. But you've been scared too. Cliff was probably scared the first time he did his hero thing." She pumped steel into her spine. "Cliff might need me. I'll jump, too."

The moment she said it oxygen became scarce. She panted, her heart pumping harder—excitement, nerves, terror, she couldn't tell. She pushed everything away. She had to think of Cliff, only Cliff.

A small smile tipped John's mouth. "Brave heart. Remember how we trained." He eyed the distance, backed up, ran a few steps, and flew across the narrow alley, hitting the roof of the hotel.

Skyler compressed her fear down into her body, the roiling sensation making her legs feel like springs. She didn't pause, just ran, hit the edge, and jumped.

Her legs were more powerful than she remembered. She sailed across the open space, not looking down, not thinking of anything but the man she hadn't trusted enough. She hit the roof hard, pain jarring her bones, shooting through her legs.

She stumbled backwards and nearly fell off.

"Whoa." John grabbed her shoulders and pulled her onto the roof. "Going the wrong way there. You okay?"

She nodded. He released her slowly, watching carefully, no doubt to make sure she found her balance. She poured every ounce of willpower she possessed into her muscles not to shake.

"Good." He turned to scout the roof. A moment later he dashed to the middle.

Skyler shook off her pain and followed.

He'd found the hatch. Opening it revealed the same ratty red carpet she remembered, about eight feet below.

"Fourth floor." John held up four fingers. "Fifteen minutes." He held up his hand three times then slid into the opening and dropped from sight.

Breath coming harder, Skyler forced herself to the edge of the opening. She slid her legs over then eased her body through until she hung suspended in the dim corridor. The hallways where she'd run, terrified, over and over in her worst nightmares.

But always at the end, strong arms plucked her from them.

No strong arms this time.

She less let go than her fingers more refused to hold her anymore. She landed with a muffled thud.

John caught her attention then held up his hand three times, reminding her they only had fifteen minutes to find Cliff.

Fifteen minutes to find her hero before a madman started carving on him.

With two fingers, John pointed at the stairwell end of the hallway.

He tiptoed to the first door on one side and pressed a cautious ear against it. After a moment, he took the handle, turned it, and cracked the door to peek. A quick scan before he closed the door with a shake of the head.

That was the plan, she remembered. Listen, crack the door for a peek, the two of them leapfrogging. She took the next door from the end while John proceeded to the one beyond her. Down one side and up the other, ending again at the stairwell.

Empty. Empty. All empty.

Not unexpected, but time was running out. If Fahrrad wasn't here, their caution was wasted.

Too bad she couldn't write a program to do this. Her thoughts tumbled giddily to cover crescendoing worry. Maybe in old BASIC. Line 10—Check room. Line 20—If empty then move to next room else call Kulinahr.

At the stairwell, John checked his watch, held up his hand twice.

Ten minutes to go.

She followed John cautiously down a flight of stairs to the third floor.

Memory assailed her. Running in the stairwell, feet pounding behind her. Throwing open this very door to enter the hallway where she'd found her rescuer.

Where she'd found Cliff.

Need for him burned through her so bright and fierce that she nearly bolted out of the stairwell to throw open that same door.

John held a cautioning arm up. He frowned at her almost as if he read her desire. She heaved a breath, trying to slow her panting, to rope in her desperate urge.

Dropping his arm, John started on the first door on the left and slowly pressed his ear to the door.

She followed, her heart skipping a beat as she passed the first door on the right. Where Cliff had been last time.

He'd checked in under an alias. Fahrrad couldn't have known this was the same room. There was no reason to assume he was being held here.

So pass the room she did, to press her ear to the second door on the left. They had a plan.

Still, she felt her stomach sink the farther they went from Cliff's old room.

How long now? Did she have time to try every yellowed knob down the ratty corridor?

Did she have a choice? Her hand paused on the next glass knob.

What if her gut was right? What if she was doing the wrong thing, ignoring it? They had so little time. In less than ten minutes Fahrrad would bring out the meat cleaver.

She choked a little on that thought.

Then a door slammed below, followed by a string of curses accompanied by the muffled sound of feet stomping up the stairwell.

Skyler couldn't stop herself. She flew toward the door, the one that had given her sanctuary last time.

John hissed, "No."

She paused.

Then, as the stairway doorknob rattled, Skyler twisted the knob and jumped inside. With a curse, John must've leaped after her because he crowded through behind her.

He yanked the door shut as the stairwell door slammed open, the string of curses getting louder.

One of the voices sounded like Fahrrad.

She froze, ice crowding her veins. *Fahrrad's recorded, oily voice. "It is only a matter of time...and a few unnecessary body parts...before I will have full access."*

"Hey!" From *inside the room*. "Who are you?"

She spun.

A uniformed guard was rolling from the bed to his feet, flinging away a cigarette and magazine.

Beyond him, on the floor at the foot of the bed, was a man. Blindfolded, gagged, and trussed up tighter than Houdini.

Cliff.

Chapter Thirty

The last time she'd been in this room, Cliff had commanded the space with his big body.

Now, bruised and trussed, he occupied one small corner. Skyler's heart broke for him.

She automatically started for him.

The guard caught her first.

"John!" She struggled to get loose.

"A little busy here." As the door started to open, John rammed his shoulder against it. Shouting came from the other side. Pushing too, from the way the door began to crack open again.

John grabbed the door frame, braced his feet on the floor, and shoved it closed.

He couldn't help her. And Cliff… Her powerful, wonderful Cliff, the man she loved, lay helpless on the floor. *How dare they?*

Fury fueled her arm as she took a swing at the guard—and to her shock, connected with his skull.

The blow rang up her arm bones. She yelped.

But the uniformed man wavered on his feet, eyes glazing.

John spared her a glance. "Roundhouse. Put your shoulder into it."

Trembling, she made a fist, twisted her elbow back, then for good measure twisted her whole trunk. She rammed knuckles into the guy's temple, putting her whole body behind it.

He went down.

She covered her mouth with both hands and tried not to empty her stomach.

Bam. The door bowed, jarring John, but he stayed firm. "Good job. Maybe you train faster than Cliff."

She managed to drop her hands. "What now?"

"Get the gun off the guard."

She fumbled it out of his holster. Holding it with two fingers and thumb by the handle, she offered it to John.

He barely glanced at it. "Get ready to shoot. I'll let go of the door—"

"No!" Her whole stomach tried to leap out at that. "I've never...I don't know how to fire one of these. Hold the door while I try to release Cliff. Maybe he can shoot."

A hard thud sent John's feet skidding back an inch. He gritted his teeth and pressed harder into the door. "Better call the prince for backup, too."

"Right. After Cliff."

Skyler skidded to her knees next to the big man. She wrenched her fingers on the blindfold's knot, tossing a glance around the room, but no knife or scissors stood out. As she was looking, another thud cracked the door.

John turned and put his back into the wood, muscles straining as he slowly closed it. "*Hurry.*"

Delicately she began to search Cliff for a knife, realized she couldn't waste time on modesty and dug around. At the rate she was going, she'd never call Kulinahr.

Hopefully he wouldn't wait to send reinforcements—or maybe the Mounties would show up.

Yeah, they were so screwed.

Then she realized Cliff hadn't made a sound or movement beyond breathing. Fear iced her. She might have a bigger problem.

"Cliff, it's Skyler," she whispered sharply. "Nod if you're awake."

His head wobbled slightly. Drugged? He'd never be able to shoot.

Then he lifted his chin, and she saw the rope was wrapped around his neck. Good news, he wasn't drugged. Bad news, he was trussed like a rodeo calf. She'd never free him before the door stove in.

He tried to nod again. Had no more success. His face contorted around the gag, his jaw elongating. She blinked. He was trying to tell her something...

He was pointing his chin at his chest. At the black T-shirt he wore.

She snaked her arm inside his shirt, grabbed the hidden pocket—and cut herself. She jerked back.

With more care, she tried again. A small, handleless blade lay flat in the pocket. She worked it out then slashed the rope at his neck. As soon as the rope loosened, he writhed and pumped, coils beginning to gap. She'd forgotten how strong he really was. She started working on the gag. The moment he had his hands free he ripped the rope away from his neck. She'd barely frayed the gag before he tore it off, then ripped the blindfold from his eyes.

His cobalt gaze blazed into hers. She hesitantly touched his face. Would he ever forgive her for not trusting him?

"Oh, Skyler." Her name was a hoarse gasp, but his arms were sure and strong as he folded her into his embrace. He hugged her desperately. "How long do we have?"

A lifetime. "Maybe a minute."

"Maybe *not.*" John's voice was punctuated with a couple grunts.

Cliff released her and got stiffly to his feet. "Who all is here?" After shaking his muscles loose, he held his hand out for the gun.

With relief, she got rid of the thing. "John. A crazy chauffeur. Reinforcements, as soon as I call." She took out her phone—and realized she didn't know how to get hold of Kulinahr. "What do I call, 911?"

John gritted out between slams, "Use." *Bam.* "My." *Bam.* "Phone."

"Right." She slid his smart phone from his pocket. "Call Kulinahr."

The prince answered himself. "Hello, this is—"

"He's here. Send help!"

"Right."

As she slid the phone back in John's pocket, Cliff positioned himself to the right of the door, on the gap side.

"You've been busy." He seamed his big body with the wall.

Skyler faded back on the hinge side. "I wish we could've been here sooner."

"And miss a last-minute rescue? Where's the fun in that?" Cliff leaned out and gave her a quick grin. "Okay, let it go."

"Finally." John released the door, stepping back to body-shield Skyler.

Good thing he had. The door slapped open so hard, if John hadn't caught it, the knob would have punched through them, then the plaster.

The first goon ran through. Skyler steeled herself for the report of the gun.

Cliff slammed it instead into the side of the goon's head. The man staggered into the room revealing a second goon. Cliff punched him, too. John reached out, grabbed the first, and spun him into a choke hold. Moments later the man sagged in his arms and John dropped him, unconscious, to the floor.

Cliff had meanwhile punched two more goons but a fourth was shoving through. John choked one.

But that left two for Cliff, plus any more still in the hallway—including Fahrrad, if he was out there.

Acid blanched Skyler's veins, adrenaline making time slow. She had to help. But how?

Pepper spray. She jammed her hand into her pocket, trying to dig out the small cylinder from a pocket that had suddenly become a finger trap.

Meanwhile, Cliff simply punched the fourth goon then grabbed the two staggering men—and knocked their heads together.

They slumped against each other as they slid toward the floor.

Skyler clutched her pepper spray, heart rattling her ribs, eyes straining wide in amazement.

John looked up at Cliff from depositing his man on the floor. "Why didn't you shoot them, you idiot?"

Cliff grinned. "Don't want to waste ammo. That's the last of them."

"The last in the hallway, you mean." With a disgusted *tsk*, John said, "Never let anyone know I trained you. I'd be too embarrassed."

"I'm your best student." Cliff grabbed Skyler's hand and pulled her out into the hallway.

She'd missed his hand, his big body beside her. She stuffed her spray back in her pocket. "I thought I heard Fahrrad. I wonder where he went?"

"Who knows? Wait up a moment." John was searching the unconscious men. "Damn it, only the one on guard in the room was armed."

"Be glad they weren't." Cliff tossed John the gun. "Otherwise they'd have shot the door open. Don't worry, I'm sure any more we meet will have rifles and more. C'mon, let's get out of here."

"Don't have to tell me twice." John took the gun and ran into the stairwell.

Cliff glanced at her. "Ready?"

"You're actually asking this time?" Giddy, she started toward the stairs, pulling Cliff beside her.

They dashed hand-in-hand toward the stairwell as the door started to shut after John. Cliff barely slowed, wresting the thing open and swinging her through. "You're smiling."

She hit the stairs down, running lightly. After hundreds of flights on the stair machine, it was easy. But just feeling his big hand again, clamped securely around hers, made her blood fizz. "Running with you...it's got its perks."

"Skyler Lynn Jones, where have you been all my life?"

Her heart swelled. She opened her mouth to reply when angry shouts vibrated the air behind the second floor landing door.

Cliff swore. He shoved Skyler past the door toward the stairs—just as the door flew open.

"Let him try to hold it shut now—you!"

A furious Boris Fahrrad stood there, fists clenching, nostrils flared, gaze on fire.

Skyler's chest hollowed, and she skidded to a stop, her knees wobbling.

Cliff turned like a big bull to block the landing. "Go!"

She hesitated. Leave him, with rescue so close? Fold like a cheap lawn chair *like his old flame?*

Her heart leaped in her chest. Digging for her pepper spray in her too-tight pocket, she started for his side.

Fahrrad raised a huge handgun.

Skyler flipped the top and pushed the button.

A stream jetted toward the dictator—just as a mercenary pulled him back to safety. The mercenary shouted, scraping at his eyes.

But two more goons took his place, bubbling into the doorway.

Cliff gently pushed her aside and absorbed the attack, barely wavering. He grabbed one guy and flung him bodily into the other. But more rose up to take their place. "Skyler! *Go get John.*"

John had the gun.

"*Oh.*" She spun and raced down the stairs.

Gunshots rang out from above, freezing her. "John!" she screamed.

His face appeared below, questioning.

"Come *on.*" She nearly threw her shoulder out gesturing him to follow. "Cliff needs help."

Another shot exploded in the stairwell. She raced back up, not waiting for John. Ice filled her chest, fear for Cliff.

A body, tumbling down the stairs, nearly took her out at the ankles.

Heart in her throat, she registered the uniform at the last minute, and jumped over the toppling man. He hit the wall and stopped. Breathing. He was unconscious, not dead.

Skyler jumped over another two unconscious men on her way up.

Cliff fought to hold the landing, more graceful than ever with the economy of motion imposed by small space. Punching, kicking, he was a refined tornado picking off the armed men one by one as they tried to get through the bottleneck of the doorway.

"What a tactician," John breathed from behind her.

Skyler felt laughter bubbling up inside. "What an idiot. Why not grab a gun and just shoot them?"

"Too confined. A stray bullet might hit one of us."

"They don't seem to care."

"They're idiots too. Hey, " he shouted at Cliff. "Let me have some." Jumping to Cliff's side, he whipped the gun into the nearest man's face. "*Freeze!*"

If the guy didn't understand the word, he understood the intent. Fahrrad's man froze for the split second it took Cliff to spin and thunder down the stairs, grabbing her along the way.

"John?" Skyler panted.

"Coming. We've done this before."

Sure enough, a single set of footsteps pounded behind them...and then a whole herd thundered in their wake.

Skyler hit the lobby running full tilt as shots popped from behind. Something whizzed past her.

Behind them, John cried out.

Cliff swore and screeched to a halt. Skyler twisted midstep, stuttering to a stop.

A split second later, John stumbled into the lobby, eyes glazed, blood streaming from a nasty head wound.

Adrenaline dumped in her blood. She started back.

Cliff snagged her arm as she tried to reach John, using it and her momentum to slingshot her toward the exit door. "I'll get him. Go!"

She surged toward the door and through it. Grabbed it and hung on, her speed swinging it completely open. Panting, she clung to the door, blinking in the low blinding sun as she stuttered to a halt. She stood there, hanging from the door, both to keep it open for Cliff and because her knees were shaking so badly she wasn't sure she could stand on her own.

Cliff came out at a dead run, John dangling limply over his shoulders. Feet crashed behind him. "Come on!" He herded her away from the door.

Just as bullets started flying past her head—from *both* directions, front and back.

She squealed her terror. Cliff nudged her from behind. Her knees buckled, dumping her to the ground. Cliff dropped John next to her and covered them both with his big body.

"No!" From the street. "They are on our side."

The crazy chauffeur-guard, Skyler realized, about the same time she realized she couldn't breathe, her breath knocked out of her. She gasped ineffectively like a fish.

The bullets stopped.

Cliff's hands went under her arms, and he hauled her to her feet.

She'd just sucked in her first breath when she was tossed to the side. Stumbling in a spin, she saw why.

Fahrrad's men ran out of the building as she stuttered back, losing her balance the more she tried to regain it.

Cliff took two big leaps to her side and grabbed her, his sure arms keeping her from falling, wrapped around her as if they would never let go.

"Throw down your weapons." Kulinahr stepped to the front of a militia that filled the street, bristling rifles.

The first of Fahrrad's men tried to retreat back inside. But more were still pouring out, so he couldn't.

He turned his rifle on the militia, and Skyler's breath froze.

Then a man to his side threw up his hands, the gun still in one, pointed skyward. He barked something.

"I surrender," Cliff translated.

The first threw down his gun and raised his arms, too. One by one, the rest followed suit.

John sat up woozily mid-street.

A field medic ran to take care of him.

"I'm fine," he croaked. "Or I will be. Someone go get Fahrrad."

Cliff solicitously guided Skyler to John. "He's not out here. He must be holed up inside."

Kulinahr strode to Cliff's side, every inch the leader. "I do not wish to send my militia blindly inside. We do not know if the madman has any confederates left."

"Or if he has set traps." Cliff eyed the hotel. "I can infiltrate through the roof."

Skyler saw the intent in his blazing blue eyes. "No! You just escaped after being tied and tortured. You can't go back in there."

He took her by the shoulders and gave her his full attention. "We have to get Fahrrad out before he does any more damage. One person stands a better chance."

She searched his cobalt gaze. No matter how her intuition screamed against it, she wasn't going to stop him. But she'd lost her pepper spray somewhere along the way. "John—give me the gun."

"No," Cliff said.

"Yes."

"No."

"Children." John managed a weak laugh. "The gun is out of bullets. Take one of Kulinahr's rifles."

"Good idea." Cliff simply reached out. Three rifles were thrust into his hand. He took one, clasped it under his arm, and started for the alleyway.

"No." Skyler chased after, grabbing onto one thick biceps. "I don't care about your damned sense of responsibility. You're not going in there alone to get yourself killed. I didn't risk my neck just to lose you again!"

That stopped him. He gazed deeply into her eyes, then smiled slowly. "You worked your tail off for me, and risked your neck for me. Any other body parts you care to contribute?"

Too little sleep and too much adrenaline, and a tank as obstinate as herself had made her blurt the truth. "Yes, you big muscled mass-without-the-m. I've lost my heart to you, too." *And apparently my mind.* "I love you."

She immediately covered her mouth. Too soon.

Now she stood before him, more exposed than she'd ever been to bullets.

Chapter Thirty-One

"You love me?" His smile broadened. "I love you, too, Skyler Lynn Jones. Do you want to get married, or live together in sin?"

She blinked back tears. *He loves me, too.* She threw both arms around him, gun and all, and would have hung on forever.

"Fahrrad," John yelled. "On the roof. We'll cover the front. You go take the fire escape."

Cliff sprang into action. Skyler, with a death-grip on him, was pulled along. He stopped.

Before he could say anything she blurted, "Don't leave me again. I couldn't bear it if something happened to you."

He swore under his breath. "And I couldn't bear it if one hair on your head was harmed. I'll be back, I promise." He gripped her arm with one big hand. "I'll finish this for you, for me, for both of us."

He planted a hard kiss on her lips.

The kiss was so hot, smoke seemed to come out of her ears.

So when he released her, she just stood there, arms turned to spaghetti, stunned. That kiss...it promised forever.

Then she saw he'd slipped out of her embrace and was getting away. She ran after him.

The rat-a-tat of gunfire shot fear into her stomach. But the cracks echoed from behind her. Fahrrad wasn't shooting at Cliff. He was raining bullets on Kulinahr's men at the front of the hotel.

While the colonel was distracted, Cliff reached the neighboring building's fire escape, the one Skyler and John had scaled just half an hour before.

If we make it through this alive, she thought, *I am buying a fire escape for this hotel. I don't care how much it costs.*

The ladder had retracted since she'd used it last. *Of course it has.*

Cliff leaped gracefully to catch the edge of the ladder, pulling it to the ground. He ran fleetly up the fire escape just as Skyler reached the bottom.

She ran less gracefully but no less effectively with muscles honed by John but built by Cliff, love, and maybe just a little by her own temper and competitiveness.

Switchback stairs took her up three stories. As she reached the top of the fourth, a rifle muzzle appeared.

She ducked, panting.

Only to realize the barrel was above her and slightly to her left.

Cautiously, she mounted the last few steps, her head gradually clearing the roof's concrete ledge to the sight of Cliff kneeling.

With the rifle braced on the edge of the building, he took careful aim. She slid over the ledge beside him, careful not to disturb his shot.

"I told you to stay," he murmured, his focus not swerving a millimeter.

"Yeah. Well, I'm your lover, not your soldier."

"How about my wife?" Cliff squeezed the trigger.

It felt like the bullet went into her lung. She wheezed, "What?"

"Damn, he moved." He squeezed off another shot.

She glimpsed Fahrrad's gun turning toward them just as Cliff barked, "*Down,*" yanked her low and ducked himself.

A battery of shots erupted over them.

"Missed again?"

"Kevlar," Cliff growled. "Next time, I'm not going for a body shot."

"Ah." Maybe it was the nonstop adrenaline, maybe it was being with Cliff at last, but she felt giddy.

"If there is a next time." Cliff checked the chamber. "Yep, empty. Why are you surprised I asked if you'd marry me? I asked before."

"I thought you were kidding. Now what do we do?"

"You say yes?"

"About Fahrrad."

"Oh. Now I nail him." Cliff edged a peek over the ledge. "While he's distracted."

"You don't have any ammunition."

He gave her a small, coy smile and reached into his pants pocket. "They searched me fairly thoroughly. Of course, they didn't realize the meaning of me wearing two T-shirts, nor did they see me hand off one to that plucky young lad. And they didn't find either shirt's secret pocket.

They found this, but they didn't think it was important." He drew out a rubber band and a square of chewing gum.

She eyed it. "You're going to take him with your sawed-off rubber band?"

He held up the chewing gum gingerly. "This is a highly powerful explosive. I had it in the palace on the off-chance I might need to blow up the HCCpi. Luckily, I was able to get out of the server room about two seconds before they found me."

He'd been captured, manhandled, fighting, and rolling around with an explosive on his person. He could've been blown up at any time. It abruptly chilled her out of any giddiness.

He read her expression as always. "Don't worry. It's extremely stable—until I activate it. Twist, then ten seconds. It's my own design."

"Lovely. How do you plan on getting it onto the next roof over? Since that must be a good fifteen feet."

"More. And how?" He held up the rubber band. "This."

"What? A weighted rubber band, go twenty feet?" It reminded her of her team's play fighting, only this was deadly serious. "Unless you designed that thing out of space age superball polymers, you'll never make it."

"Oh, ye of little faith. I was rubber band shooting champion of my public school four years in a row."

"I don't think that's a real thing."

"It should be." He activated the explosive with a twist, balled it around one end of the rubber band then drew the band taut. "If I can just get this to stretch far enough…"

He popped up with a twist, facing Fahrrad, and released the rubber band with a twang. Immediately he dropped back behind the concrete edge of the roof.

The explosive shot up into the air, at exactly forty-five degrees, the best trajectory possible. It arched way, way up.

"It'll never make it," Skyler breathed.

"Faith," he retorted.

"Not even Belva could make a shot that far," she said.

He smiled. "Who do you think taught Belva to shoot?"

Skyler blinked and lost sight of the rubber band and its little payload. She waited, her blood whooshing in her ears. Nothing. She dared a peek. "Cliff, I don't think that was explosive—"

A concussion wave tore the word from her mouth as, with a boom, the roof of the hotel burst into the air in a cloud of dust. Waves of heat hit her. Cliff tugged her down, hugging her in his protective arms.

But not before she'd seen Fahrrad tumble off the hotel, falling like a rag doll. She struggled from Cliff's arms and popped her head over the roof, searching below, not sure she wanted to see, but needing to.

The dictator had fallen into an open industrial garbage bin. Airbagged by plastic bags of waste, he was already scrambling to get out.

But Kulinahr's men flooded the alley before he could get away. After a brief struggle, they took Fahrrad captive.

"I'll learn to trust you," Cliff murmured into her hair. "You should learn to trust me, too."

She just nodded, snuggling into his embrace in profound relief.

*   *   *

Skyler sat in her office at work, deep into a coding project she herself had picked. She had the luxury of plenty of time to finish it, because she herself had set the deadline.

She was her own boss, now, and she loved it.

"Hey, Skyler. Aren't you hungry yet?"

Or mostly her own boss. But being her boss wasn't the only thing she loved. Joy surged through her at the deep male voice, even as she affected an irritated sigh. "I'm almost done." She looked up and beheld her nominal boss filling her office door like an avenging god.

Sir Humphrey Hawkesclyffe, as gorgeous today as he'd been when she first met him.

And as hungry too. He pouted. "You said that an hour ago."

"Just one more thing—"

"C'mon, Skyler. I have reservations."

"Cancel them." Making a decision, she stood, stretched, then sauntered over to him. "I'm in the mood for a workout...or two."

His eyes darkened, catching her innuendo.

But then he shook his head. "We need to talk."

She chilled. That didn't sound good. And why now, after all they'd been through? She swallowed a lump of anxiety and cautiously asked, "What?"

"I have something I have to get off my chest."

He shut the door.

Her legs almost buckled. If "we need to talk" and "something to get off my chest" were bad signs, closing the door was the worst.

But she still had her cloak of professionalism, tattered but available, even though she thought she'd never need it again. She donned it now, but it was uncomfortable, like using an old toothbrush. "Let's sit." She led him to her conversation grouping, sat on the couch, and patted the cushion next to her hopefully.

He just stood there, freezing her soul.

She'd thought, after they'd gotten things stable in Middle Yemen, that their relationship was stable too.

Then he sighed and heaved himself beside her and her heart thawed.

His cobalt gaze searched her face. "I have to apologize."

Relief flooded her. "Okay, that wasn't what I was expecting after your buildup."

He flashed her a quick grin. "After we argued, last time I went to Middle Yemen, I should have called. But I wasn't sure how you'd take it, and I was thousands of miles away. I was afraid that if things didn't go well, I wouldn't be there to fix it."

"You couldn't. You were a little busy with a counter-coup."

"True." Another grin. "Thanks for remembering. The point is..." He dug something from his pocket, slid off the cushion onto one knee, and held it up to her. It was small and covered in dark velvet and for a moment she didn't understand.

Then he snapped it open, and she was blinded by the flashing awesomeness of a two-carat diamond platinum halo engagement ring.

"The point is, I didn't know you well enough to just blurt out what needed to be said. But I want to. Desperately. I want...well, I want a lifetime to know you better. Skyler please. I've asked twice now. Will you marry me?"

"I didn't think you were serious." She held a hand to her chest. Her lungs weren't working quite right, and her words were breathy.

"I've never been so serious. If you're not ready to be married, we can have a long engagement. But at least give me hope. Will you marry me?"

"There are so many things we haven't discussed. My job...I like it here at HCC. I don't want my personal life to ruin my professional life."

"Why can't one make the other better? Are you worried that I own the company? Everything I have will be yours. We'll make it Hawkesclyffe-Jones Computers. Or Jones-Hawkesclyffe, I don't care. I just want you in my life, Skyler, now and forever. Last time, dear heart, because my ego won't take much more of this. Will you marry me—?"

"Yes." She stopped him by pressing her hands to cheeks just starting to stubble. "You incredible, insufferable, always-hungry, brilliant man. I'll marry you."

He whooped and lifted her off the ground.

After her stomach settled, she grinned down into his face. "Now, you mentioned restaurant reservations?"

"Yeah. Five-star, six-course meal." He settled her on her feet and took her face in his hands. "I was going to propose over dessert. But since you mentioned working out..."

She waggled her eyebrows. "Hannah left us a cake at home."

"Then let's eat in, okay?"

"Okay." She gave him a quick kiss and went to grab her purse. "But I get to drive."

"No, I'll drive." He opened the door. "My car."

"If you meant it, *our* car. You got to drive last time."

"I'll race you for it."

"With your long legs? I'll let you have the last piece of cake."

"Darn it, Jones. You know how to hit a man's weaknesses. But I have the keys." He took them from his pocket and dangled them, tinkling. She snatched; he evaded.

She smiled prettily at him. "If I drive, the doctor will come back and check on how well your burn is healing. Reward you if you've been good."

He stopped as if felled. "Right. You drive." He tossed her the keys then grabbed her hand.

Hand in hand, they walked out of the building together.

Continue reading for an excerpt from Falling ~~on~~ for the Billionaire.

About Mary Hughes

Mary Hughes (written Hug-he's but possibly pronounced throat warbler mangrove) writes smart and sassy stories of action and love.

She's a bona fide computer geek and performing flutist. (And piccolo, but we don't talk about that.) When this USA Today Bestselling Author isn't busy finding the missing </> tag or blowing her lungs out, she's reading or binging on The Flash, Instinct, Wynonna Earp, or Agents of SHIELD...and petting the cats that inevitably end up on her lap.

Find her online!

Newsletter http://www.maryhughesbooks.com/Newsletter.html

Facebook http://www.facebook.com/MaryHughesAuthor

Twitter http://www.twitter.com/MaryHughesBooks

Instagram https://www.instagram.com/maryhughesbooks

BookBub https://www.bookbub.com/authors/mary-hughes

Goodreads http://www.goodreads.com/author/show/279140.Mary_Hughes

Website http://www.maryhughesbooks.com/

Blog http://maryhughesbooks.blogspot.com

Falling ~~on~~ for the Billionaire
© 2016 Mary Hughes

Zan is a billionaire media superstar tired of high-gloss, meaningless dates. Vicky's a junior college teacher who loves him from afar—until she's roped into playing wingman for her international-model sister, who's trying to win him back.

So when Vicky trips and lands in Zan's lap, her face is hot. But soon, that's not the only thing heating up.

Enjoy the following excerpt from Falling ~~on~~ for the Billionaire:

Zan stopped—coincidentally right next to Vicky—and frowned, putting his hands on his hips, as if in consternation, gazing where her sister had just disappeared. "Darn. Missed her."

Then he turned to Vicky. Smiled expectantly at her. "Hi."

"Hi." A delicious pink blush rode her cheeks.

He found he wanted to kiss that pink skin. "I'm Zan Sinclair. You're Vicky Brooks? I'm acquainted with your sister."

"I know." Her voice was breathy, oh-so-sexy. "She said."

Her lips were a perfect natural rose. He wondered if they'd be petal soft if he kissed them....

"I'll go get her for you!" Vicky scooted off.

Lost in her lips, he was totally unprepared for her flight. He stood there in surprise. He was wondering what he should do now when she trotted back with her sister in tow.

Ronnie didn't look happy until she caught sight of him. Then her whole face changed, and she hove out in front of her twin like a barge.

And Vicky...stopped. She began to turn. He clenched fists. She was going to run away *again*. He had only seconds to act or lose her.

He covered the distance in two strides, catching Ronnie by the upper arm with one hand and Vicky by the shoulder with the other.

Her slight body was warm and soft under his fingers. A distracting surge of sheer need flooded his system. She looked up into his face, her eyes big and blue.

Her pouty pink lips trembled.

His whole body hardened, instantly ready. He almost ignored the people milling around them to yank her to him, to feel her heart flutter against him, to embrace her, to *kiss* her...